Shanidar

Shanidar

A NOVEL BY
HASHIAN

WYNWOOD™ Press
New York, New York

Library of Congress Cataloging-in-Publication Data

Hashian.
    Shanidar: a novel/by Hashian.
        p.   cm.
    ISBN 0-922066-38-8
    I. Title
PS3558.A72344S5 1990
813'.54—dc20   90-33194
                                                                    CIP

Copyright © 1990 by Hashian
Published by WYNWOOD™ Press
New York, New York
Printed in the United States of America

To those
brave and silent men
who live and die quietly
in lonely special service
to their country

and

To my
inspiring friend Bette Briggs,
with love and appreciation

An Important Word About This Story

The United States has had the immediate and total capability of finding and rescuing American hostages held anywhere in the world.

This astonishing statement—astonishing in that the United States has done nothing of the kind—is based entirely on an awesome array of military, technological, and human resources created and husbanded since World War II, much of it unheralded, some of it necessarily covert.

The use of this capability was brought to bear by only one American leader, President Carter, whose magnificent design to rescue our embassy hostages in Teheran was thwarted by the most inconceivable and incomprehensible development in that highly complex operation—mechanical failure and the lack of American equipment. The concomitant loss of our covert Teheran operatives, both American and Iranian, has never been told.

But that is another story. This novel is mostly fictitious. It is based totally, however, on the capabilities and instruments, both organizational and human, that exist today in the arsenal of our great democracy. Only the specifics involving actual methods and means have been shrouded carefully to protect what the United States has and can do—if it wants to.

To explain why nothing has been done is not the purpose of this tale. The domestic and international considerations, the political and policy ramifications, and the human equations of life and death, all impact heavily on those in the seats of power who have the ultimate and lonely responsibility of making such decisions. Unless we know all the facts, we cannot and must not pass judgment.

The Author

Acknowledgments

For their assistance and/or inspiration:

George Maranjian, River Vale, New Jersey
Sir Thomas Ramsey Galt, London, England
Capt. Steven J. McManus, AUS, Washington, D.C.
Branch R. Fahnestock, McLean, Virginia
Rutherford S. Hopkins, McLean, Virginia
Dr. Mary R. Haack, Washington, D.C.
Col. George Juskalian, USA (ret), Vienna, Virginia
Staff Sgt. Steven M. Petrie, Special Forces, USA, Topsfield,
    Massachusetts
Jackline Abramian, Watertown, Massachusetts, and Parideh
    Abramian, Tabriz, Iran
Thomas W. Neff, Jr., Massachusetts State Police, Newbury Bar-
    racks
Bill Thompson and Richard Re of Wynwood Press, New York,
    New York

                              and

Tad Hashian, whose sharp observations helped to channel
    his dad's latest effort at telling stories

Shanidar

Chapter 1

Geoffrey Maran hurried down the corridor to the communications office to make one last confirmation of the fact that his archaeological expedition had not been heard from for nearly two weeks. Working for a lifetime among generally impractical people who seemed to have a penchant for placing themselves in perilous predicaments had turned his head of hair snow white years before he became head of the Department of Anthropology at Columbia. And today was no exception. If there still was no word, he would have to call Baghdad to secure information as to the protracted silence of the thirteen Americans, led by his old friend Jonathan Caldwell, in the mountains of northeastern Iraq.

A slip of a young woman whom Maran vaguely remembered as being called Lizbeth, rose from her desk with a smile and a "Can I help you, Dr. Maran?"

"Any word on the teletype from Iraq?"

"I've been watching it closely, sir. Nothing, and they were sending us status reports every three days."

Maran nodded. "I need to send a radiogram or cable or whatever is the fastest way to get there, a message to the director of the Directorate General of Antiquities of Iraq in Baghdad, Naji al Hasil. Express my concern for the safety and whereabouts of the expedition, not having heard from anyone there in two weeks. Suggest he could combine the trip there with his periodic sondage of the digs. Close with this line, please: 'I beg of you to hasten a reply.' Sign it 'Papa.' Thank you."

In the late afternoon of the third day after the message was sent, Maran got his answer. "Cave deserted. No sign of archaeologists. Two police assigned to guard area found shot dead. Conducting investigation. Hasil."

"Not a word of this to anyone, young lady. Is that understood?"

"Yes, sir."

"All right. Now, put in a call to the White House. I want to speak to the President. If he can't come to the phone, I'll speak to his chief of staff. If he isn't available, I'll speak to the director of information or communication or whatever they call that person.

"They'll ask you to state the nature of the call. Other than saying it's from Columbia University and that it's urgent, do not say more . . ."

Lizbeth couldn't get through to the President or his chief of staff, but she did reach a David Demery, director of communications. She put Maran on the line.

Maran identified himself and spelled out the few facts he knew, withholding the information about the dead police.

"Could they have gone off on a side trip, Doctor?"

"Highly unlikely, Mr. Demery, but even if that had happened, someone would have stayed at the cave. It's their base of operations and the locus of the entire expedition."

"Are you sure you are not making more of this than you should? Is there anything else you know that makes this a matter of urgency?"

"I didn't want to alarm you if it wasn't necessary, Mr. Demery, but I'll have to tell you. The two policemen assigned as guards by the government were found shot to death."

"My God, man! What are you saying . . .?"

"Yes, sir, I'm sorry, sir, but that's the size of it. The Iraqis are conducting an investigation, but I don't know what they'll find."

"All right, Doctor. Would you be good enough to stand by and keep this line open until I can reach the President?"

Maran mumbled an "of course" and held on for nearly six minutes before the familiar voice of the President broke the silence.

"Thank you for waiting, Dr. Maran. Would you be kind

enough to repeat what you told Dave so that I have it firsthand from you?''

Maran went over all the facts, including his growing concern during the two weeks of silence.

"How are you counting the time period, Doctor? Did you start counting from the first day after the last report or from the day the next report should have been received?'' Maran was impressed by the President's acuity.

"The day the next report should have been received, Mr. President, but I added the three days it took to obtain a reply from Baghdad. So it's exactly two weeks to the day, sir . . . or two weeks and three days . . .''

"Do you have any suggestions about where to start or what to do, Doctor?''

"I'm very sorry, sir. I don't know for the life of me where they could be or what happened. I would suggest one avenue, sir—obtain permission from Baghdad to send in an investigative force.''

"Thank you, Dr. Maran, thank you very much for your concern and assistance.''

"You're welcome, Mr. President. I only wish I could be of more help. Bye, sir.''

Maran called the university's press office and sat down with the director, Doc Avery, to work up a contingency news release if the media badgered the university for ''its side of the story.''

It wasn't every day that the daughter of the President of the United States disappeared while digging for humanoid bones in a wild mountain range thousands of miles from her country.

Chapter 2

The President of the United States sat with sagging shoulders at his desk in the Oval Office, facing the solemn faces of the chiefs who headed the NSC, the CIA, the DOD, the DIA, and State, together with Dave Demery. He could tell immediately that there wasn't going to be any good news.

"Let's start with you, Roscoe," the President said, nodding to the secretary of state, Roscoe Barnes.

"I talked directly with our embassies in Iraq, Turkey, Syria, Jordan, and Israel. Not a whisper, sir. Not one of the ambassadors had heard the slightest rumor about the lost expedition. I've asked them, of course, to mount a discreet but extensive inquiry about any missing group of Americans that may have been sighted somewhere."

"No contact with Iran, of course . . ."

"None. We did ask the Algerians to keep their ears open about Americans in that area, but that's a long shot. I hope you realize, Chief, that that cave in Iraq is less than twenty-five miles from the Iranian border."

"So, we have the possibility of contending with those crazy bastards in Iran, eh?"

"Let's not take that approach yet, sir." Tom Brockway, the CIA director, was not one to leap into anything without a long, hard look. "We haven't heard one word from anywhere at this point, and I believe it behooves us to wait and see. The fact that no dead Americans have been found is a definite point in our favor."

Bill Woodley of the DIA said his agents in the area had followed closely the investigation by the Iraqi government. Mounted and foot soldiers combed the entire area on both sides

of the cave, north to the Turkish border and east to the Iranian
border at the pass, and didn't even find a footprint, hoofprint,
or tire track.

"What recourse do we have, Tim?"

Timothy Rand, the almost seven-foot former tight end who
headed the DOD, held his open palms upward. "We have the
range of military and naval forces to handle anything that
threatens us, but we can't apply any attempt at a solution until
we know what the problem is. At the moment, we are helpless,
sir."

"What do you have to say, Dave?"

"I believe we had better prepare a statement for you, sir. This
isn't going to stay under wraps for long—it must be all over
Iraq by now, at least, with all those troops participating in the
search.

"If we only knew what the facts were in the disappearance,
I'd feel much better about what to say. The paucity of information is absurd and a little scary."

"Prepare one, Dave, and we'll get together this afternoon
and kick it around."

"I thought we might need one, sir, and I've got a draft copy
with me."

"Excellent. Read it out loud, please."

"Columbia University has informed the President that the
archaeological expedition, consisting of ten graduate students
and three professors of anthropology, at a cave site in Iraq, has
not been heard from for nearly two weeks. The Iraqi government is conducting a search. The President's daughter is among
the students missing."

Woodley asked Dave to repeat the statement. When Dave
had done so, nothing more was said.

"This shouldn't be issued," Dave volunteered. "It would be
used only as the official reply if we receive a query from the
media."

"What if they want to know other related facts about the
expedition . . . such as when did they go, what are they looking for, and so forth?"

"I'd refer them to Avery, the PR man for Columbia. Say, I'd
better have his phone number on the statement, just in case

we're asked such questions. I'd also better let him know that
we would be referring calls to him."

"Fine, fine, Dave. Good work. Tomorrow, then, gentlemen.
Same time, same place, and let's hope it won't be more of the
same."

When Brockway returned to his offices in McLean, he put in
a call to the NASA complex in Houston.

Chapter 3

The odd, double beeps that emanated from the neon light
fixture in Jackson Harding's kitchen weren't the kind of sound
he liked to hear these days. It meant a lost weekend for him, if
not more, including a dash to some forsaken corner of the earth
where humans were testing each other's ability to survive.

He picked up the little black receiver that was resting by his
store of black pepper in the cabinet next to his stove, and responded with his call numbers. It was Brockway, just as he had
thought. "Yes, sir?"

"I think I've got a job for you, Jake. Think you could stand a
quick trip to the Middle East?"

Harding made a gagging sound into the transmitter.

"The President's daughter has disappeared in Iraq."

"Holy shit!"

"And so have all twelve Yanks with her."

"Where?"

"She was one of ten grad students picked to go dig up some
more human skeletal remains in a cave in the upper northeast
corner of Iraq. All the students and the three professors with
them have vanished."

"Are we sure they're not off on an academic toot of their
own?"

"No chance, Jake. The two Kurdish police guards stationed with them by the government were found at the cave, shot to death."

"Hmmm. How long have they been missing?"

"Three weeks now. And it should be hitting the news any day."

"What do you have in mind?"

"I'll get the papers cut to break you loose down there. I'd like to see you by midnight tonight. We can brief you and ship you out there to see what's going on."

"Why me, sir . . .?"

"You know damn well why, Jake. Not only do you have a handle on most of the languages over there, but you also happen to be a student of physical anthropology. That's a combination I wouldn't find anywhere, and it fits perfectly this particular set of facts."

"It seems to me that every goddam situation is tailor-made for my ass, sir, meaning no disrespect."

Brockway laughed. "If you hadn't complained, I would have worried about you being sick or something. OK, get that tailored ass up here and we'll kick it around. And, Jake . . . I don't like the smell of this thing one little bit."

So, Brockway didn't like the smell of things, did he? Jackson Harding got a can of beer, parked himself at the kitchen table with his feet propped up on it, and stared at nothing in particular, sipping at the silvery can, thinking. The United States, with more than two million military personnel stationed in every strategic spot on the globe, armed with an array of weapons systems unmatched in the history of the world, was once again in a position of helplessness, depending on the will and whim of persons unknown to resolve what could be described as fatally poisonous tick bites on a handful of its citizens. The catch was that the ticks were still imbedded. Any attempt to tear them off would kill the victims. And there was the rub. The United States was considered a toothless tiger, unlike the Russians and the Israelis. When a Russian was taken hostage in Beirut, they shot the abductors and retrieved their man. When the Israelis faced a long string of similar situations, they stormed the strongholds of the abductors and killed them all, rescuing most of their people.

Harding sighed. Since the United States first displayed a national lack of unity in international affairs, in the 1960s, picking on America and Americans had become a way of life for the fanatics of the world. It was easy to blame Americans for every ill, every misadventure, every political debacle, much as the British Empire had been at the turn of the century. But the United States was paying the price for its consistent and constant hand-wringing over the plight of a handful of hostages, unmindful of the damage such a stance was inflicting on its reputation as a strong, purposeful world power. Americans were fair game and hostage-takers had little fear of retribution of any kind. Hell, we had had the names and pictures of all those responsible for blowing up the U.S. Marine barracks in Lebanon, and we had known exactly where the culprits were to be found. But we sat on our hands, lest the American hostages be harmed. We lost more than 240 young men in that one bomb blast and worried about what would happen to six American hostages if we had exacted a price for those dead Marines.

Harding knew what he had to do. It was the sort of thing he had done so many times for his country—find where the Americans were being held. But . . . He sighed again. So what? Time and again in the past he had provided precise information at great personal peril to resolve similar situations, only to have his country sit on its hands rather than take action.

Jackson Harding snapped out of his reverie. After all, it was a problem of definition when it came to truth.

Chapter 4

The story broke the next day, with Russian and Israeli news agencies reporting a broadcast by Baghdad radio that said all thirteen members of the American expedition at the Shanidar Cave, authorized by the Iraqi government, had disappeared from the site at least two weeks ago.

That was in the morning. The media had no sooner collected all the information they could gather on the disappearance than there was a wild scramble back to the press room at the White House in the late afternoon. A shortwave message had been picked up saying that the Americans were safe but would be held for ransom, the terms of which would be announced in a week or so.

There was no indication of who was behind the abduction or what the Americans were to be ransomed for.

The White House press spokesperson, Chriss Williams, had the worst time of her life trying to provide answers to questions that had no answers. After twenty-five minutes of fruitless jockeying and parrying, the press corps dwindled away, finally convinced that what they had gotten was all there was.

President Randolph was as frustrated as the press corps. The terse, uninformative radio message, delivered in excellent English, didn't provide a clue beyond what was said.

The press had a wonderful time that first day, the tabloids especially:

WHERE IS SHE ? ? screamed the *Daily News*.

PAT HAREM BOUND? howled the *Herald*.

SAY IT'S JUST A PRANK, PAT, pleaded the *Chronicle*.

PRESIDENT'S DAUGHTER KIDNAPPED, stated the *New York Times*. (The *Times* rarely fooled around.)

WORLDWIDE SEARCH LAUNCHED FOR PAT, proclaimed the *Washington Post*. (The *Post* always tried to be one step ahead of anyone else.)

RANDOLPH READIES ROUNDHOUSE REPLY, predicted the *Tribune*.

STRIKE FORCE POISED TO RESCUE PAT, guessed the Detroit *News*.

And so it went. The broadcast media provided a mélange of all the stuff appearing in the printed press, coupled with somber-toned anchors and analysts highlighting a variety of "facts" not yet fully established, and intoning ramifications that would affect everything from world peace and the certain collapse of the stock market to a ban on future archaeological digs.

The President, experiencing his first real encounter with a press gone wild, was deeply impressed.

"Incredible," Randolph kept repeating. "Incredible!" "Unbelievable!" "Stupefying!" "Incredible!" He was at a loss for words, really.

Dave wasn't showing much reaction. "Wait till tomorrow, Mr. President. Each organization will try now to outdo and outguess the rest. The results will be a reaffirmation of that old yellow journalism adage, 'Never let the facts stand in the way of a good story,' you can bet on it."

"Dave, I'm going to call off the meeting. Let's wait until tomorrow and hope they'll try to reach us with something we can work with."

Tomorrow came and went without another word from overseas, but the media had another field day. The newspapers and television ran pictures of all those missing, devoting extra space for the image of Patricia Randolph from the University of Texas at Austin, listing her address as the White House or Albuquerque, New Mexico, where she was born and reared.

The background and scholarly achievements of the three leaders took up space with the pictures of Dr. Jonathan Caldwell of the Department of Anthropology at Columbia; Dr. Ursula Baines of Georgetown University; and the director of the Peabody Museum at Harvard, Robert T. Gilmore, the graying protégé of the late, great Harvard anthropologist, Ernest Albert Hooten.

Practically every layout of the nine other students was in alphabetical order: John T. Berry of Enid, Okla., Yale; Bernice Carter Ferrick of Tarpon Springs, Fla., University of Alabama; Edwin Genereau of Amesbury, Mass., Stanford; William Isenstein of Seattle, Columbia; Donald K. Kenyon of Baltimore, University of Pennsylvania; Peter Labelle of Palmer, Mass., Harvard; James Nasvik of Pittsburgh, University of Chicago; Robert P. O'Meara of Charlottesville, Va., Berkeley; and Charles W. Spooner of Terre Haute, Ind., University of Michigan.

There were brief biographies under each photograph, supplied by Avery at Columbia, and interviews and photographs of some of the parents.

With information so scant, hope that everything would come out all right was the primary theme of the interviews. After all, the President's daughter was involved, and none could perceive dire consequences—not with such a major bargaining chip.

The President certainly wasn't going to allow anything to happen to his daughter.

Chapter 5

To put it bluntly, he was scared. It was nearly midnight and he was alone on a white sand beach stretching for thousands of yards in either direction. A full moon etched his striding form alongside a languid sea that whooshed up and gurgled back in perpetual indecision. The sand to his right swept gently inward and upward for about a hundred yards, cresting with long tufts of grass in casually distributed clumps.

Perhaps it was his total nakedness that was making him so apprehensive. His only attire was a G-string suspending a white patch of linen encasing his privates. No wristwatch, no head covering, no footwear . . . Christ! There's something about traipsing around bare-ass outdoors and in strange surroundings that adds to one's feelings of vulnerability. What the hell am I doing here? was the question Jackson Harding asked himself over and over again after he had been dumped on the beach ten minutes ago. Of course, it was a rhetorical exercise. He knew what he was there for. The question always was the why. And he knew that answer, too: He could never say no to them, prompted no doubt by the subtle flattery of being asked to do something out of the ordinary for one's country. It was going to be the death of him yet, but to hell with it, you can't live forever, he kept telling himself.

He broke into a jog to help release his growing tension and had not gone five yards when three heads rose above the grass line up ahead to his right. He didn't break his lope, acting as if he hadn't seen them, until the bodies attached to the heads emerged and three heavily armed figures moved down the sandy slope to intercept him.

Harding slowed to a walk and raised his right hand as he approached the trio.

"Hello. It's a nice night for a walk," he called out haltingly in Arabic.

"Daylight would be safer." It was the proper counter to the coded words, also in Arabic, spoken by the tallest of the trio. "What's your name?"

"Ibrahim." He gave it the Arabic pronunciation.

All three seemed to relax ever so slightly. The tall one stuck out his hand for a quick handshake and a slight tug to move the group back to the dunes, the short snouts of their Uzis seemingly sniffing and measuring the yards ahead. Once behind the dune, one of the trio, on closer look a woman, went to a small duffel bag and produced some beige-colored clothing.

"Here, put these on," she said in English that suffered the American twang.

Harding slipped on a short-sleeved shirt stripped of its buttons and began to step into a baggy pair of pants, with a frayed rope for a belt, and open sandals. As he was about to tie the rope, she gestured toward his hips.

"Take off that thing." She sounded like the Bronx, for sure.

Harding paused for a fleeting instant before he realized she was referring to the G-string. He removed it with a sharp tug, snapping the cord. The other man took it from him, scooped out a hole about two feet deep and buried it. "Let's go."

Ibrahim fell in behind the tall one, followed in single file by the woman and the other man, whom they called Harry, moving quickly inland over the flattening dunes, now totally covered by tall grass. In ten minutes they reached a gray Mercedes station wagon sitting on a narrow dirt patch that passed for a road. The tall one and the woman got into the front after indicating the rear seat for the newcomer.

"Where're we heading for?" Harding asked, this time in English.

"Al Qubayyat."

Harding nodded to himself. That would be in just about the right direction, the high country near the Syrian border, maybe fifty kilometers or so. "Any special instructions?"

"No. You'll be on your own once we drop you off. Need anything?"

"Can't think of anything . . . except a compass, and that's out of the question." The last thing that should be found on him if he were stopped and searched was any possession that would be out of character for a seemingly penniless vagabond.

The Mercedes moved at a good clip, doing about 90KPH, its diesel purring at that speed, raising a cloud of dust that was visible for miles in the light of the moon. The road was paralleling a river now, and the terrain was humping up into low hills, creating an ever-deepening valley for the water course as the car traveled inland.

"We'll have to slow down soon . . . sort of tiptoe through the outskirts of Halba. Can't afford to draw attention to ourselves." The Tall One made the announcement to no one in particular. In this part of the country, drawing attention meant scrutiny by the Lebanese Forces, the name for the Christian militia that dominated the land from the western slopes of the mountainous spine running the length of the land and aproning the sea.

The eastern slopes of Mount Lebanon, from Jabal Aamel in the south to Jabal Akroum in the north, were dominated by Moslems—Shiites and Sunnis—with a sprinkling of Druze forming the ferment of the Beqaa Valley, a valley that had spewed its poison of hate and vengeance on a tortured land for more than fifty years.

No sooner had the words been uttered than an arm-waving figure appeared suddenly on the roadway ahead, flanked by two others with rifles leveled at the approaching car.

"Can't stop . . . we've got weapons and someone without papers!" With that observation, larded with some mumblings concerning excrement, Tall One jammed the accelerator to the floor and headed straight for the human roadblock. The riflemen allowed the car to get to within fifty yards before they scrambled to the left shoulder and opened fire. The woman had her window down and began firing across the hood of the Mercedes as Harry opened up from the side window.

The windscreen shattered in a dozen places and disintegrated. Tall One's head erupted into bloody shards of bone and hunks of hair; Harry gurgled something in Hebrew and slumped back with the death rattle in his throat; and the woman moaned softly as she tried steering the wagon, now careening out of control down the embankment toward the trees and the river.

Harding braced himself on the floor in the rear with Harry's body bouncing heavily on top of him. After a jarring blow to his shoulder, he realized that the dead man's flopping head had become a dangerous element in the wild, plunging descent of the car. Even as the sounds receded from the roadway, he could still hear the snapping reports of the rifles, the bullets whizzing through the jouncing wagon as it finally came to a crashing, snarling halt among the cypresses on the riverbank, its spinning right rear wheel hanging over the embankment.

"Anyone alive?" The woman's voice broke the suddenly heavy silence.

"I think so."

"Are you hurt? How's Harry?"

"I'm OK. Harry's bought it. Are you OK?"

"Hurt my knees and elbows. Don't think I've broken anything. Got to get the hell out of here, quick like. They'll be down looking for us."

"Looks like we're almost in the river," Harding said to the face that appeared over the top of the front seat. "We'd better slip into it if those bastards don't get to us first. See if your door will open. I can't open this one."

The front passenger door did open, and the woman, followed by Harding, dropped about four feet into the surprisingly cold waters of the shallow stream. She was still clutching her Uzi. The banks were steep with water erosion, providing cover for the two, now hip-deep and wading upstream close to the embankment. The almost full moon cast a strong, eerie light over the scape.

"Looks like a small bridge up ahead, probably for the road we were on."

The woman emitted a small grunt in answer and then tugged him to a halt. "I think they've reached the Mercedes. Those shouts . . ."

"Yeah. You're right. Let's move to that overhang there," he said, pulling her toward him and the base of a tree whose roots were half-exposed over the bank, the tubers reaching thirstily for the water.

They crept into the dank, dark protection of the bank, which turned out to be slimy with a faint odor of petroleum, and waited. For some reason, the three riflemen did not split up to inspect the bank in both directions from the car wreck. They worked their way toward the spot where the two were hidden, talking volubly in Arabic about whether there could have been more than two in the car. One was certain there were at least three, but he was losing the argument in favor of returning to the road and making their report. Their voices faded as they turned away from the stream and headed back.

"Well, that seems to be that. What the hell do we do now?" Harding announced as silence settled over the two crouching figures.

"We get out of this cold water, for starters, and maybe we can think of something," she said, turning her words into action. Once out, they separated briefly into the brush to take off their pants, wring them out, and put them back on for their body heat to do the rest.

"I've got to get something from the wagon," she said in the darkness and left him to follow her back to the wreck. She paid not the slightest attention to her dead cohorts, now stripped naked and laid out by the riflemen in the brush alongside the car, and opened the gas tank lid. She stuck her hand into the opening, fished around a bit, and pulled out a packet, which she said was money she would need.

"Well, here we are. I think we're about three or four kilometers from Halba and about twenty-five from Al Qubayyat. Were you going to meet anyone there?"

He stared at her for a moment before replying, "You were involved to the extent of getting me to where I had to be. That's all you have to know. I'm going on my way . . . alone."

"I'll be going with you as far as Al Qubayyat in any case, whether you like it or not." Her voice was low, with a hardness he hadn't heard before.

"It's out of the question, lady."

"Why?"

"How do we explain a penniless beggar with a woman tagging along, eh?"

"We won't have to, because you'll change your act. You'll stand straight, walk with purpose, and give me indifferent attention as I tag along two paces behind you."

"Yeah? When we're stopped, as we sure as hell are going to be, who are we, where are we going, and where are our papers?"

"We'll figure out something, mister. My immediate problem is going to be clothes. I'll need a black, ankle-length dress, a *shawlwar* and a *chador* to pass as a Moslem woman."

Harding didn't reply. He was putting his life on the line, taking as many precautions as he could to succeed in his mission, and she, an ally, was not only giving him lip but destroying his one formula for his past successes—a one-man operation. He was keyed up and ready to handle the unexpected, but his entire being, his total experience, was predicated on working alone. Ever since his linguistic aptitudes and apparent acting abilities had been recognized as useful tools by his agency, his covert duties had taken on a totally different cast, so to speak. Suddenly he was no longer working in ordinary business suits or military attire from the cultures of his clandestine environment. He was more apt to be in the sloppy, flapping garments of a Moslem fellah in the Middle East—as he was now—or a peon in Central or South America, or a head-banded fisherman or coolie in lands Columbus had broadly dubbed Cathay in his romantic ignorance.

When the Trident sub had put him ashore in the dark of night off the northern Lebanese coast without a stitch of clothes on, to foil identification if he were caught, the plan was a simple one: meet the people on the beach who were to transport him to a prearranged meeting place with a contact who would set him up for a lonely, furtive trek to the Irani-Iraqi-Turkish border.

Now he wasn't at all sure he would be able to pull off his mission: Find the Americans.

Chapter 6

President Randolph was not in a mood to be trifled with. A big jump in the cost-of-living index had been announced that morning; his policies involving Greece, Zamboanga, and Bolivia had touched off riots; his daughter was a captive somewhere of unknown forces; and the relentless *Washington Post* was giving him a hard time—as if he needed more—about the color of his socks. He closed his eyes for a moment and tried to visualize who among the people sitting around the table in the Cabinet Room could have leaked the latest bit, about his socks being mismatched at last night's state dinner. Dark green and black are hard to tell apart in a dimly lit bedroom, but they become startlingly obvious when you are sitting in front-row chairs in the East Room during the entertainment. Oh, well, if that's the best or the worst they can write about, it wasn't any big deal. But, still, it would be nice to find out just once who had a pipeline to that newsroom.

He opened his eyes with a start as he realized that that same pipeline might report that he had dozed off during the cabinet session. He stared around at his Secretary of State, sitting next to him on the right, and wondered if any of the situations abroad would have a line of action or a solution today. Of course not. Here he was nearly two years in office, and his high-powered team of national security and foreign affairs experts was still talking about the same problems. It wasn't that he was impatient. Hell, these were the same agenda items, almost to the letter, that had bedeviled his predecessors to a greater or lesser degree as far back as Kennedy and Johnson. No, it seemed that old problems never die, new problems keep adding on. Like that stupidity in Iraq. Absolutely no good reason why any of that should have happened. What were they thinking of? And what was the State Department thinking of when it provided the passports and channels for it to happen?

Now, where was he . . . oh, yes, about the mismatched socks. The news leak wasn't really what bothered him. All it did was bring up that persistent and odious comparison to Buchanan, Lincoln's bachelor predecessor in the White House. Of course, if he had a wife, his socks would never be mismatched, went the drivel in what the media called news. And on and on about how the nation missed having a First Lady, and how much she could have added to the President's social effectiveness, and how important it was to have such a person at the President's side. And the stories would hark as far back as Wilson's administration to make their dubious points.

The media had left him alone the first year of his presidency, giving him a year of grace after the tragedy that had rocked the nation. Two days after he had won the election, his wife had died suddenly from a massive pulmonary embolus while being treated for a chest cold she had picked up during the campaign. As the president-elect, he had stumbled through the preliminaries of cabinet and staff selections, but the awesome responsibilities of his new job had been the best relief from the loss that had overwhelmed his senses. From the day he was sworn in, he had tackled the problems of the nation and the world as if his life had depended on it, leaving him little time even for his eighteen-year-old autistic man-child, one of two offspring in his twenty-three-year marriage.

His daughter, twenty-two-year-old Patricia, was currently giving him aggravated fits, and he was feeling totally helpless about her. The situation wouldn't have been at all serious if she weren't the President's daughter, but she was, and everyone knew she was, and everyone was squawking about her, and none could offer a remedy or a way out. It was going to be a . . . now, what? Brockway, the CIA chief, had posed a question to him, and the president had to ask him to repeat it.

"Are you prepared, sir, to accept the consequences of suspending relations with Greece?"

"I certainly am prepared to accept the consequences. We've discussed this matter for nearly five weeks now. Shall we move to the next item, please?"

An hour later, the President was alone with the heads of the NSA, Secret Service, and CIA, his national security chief, and his chief of staff, in the Oval Office.

"Let's get started, gentlemen," the President said. "I want to know every detail as to what we've done so far and what we've accomplished. You start, Tom," he said, nodding to the CIA chief.

"We got our man to Naples by way of supersonic aircraft from Andrews and put him ashore on a beach in northern Lebanon . . ."

"Why couldn't he have gone in directly by ferryboat from Cyprus to . . . to . . ."

"Junieh, sir?" The President nodded.

"It would have been a seven-hour trip from Cyprus, sir, and he would have had to undergo the scrutiny of a thousand eyes on landing, including a body search by the Lebanese Forces. They're the government's principal Christian militia. Frankly, we couldn't get him in any other way without running the chance of being spotted. That part of the world is so paranoid,

so involved with intrigue and double-dealing and triple-dealing
that merely saying 'good morning' can raise eyebrows.''

"What about Turkey as an avenue of entry?"

"No good, sir. Our air base at Adana would have been an
excellent jumping-off point in our investigation, but the civilian
help doubles its income by being eyes and ears for practically
every friend and foe of the United States around the world.
Goes back to when the world suddenly realized we were using
the base for high-altitude surveillance, among other things,
when we lost one of our airplanes over the Soviet Union.''

"Oh, yes, I remember. The U-2 incident. Well, I presume
we're going about it the right way."

"Yes, sir. It's the long way around, and the distances that
need traversing also create the problem of discovery, but there
simply is no other way. We thought of dropping him in, but the
combination of terrain, the necessity of carrying things in with
him, and the chances of being spotted, ruled that out.''

"Is he ashore now?"

"The Navy succeeded in putting him ashore, sir, undetected
as far as we could tell.''

"Tell me again, why all the secrecy in putting our man
ashore?"

"In a nutshell, Mr. President, we are not at all certain who is
behind the kidnapping, or whatever you want to call it. The
only people we've brought into our confidence have been the
Israelis.''

"We have no idea who's behind this?"

"We can't be sure, sir. The locus is the geographical juncture
of Turkey, Iraq, and Iran. The area is also proximal to Syria and
Soviet Armenia. On top of that, we have indigenous popula-
tions of Kurds, Circassians, and at least fourteen Moslem factions within all these groups, making such a hodgepodge of
affiliations and followings that it would be foolhardy to assume
anything at this time without absolute proof.''

The President drummed his fingers on the desk top for a
second, assimilating what had just been said. "What's this one
man going to accomplish?"

"We're not sure, sir. He has been apprised of all the facts, he knows the country and the languages, and he is one of our most resourceful agents."

"You must have given him some instructions?"

"Yes, sir. We told him to get to where they were when last heard from and find out where they are or what happened to them."

"You mean to tell me you slipped an American man into the Middle East, on some beach, and told him, literally, to go find 'em? Are you mad? What kind of a paragon is this guy? Who dreamed up such a scenario?"

Brockway smiled at the President. "I don't blame you one bit, sir, for reacting the way you have. But hear me out, please. We've actually put nine men ashore, if you please, sir, in this one person. This man speaks nine languages fluently, including three English accents: Oxonian, Bostonian, and Oklahoma Panhandle. He is expert in the martial arts, knows how to handle firearms, flies jets and copters, is as much at home underwater as on land, and relies on his wits rather than brawn to get things done . . ."

"What's his record to back up all this?"

"Mr. President, he has been one of those people we send anonymously to places we're not supposed to be or know about. He is one of those people who act as our eyes and ears, who send back or come back with the vital intelligence we need to act on or not to act on in any given situation. He is one of our invisible stethoscopes, one of our invisible eagles peering into areas that would be absolutely barred to us otherwise."

"Let me ask again, what's his record?"

"Excuse me, sir. In the past nine years, he's been the lone agent involved in the Algerian sinking, Mannheim explosion, Singapore, Hong Kong intervention, Cyprus revolt, Islamabad, and Beirut South, and in two-man teams in Caracas, Libya, Aden, and Athens—all familiar to you, sir, in overall and public information."

The President looked impressed. "He pulled off the Mannheim raid?"

"Not the raid, sir. He nailed down the actual people responsible for the terrorist bombing, located exactly where they were to be found, and provided the timetable for their apprehension."

"Sounds too good to be true, Tom. Who is this man?"

There was a long silence, and the President's eyes slowly widened as he realized that his question was not being answered. "Well . . . ?"

"He's one of several men who have been operating under code names ever since the SOB was established way back in the 1950s under Dulles. Their real names have never been part of our official records, sir. They're numbered operatives."

"You are not going to tell me this man's name?" The President had a weak smile on his face.

Brockway squirmed slightly in his chair, then said softly, "I know his code name, sir, and 'Mother Hubbard' out at Fort Meade knows his real name . . ."

"All right, all right, that's enough. I just want to know three things right now to satisfy my curiosity. If we are operating without records on such men, how do they get paid?"

"They don't," Brockway said with a wide grin. "These people are very special Americans. They have real cover jobs in ordinary federal agencies with understandings established to allow them one or two days' leave of absence on special assignment to the White House, usually over weekends."

"Hmmm. Sounds a little bit like history. The Iran-Contra Affair. My second question: What does SOB stand for?"

"Special Operations Branch." Brockway sounded a bit sheepish.

"How esoteric. OK, if the Israelis are helping us out in this situation, would it be too much to ask what the Israelis are calling him?"

"Certainly not, sir. He's being called Ibrahim."

Chapter 7

"I suppose you're a Yankee fan?"

"What makes you think that?"

"I detect the Bronx in your accent."

"That's pretty good. I thought I had lost that some time ago. Nope, I never gave a damn for the Yankees." She wasn't going to elaborate beyond that, judging from her subsequent silence.

They were trudging along the side of the road, she two paces behind him, dressed in a loose-fitting black jumper and *shalwar* with a black twist of cloth on her head. No veil. That's all they could scavenge from a line of clothes drying in the yard of a mud-pack hut about a mile from where they had left the river. She had clipped a one hundred–piaster Syrian pound note to the line. Losing such clothes would have been an economic catastrophe to such people.

At the rate they were going, it was going to take two days to reach Al Qubayyat. He had to hitch a ride for certain, but the presence of a female made it almost impossible. Arabs and other travelers on these roads were quick to provide a lift to pedestrians but never if a woman was involved. He couldn't shake the fact that she was a hindrance.

"This setup is not going to work, lady." He had yet to ask her her name. "We've got to hitch a ride, and no one's going to pick us up with you along."

"I was thinking the same thing, but we'll never pull it off either if we become two guys."

"Incidentally, you don't seem to have any kind of an accent that could tell me where you come from in the States. Where're you from?"

Harding shook his head. The less she knew about him the

better. That was certainly a rule she could understand and knew very well. Else, she wouldn't be in the business she was in. What the hell was she doing asking questions? Oh, well. "I could have spoken English with a definite British accent, or English as if I were born and reared in Boston, Massachusetts, or English of the kind I have spoken. It's Oklahoma Panhandle American, the only English spoken in the U.S. without a tell-tale accent of any kind. How's that? Do you still want to figure out where I'm from?"

"I really don't care, mister. I was merely curious since you pinpointed me, and I've been away from the States for fourteen years."

"I was wondering about that. I'm supposed to meet some Israelis, and one of them turns out to speak English like an American. Are you one of those . . ."

"I'm one of those whose parents emigrated from the States to live in a kibbutz, and I'm serving my hitch in the Israeli military. I . . . I happen to be a small-arms expert." She tagged on a small, deprecating chuckle after that one, patting the Uzi she still had stuck into the sash under her voluminous folds.

"Were those two guys we left back there friends of yours?"

"You could say that. When you hide together, fight together, share whatever you have to eat and drink, and smell each other's shit because there's no room or chance for modesty, yup, you could say that."

They continued to plod on for another minute or so, not looking back even as the hum of an approaching vehicle grew louder in their ears. The Rover slowed down and came to a stop just ahead of them. It was the same vehicle, with the spare mounted atop the hood, that had raced by them much earlier, at the crack of dawn.

"I say, old chap, would you and your missus care for a lift into town?" The speaker was obviously English in accent and even looked the part, in the uniform of a brevet major with a UN arm band. He was tall and stocky with light hair.

The man called Ibrahim made gestures indicating his desire to ride toward town, obtained some assenting nods from the driver, and hopped into the rear section, dragging the woman along. He wasn't about to admit knowing English.

The Rover took off with a roar into the sun, now almost at its meridian, consuming the kilometers in giant gulps, the same kilometers that would have cost Harding hours instead of the Rover's minutes.

Ten minutes on the road in total silence was finally snapped by the driver: "Expected four of you." His blue eyes scanned the pair briefly, but his question-statement brought blank stares from the hitchhikers.

"I may be talking to myself, for all I know, but we had almost given up hope that the whale gave up Ibrahim and the Israelites clothed him."

The hitchhikers grinned at each other for the first time since Harding had come ashore. "I'm Ibrahim," he said as he reached over and her Uzi suddenly appeared in full view on his lap.

The driver stole a furtive glance at the machine pistol as he barreled along the empty road, then: "What kept you? Where are the others?"

She filled in the details in a few clipped sentences, then asked what her chances were of getting back south.

He shook his head. "You'll need wheels and a male escort. We'll have to see about that once we take care of Ibrahim."

Taking care of Ibrahim turned out to be a casual affair, once they reached their destination, a large, two-story white brick structure that had once been a storage building of some kind and was now serving as the perpetual peacekeeping mission of the UN. The driver had let off the pair just inside the limits of the city and told them to find their way to the rear of the UN building located on the same main street they were on.

With prearranged difficulty, they were allowed entry, satisfying interested eyes that the man and the woman weren't anyone of import.

Harding was directed by a tall Sikh to a flight of steps while the woman was waved to a door on the street floor.

He stuck out his hand to her. "You've got guts, lady, and I'd like to shake your hand. What's your name?"

"It's Lenna, with two ens," she said, breaking out in a broad grin, exhibiting a fine set of white teeth and a sparkle in her dark eyes. "What's yours?"

"Sometimes I answer to the name of George, but don't hold me to it."

"See you around," she said, waving an arm at him as she disappeared through the door.

See you around, Harding thought. She's like a schoolgirl waving to a chum after school lets out. See you around, all right, when hell freezes over. His eyes were fixed on a thin young man, thirtyish, sitting at a table in a bare room. Shit, this guy's a kid. What's he going to do for me? He stuck out his hand and exchanged names as they shook.

"I'm Forbisher, sir. My orders are to get you on your way with whatever you need."

"What I'll need will depend on what you can do for me in terms of transport. What's your geographic jurisdiction?"

"The Lebanon-Syrian border here is my bailiwick, but we're an outpost of a unit headquartered in Aleppo, to the north."

"How far east do you range?"

"Directly to the Iraq border. We share our peacekeeping duties with the Syrian and Russian units assigned to the area."

Harding thought that over for a moment. "Any way I can hitch a ride to the Iraqi border?"

Forbisher scratched his black hair. "We could get you there as a replacement in our unit, but you'd have to be in uniform . . . certainly not the way you're dressed now . . . and your presence would be highly visible and accounted for."

"Yeah, I see. Do you have a repair depot for your Jeeps and trucks anywhere close to the Iraqi border?"

"At Dei ez Zor. That's about a hundred kilometers from the border."

"Forbisher, right now, I'm about 725 kilometers from where I want to be, as the crow flies, and Dei ez Zor reduces that distance by 350 kilometers. Can you get me to Dei ez Zor right away?"

"Certainly. You must understand that it's in the middle of nowhere, a real desert area, but I guess you know that since you can rattle off distances as if you've lived here all your life . . ."

Harding grinned. "I've been around, and I also put in a few

hours studying the entire area since I'm not really sure where I'm going to end up."

"Excuse me, sir, but any new word on the situation?"

"Nope. Not a single word in weeks. Driving everybody up the wall."

"Your president must be going crazy."

"I wouldn't know that. You'll have to set me up as a mechanic. I think a Syrian mechanic would be best. I'll need some metric-gauge tools and . . ."

"We'll have all that and provide papers for you. Will you need any personal arms or special weapons?"

"No, nothing like that. I would like an accurate compass, though. Something old and banged up and much the worse for wear. And I want to see your garage here . . . You have one, what?"

"Quite. It's located behind the next building to this. I'll take you there. You know, it's not going to be a joyride to Dei ez Zor. You've picked just about the worst time to be traveling here. Temperatures out there go as high as 125 degrees Fahrenheit before noon and stay there until the evening. Then, if you're not prepared for it with suitable clothes, you shiver your skin off in the coldness of the desert night."

"I know, old man. Can I start off before nightfall?"

"We'll try. You'll be traveling alone, of course. Right now, why don't you gather some shut-eye for a couple of hours? We've a room in back here that'll do you just fine while we're getting things together."

Harding took the advice and had just closed the door to the cell-like room when it was opened by Forbisher: "You won't be taking showers or other ablutions, you know." He grinned and pulled his head back as he closed the door.

No kidding, Harding thought. He was now in a part of the world where showers for cleanliness were nonexistent and baths were more than likely taken or given as a matter of medical necessity. He knew that the dirtier he was or became, the more certainly he would be accepted as one of the populace. There were public bathhouses in most cities and larger towns, but generally, the old phrase, the Great Unwashed, was a simple matter of fact embracing the entire area: the subcontinent, the continent. This element of his assignments was the one aspect he hated. He smelled so badly in a matter of days, he couldn't stand himself. Worst of all, sores would break out around his privates and under his armpits. Most amazing to him, the aromatic people with whom he came in contact never seemed to be repelled by the aroma he knew was emanating from him.

He remembered that on one assignment a few years back, he had had to go directly from the carrier deck to shore to take up a position in a certain marketplace, dressed in the garb of a beggar. The special-assignment unit on board had sprayed him with a foul-smelling chemical compound that gave off the stench of weeks of dried sweat and urine. Incredibly, in such a condition, he was always able to smell the lye and soap mixtures of a washed and bathed European or North American.

He wasn't aware of how long he had dozed off when Forbisher shook him awake to tell him that all was in readiness in the garage. The Englishman was a precise man, Harding noted, with a habit of bending an elbow and geturing with his hand. He did just that in indicating that Harding should don his sandals and follow him. They went down the same stairs Harding had used, through a side door, into an alley, and across to another building, with a collection of trucks and Rovers.

Harding went to the first vehicle with its hood raised, stuck his hands into the bowels of the engine cavity, and managed to muck them up with black grease and carbon. He scraped his fingers across his palms, getting the black under his nails and around the cuticles. He didn't stop rubbing his hands together even as he spoke. If he was to be an auto mechanic . . .

"I say, old man." Harding's British accent was flawless. "Who was the driver that picked us up on the road this morning?"

"Why, Jones-Armitage, of course. He was with us all night waiting for you to appear. At daylight he volunteered to go out on a scout for you."

"How many knew I was coming?"

"Amesbury and me received the signal from Whitehall, in code, of course. You're certainly mucking up your paws, old boy."

"And Jones-Armitage?"

"We carry him along, sir. He's not an Englishman, really. Left over from an oil company crew two weeks ago. We give him our cast-off clothes, give him the run of the place, feed him, and he runs our errands, does the laundry . . . Why are you looking at me like that, old boy?"

"Where is he now?"

"Why . . . why . . . he accompanied that Israeli woman to the bazaar to pick up some things and get a bite to eat . . . Wha . . . what's the matter?"

"My God, man, I hope we're not too late! Let's find 'em, quick!"

As Harding dashed for the door, Forbisher leaped into a Rover and caught up with him. "We'll be in the area in two minutes. I think we should try Hakim's teahouse."

The Rover roared down the narrow main street, its lights flashing to warn pedestrians, and they came to a screeching halt in front of Hakim's *chai khana*, which was part of a solid row of two- and three-story buildings, all with drawn-up steel roll shutters.

They stormed into a crowded setting of small, rickety tables, small chairs, and heavy smoke hanging across the room from all the water pipes and cheroots that were being smoked. All heads were turned toward the two figures that had burst in, at first, and then toward a table at the far right. The customers knew instinctively that the sudden appearance of an Anglo could mean only one thing—another Anglo—and the other Anglo was a she sitting with her mouth agape, startled, as she recounted later, by the leaping departure of Jones-Armitage, when the screech of tires was heard, and the immediate appearance of another Englishman with Ibrahim.

Lenna, who had changed into western garb at Jones-Armitage's insistence, didn't show the slightest emotion when she realized what had happened. For certain, the cover for the project was blown. Harding decided that to show anger at this stage and under the immediate circumstances would be a waste of time. Those variegated assholes. Neither Forbisher nor Amesbury could recall what "Jones-Armitages' " real name was before they dubbed him with the names of a once-famous music hall duo. Oh, yes, Forbisher said, he did speak English very well, right from the start. Oh, yes, he's been part of the mission, ex officio, you might say, since the rest of the civilized world forced a real truce in the Middle East. Oh, yes, he lived in the barracks with the British marines. Yes, I must assume he knew everything about your arrival . . .

Harding stared at the floor for a while, then turned his gaze to Lenna: "You can see now why we had a reception committee on the road. And you can grasp the fact, I hope, that you could have disappeared tonight for good if we hadn't come along."

"What made you suspicious of him?"

"His accent. Some of it was Cantabrigian and some was Oxonian, obviously not a natural learning process. What threw me off, temporarily, was the fact that he knew about us to the letter. And get this: He's been here exactly two weeks!"

"Then we took an awful chance after we got into the Rover with him."

"I didn't give him much choice. I laid out your Uzi in plain sight. He knew he would be the first to die if he deviated from our destination. You see, he must have decided there would be other chances to get rid of us."

Forbisher, completely abashed, suggested that under the circumstances there was no option but to call off the project.

"We'll continue as planned, if you don't mind, with some small alterations. We'll let them think the project has been called. I'll take the Rover back the way I came instead of heading north to pick up the highway to Homs. After I go back and pass the town of Bire, there's a secondary road off to the right that takes you to Menjez and connects up with the road going north at Chadra. It'll take longer, but I don't see how else I can pull this off, short of helicopter support, and that's out of the question."

The glum looks of the Britishers and Lenna didn't make Harding feel any more certain. "I think I should have some weapons, though. We don't know the enemy, but they seem to know exactly who we are. I've got to even the odds a bit."

"I should be going with you." Lenna's voice was low, matter-of-fact.

"Why not? I can certainly use a small-arms expert."

"What made you change your mind?"

"The circumstances, my dear, the circumstances. A completely clandestine one-man operation is one thing. Since somebody somewhere knows about me and is intent on stopping me, a tough bird like you is welcome," he said with a growing smile on his face. "I know it's going to be a tall order, but see if you can look as much like a man as possible before we take off."

She didn't take her eyes off his, and stared him down, responding coldly to the wave of his arm in the general direction of her upper torso.

It took another hour to get the items and plans in order. Forbisher agreed that nothing would be transmitted to the outside world about Ibrahim, and not one word would be committed to paper. As the sun went down in the distant Mediterranean, the two figures in the Rover headed back for the sea.

Bullshit, Forbisher, Harding thought. Anything I do from now on will never be privy to you and your Jones-Armitages, Philbys, and Burgesses, and all the rest of that motley bag of British traitors.

Chapter 8

"I must apologize, Mr. President. My conduct yesterday . . ."

President Randolph made no oral response but smiled at the CIA director.

"It was impossible for me to reveal our operative's real identity in the presence of others."

The President raised a hand. "No apology necessary, Tom. I

realized later I had made a gaffe and I couldn't salvage the situation for you. What's the situation today?"

"Not a word, sir. He was put ashore yesterday morning, and our man is somewhere over there working on it."

The President wasn't impressed by the definitude of the answer. "Who is this man? Can you tell me now?"

"Jackson Harding. He's about five-ten, powerful and coordinated, going on thirty-six, unmarried, naval academy graduate with top honors, doctorates from Berkeley and Columbia in languages and minors in anthropology at Harvard. He speaks a string of languages fluently. What makes him especially valuable out there is that he speaks four Arabic idioms in addition to the idiom used across the Middle East and North Africa on radio, television, and in the print media."

"Well, I hope he's the answer to this mess. Did you obtain the complete list of people involved?"

"Yes, sir, I did. You know some of the names already, but this should give you everything you want to know."

The President accepted the paper that contained the names of his only daughter and everyone with her. He scanned the names of the leaders of the expedition—Caldwell from Columbia, Baines from Georgetown, and Gilmore from Harvard—and wondered if they were being of any help to his daughter.

Her name fairly leaped out at him as he stared at the sheet of paper: *Patricia Ann Randolph, University of Texas at Austin*, paired with Bernice Carter Ferrick, University of Alabama.

There she was, among ten archaeological aides selected from ten major graduate schools with outstanding departments of anthropology, given the honor of working in a remote mountainous wilderness. The magnet was a cave discovered to contain skeletal remains of nine Stone Age people who had lived there more than forty thousand years ago. The finds were made in the 1950s, in the Shanidar Cave in a tiny portion of Iraq jutting into the junction of Turkey and Iran.

"What made this cave so important, damn it?" Randolph was exasperated.

"As I gather, sir, up until the skeletal finds at Shanidar, only relics and artifacts of the Stone Age had been found in Iraq. The finds at Shanidar are similar to the finds at Mt. Carmel in Palestine. Mt. Carmel had provided purely physical evidence, that is size, configuration, weapons, tools, and so forth.

"Then a Dr. Solecki and a small crew, under the auspices of the Smithsonian, spent nine years unearthing remains and other artifacts that give us for the first time the other side of the coin—the 'human nature' of these Neanderthals.

"Turns out they weren't simple, shuffling brutes. Solecki found some positive indications that these cavemen had cared for their old folks, nursed their sick and wounded, and, get this, buried their dead with flowers!

"Well, everything had to stop with the advent of the 1960s. It was bad enough conducting archaeological examinations with wild Kurdish tribesmen constantly nagging at the expedition. They had to have a police detail with them at all times. With the political upheavals and the warfare between Iran and Iraq, and Iraq and its own mountain Kurds, precisely in the Shanidar Cave region, you would have needed an armored column to get there.

"Sir, it's been nearly five years since a shot was fired in anger in that entire region, and the cave at Shanidar begged for renewed excavation to see what further light could be cast on the past.

"So, to raise funds for a new expedition, Dr. Jonathan Caldwell at Columbia offered to take along an outstanding graduate student of anthropology from any university that donated at least $25,000. He got ten universities to support the project . . . and your daughter was at the top of the list as an outstanding physical and cultural anthropologist at Texas."

She would be, the President thought. Pat had always been an achiever. From kindergarten through college, she had obtained the highest marks, grades, and honors. Her interest in the Middle East had drawn her to the university in Austin, which was internationally famous for its Middle East studies and collections—not to mention the most complete collection of Robert Burns manuscripts and first editions, tucked away in the Tower. He shook his head. "How's the media handling this abroad?"

"I'm having a complete report sent to you today, sir."

"Dave says this is one story that will never die down, until the final curtain."

"I'm afraid he's right, sir. You don't have to be an expert on the media like Dave to come to that conclusion. This one has everything."

"Everything?"

"If you'll excuse me, sir, we have here a beautiful young woman who happens to be the daughter of the President of the United States; she's disappeared in a remote mountain fastness with a group of young Americans on an archaeological dig; and she's being held for ransom."

The President had buried his face in his hands, uttering not a sound. Brockway realized he had never seen Randolph in such a posture of emotional distress in all the years he had known him—in the Congress, the Senate, running NASA, as the vice president . . .

"How are the parents of the other youngsters taking it?"

"It's been really rather tough on them, too. As you know, we brought them to Washington to keep them abreast of developments, and they're not saying much of anything right now, but I detect a growing tinge of resentment against you for letting this thing continue for so long."

"We've only been aware of the facts for about three weeks now." He sounded a bit plaintive.

"I know, sir, but you know about human feelings. They're rarely based on logic."

Chapter 9

There was no question in his mind as to what he was going to do next. It was going to be back to the drawing board. Even as he had outlined his plan to attempt to throw off "Jones-Armitage" and his cohorts by *seeming* to head back, he actually was.

Lenna realized that the plans had changed somewhat when he drove with the Rover's headlights on, despite the full moon. Her suspicions were confirmed when he didn't take the right turn to Menjez and back to Chadra and the main highway east. She didn't say a word for the length of time it took the Rover to pass the spot where the Mercedes had plunged down the ravine and lodged among the trees on the riverbank.

"You're taking me back?"

"We're both going back to the beach."

"Uh, uh . . ."

"There's no need for secrecy. Thanks to the British back there, we were dead ducks from the moment we joined up on the beach."

About an hour before dawn they were on the shore of the Mediterranean. Harding made no attempt to cover up. The area was desolate to begin with. He drove on the flat, hard sand beach, splashing through water in some areas, and kept on past the point where he had been intercepted by Lenna and her friends. He brought the Rover to a halt at a rivulet of fresh water coursing in a shallow bed of pebbles and sand to the sea.

"I buried the transmitter here," Harding said by way of explanation to Lenna. "Couldn't chance anyone seeing my footprints, so I walked up this water bed." He made no attempt to hide his tracks, going directly to the high ground covered by grass tufts, located the spot he was looking for, and went to his knees to scoop away at the soil. He pulled out a small plastic satchel, unlocked the seal, and removed a black casing about the size of his fist. After he pulled out a foot-long antenna from the casing, he snapped off a small cover, revealing a button, and pressed it three times, repeating the triple signal at approximately ten-second intervals.

"What're you doing?"

"I'm calling for a copter." She responded with a quizzical frown. Harding stared out to sea for a moment, then decided that perhaps it would be better if he were to bounce his thinking off her to see if he was thinking straight. She was a smart one, no question about it.

"If the people out to stop me know who I am and where I'm heading, what's the percentage in secrecy at this point? I've lost a whole day and was about to go inland with my cover blown. Now, I'm back where I started from, but I'll use a copter to get me to Shanidar. Then I can take it from there, cover or no cover."

"Sounds good to me. But have you thought about what you do once you're out there?"

"Certainly. I knew that before I left the States." Harding kept looking at her intelligent face and accepted the obvious. She wanted to know.

"I'll tell you. I'm simply going to track the lot as far as I can and play the rest of it by ear. I'll have some help," Harding said, waving the transmitter.

"You know, it's not going to be easy."

"Tracking thirteen people plus the abductors won't be difficult until they take to some transport other than ground."

"Have any idea who the abductors could be?"

"If we had any idea, I wouldn't be here. I'm supposed to find out."

There was another long pause, as both of them seemed to concentrate their thoughts toward the briny horizon, now beginning to take shape as the sun tried to break the night behind them, the water running from slate black to dark blue.

"Are you still planning to take me with you?"

Harding had thought about that, too. "Since it's no secret, as I said in Al Qubayyat, you would be welcome as a gun hand . . . although I would have preferred one of your friends we left back there by the river." The instant he said it, he knew he shouldn't have.

"You big, dumb shit, you're nothing but one of those antediluvians, a throwback to the Dark Ages, a . . ."

"Hold it, hold it, cut it out, I . . ."

"Forget it, mister, I'm not going anywhere with you." Her eyes were glinting in anger.

"Fine, fine. It's OK with me, but all I was trying to say had nothing to do with your capabilities to carry your end of it. I just happen to be one of those male idiots who has an instinctive reaction to protect a female in possible peril of some kind. In the midst of some action, I might be distracted by thoughts of protecting you instead of letting you fend for yourself . . ."

"I've never needed protection . . . and I can die as quietly as the next guy."

"OK, OK, let's forget what I said and start all over again: Lenna, you would be welcome as a gun hand." He wrinkled his nose: Who said anything about dying?

"Good. I was worried about reporting back to base."

"Worried?"

"Nothing important. Goethe said it: 'A woman can stand almost anything except a succession of ordinary days.' " She grinned broadly. "I know, I know I changed it."

"And I remember Shakespeare . . . Oh, the hell with it, here it comes."

The Apache gunship from a guided missile cruiser offshore whined up to the beach and settled down fifty yards from the duo with the kind of unholy racket that only copters can make, with the air turbulence they cause. The rear door opened, and a lieutenant jaygee jumped down and met the approaching pair. Salutes were not exchanged.

"I expected only one person, a man," the lieutenant said by way of introduction, shouting over the noise from the still-running engines.

"That's right, that's me. I've picked up an ally. This is . . ." Harding turned to her, his hand out.

"I'm Lieutenant Lenna Levin, 21st Armored Division, Israeli Defense Forces." She saluted.

"Lieutenant Fernando Garza, U.S. Navy." He also saluted, and waited expectantly. Harding got down to business.

"We need a lift directly to a pretty rough spot on the map, mister. It's going to be just about 755 kilometers from here. You can set your bearings for longitude 44 degrees east, latitude 37 degrees north. That should be close."

As they hurried to enter the gunship, Lieutenant Garza asked if the destination was Turkey.

"You must be familiar with Adana in Turkey. Yes, it's Adana's latitude, but we'll be setting down in Iraq at those coordinates."

They were arranging themselves in the squat attack helicopter and Lieutenant Garza was giving directions to the pilot when the beach erupted with a shattering roar about thirty

yards to the left. The pilot didn't waste a second turning up the
RPMs and lifting off and away as a second explosion gouged
another hole in the sand, ten yards from where the copter had
been, destroying the Rover.

"It's 90mm stuff . . . and I can see them," the copilot
shouted. Lieutenant Garza shoved a negative waving hand between the pilot and copilot, signaling them to abort any move
to return fire.

"What the hell's going on?" Garza shouted at Harding.
"You're obviously no Ay-rab and . . ."

"Hold it, Lieutenant. We don't have much time right now.
Get the pilot to head for the coordinates I gave you, and I'll
need an ETA. I have no idea how fast this gunship can travel."

Lenna touched Harding's arm as Garza talked things over
with the pilot. "How do you think our friends caught up with
us so quickly back there?"

Harding shrugged. "Their people must be everywhere. My
guess is that they made radio contact somewhere near the
beach and were able to deploy some firepower when they saw
us in the Rover. They must be damn well organized."

"We should be at your destination in about ninety minutes,
give or take ten minutes." It was Lieutenant Garza.

"Good. That'll get us there before noon, and we'll have at
least six hours to poke around and get a heading. Lenna, let's
see those duffels with the arms Forbisher packed for us."

There were four .44 magnum automatics, two Bren machine
rifles the English had come out with less than a year ago, two
high-powered Belgian hunting rifles with scopes for day and
night use, a grenade launcher, an assortment of plastic explo-
sives in innocent-appearing bars, three glistening bowie knives,
and seven assorted cannisters of ammo for the weapons, including two boxes of grenades, one for hand, the other for
launching.

Harding looked at Lenna after the arms were sorted out. She
said it for him: "What a collection of junk! I can't believe it.
Other than the Brens, we might as well have checked out one
of those Army-Navy stores back in the States."

Harding shrugged, pulled out a pad from the copter's seat-
back folder, asked Garza for a pen, jotted down a few words

and numbers, and told him to have the message filed pronto.

"It . . . it's not addressed to anyone, mister . . ."

"That's OK, lad. It's in code, and the first combination spells out where and to whom it's going. Don't worry about it. Get that off and let's have a confab."

Harding and Lenna were seated facing forward; Garza was seated with his back to the pilot's compartment. He turned back to his passengers even as the copilot began sending the message.

"Once we reach the area, we'll have to do a quick bit of hovering until I locate the exact spot to put down." Garza nodded. "The pilot knows where to go once we get off?"

"Yes, sir." Harding noted that Garza had "sir"ed him for the first time.

"Good. I hope your services as transport for me will not be required again. Do you think anyone could get a fix on us at this altitude?" Harding had been startled a couple of times when his eye caught an escarpment at the window level of the copter.

"I'm sure not, sir. We've been hugging the deck as much as possible, but where we're heading seems to have some mountains."

"You're right, mister. The terrain will be extremely rugged. The peaks won't be much higher than nine to twelve thousand feet. It'll be the Zagros Mountains on the Iraq-Iran-Turkish border."

Garza nodded, and then a light of understanding and discovery lit up his face: "Egad, man, you must be tracking down the Presi—"

Harding stopped him. "You're right, lad. The whole world knows about it, including some who shouldn't have known I was here. Do me a favor, will you?" In response to Garza's energetic nods, he continued, "Don't respond to any questions or conversations arising from British sources."

The pilot leaned around. "We'll reach the coordinates in two minutes. Pick out your landing spot."

The gunship had slowed its forward speed. Harding slid open his door and looked down on some of the wildest terrain he had seen from the air. Dominating the view was a sharply delineated white-water river slashing through the steep, rocky ground. That must be the Greater Zab, he thought, using the river course to obtain his bearings. Yep, there it is, Shanidar Cave, with its unmistakable triangular-shaped opening, about sixty feet high at the apex and wide enough at the base to handle about twenty cars abreast. A roadway from ancient times wound its way past the area below the mouth of the cave.

Harding tapped the pilot on the shoulder. "Make a sweep in a twenty-mile radius with that cave as the north apogee . . . slow her down . . . that's it . . . I'm going to take a peek and tell you where to put me down . . ."

He held on carefully to the sides of the open door frame and stepped down onto the starboard runner to scan the ground below. The pilot began the sweep by heading straight for the cave and turning ninety degrees to the left to begin the slow, steady circle.

Almost immediately, the long, high mountain lake was visible below, formed by the new high dam at what was once the head of the Bekhme Gorge on the Greater Zab when Dr. Solecki made his discovery trip in 1951. It shimmered in the noonday sun, about thirty kilometers long and six kilometers wide, serving as a vital water source for the parched plains and the mighty city of Baghdad in the summer months. Harding marveled at the fantastic amount of water in all forms and shapes—rivers, rivulets, rills, ponds, lakes, basins—he saw sweep by below him, interrupted at one point by a large city—Rawanduz, for certain—straddling the river of the same name at the nadir of the vast circle the gunship was making.

On the sweep back north, now across the lower mountains of the Zagros-Taurus range, which defined the impassable border with Iran, Harding brought his right leg back into the compartment, nodded at Garza to get closer to him, and said Garza was to relay the set-down command to the pilot when Harding gave it.

The gunship was coming up to the Shanidar Cave, dead ahead in the west now, when Harding made up his mind.

"Set her down anywhere," Harding pointed downward, "and get the hell out of here, quick." He touched Garza's arm.

"Send out this message," he said, handing over another piece of pad paper.

The copter touched down for no more than four seconds, giving the debarking passengers just enough time to pull out the three duffel bags before it rose in thunderous farewell, heading for the mountains to the north and Turkey five minutes away.

The looming, yawning mouth of the cave at Shanidar beckoned the pair.

Chapter 10

"There are no provisions for voice transmissions, sir."

"Then?"

"We are committed to a simple series of dots."

"Dots?"

"Yes, sir. Harding has a powerful microchip transmitter with him, only slightly larger than a telephone beeper. It was developed for our exploration team on Mars."

"Does he use Morse?"

"Definitely not, sir. We have a simple series of dots created only for this mission, which we felt he might need in certain circumstances."

"What if we have to get to him? How do we know exactly where he is at any given time?"

"We don't know where he is at any given time, but he can let us know simply by repeating a signal at short intervals, the signal not longer than a minute in time span."

"I'm curious, Atwater. Tell me exactly how that works."

William Atwater, the taciturn Secret Service chief, was feeling uncomfortable in the unexpected limelight of technological consultant to the President.

"Let's say Harding needs a copter. He presses his signal button three times in rapid succession. That's the prearranged code for a copter—three dots, Mr. President.

"Then, if he repeats the three dots every ten seconds or so, we are able to pinpoint his location as well as the reason for the transmission."

"I take it the signal can be picked up by unwanted ears. You keep transmissions under a minute . . ."

"Well . . . well, sir. It is impervious to pickup by any and every type of ordinary or sophisticated listening device known to science, military or civilian . . . except one."

"One?" A trace of a glower appeared on the President's face.

"When the Mars expedition was in progress, one of the Houston staff had to stay home because of a flu attack and almost fell out of bed when he recognized dot signals from Mars coming from somewhere in his house . . ."

"Really?" The President was grinning now. "Had he violated the rules or something by bringing home a receiver?"

"No, sir. He found the signals emanating from one of those 'learn-to-spell' computer gizmos he had bought for his eight-year-old, who was using it at the time."

"Yeaaah . . ."

"Of course, we never told the outfit in Texas that makes and sells those things that a magnificent coincidence had created a million-to-one chance that one of our covert operations could be blown by its spelling machine. They've sold over six hundred thousand of them already, sir. By keeping any location transmission to less than a minute, we feel we can eliminate any possibility of the exact locus of the transmission being pinpointed."

"Why didn't you have the chip changed and the receivers modified?"

Brockway interjected: "There are at least eight hundred transmitters planted in strategic spots around the world, sir. We couldn't possibly retrieve them all. And an unchanged transmitter could place one of our operatives in jeopardy if the need to use one arose."

"All right, tell me about Harding."

"The copter landed him and another agent in the Zagros

Mountains yesterday morning. The Navy says that the cave he was looking for was in sight."

"What are you telling me? What copter? What other agent? Have I missed something here?"

Brockway groaned inwardly. It seemed to him he was always apologizing to Randolph: "I'm sorry, sir. An 'Eyes Only' report was sent to you first thing this morning . . . and . . . and we assumed you had read it."

"Oh, I signed for it in my bedroom just as I had turned on the shower. I left it, unread, on the pillow . . . Wonder if they've made the beds yet . . . Alice!"

A startled woman of middle age opened an Oval Office door and responded with a quavering "yes, sir" to the President's singular action.

"I'm sorry, Alice. I think I'm losing my marbles. I should have buzzed. Please excuse me. Would you kindly retrieve an 'Eyes Only' report from my bedroom and bring it to me immediately?"

Alice, all smiles now, left.

"Well, shall we go on, gentlemen? Let's have a rundown from you, Tom, first, then I want to check a few things with you, Bill," the President said, talking to Atwater.

"Harding was contacted by the Israelis as planned, and he got as far as Al Qubayyat, where . . ."

The President slumped ever so slightly, realizing that with twenty-four months on the job, he still hadn't convinced his closest cabinet and staff members—with the possible exception of Dave Demery, his communications chief—that he didn't damn well know everything. He had to interrupt immediately. "Where's Al Kub yat, or is it a person named Al?"

"Sorry, sir. It's a small city in northern Lebanon where the UN peacekeeping forces have a British Marine unit. The Israelis were to run Harding to this British unit, which was prepared to help him in any way he wished to get him to wherever he wished. We set this up with British, Russian, Syrian, and French units in the Middle East UN forces . . ."

"I thought the Israelis were the only ones in on it."

"Let me explain, sir. The Israelis are totally involved with us through their covert operations unit and their commando

squads. As of this moment, they know as much as we do . . .
yes, sir . . . what I'm about to fill you in on. The other UN units
will be contacted by Harding only if other means at his disposal
fail . . . and they won't know about anything he's up to.

"I'm sorry to report, Mr. President, that as a result of Harding's first communication with us, we've had to divest ourselves of further British involvement in this matter . . . at
Harding's adamant request."

"Don't tell me the British did it again?" Randolph knew instinctively he didn't have to ask the question. Since the end of
World War II, the vaunted and valued friend of the United
States had spawned a series of British traitors who had sapped
the shared military and scientific lifeblood of the two nations.
The President shook his head in abject sadness. His own
daughter was now involved.

"Yes, sir. The British station at Al Qubayyat apparently had
a deep mole since the first day we learned of the abductions.
We have now warned every and all UN stations throughout the
Middle East to check all their personnel and procedures as the
result of this situation."

"How was the mole discovered?" He bet with himself it was
Harding.

"It was Harding, sir. He spotted a chap with two British
accents. A few questions, and the jig was up. But, the mole
tried to nip the Harding project in the bud. His gunmen shot
up the car before it reached Al Qubayyat. Two of the three
Israelis were killed. The third Israeli, a woman tank commander
and a sharpshooter, has now teamed up with Harding."

"Why? I thought Harding operated alone."

"That's right, sir, but thinking along the lines Harding would
take, since the unknown enemy seems to know all about Harding through our British friends, the need for secret and solo
action no longer exists.

"That's why he drove back openly to the Lebanon coast and
signaled—three dots, sir—for a helicopter. We sent out an un-
marked gunship from the carrier *America* to pick him up and
take him to wherever he directed."

Brockway recounted how the copter had just missed being

hit by ground fire on the seacoast and how it had gotten Harding and Lieutenant Levin to Shanidar.

"Were they spotted?"

"Not according to the officer on the gunship, sir. They arrived at the cave site in ninety minutes, flying below radar range, and the pilot dropped the pair in sector number 16. Of course, thousands of eyes must have seen the copter, especially in the Shanidar Valley, but anything beyond that would be anyone's guess."

"Since the abductors seem to know about Harding, he's going to need help if he's going to accomplish anything," Randolph said, staring into space. He turned to Atwater. "All right, now. Tell me about your two men."

"Patricia doesn't know about them."

"Good. We can't afford to let anyone know . . . Does Harding know?"

"Yes, sir."

"They're armed, of course . . . ?"

"They were. We don't know about that now."

"Are they reliable?"

"They wouldn't have been selected for the Service if we didn't think they would be, sir. The only negative we have about them is that they are relative neophytes."

"Neophytes?"

"Sir, we had to select two agents from the ranks who could pass as grad students. That limited our choice to people about thirty or under. I assure you, sir, they're outstanding young men."

"Who are they? Can you tell me?"

"Certainly. The twenty-nine-year-old is Robert O'Meara, a Berkeley man, so he's the 'anthropologist' from the University of California at Berkeley. And Donald Kenyon, he's twenty-seven, is a Penn graduate, so he's our 'scientist' from the University of Pennsylvania. The Peabody Museum at Harvard gave them a crash course in archaeological manners involving a dig, sir."

"I think you are right in having selected younger agents for the cosmetic effect, if nothing else, Bill, but I hope you realize that there are more grad students over thirty than under thirty."

Atwater grinned. "Your daughter really was adamant about not having the Secret Service tag along, and thank God we came up with the cover we did."

The President nodded. "The abductors probably would have killed them outright if they had known, you're right."

Chapter 11

The two stood motionless on the ancient roadway where the gunship had dropped them off. They were looking upward, about nine hundred feet, at the triangular opening in the sloping mountainside of the cave at Shanidar or what the locals had been calling Shkaft Mazin Shanidar or the Big Cave.

"Jeez, that's a biggy. Do you know how far back it goes?" Lenna was impressed.

"Yeah, it goes back about half the length of a football field, and its ceiling is over four stories high."

"What's it shaped like inside, a tube?"

"Oh, no, Lenna, you'll see when we get up there. The inside spreads out to almost sixty yards in width. That's a ballroom!"

"OK, wiseguy. How do you make a cave this big?"

"Let's talk as we climb up there. That's the path over there to our left. It's not going to be easy . . . OK, lemme see how I can describe this.

"Picture this area billions of years ago, steaming, hot and cooling rock formations with some long slabs of limestone standing on their sides in all this hot stuff. Or, better still, picture the slabs of limestone as long sticks of chewing gum in this flat area of cooling rock. OK?

"Remember now, the sticks of gum (limestone strips) are lying on their edges, not flat.

"Bang! A cataclysmic upheaval of the earth's plates flings the area upward across hundreds of miles. In this area, the whole surface is pushed upward like a giant drawbridge until it has a slope of about sixty or more degrees.

"The limestone slabs, once vertical on their sides, are now almost horizontal to the earth. And crunching pressure on the ends separate two of the strata to bulge apart, one up, the other down.

"Got it? Take two fairly soft sticks of gum. Hold them flat together and apply pressure to the ends toward the center. Sometimes, the sticks will part, forming a space between them. That's what happened to the limestone layers here."

Lenna, following Harding up the winding path, grunted acknowledgment.

"What happened here—and it's the same for most cave creation . . . the dolomitic limestone . . . that's where it gets that light, gray-brown color—is that both strips of limestone bulged equally as they were being tipped over on their sides to become the roof and the floor. Over the eons, the lower bulge gathered a succession of floors with layers and layers of material, creating new strata of living space and preserving what is now being dug out as artifacts and relics.

"Shanidar became a very special cave for three reasons. Its opening is almost due south, giving it heat and light, especially in winter; the north winds never get to it; and it has a constant supply of spring water just outside and upward about four hundred feet.

"Just this, and I'll shut up, my dear. The square footage of floor space at this point in time is roughly equivalent to a dozen average-sized seven-room homes. It's been home for mountain folk in these parts for centuries . . . living here with their sheep and goats."

It took them more than a half-hour to work their way up the path, finally rounding a standing ridge and seeing the opening close up for the first time.

Carrying their duffel bags, they entered the cave with somewhat the same reverence they would have felt entering a cathedral or temple. The first thing they noticed was that the cave's ceiling was totally covered with a heavy concentration of black soot and cobwebs, the residue of man's cook and heat fires down through the ages.

Harding's anthropological training created a stir in his breast as he immediately cast his eyes over the dusty, filthy floor where goat and sheep dung was in evidence, looking for tell-tale clues of Paleolithic occupation, such as a flint. He stopped almost as soon as he began, to look sheepishly at Lenna. "Walk over here, carefully. I want to show you something."

They took about ten steps toward the interior, and Harding gestured toward a deep trench in the cave floor that he knew had to be there from the digs dating back to when Professor Solecki had made his discoveries.

"These trenches go down about forty-five feet to solid bed-rock. The archaeologists keep digging away with great care to see what the various layers of dirt contain. Tremendous labor and tremendous patience.

"They had found the remains of nine skeletons here before they had to quit because of political turmoil back in 1960." Harding suddenly shut up as they both perked up at an unde-finable noise and edged back to the cave opening.

"There's two of them . . . and they're coming up here." Harding motioned to their bags, and each picked up an automatic. "I noticed coming up the path that you have to get around the nose of a jutting ridge before you can see the cave. Let's wait for them at that point."

They stayed hidden until the twisting upward path pre-vented the climbers from seeing the cave opening. They then crept over to the vertical ridge with their guns at the ready.

Two heavily armed Kurds in deep conversation, with ban-doliers crisscrossing their chests, stopped short at the sight of the odd couple when they came around the rocky protuberance on the path. Both pairs stared at each other without a word. Harding kept his mouth shut. He had to hear a dialect first to see who was who and what was what.

"Who are you?" The taller one addressed Harding. It was in the Mukri dialect. Good. He could handle that.

"We are looking for some lost friends, and who are you?" The Kurds had relaxed perceptibly when they heard him speak.

"I am Achum al Benri Beg. This entire land was mine to rule at one time. Who are these friends you are seeking?"

"They are Amerikatse, mostly students, who had permission to seek the bones of our ancestors in this mighty cave."

"Are they supposed to be here?"

"Yes. They were all here until three weeks ago. Then they vanished like shadows in the night. Did you see them, or have you heard from anyone as to where they could be?"

The Kurds looked at each other for verification and shook their heads. "Are you sure that here they were? There does not seem to be any sign of alien peoples having stayed here."

"Yes, they were here, thirteen of them to be true. And they lived here for more than one moon before, poof, they were gone. And no word from them that they were going and no word from them since they went poof." Harding sneaked a look at Lenna as he babbled on. She had a wisp of a smile tugging at the corners of her mouth. He noticed also that she had stuck her automatic back into the folds of her sash. Not good, he thought.

"Did these friends of which you speak dig this big hole?" The Kurd was indicating the yawning trench area that still held the safety fence rigged around the perimeter of the jagged gash in the floor.

Harding broke out into a big smile. He'd have to throw this sucker off stride. He couldn't be from around here and not know that the trench had been there for over thirty years. Or was he testing him? Still smiling, Harding's eyes never left the Kurd's as the click of his gun being cocked echoed like an agate falling on a marble floor. The rifles the Kurds were carrying—they looked like World War II German Mausers—were still hooked through their arms, the heels behind their shoulders and the barrels pointing toward the ground.

"You are not pleased by something I say?" Harding knew the Kurd to be one of the fiercest of fighting men, and fear was rarely in their lexicon of combat reaction. This Kurd was still staring into Harding's face. "It is not polite or courteous to step by the truth, *aga.*"

"And who is to say what is the truth? Would you be offended if I were to point out that you do not rule this region, and that you have never been in this cave?"

"I could hardly be offended by the truth, *aga*. How did you know I was testing you?"

"Truth speaks with most miraculous tongue, stated and unstated." God, he loved speaking in these Indo-European dialects. So poetic, Harding thought, but what bullshit!

"Very well. We were sent here to see if anyone was examining the cave and asking questions."

"Who sent you?"

"The director of antiquities in Baghdad has not lined my pockets with gold, but he has allowed a few coins to fall in return for my occasional visits here."

"And, now that you've found visitors here, what are you expected to do about it?"

"Nothing, *aga*, other than make a report by wire from Rawanduz down in the valley."

"Then go with Allah and peace be unto you." Harding brought up his right hand to touch, in succession, his heart, his mouth, and his head, in farewell.

The Kurds responded in kind, turned around, and went back down the path without once looking over their shoulders.

"I'm not sure about what just went down, Lenna, but if I try to figure out everything that's going on, I'll be in a restraining jacket. Let's take a hard look in here and see if we can come up with something that might give us a clue or a whisper."

They split up as they scouted the floor on opposite sides of the wide trench in the middle of the cave. It became darker as they moved deeper into the interior, but they could see well enough to determine that there wasn't a sign of anything that indicated that anyone other than shepherds and animals had been there.

"Damn. I wish we had a flashlight. I think I ought to examine the depths of the trench."

"How about a torch? I know how to make one . . ." Lenna had a good idea, but they couldn't find anything among the twigs and branches outside that would burn steadily. They had nothing like oil or paraffin to dip the wood into. The trench had to be ignored. Harding kicked himself mentally for not having thought of bringing some kind of portable light with him.

He stepped outside with beeper in hand, snapped off six dots in rapid succession in three sets, separated by ten seconds each, and went back into the cave. "Let's chew on something to eat, get some sleep, and start off in the morning for points east, what say you?"

For a place to sleep, they chose the first step down in the trench, about two feet deep and three to four feet wide, giving them some invisibility from the opening as well as a good vantage. Harding had noticed that the cave floor was much higher in the center, and the trench had been started there, giving anyone peeking out of it a good view.

Each used the dubious cushion of a lumpy duffel bag for a headrest, lying about three feet from the other.

"We're going to have some aching bones in the morning, but we won't have too much time to worry about it. I've called in the gunship to pick us up at dawn . . . or just before."

"Is that what you were doing? You like your work?"

"What we're doing now or what I do for a living?"

"Aren't they one and the same?"

"Nope."

"Don't want to talk about it?"

"What's there to talk about? I test special craft and instruments in a paid job, and I do this sort of thing—whatever you want to call it—on the side."

"Have you been trained for this?"

"You might say so. I was trained to fly combat aircraft from carriers and was taught how to survive in most any terrain and how to defend myself with only my body as a weapon of offense."

"Where did you learn to speak Kurdish?"

"That's like asking if one speaks Chinese. You don't speak Chinese or Kurdish. You speak a distinct dialect that makes it almost impossible to speak or understand any other dialect even though it's called Kurdish . . . or Chinese as the case may be."

"How many languages do you speak? I know you speak Arabic . . ."

"Ahh, forget it. Tell me, what are you doing in this line of work?"

"It's better than driving one of those stinking-hot armored attack tractors we use in desert regions. The temperatures get up to one hundred fifteen inside, and if you stay aboard more than twenty minutes with the hatch closed—for battle conditions—you're ready to pass out, if you haven't already."

"So, how did you get into this business?"

"I signed up for the Netanyahu Institution, where they select a few candidates for some real training in antiterrorist skills of all kinds, both physical and psychological, with some hands-on training in a host of ways to dispatch a fellow human, with or without noise."

"Wonderful, wonderful. What a world we're in. And we're supposed to be the good guys!"

"It doesn't matter, George. A long time ago, I think we substituted that phrase, survival of the fittest, with survival of the meanest."

"Well, for one thing, I'll remember never to make a pass at you. I'll end up flying on my head or have a knife at my throat . . . Which would it be, Lenna?" It was dark now and Harding was staring up into the darkness as he talked.

"That would depend entirely on what you had in mind, dear boy."

"A pass is a pass, Lenna. What exotic method would you use to foil the fellow?"

"If he made a pass with marriage in mind, I'd have him decked in one second flat. If he were seeking warmth and touchy touchy . . . that's another matter altogether."

There was a long moment of silence. Then the sound of shuffling cloth and bodies on the hard, dirt floor of the trench subsided to an occasional "ah" or an "oh," followed by the sounds of two humans of the opposite sex expressing carnal appreciation for each other in that life-honored celebration of the body.

Harding continued to hold her, once all activity had subsided to that quietness following the act. The tenderness he felt for her was tinged, however, with a slight revulsion for his actions. The sounds she had made had been barely audible, and if she had not finally whispered that "three times is enough" and had not gently pushed him away, he would not have known that she had been satisfied. Now, remorse had set in. He had indulged in a purely physical act triggered not by deep affection and long, associative chemistry but by a combination of unexpected though veiled obtestation and pure opportunity. Such feelings of compunction made him hug Lenna all the more, stroking her hair occasionally. It was a rarity for him to indulge his physical needs through mere chance. Women were not toys to him.

His stern upbringing by an "uncle," a transplanted Brazilian army colonel of Armenian extraction, in the Massachusetts hills near Worcester had made him different from most of his young peers. He had not been allowed to play with the boys in the neighborhood after school. He had to stay in and study his lessons and read the great authors, beginning with the forty-nine Harvard Classics, and be coached in Portuguese, French, Turkish, and Armenian, the languages his mentor knew. For physical exercise, he would jog with his guardian every morning, rain, shine, or snow, at five o'clock, for an hour, and was taught how to fence, both French and Italian style. Sundays had been his only relief, after attending the three-hour Armenian high mass in the morning. It was a regimen that had not been a burden on him, since he had not known any other way of life.

His parents had died when he was a little boy, and he had been handed around from foster home to foster home until Colonel Zartarian had taken him in at the age of ten. Instinctively, the boy had realized that the stiff-backed, mustachioed man cared for him, because of the close attention he paid to the boy's every need, physical, spiritual, and cultural. Discipline was the rule of life.

His "aunt," a woman whose one and only child had died in infancy, was quiet and subservient to her husband and had wasted little affection on her ward. Thus, the boy had grown to manhood subconsciously seeking a woman who cared for him with the generous, giving love of a mother. His first sexual experience had been the time he had kissed thin, blond Lillian Carlson in the library stacks—his only experience while attending the Naval Academy, where he was graduated first in his class. Once his fellow pilots at Pensacola, where he was being trained as a carrier pilot, realized that he didn't have a girl friend and had never been laid, they quickly dubbed him with a couple of wry sobriquets, Jake the Rake and Hard-on Harding.

His shyness and diffidence in the presence of women attracted the opposite sex in droves, however, coupled with his good looks. When he was hospitalized and then on recuperative leave in Frankfurt—after losing a wing and crashing on a sweep over Lebanon—he experienced his first serious liaison, with an Army nurse who tended him, a stunning brunette with large brown eyes, named Nadja Vidach. Nadja became the first in a series of four "relationships" that ended abruptly when he made the mistake of believing that "this is it" and proposed marriage. After all, she had slept with him . . . Wasn't that the ultimate indication and measure of love? Thereafter, he found excuses to walk away. He wasn't going to be rejected ever again. They became too bossy, anyway, once they realized that he was a real man and that his slowness to touch their bodies was not to be mistaken for homosexuality. Not by a long shot.

Well, he knew he didn't have to worry about Lenna. She certainly knew the score.

Chapter 12

Dave Demery was called to the Oval Office that morning, the morning after the whole world heard a shortwave message near midnight declaring that the Americans would be set free in an exchange. He was waved in by the secretary, who was expecting him.

The President was with Brockway and Roscoe Barnes, all with long faces. Dave wondered whether it was because of the hour—five o'clock in the morning—or because of the news . . .

"You've heard?" The President sounded brisk.

"Yes, sir."

"We need a statement."

"I worked one up for your approval, sir. I have six copies here."

"Good. Read it out loud."

"It's short and sweet, sir: 'The American people will never negotiate with anyone seeking to gain their ends through acts of terrorism. The immediate and unconditional release of the thirteen teachers and students is demanded. The United States cannot and will not retreat from its time-honored position of never negotiating with perpetrators of violence and threats of death.' That's it."

The President thought for a moment, rereading what was handed him.

"I would strike out the last seven words, beginning with perpetrators, and substitute 'criminals' and a period." It was Brockway.

"I like that," Dave said.

"Fine. What do we do now, gentlemen? What's the latest from our man in the Middle East?"

"He's at the cave at Shanidar, sir. He signaled last night. It's deserted and there didn't seem to be any clues. Not a hair."

"Do we know what he's going to do next?"

"Yes, sir. It's way past noon back there. A gunship was scheduled to pick him up at daybreak and take him where he directs."

"I assume the Sixth Fleet knows about the ransom by now. I wonder if the word was out in time for the gunship to get the information to our man?"

"It wasn't, sir. Missed by an hour. He'll know the next time he needs contact . . . I don't think this news is going to make much difference to him."

There was a long pause.

"Is *he* safe?"

"Yes, sir."

"The media can't get to him?"

"No, sir, he's in a safe house tucked away in Greene County
. . . New York."

"Does he still feel as he did when apprised of the situation?"

"Definitely. He wants to be swapped."

"Good man, but we can't take him up on it . . . God, I wish
we could!"

"I know, sir. Do you think Pat would have it any other way,
if she knew?"

"I wonder how much she does know. I'll bet they've told
her."

"You're probably right, sir . . ."

"Damn it, Tom, must you constantly 'sir' me in private?"

"Habit . . . I didn't get to be an admiral by forgetting my
manners. Sorry."

The President wondered how much of the manners exhibited around him by staff and visitors was dutiful regarding a
president, and how much was servility with a touch of men-
dicancy. He guessed he'd never know for sure.

"I suppose the parents don't seem to care about international
niceties or the integrity of the United States when it comes to
the lives or welfare of their kids . . ."

"That's about the size of it, Mr. President."

"I'm certainly in accord with them on that, Tom."

"I know it's tough. Do you act as the President of the United
States or as the father of a daughter in mortal danger?"

"How much time do we have? . . . Oh, that's right . . . No
time limit indicated."

"Did you know that Harding knows the young man personally?"

The President registered alert interest with a low, sharp
"What?"

"Yes, sir. They've had a continuing chess game the past
three years, when Harding has been available."

"How did Harding get to know him?"

"The kid was interested in our space program, and we had
him at the Houston facility, where he met Harding . . . Yes, sir,
Harding's on detail there from the Navy . . . Harding spoke to
him in impeccable Farsi, the Persian dialect of literature and the
official language of Iran, and they became fast friends."

"And what's with chess?"

"Apparently they made a pact to keep in contact as much as possible to keep up each other's command of Farsi, and chess seemed an excellent excuse."

The President shook his head again. "All right, enough of this, Tom. I'll see you tomorrow, this time with the entire crew, and hope you will have something concrete."

"I certainly hope so, sir. But, just one other thing. The media keeps pressuring the press office about possible alternatives, if only shadings, about the position of the Administration in this matter."

"The goddam press. They won't leave well enough alone, and the Lord knows, there's nothing well enough about any of this. I wish they'd concentrate on the color of my socks . . ."

"Thanks, Tom, I'll get Dave to work up an announcement to reiterate my position that the United States cannot participate in or agree to the ransom of a single American for anyone in the world, including Mohammed Riza Pahlavi II, son of the late Riza Shah I, Shah-in-Shah of the Persian Empire and Pretender to the Peacock Throne."

Chapter 13

It wasn't quite light enough to see, but the gunship settled down on the roadway below the cave with unerring accuracy. Again, Lieutenant Garza was there, beckoning, and Harding and Lenna, who had descended what turned out to be a perilous path from the cave, jumped into the craft with their duffels.

"We're only going a short way, Lieutenant," Harding said after the greetings subsided. "Head due east and watch for a five-foot stone marker, near a grove of trees. It should be light enough by then.

"It's the Topzawa stele—out there in an open plain. Should be coming up . . ."

"There it is," Lenna yelled. It was slightly to the right of the copter's direction.

"Change heading three points north." The gunship was now heading east-northeast, staying as close to the mountaintops as possible.

In no time, they were approaching a broad mountain valley dotted with trees, rock outcroppings, and clumps of bushes. No signs of life, but another monument, this one about six feet in height, was clearly visible way down the valley.

"Let us off right here, right here!" The copter settled gently to earth with its usual racket and was off and away to the north again, leaving its two recent passengers to fend for themselves.

Jackson Harding felt fairly secure in his assumption that there wouldn't be much of anybody in the vicinity of the beautiful valley he had descended on. This was once populated by the brutish Kurds, who also enjoyed a simultaneous and antithetical reputation as people of great generosity, honor, and hospitality. They might steal everything you own and slaughter you in the bargain, but they would protect and defend you to the death if you called them brother and shared your bread and salt.

More than a decade ago, the enlightened government of Iraq, in a death struggle with Iran, its arch enemy, could not handle the sudden rebellion of its Kurdish population in the northeast, historical land of the Kurds dating back a couple of thousand years. Harding stared across the landscape and shook his head. This land of rushing streams, woods, and mountain sheep and goats, site of the Baradost Tribe of Kurds, had few if any humans extant. The tribesmen had paid for their rebellion almost to a man, when the government had attacked them with chemicals—poison gas.

"We're not going to meet too many people here. Most of 'em died in the eighties," Harding announced. "Won't find any sheep or goats around here, either. It takes a long time to rebuild any population from scratch."

These pontifications required some explanation, and Harding went into a long-winded soliloquy for Lenna's sake. He ended up, after a pause, with a plaintive: "I wish I knew what I was doing."

"Come on, George. You seemed to know up to now. Want to let me in on it?"

"Lenna, we have an Iranian connection, absolutely no doubt about that. The real question is, what faction is involved and directing their operation? On top of that, is the Iranian Government involved? If it is, it would be an entirely different ball game. And all that brings me to the question at hand: What arms do we take with us and what do we cache? I could answer that if I knew what to expect . . ." Then he said something out of context that escaped Lenna: "Why haven't they hit us before now?"

"I'm hungry," Lenna said by way of response. "We haven't had anything to eat since yesterday, and we aren't going to take another step, make another decision, or worry about another goat till we eat." With that, she went to one of the duffels and pulled out some dry unleavened wafer bread, some goat cheese, beef pemmican, olives, and halvah, all in small plastic bags, and ordered Harding to fetch some water.

They were seated under a huge tree in a stand of oak and munching happily when Harding asked, as a bit of small talk, where she had collected such good chow. She opened her mouth to answer, gagged, and stared at Harding.

"I . . . I bought the stuff at the bazaar in Al Qubayyat," Lenna said in a hushed tone.

Harding picked up on his cue. "Jones-Armitage was with you when you did your shopping, right?" In a flash, she dived for the duffel bag with the food and began pulling out everything in it.

There were two of them, made to look like inch-wide buttons at the ends of the bag. Jones-Armitage, or whatever his name was, had taken no chances, just in case he missed. The two beepers, equipped with tiny fission batteries, complete with selenium cells for almost perpetual operation, had Harding under constant tracking and surveillance.

Lenna stared forlornly at Harding. "I'm truly sorry. I never thought . . ."

"Forget it, Lenna. I knew it all the time."

"You . . . You knew it . . . You knew about the beepers?"

"Certainly. I checked everything before we left Al Qubayyat. Found them immediately but left them there."

"Why, for heaven's sake?"

"Look at it this way, Lenna. We are at the doorway to a gigantic land mass slightly larger than the state of Alaska, with more than six hundred thirty-six thousand square miles, called Iran. When we step through that door, Kaleshin Pass, by the way, which way do we go to find them?"

"Jones-Armitage made me change my plans and almost killed me in the bargain, but he gave me a new course of action." He paused for effect.

"Do you want to tell me, or am I supposed to play twenty questions?"

"Sorry. My plan is now to let them come to me. If we survive the meeting and we have at least one prisoner, everything is fine. If we don't survive, Washington will have to take it from there. We will have done all we could."

"How will they know if we fail? It would take quite a while before they could assume we had . . ."

"My transmitter. I squeeze off some dots at sunset to let them know I'm alive. If I'm not heard from two days in a row, I'm dead." There was not a trace of emotion in his voice.

She shuddered. "You know, I've been in the army and I've seen death and destruction, but I can't get over your matter-of-fact attitude about yourself. Doesn't it matter to you whether you live or die?"

"It sure does."

"What, to live or to die?"

"Look, lady, you know as well as I that we're going to die sometime. We're born to die. All I do is try to live as best I can, do the most good I can for my family, friends, and country, and never think of death, because you're never ready for it. Why should I attempt to guess when it's going to happen to me and let it color my actions and thoughts?" Harding felt a sharp tug of loneliness as he finished speaking. Lenna had brought up a subject that he had been careful to avoid in his thoughts as much as possible lately. He had little home life, no steady girl friend, and practically every weekend, with a Friday and a Monday tacked on each end, he was flown into some unlikely situation that could mean his hide. Harding had come to inure his senses to the precarious spots in which he found himself on too many occasions. What bothered him was the simple prospect of being called upon, rather than the danger itself.

It didn't seem to matter what party was in power or who was directing the agencies that called on him, he was always tapped, thrown into the breach, recovered, debriefed, thanked, and whisked home to report the next day to his cover job as if nothing had happened.

And she was asking whether he cared if he lived or died. It might be far more dangerous on a daily basis to walk across a square in Rome or Paris, but you didn't think of fortifying your soul to do it. You fortified your soul and your gut when you went on a tour such as this one, to the point of numbness. You didn't even think about it . . . unless some idiot brought it up.

"It gets dark suddenly in mountain areas, Lenna. I saw the copter's altimeter when we jumped out. It indicated we were at 6,400 feet. That means we have approximately ten hours of daylight left. Let's unpack the weapons."

They removed all the arms, stacked them in neat rows, allotted matching ammo to each stack, and sat down to gaze down the valley, about a half-mile long.

"OK, Levin, where do you think we ought to set up to repel an attack?"

"I've been looking, believe it or not, ever since you told me you were baiting them to come to us. I like that grove of oaks over there," she said, pointing to a thicket about one hundred yards away and sitting on a knoll. "It gives us a command of all approaches to this spot."

"Exactly what I had in mind. Let's move over there but leave the empty duffel bag with the beepers right here." The wooded knoll would be an excellent vantage from which to see who homes in on the beepers . . . if anyone.

"I don't know how many they'll send," Harding went on.

"They must know there's at least two of us. Those new Brens may be the ticket, do you agree?"

"Yes, if a horde were to attack us," Lenna said. "Maybe we ought to keep them in reserve and try to knock 'em down with the rifles, depending on the numbers, of course."

"All right. Unless they've already spotted us, we will have what strategists refer to as the element of surprise. In any case, they won't be coming till dark. It's too wide open for anyone to approach unseen in daylight."

"You mentioned taking a prisoner?"

"That's the whole point of this plan. We wait until this unseen enemy shows itself by trying to wipe us out. We wipe them out, hopefully, but we grab at least one prisoner and try to shake out where they've taken the Americans."

Lenna thought about that for a moment. "It's going to be difficult picking and choosing and deciding how many are left . . . in a nighttime firefight."

"That's right, so we shoot low and hope to cripple our targets rather than kill them. In that way, we won't have to worry about how many are left as prisoners. How does that grab you?"

"Sounds fine, George. Now, all we have to do is wait . . . or do we . . ."

A figure on horseback, halfway up the valley, had appeared on the rounded ridge to their right, riding slowly but steadily toward them.

"Forget him! Look sharply beyond and on both sides of the valley for movement of any kind . . ."

Harding's eyes swept and reswept the area almost a half-mile away behind the horseman. Nothing . . . nothing . . . "Do you see anything?"

"Nothing . . . He's broken into a canter . . . What do you think?"

"I think he's going to go right by us down there where we were."

The rider, sporting a black sheepskin calpac, black tunic, and breeches atop a dappled gray mare of undetermined breed, seemed totally oblivious to his surroundings as his mount continued its three-beat gait past the watchful pair looking down on him.

"He'll be back in less than a couple of minutes."

"Yeah? Anybody you know?"

"Yes. He's got to be the scout. He must be carrying some kind of a sensor receiving signals from the beepers. I'll bet his receiver went dead as it passed through the cone of silence these directional transmitters have. It will have picked up again just beyond the copse, pinpointing the location of the beeper." Harding sounded satisfied with his summation.

The rider did not return. They watched him ride to the end of the valley, where it merged upward toward the slash in the escarpment, replete with trees. The rider disappeared. Lenna watched the area where the rider had vanished, and Harding watched down the valley for the rest of the six hours of daylight remaining. Nothing.

Neither had spoken a word during the entire wait. It became dark in a matter of minutes, and it would be a while before the waning moon provided some light in the valley.

"They'll be coming for us either before the moon comes up or after it goes down. The scout must have taken a hidden route back . . . if I'm right, old girl."

Lenna nodded. If Harding was right about the rider being a scout homing in on the beepers, then it made sense that the rider would have found another way back to his attack force, if that was the plan.

"Grab some food and whatever arms you want, and go sit at the far end of those trees," Harding said, in a low voice. "I'll stay here. Join me when the moon comes up. Might as well be separated in this total blackness just in case they're able to sneak up on us. Wish we had a Very or some phosphorus."

Lenna gave Harding's arm a squeeze by way of assent and moved off after collecting a few items. The moon crawled over the mountains about an hour later, and the entire valley was bathed in its dim, cold light, light enough to be able to see anything that moved. Lenna napped for three hours and played sentry while Harding did the same for the next three. The moon slipped behind the mountaintops to the south.

They split up again after Harding ventured that if anything

was going to happen, it would happen in the deep darkness before dawn.

In about ten minutes, they heard them. The clink of metal on a rock, a rustle of a branch, the crack of a small twig . . . then the sounds of a concerted stampede of feet as the unseen made a dash toward the unknown, heading for the sound of the beepers.

As far as Harding was concerned, they made a fatal error. A flare went up to light the arena in stark, harsh brightness. He counted sixteen of them, all fairly bunched in a ragged line approaching the trees below him and Lenna. They were still about twenty yards from the first tree when Harding opened up with his Bren, followed within a split second by Lenna's. The flare was still winking its last gasp of light when the two stopped firing, three seconds after they started. There wasn't a target left standing.

Harding started crawling toward Lenna and met her halfway in the blackness.

"Not a sound and no more movement until it gets light. We don't know what was there beyond the pale of light." It was an hour and a half before the sun came up. The moans and occasional cries of the wounded had punctuated the darkness the entire time, and Harding wondered if any would be alive by the time he could venture a look.

When the bodies of the men were clearly visible in the growing light Harding felt some uneasiness. It was truly deathly quiet down there. He held up a hand to warn Lenna to stay still, and both remained crouched at the base of the trees they had used for cover. Three hours went by. Harding had not seen movement of any kind among the downed men, or heard a sound. It was an extreme rarity, in his experience, to sweep that many men in a three-second burst and kill all of them outright. Hell, you'd be lucky to wound every single one of them . . .

He stood up, exposing himself to the grove below. "Come on, Lenna, we're wasting time. I think we've been outsmarted again." Filling their hands with a couple of .44 magnums, they strolled down the knoll to the bodies.

Each was a corpse with its throat slashed. Eight of the bodies had bled from the throat, indicating that they had been wounded by the gunfire but were alive when the throat slasher had done his final deed.

"I'm fairly certain we're being watched from afar, but to hell with it. We can't stay here forever. Whoever's in charge of this operation knew he had to take no chances of anyone talking . . . cut 'em up in the darkness while we were waiting for light. Damn . . . !"

He knew without looking that there wouldn't be any indication of who they were or where they came from, so he didn't touch any of the bodies. They made their way back to the knoll silently after Harding had retrieved the decoy duffel bag and crushed the beepers.

"Let's collect our gear and get going . . ." The neigh of a horse stopped the pair in their tracks. There were six saddled horses, their reins trailing, ambling toward the bodies.

"What unmitigated luck! Lenna, we've got a ride if we can catch two of 'em. Whatever you do, don't go near those two white ones. Try for one of the others. Don't run . . ."

Both assumed a saunter and angled toward the beasts. The white ones snorted and pranced, ready to run, but Harding walked directly up to a pair of roans and held their reins. He was grinning for the first time since Jones-Armitage had said the right things in the Rover two days ago. He wasn't accustomed to saddles without pommels, but he draped the duffel with the arms and the food across his mount while Lenna took the other bag.

"What was the matter with the white horses?"

"They're Arabs, Lenna. We would've chased them all day, and if we had caught them, they wouldn't have let us ride them. Each belongs to one man. It was the Arabs that came looking for their masters, and the others followed suit, lucky for us. Hey, can you ride a horse?"

"I learned to post when I was a kid, but I've rarely had an opportunity to ride one of these animals lately . . . I'm sure going to die trying, though. Shit, forget that last line . . ."

"OK, let's go, but let's see if anything we try throws off those bastards. We won't ride down the valley to Kaleshin Pass. Let's ride back toward Shanidar and see if we can find the path back, skirting the valley, that the lone rider took yesterday afternoon. It's worth a try, and it would keep 'em guessing as to what we're up to, OK?''

"You're the boss, ole buddy," she said, tossing a light salute in his direction.

They grinned briefly at each other. The sun was blazing at high noon when they found the trail they had thought might be near the head of the valley, and picked their way eastward through the tree line for ancient, bloody Persia.

Chapter 14

Cushing Chatterton Randolph didn't feel too much like the President of the United States. He felt more like a hounded criminal who had committed some heinous misdeed and become the target of the merciless media. He wasn't one given to headaches, but he was sure something was going to snap if he didn't get some relief from his fears about Patricia. The listening towers at Annapolis and the responder grid in North Dakota hadn't picked up a single dot from that fellow Harding, and for all he knew, the poor devil was dead somewhere in those godforsaken mountains. No, he had to put an end to such melancholy. He couldn't, shouldn't allow his spirits to sag because the *Washington Post* was at it again.

The unelastic demands of headline writers, who had created and used a series of presidential acronyms such as FDR, HST, JFK, and the nickname Ike, hadn't been satisfied with CCR where he was concerned. Depending on the slant or subject matter of the story, they had also come up with his college nickname, Chat, and his high school sobriquet, Cushy—take your pick. The *Post* was calling him Chat today in the morning editions.

Allison Arnold Davis was in the news again, even though she had been smuggled, literally, almost daily into the White House to prevent just the kind of "news" copy one could expect from the hungry gossip mongers who had the audacity to describe themselves as journalists and who turned out their olio of fact and rumor under the highly dubious banner of "the people's right to know."

The long memory of these vendors of claptrap went back to the small formal dance held at the White House itself on the eve of Randolph's inauguration two years ago, when he had appeared briefly with his daughter Patricia and the "Boy Wonder," as his autistic son was called behind the President's back.

Allison Davis, the 36-year-old never-married sister of the Speaker of the House, had been one of the special guests invited to the small soiree that evening, and even though the president-elect had not danced with her, the fact that she and Patricia had flanked him at the dinner was enough. But not a word beyond that. The media had restrained itself from the obvious vulgarity of mentioning anything "going on" between the redoubtable Miss Davis and the President. Good heavens! Mrs. Randolph had expired only two months ago. But it remembered. The media kept a file, no doubt about that, he thought, a scowl attempting to form on his face.

His eyes scanned the faces of his cabinet, convening for its weekly session with "The Boss," as he found out they were calling him, all because he had ventured smilingly at his very first cabinet meeting that he had the "only vote here" when the secretary of HHS had responded to Randolph's request for an opinion by saying, "I vote . . ."

His eyes came to rest on his secretary of commerce and labor, Madame Kunhardt, who had introduced the Davis woman to him years ago as a possible press officer when he was running NASA. Allison had the goods, and her unswerving dedication to her work and total loyalty to Randolph had caused him to take her with him to whatever position he assumed. It hadn't been difficult at all for Randolph to stay away from the lovely Allison, because she wouldn't allow the slightest familiarity from anyone, including Randolph. They had become fast friends in the interim.

With the death of his wife, Allison maintained the same relationship, with one exception. She became a sort of busybody where the President was concerned. She was solemn and purposeful in the trying days of the funeral, taking over the arrangements, comforting the shocked children, and parrying the myriad attentions, good and bad, from the well-intentioned—including those from the dead woman's divorced sister, Joan, who found herself persona non grata with a now-resentful brother-in-law who couldn't forget that Joan had made several blunt sexual overtures during his marriage.

Allison had to forsake the spot as director of communications in the White House for outward appearances—the press was licking its chops—in favor of Dave Demery, a levelheaded, smiling, tough young man who had guided the public affairs of the Senate Majority Leader and run a slam-bang nomination campaign for him, only to lose by inches to Allison's efforts on behalf of Randolph. It was Allison who had recommended Davis for the job, and the President thought it was a great choice.

But Allison hadn't kept away from the President, even after she took over as assistant to the president of Georgetown University. She became a sort of overseer at the White House, checking up on and checking out the two children and raising the hackles of the White House housekeeper by recommending menu and schedule changes, of which she had sternly sought and won approval from Randolph.

When Patricia disappeared with her colleagues, Allison was the one who provided him with a calming voice and optimism, especially in the evenings, when physical and mental exhaustion brought a dusting of depression on the President's outlook.

Well, in any event, that pipeline to the *Post* had to be stopped up. He was "Chat" today in the headline: CHAT CALLS ALLISON FOR CHAT.

The article consisted of total conjecture, but it did contain some specifics. They certainly had sat in the upstairs drawing room; they certainly had been served decaffeinated tea; they certainly hadn't touched the chocolate cookies; she certainly had arrived at eight o'clock, and she did leave at ten-thirty. The writer had woven the facts into a series of guesses as to what they had talked about. Certainly they had talked over the fate of the missing Patricia and what was being done to rescue her. Certainly they had talked about the furor raised by the insistence of the United States on putting a ceiling on the trade imbalance with Japan . . .

"Yes, of course, Charles, I'm listening. But I don't believe we know enough about that to proceed in the manner you suggest," he piped up, responding to the Energy secretary. "I think we ought to hear what the impact of your idea would be on our transportation industries. What say you, Madame Kunhardt?"

The President smiled at Kunhardt, another handsome woman who always "knew what time it was." Gad! Half his cabinet consisted of women and there wasn't a "dog" among them. And they were the smartest, toughest people he had ever worked with. Yep, it wouldn't be long now before . . .

Where was I before someone had the nerve to ask me a question, he thought. Oh, yeah, my rendezvous with Allison. Of course, the *Post* article was bullshit, but there was enough verisimilitude to give it the ring of total authenticity. He *had* to find the son of a bitch who was talking to the *Post*.

Wouldn't they have had a field day if they knew that he had held Allison's hand as they sat on the sofa and he poured out his frustrations about Patricia. "I think our gambit with Harding has failed, Allie. He seems to have disappeared in those mountains. Unless he contacts us, we don't even know where he is." Allison wouldn't accept his pessimism, insisting over and over again that it was too early to come to any conclusion.

The media probably wouldn't have understood at all that practically three-quarters of the time had passed in total silence between the two, the clasped hands doing all the talking necessary. A smile spread across his dark, chiseled face as he sat at the table thinking of her . . .

"Please, Mr. President. Why do you find the loss of six hundred thousand jobs amusing?"

"Huh?"

Chapter 15

The mountains of the Zagros-Taurus range, forming a crescent from Turkey down along the border between Iran and Iraq, weren't high as mountains go—about ten thousand feet on the average—but they were loaded with water obstacles on the western side and dry, sullen slopes, ravines, and treeless sweeps of rocky ground, which eventually became desert, on the eastern side. In the vicinity of the Kaleshin Pass, the two riders weren't at quite four thousand feet when they broke out of the northern ridge flanking the valley and crossed the unseen line that separates the two countries. Darkness overtook them.

"We're in Iran."

"How do you know?"

"That thing you thought was a man . . . can't see it now in this light . . . that's the famous Kaleshin stele, and it's just over the line in Iran. It's a monolith, about six feet high, carved from stone with flat sides, set in a hole cut in basal rock. It's covered with cuneiform writing which commemorates some great victory over some despicable enemy in ages past."

"What's it doing out here in the middle of nowhere? Is it the same sort of thing we spotted back in Iraq from the copter as the point to turn?"

"Yup, the Topzawa stele. The archaeologists keep taking latex impressions of the writing for further study. These steles are erected on the actual site of battle, usually on the spot where the leader of the vanquished was beheaded. In the light, you'd be able to see the great number of bullet scars on them. The Kurds keep using the steles for target practice."

"How's your butt doing?"

"It's not my butt. It's the inside of my legs at the knees. No matter how many adjustments I make on the stirrups, it doesn't seem to be right. I'm sore. This nag has a bristly hide."

"It's OK. We'll have to stop somewhere along here before the moon comes up . . . Can't see a damned thing, now."

"Do you think we made it without being spotted, George?"

"I have no idea, but I'm sure they'll let us know in their own good time. Let's lead the horses for a while."

They dismounted and walked only a few feet before they stumbled on some rock outcroppings. Further groping showed they had come upon some boulders that were higher than they could feel in the darkness.

"Let's camp here between these two big ones. The horses had plenty of water during the day, and that'll have to do till morning . . . Better tether them carefully, huh?"

Lenna groaned as she settled her back against a rock. "Oh, does this feel good . . . talk about aches and pains on that horse! Ya hungry?"

"Sure am. I'll get your magnificent cuisine and spread it out for you, but I'm not eating just yet."

"What do you mean you're hungry but you're not going to eat?"

"I'm going to take a careful walk down this opening to the pass and see if I can pick up the tracks of the riders we killed." Harding couldn't see her face in the darkness, but he knew she needed a better explanation than that. "I can't do it when the moon comes up—the rational thing to do—I may be seen by whomever is dogging our trail. Sooo, I do it in pitch darkness, using my sense of smell, hoping that the horses left droppings along the way."

"What's that got to do with eating or not eating?"

"Your sense of smell is at its peak when you're hungry . . ."

Lenna shook her head. "Where does this man get this stuff? Unbelievable!"

"Unbelievable or not, you've got to help me. Give me exactly a half hour out there and then produce a double rapping sound on one of those ammo cans with a knife handle. I've got to get a signal from you so I can make my way back. I've got to get back before the moon comes up. OK?"

"What's a double rap?"

"A tap-tap on the top of one of these cans, and repeat the sound at five-minute intervals."

"Gotcha. Go."

Harding knew he was taking a calculated risk. The tapping sound could just as easily attract the enemy as help him find his way back. But he figured the enemy would be in the dark, literally, not knowing what the sound meant, whereas a moonlit excursion would leave him totally vulnerable.

He had watched the broad path at the beginning of the pass on the Iranian side and had seen the fresh hoofprints of horses that could only have belonged to the dead men back there. He and Lenna would have seen anyone in the pass during the day. By scuffing his toes lightly he was able to feel the roughed-up floor of the lightly sodded ground. The going was extremely slow, and he finally realized that he hadn't gotten a whiff of anything and his half-hour was probably just about up.

Tap-tap. He heard it, surprised at how close it sounded. He had turned about three-quarters of the way to head back when he heard it again.

Tap-tap. Damn it, she was supposed to do that at five-minute intervals.

Tap-tap. Harding was about to break into a run to home in on the signal when he stopped short.

Tap-tap. He cocked his .44 magnums, touched the handles of his two knives, and sprung the latch to free the easy withdrawal of the four grenades.

Tap-tap. Lenna was certainly at the point of a gun, or the signal had been squeezed out of her before she had had her throat cut.

Tap-tap. "It's OK, Len. I'm almost there." The moment he stopped shouting he darted without a sound to his right and kept creeping away from what he estimated would be a direct line back to the rocks from which the tapping sound was emanating. Shit, the moon would be up soon and he'd be out there in the open.

No more taps. Good stuff, that Lenna. She had given them the signal but had not told them the intervals . . . How in hell did they find Lenna . . . in the dark, too? . . . And how many were there? . . . And how was he going to get to the rocks and "correct the situation" as they'd say at the academy?

When he felt he had gone far enough to the right, he estimated the quadrant to his left where the rocks should be, and began a careful, silent pussyfoot advance. His highly sharpened senses in the deep darkness signaled something ahead, and he shrank quietly to the ground, not knowing why he did it.

"The unbelieving dog should have reached us by now." The whispered words were in Azeri.

"I know. His braying could not have been more than twenty steps from us."

Harding rose ever so slowly, one of his Bowies now in each fist, waiting for one more exchange between what seemed to be two men, and two only about a breathtaking yard away.

"By Allah, I think something has gone wrong." Target number one fixed.

"I think you are re— What are you grunting . . . aaah."

Harding hoped that their final notes of surprise, uttered almost at the same level as their whispered exchange, had gone unnoticed. He had dispatched the pair in total darkness, taking the awful chance that his knives might miss their throats and they would sound the alarm.

He crept forward and bumped his head against a large boulder. His hands caressed the barrier, and he realized it was one of the big ones he had encountered at first, also in total darkness. He knew where he was now. If he went around the huge rock to his right, the horses should be tethered there, if they hadn't been moved. If he went to his left, he would be entering the area between the rocks, where he had left Lenna. He went to the left. The horses, if they were still there, might have snorted or whinnied at anything underfoot in the darkness.

He stopped in the squatting position at the mouth of the opening and drew both .44s.

"I say. Your boyfriend didn't buy our signal, apparently . . ."

The voice sounded odd. Harding knew he had never heard it before.

"Won't need you anymore, bitch. I'll have a jolly good time with you once we dispatch that American bugger."

Harding fired twice. The first shot, from one gun, was primarily for illumination from the muzzle flash. The second shot, from the gun in his left hand and following almost instantaneously, was aimed at the face of the speaker, who was limned for a fleeting instant standing in the middle of the area, looking down, arms akimbo, at a form on the ground.

Harding had missed. He knew instantly, when three quick shots whizzed by him as their powder flashes retreated into the open spaces beyond the rocks . . . and all was suddenly quiet.

Harding scrambled after his target into the darkness on the other side of the rocks. Not a sound, not even a natural night sound. He hurried back the way he had come and miraculously found the rocks. Lenna's hands were swollen and dark blue from the savagely tightened bands of goatskin around her wrists. Her ankles were similarly tied, and a filthy piece of black wool had been stuffed into her mouth, with a thong tied around her head to keep the gag in place. Harding had to grope to find the thongs in the dark and didn't notice the deep blue of her hands and feet until the moon finally shed its weak light two minutes later.

Lenna's face was covered with blood. She hadn't uttered a sound as Harding untied her and sat her up. She didn't utter a sound as blood began to flow from her nose and mouth. She didn't make a murmur when he noticed her torn blouse or when he gasped at what he saw as he attempted to tidy her up.

Harding squeezed off three dots on his transmitter, waited for ten seconds, and did it again.

Chapter 16

"He's in Iran?"

"He was in Iran, sir, just over the border from Iraq. He ca—"

"Did he get a line on Pat?" The President's anxiety expressed itself in impatience.

"Nothing on Pat, sir. He had to—"

"Wait a moment, Tom. You say he was in Iran but now he isn't?"

"Please, Mr. President, you're not allowing me to complete a sentence. He was on to something, apparently, but was ambushed by a band led by the same mole he unmasked in Al Qubayyat, a fellow called Jones-Armitage, sir. That's a hyphenated last name."

"What happened?"

"The Israeli officer with him was badly hurt, and Harding called in the copter to get them out."

"You mean, he's given up the search?"

"Emphatically no, sir. We had a briefing from Harding on the scramble system. He had allowed Jones-Armitage to trail him to the Shanidar Cave and the Kaleshin Pass across the Iran-Iraq border. He had hoped to get a line on the abductees by having J-A come to him, but this guy Jones-Armitage is good, to say the least, sir. And we know who he really is."

The President straightened up in his chair a bit, the leather squeaking.

"His real name is Stefan McMahan. He's an Irish-Polish American from Detroit, Hamtramck to be precise. We were able to nail down his identity through a startling coincidence, sir. He had applied years ago to my agency for an appointment as an agent of some kind. He didn't care what as long as he could work for us. Really gung ho. We were able to correlate the physical description of McMahan given by Harding with the computer reference we'd kept on him—we never throw away a thing, sir. McMahan had become fast friends with one of our case workers, who had recommended McMahan and who had mentioned in passing about ten years ago that McMahan had finally latched on to a job in the Middle East somewhere with Dutch Shell. That old information dovetailed with the sudden appearance of Jones-Armitage."

"Tell me why McMahan wasn't hired."

"He had a couple of things we couldn't square away, Mr. President. First, he had no grasp of any foreign language, not even Polish, and you know, sir, we try to bring in prospective operatives with fluency at least in one language other than English."

"What else drove this apparent hotshot away from our doors, Tom?" Randolph sounded dubious and Brockway was beginning to feel uncomfortable.

"Well, sir, to put it bluntly, he was at least eighty to one hundred pounds overweight on a six-foot frame."

"You mean he looked like one of our smaller footballers in the NFL? Was he checked out for agility, for quickness, for speed of foot?"

"I'm surprised you would ask that Mr. President. That's exactly what we learned about him from our UCS man. He was all that and more. Terrific!"

"All right . . . ?"

"We can't have covert operatives in this business who would be instantly recognized regardless of what they wore and where they were. You see, sir, you can pad a thin man for purposes of disguise on occasion, but a big, tall, rotund chap is always a big, tall, rotund chap."

"I don't necessarily follow that logic, Tom, but OK, he's now pushing us around, I take it."

"He's making every effort to thwart Harding by killing him."

"Do you think this means that McMahan fears Harding because Harding seems to be on to something?"

"It's hard to say, sir. The only thing we know for sure about the abductors is that they are either Iranians or have an Iranian connection. But the fact that they could be Iranians of the Hezbollah or the Mujahedeen Khalq gives me cause to worry, sir. I can't spare you in something like this. If I were to kid you along and then something dreadful occurred, you could turn to me and ask me why it happened."

"Thanks, Tom. That's the way I want it, I kid you not. Now, what's the worrisome significance of the Mujahedeen Khalq?"

"They came into organized existence back when that madman, the Ayatollah Khomeini, the self-righteous Moslem mullah who grabbed political power in the 1970s after our Iranian prince's father was kicked out in a bloody revolution. Their name means People's Holy Warriors, and they are madmen, radical socialists who would destroy everyone to get their way. Even other Shiites shun them."

"And the Hezbollah?"

"We've ruled them out, sir. They consist of Arabs concentrated in Lebanon. I can't see them operating on Persian soil."

"Tom, how could an Irishman, or better still, an American like McMahan, be working with or for the Mujahedeen Khalq? They hate us."

"I didn't get to that aspect, sir. McMahan was a hard-nosed conservative in politics as a young man. He had worked hard for the election of Jason Chase Clay of the America Right Party, lost heart when Clay didn't carry a single state, and showed up in Ireland. That part of his past was verified just this morning by laser transmission from London."

"I thought we weren't going to have the British involved in anything. Isn't that what Harding asked us not to do?"

"We worked only with our embassy in London, sir. The embassy made some inquiries through our consulate in Dublin. The chief of police, believe it or not, gave our people a list of persons they suspected or knew for certain to be active in the Irish Republican Army. McMahan was on the list years ago. The police were going to arrest him and deport him to the States when he disappeared. Then he shows up in the Middle East working for an oil company. Our UCS man, his friend, spotted him out there and happened to mention it when he was debriefed. McMahan never knew his friend's UCS connection. Incidentally, he was calling himself John McMahan then."

"I can't believe all this."

"As you know, sir, the IRA has had a reputation for working hand-in-glove with the Iranian and Libyan terrorist groups . . . mainly helping to train them. They were probably instrumental in subverting the uprising in Iran last year."

"That was a bloody business." The President sighed at the recollection. "And the United States was blamed, of course, and your outfit specifically, Tom."

"You know, Mr. President, we haven't been involved in the slightest with any of the flare-ups around the world in the last year or so. Yet, we have been tied, by every possible nincompoop with access to the media, with the overthrow of the Commie government in Nicaragua, that wild succession of bombings after the Chinese took over Hong Kong, the destruction of the Panama Canal, the assassination of all known black leaders in South Africa in one week's time, the revolt of the Soviet generals, and, of course, the unsuccessful attempt to topple the Islamic government in Iran to restore the monarchy."

"You've got to admit, it was easy to point the finger at us for the Irani uprising. Young Pahlavi leaves the U.S., shows up in Paris, disappears, and shows up with a parachute battalion south of Teheran, supported by an amphibious landing at the Persian Gulf port of Khorramshahr and an armored column at Halabja, with the Iraqis closing their eyes."

"It would have worked if there had been even a modicum of support from the general populace. No one lifted a hand. The tank column didn't get the gasoline from the invaded area, the sea invasion was sunk by mines—someone had inside infor-mation on the attack, and the chutists were surrounded and chopped to bits in three days of fighting. The prince was lucky to escape in a chopper that the whole world said was sent by us."

"How did that information get out, Tom? We *did* send in that chopper, didn't we?"

"Yes, sir. We followed the entire operation closely, out of sheer interest, without providing any advice, equipment, or intelligence. When we saw how things were going, I felt it was the humanitarian thing to do for the young man."

"I wonder if this present situation with my Patricia isn't pay-back time, Tom?"

"Mr. President, until this morning I couldn't have sworn to it, but after learning about McMahan I'm afraid the fat's in the fire, to coin a phrase."

"In other words, we are really dealing with those mad hat-ters in Teheran, and sanity, logic, decency, honesty, honor, or truth will not play any part in the resolution of this mess."

"I'm afraid you're absolutely correct, sir."

"Where do we stand, Tom? Does Harding have a plan now?"

"If he isn't back there at this moment, he's on his way, sir."

"What's his plan?"

"Mr. President, Jones-Armitage—I mean McMahan—has had the upper hand right from the start. When Harding realized this, he played the puppet to see if he could gain some steps. Nothing worked.

"So, he's going to use all and any assistance he requires from our military air and naval forces to find the archaeologists. It's going to be a blatant and unabashed foray into Iranian territory, I'm afraid.

"And you, sir, will have absolutely no knowledge of this. As the President of the United States you must not be privy to such information, you cannot have approved of it in advance, you cannot have approved it if you learned about it while it's under way, and, most of all, the Congress cannot be apprised of it."

"I'm going to discuss this with the Speaker and the Senate leadership."

Brockway showed his dismay by bringing a hand to his forehead.

"Yes, Tom, I'm going to do it. I will insist, however, that there be no staff assistants present, and beg them for absolute secrecy."

Brockway calmed down. "It just might work, sir. It'll keep you honest in their eyes in any event, and you certainly have an in with the Speaker." Randolph ignored it.

"I know what I'm going to do, Tom. I will ask these people to attend your daily briefing sessions with me. Most of them will be too busy to come, but I will promise to keep them informed."

"You are definitely asking for some highly dangerous leaks, Mr. President."

"I know, Tom, I know. I'm going to leave it up to you as to how much you tell us at these sessions. We can always talk privately before or after the sessions."

"Very good, sir. Now, about Harding. He's at the air base on Cyprus—or was—when I talked to him four hours ago. He plans to go back to Kaleshin Pass immediately in a small transport chopper, but he's not going to assume anything passive from now on about McMahan and company. He wants a gunship, armed to the teeth, to fly cover for him, with the privilege of calling in additional support if the situation warrants. He feels that there must have been about twenty-five or thirty in

the party of abductors and victims, and they must have left
some clues as to what direction they took and a possible destination."

Brockway noticed the growing irritation on the President's
face. "That was his plan all along, sir. But he was setting out to
do it under total cover to give the abductors a sense of safety
and its concomitant carelessness. We had no idea that the slop-
piness at the British UN base had blown his secrecy even before
he was landed on the beach. So he's going in flat out, with all
the support he needs, to see if he can do something about a
rescue."

Randolph pondered Brockway's dissertation for a moment.
He seemed satisfied, finally, and changed the subject. "What's
happened to the Israeli who got hurt?"

"Lieutenant Lenna Levin was flown directly from the Iranian
border with Harding to the hospital at our air base at Adana.
They got in touch with the Israeli command in Jerusalem to
explain her condition. The Israelis wanted to treat her themselves, and she was back at her own base hospital within forty
minutes."

"Is she going to be all right, Tom?"

"After a while, sir. Apparently they punched in her face to
make her talk as to Harding's whereabouts, and when she
wouldn't, they found another way to loosen her tongue."
Brockway grimaced and went silent.

Both men sat looking at the floor for seconds that seemed like
hours.

"What did they do . . . ?"

"They stuffed her mouth so her screams wouldn't be heard,
and slowly peeled off about six inches of skin from the breasts
before she nodded assent."

"I'm sorry I asked. I'd like to shake her hand someday."

Chapter 17

Harding was feeling a lot better now as the little two-seater with the ram-jet power source whisked him back to Kaleshin Pass. He had feelings of remorse alternating with fury at what had happened to Lenna. The flight to Adana to get her some help had seemed like an eternity. He had held one of her hands all the way, staring constantly at her broken face. Her nose was almost flattened and her cheekbones were smashed. Lieutenant Garza had administered some morphine to deaden what must have been excruciating pain, both from her face and chest. Harding had read of aborigines and some American Indian tribes literally skinning an enemy alive, but he had never expected to see the real thing in the twentieth century. Lenna had great difficulty forming words, but she kept repeating a sound that seemed to be "George." She sure had guts.

Every so often he spotted the helicopter gunship about a thousand feet above, sporting about, circling, climbing, constantly on the alert, constantly returning to the cover position of the slower two-seater Harding was in. At Harding's request, they had found a couple of chopper pilots who spoke the same American Indian tongue—in this case, Oglala Sioux—among the three services operating in the area. One became Harding's pilot, and the other joined the gunship as the copilot. Harding figured they'd be able to communicate freely in the air without any fear of unwanted listeners understanding a word of it.

"I want you to reduce your airspeed once we get to the pass and travel in tight circles so that I can look for something . . . I don't know what . . ."

The pilot nodded, pointed ahead, and looked at Harding with puzzlement.

"Bring her down, bring her down . . . I want to check that
. . . And let them up there know what we're doing."

As the pilot spoke to the gunship in the high-pitched, halt-
ing, singsong Oglala dialect of the Teton Dakotas, the copter
settled to earth near a collection of bodies, each one in its own
pathetic repose of death.

Harding leaped down and walked quickly among the
corpses, checking to see if anyone had touched them since he
last saw them. The carrion eaters, both aerial and surface, were
still missing from the land of poison gas, and the natural san-
itation they would have provided was absent.

He stared and pondered and looked as he slowly made his
way through and around the ghastly scene. Then he spotted
what he was searching for, finally. The dead men were not in
uniform of any kind. The clothes were nondescript, for that
matter. But he found what he had missed before.

The high-crowned sheepskin calpacs they had worn had
mostly fallen off when the men hit the ground. But each cap
had a dark-blue circle of piping about an inch up from the
band. It identified the village where the calpacs had been made,
and it also indicated that the wearers came from that village . . .
usually. The piping was almost invisible because of its shade of
blue against the black sheepskin.

Harding clapped his hands. Now all he had to do was find
out where they made those caps. At least it was the first tangible clue he had found. Better check the others. He ran back to
the chopper, thumbing up as he climbed in.

"Stay at around a hundred feet and start those sweeps."

The copter began its lazy circles across the mouth of the pass
and onto the gentle slopes that widened to the plain below.

"Bring her down near those rocks . . . and don't forget," he
said, pointing skyward.

Harding was on the ground again, this time walking to the
spot among the huge boulders where he and Lenna had squan-
dered their luck only the night before.

Sure enough, the two men he had killed with his knife were
still where they had died so ingloriously. One of the bodies had
a calpac with the same blue piping. Good. The other was wearing a burnoose with nothing apparently special about it. Har-

ding strolled into the area between the rocks and scanned the ground. Ah, the ants were alive there. They were busily swarming over the heavy residue of Lenna's blood. He picked up three bright shell casings, being careful not to touch the flat surfaces, and stowed them in a small bag he created from the shirt of one of the dead men. He'd get them dusted to check on the possible identity of the bastard who cut up Lenna.

He ran back again to the chopper; it took off, and even though the pilot began making the sweeping turns, Harding wasn't watching. He was scribbling a message, and when he was ready he switched on the mike, pressed the scrambler button, and rattled off a request to Brockway to see if either Texas or Harvard's anthropology department could come up with a possible location in Iran, probably northwestern Iran, where calpacs with that particular blue piping were made. Rush.

"Ask Lieutenant Garza in the gunship if he's seen anything telltale from his vantage." Sometimes the difference of several hundred feet altitude could make visible something on the ground that a closer look would miss.

"He says you must be on to the tracks . . . Are you, sir?"

"Ask him, what tracks, where?"

"On the left side of the opening plain, he says."

Harding craned his neck, directing the pilot to provide him with a side view of the area to his left. He spent a good five minutes peering and squinting and finally gave up.

"Take this crate up to nine hundred feet, and let's take another look-see."

The little copter climbed, and slowly Harding began to make out the barely noticeable slur on the hard, desert floor below, as if a nearly dry paintbrush had been swept across the earth and sparse vegetation. He calculated a width of about thirty feet. Neither rain nor the lack of it had obliterated the traces of man and his acquisitions passing by.

"Keep your eyes on what we see from here, and land me on it. Pick out that black boulder as your guide and set her down to the right of it. That should put us on the mark." He pointed up again to remind the pilot to tip the gunship that they were going down. The trail, so visible from a thousand feet, disappeared as the copter chopped toward the ground. Harding motioned to the pilot to step out with him. They looked carefully about them.

"I thought perhaps that since your antecedents are Native American you might have special talents as a tracker, lad . . . Standall," Harding said, picking up the pilot's name from the little name badge on his tunic.

The pilot laughed. "Sir, I grew up in the outskirts of Pierre, and I know as much about reading sign, as they used to call it, as a blind man . . . Though I know that that sure as hell ain't the print of a fucking horse," Standall said suddenly, pointing to a large depression almost between the two men.

Harding recognized it for what it was immediately. It was the imprint of a camel—the large, almost round, pad with two small hooves sticking out in front. "Are there any more to confirm this isn't a chance imprint?" The two scrambled about in all directions, and sure enough, as Standall cried, "They're all camels, and now all we have to find is some camel shit to prove it. Do you know what camel shit looks like, sir?"

"Excellent question, Standall. They are very much like sheep and goats in their digestive system. They squeeze out every bit of nourishment and eliminate dried up balls of waste." They looked some more.

"Look at this, Standall. Would you say these camel tracks on the rim of the trail they made seem to have a much shallower imprint than those in the center of the trail?"

"Sure do, sir. Do you know what that means, by any chance?"

"Sure do, lad. Let's saddle up and get out of here."

Harding assured the pilot that they didn't have to find camel shit to prove the tracks were made by camels, and they lifted off.

"What's our PNR, can you figure it now?"

"We can go in a straight line another two hundred miles, or approximately another two hours, before we reach the point of no return."

Harding studied his map. "All right. Tell 'em we're going to climb up there with them and follow the trail. If it heads into Oshnoviyeh—that's ten miles from here—we turn back. If it bypasses the town, we follow it until we reach the PNR and turn back. Clear?"

The pilot nodded as he passed along the message to the pilot in the gunship. The trail passed Oshnoviyeh to the south and kept a steady heading, south by southeast. No doubt about it now, the trail was heading for Mahabad, about fifty miles farther south. Would it stop there?

"Tell them to keep totally clear of Mahabad. Now, fly due south until we reach a mountain peak, it'll be Kutchuk Darreh. When we reach it, bank ninety degrees east, and that should take us just south of Mahabad. Go!"

Once the turn east was made, they looked for the trail they had followed. Couldn't find a glimmer. Harding then ordered the copter to turn north once they were well east of the city, and they scanned the earth below for signs of the trail going eastward. Nothing.

"All right, lad, let's head home. And tell 'em up there."

There was a sense of elation coupled with doubt as he realized what he was up against. Patricia was being held in Mahabad, maybe . . .

The entire situation was getting to be a puzzlement. Harding became aware that there were elements that he just couldn't explain. Camels in the Azerbaijan province of Iran, for instance. There were plenty of camels in Iran, but they were way to the south in the arid midlands—Isfahan, for instance. Those hoofprints were camels, though, no doubt about it, but why use them as the mode of transport in a chancy caper such as this? They weren't what you'd call swift—unless they were those speedy dromedaries they called meharis. Meharis could outrun horses.

And why Mahabad, historical stronghold of Kurdish unrest and certainly an area that has never had close ties with any Iranian government, neither the shah's nor the fanatical mullah's? It didn't seem exactly the right place to bring abductees to be exchanged for a monarchical pretender. Or was it? What would be the percentage for the Kurds to have in hand the political thorn in the side of the Teheran government? Would Teheran grant Kurds their political autonomy in exchange for the young shah? Harding doubted that scenario. The young prince was not enough bait, not important enough for the gov-

ernment to give away the second most populated area of the
country to be ruled by a collection of warriors, goatherds, farmers, and rugmakers. And the Kurd was intelligent. He would
not get involved in such a swap, knowing full well that the
reputation of the Teheran government for dishonesty and chi-
canery was well earned, and once the swap was made, the
Kurds would be overrun by Iranian tanks.

Harding came to a reluctant conclusion. He would have to
slip into Mahabad and find out for himself what was going on.

Chapter 18

Allison Arnold Davis was having the time of her life. It
seemed that everyone in Washington was taking potshots at
her, and she was positively delighted. Of course, the *Washington Post* was leading the charge with a marvelous, almost daily,
collection of half-facts and innuendo, aided and abetted by its
morning competitors, the *Washington Times* and the *New York
Times*. The national weeklies and the cable networks weren't far
behind with cover stories and interviews provided by everyone
but Allison. What gave her the greatest kick out of all this was
the mounting fury of her brother John, the canny Speaker of
the House. Older by sixteen years, John Spangler Davis had an
atavistic sense of decorum that transcended time and dictated
the outlook that it was unseemly for a single woman with her
connections to be spending evenings alone with a man, especially the President of the United States. "There's bound to be
talk," he had warned in the understatement of the century.

She had thumbed her nose at all of this, figuratively, and
today she was almost skipping in glee that the President had
invited her to dinner, alone, at the White House. It would be
the first time they had had dinner there without scores of other

diners present. Dinner guests were always posted as part of the President's daily schedule of events, and the invitation was no secret, of course. She wondered what everybody was going to make out of that. She was grinning at the thought. She'd find out what went on between the President and her tomorrow morning when she turned on her TV or read the papers. Just before she left for the White House, she took one more look in the mirror to make sure she looked OK. She pirouetted with her arms folded up and back, smiled at what she saw, and ambled downstairs to the car, wishing she had bigger boobs . . . as an afterthought.

The President was his usual gracious self at dinner but seemed to be impatient to be alone with Allison. He kept casting wary looks at the servers and stewards and heaved a sigh of relief when he announced they would have brandy and coffee in the Yellow Oval Room upstairs.

"Our people think they've located Pat's whereabouts," Randolph blurted out once they were alone. "They think she's in a town called Mahabad . . ."

"Goodness, what wonderful news. Tell me all about it, Randy." She had made up her own nickname for the President, something the media was not aware of.

Randolph gave her a summary of the report and the conclusions drawn from the lack of a trail beyond Mahabad.

"There must be roads leading in and out of that town. Why couldn't the caravan have taken to a highway?"

"Exactly the question I asked Tom. He says that such a group of camels would have to string out in single file along the side of a roadway. If they're herding prisoners, you run the risk of having them cry for assistance to passing vehicles . . . or even trying to break away. So, the best method for them is to ride cross-country as they've been doing."

"Mmm, that makes sense. What're we going to do now? Can you tell me?"

"I'd tell you anything, m'dear," Randolph said, breaking into a grin. "Our man Harding is going back in there alone and in disguise to see what can be done."

"My God, Randy! This man is simply going to walk into this strange town and ask questions?"

"Not quite, my dear. He will be slipped into the area—someplace he chooses—and take up a likely position in the marketplace to watch and listen."

"Oh? This agent of ours is an Iranian?"

"No, Allie, he's an American, and I think Tom said his ancestors came over here from Anatolia to escape the Turkish massacres around 1915."

"An Anatolian? Never heard—"

"Allie, he's of Armenian descent. Anatolia is their ancient homeland in the eastern portion of Turkey. Part of it is a Soviet republic now . . . you know, where they revolted for independence and were squashed by the Red Army back in . . ."

"Randy, please tell me, how is this man going to get away with it if he isn't one of them?"

"He is, in a way. Allie, he speaks a string of languages fluently, they tell me. Listen to this, I memorized it just to reassure myself that we had a real hotshot working for us: His thesis for his Ph.D. in languages at Columbia was 'The Influence of Arabic on Farsi, Turkish, Kurdish, Armenian, and Spanish.' Enough said?"

"Goodness, gracious me," Allie chuckled. "But tell me, if Mahabad is basically a Kurdish town, will Farsi be enough to get him by?"

The President was pleased. "He speaks several dialects of Kurdish, my dear. I tell you, he's a gold mine." Randolph was so pleased with himself, he leaned across the sofa and gave Allie's arm a long squeeze. Allie glanced down at the hand, and before he could let go, her hand was over his, and the two moved themselves closer to each other, not letting go. He stared into her gray-green eyes, now wide and expectant. He touched her lips with his, pulled back, freed his hand to embrace her, and kissed her long and soundly. She moaned softly as the kissing wouldn't let up and the hands of each sought to tenderly caress the other's back. They finally disengaged their lips and simply held on to each other, not saying anything for a full minute or two.

Randolph broke the spell and the silence. "I hope we know what we're doing."

"If we don't, no one does, Randy," Allie said in a soft voice. "I've been wanting to hold you for such a long time."

"My feeling exactly, Allie. I want you to be my wife."

"I've wanted that for a long time, too, Randy."

He clasped her again and kissed her. Then he pushed her away slightly and adopted a sober mien. "We'll have to put everything on hold for now . . . until we get Pat back."

"Of course, of course, darling. I'm going to help as much as I can. If only I were a member of the family so that I could be around."

"I know. I've wanted that, too. We'll just have to work out something, but in the meantime our fortunes seem to be riding on the back of this character with the unlikely name of Jackson Dertahd Harding.

"Incidentally, I've got a confession to make. When we were holding each other I had the weirdest feeling that we were being watched . . ."

"You mean the servants could have . . ."

"No, no, Allie. Kissing you tonight was the first time I've done anything like that in the White House. I almost broke off at one point to look at the door to Lincoln's bedroom. So help me, Allie. I felt he was watching us."

"I think he would have approved, if he were watching."

"I hope he wasn't reading my mind, my dear."

"I was."

Chapter 19

All he wanted was to be alone. He had to psych himself into a frame of mind that would enable him to carry off what he proposed to do. Like an operatic tenor working himself up to have "tears" in his voice as he sang *Pagliacci*'s famous aria, or a Grand Masters golfer concentrating to become part of his club to sink the thirty-footer, Harding was shifting all his mental gears to speak the Kurdish dialect of the Mukri tribe without a glaring slip. He was crouched in a corner of the ready room on the super flattop *America*, his eyes closed, his mind racing.

And he did not look the same. In fact, it would have been difficult to recognize him unless one was actually expecting to see Jackson Harding. The SOB special team on board had seen to that, since the possibility of meeting Stefan McMahan was certainly there. Harding's nares had been expanded with plastic tube inserts, widening and flattening his nose; a molded yoke of plastic resembling a "U" had been inserted under his gums in the lower jaw, broadening his mandible, and he had been completely sprayed with a henna dye to cast him with a swarthiness typical of the inhabitants of that *shahrestan*. He would be endowed with the special odor of unwashed people when he was about to leave.

The plan was set. Eight gunships would make a beeline from the carrier off Cape Andreas on Cyprus to the Iraq-Iran border, flying in full radar visibility. The mountains there were in the 9,000-foot category, almost due east of the carrier. Once the choppers reached the Gerkah Darreh at 9,400 elevation, they would swoop down into the valley leading northeast to Mahabad and Lake Urmia, farther north. The choppers would blossom-roll toward the ground, with the first one, containing Harding, hovering just long enough for him to drop off, and all the gunships would climb and head west as if they had been on a training exercise. It wasn't going to fool anyone, but then, there would be no proof of anything having happened.

The exercise went off without a hitch. Jackson Harding found himself alone on the side of a wooded hill with a large stream to his left and the assurances of Lieutenant Garza (can't seem to shake him, thought Harding, when he met Garza again) that if he followed the river, Mahabad would show up on his right within an hour, at the most.

Harding was a "Kurd" now. He walked with purposeful strides, his bearing on the arrogant side, clothed in the dress of the area, with a flat calpac of goatskin, a leather jacket without sleeves, long, loose pants tied around his ankles, and *kaloshes*— sandals cut from discarded automobile tires. Harding noted the almost rolling motion he attained with his new "shoes," the soles retaining some of the tire round. Shit. Talk about rolling along . . .

He was wondering about whether to play it straight and head directly for the center of town, where there was sure to be the main town well, or to go directly to the bazaar and see what was up. The decision was taken away from him with a fortuitous offer from a goatherd approaching him from the rear.

"Hey, banjo. Help me with this herd into town, and I'll give you your supper, eh?"

Harding seemed to hesitate, then shrugged and agreed. The herdsman explained that his son, who was helping him, had to return home because of a bad cut he sustained on his foot that wouldn't stop bleeding. Harding was assigned the drag or the tail end of the herd of twenty or so animals. He was catching quite a bit of dust, and the owner really didn't need anyone to help with the herd. It was following the bell ram. He was serving as a sort of tail gunner, making sure someone didn't rope off and disappear with one of the animals.

And Harding counted himself fortunate that the boy had cut his foot. Three trucks filled with soldiers roared up from the direction of Mahabad, obviously rushing to the area where the gunships had been sighted, to see what was what. He certainly would have been stopped and questioned. Harding felt comfortable about his disguise, but why take chances in a meaningless encounter of this kind? The trucks slowed down when the leader saw them and then speeded up. Stupid goatherds were not likely to do more than waste time for them.

Toward nightfall the goats and their herders were in the outskirts of the town. Harding's queries yesterday had elicited the information from the geopolitical section that the city contained about 240,000 Kurdish inhabitants, mostly shopkeepers, moneylenders, and workers in a tannery, a rug sales depot, and a caravansary. The latter was what had intrigued him. Apparently, Mahabad was the northernmost terminal for camel caravans from the south and midlands. It was the cheapest form of transportation, and certainly the oldest.

The goatherd and his flock streamed directly into a long side street in Mahabad with mud-brick buildings and not a few large goatskin tents. He seemed to know where he was going, and Harding followed, content that wherever they ended up would be good enough as a starting point for him. Ah, if the boys back home could only see him now. The one-liners would be zinging past his nose, especially the one about being a shit-kicker because he had done just that, or stepped in it, several times during the trek into town.

Finally, near the edge of town, they brought the goats to a large fold behind a two-story building, where they were penned up. Harding was invited in to what turned out to be the herder's brother's house, where he was made welcome, told to sit, and served food—consisting of unleavened bread, goat cheese, olives, yogurt, rice pilaf, and bits of boiled lamb. A watered yogurt, with bits of cucumber, mint, and a touch of garlic, was served after the solid food, and supper was over, the woman servers departing quickly to allow the men to express their appreciation of the repast with loud belches.

It took Harding some doing to work up a belch since his system was not used to it. It would have been a deep breach of etiquette if he had not belched. He worked up two belches, apologizing for his inability to manifest his great appreciation for the good food because he had recently suffered from an attack of dry bowels, and belching was almost impossible.

Everyone was pleased and they said goodnight to Harding. None had requested to know his name, none had asked where he was from, and none had asked about his business. If such questions had been asked, they would have been forced to invite him to stay overnight as a matter of courtesy. But not if they didn't ask those questions.

Harding had checked the location of the house, just in case, and headed for the caravansary. The goatherd had told him that the caravansary was on the other side of town and that they weren't going there, when Harding had asked if that was the destination of the flock. It was dark and the air was getting colder as Harding approached what was certainly the place where they put up camels and horses for the night. It was a tall, plain-sided building with a large courtyard to accommodate the big beasts of burden. It had a hand-operated well in the center with two large troughs spoking out from the water funnel.

And there they were, about twenty dromedaries sitting with folded legs on the earthen floor of the yard, chewing on their cuds with their own special expressions of a patient scowl.

Harding strolled into the courtyard through the gateless opening, went straight to the well, and cupped up handfuls of water from the nearest trough, the same from which the camels must have drunk. He knew he had to do that, since in that part of the world, water was water and you didn't decide between an animal's water and your own. The water had a slight odor to it. It had to have, if the camels had lapped at it. Their saliva was the most foul-smelling of any animals', something they seemed to know because an angry camel would spit on you, and you smelled bad until you could scrub it off.

Without looking around or seeming to have any interest in his surroundings, Harding walked out and sat up against the outside wall of the inn, his legs drawn up, and went to sleep. He had not gone unnoticed, he knew.

In the half-light of the morning just before dawn, rough hands shook him awake. He muttered some imprecations in Kurdish, seemed to come awake, and stared into the face of Stefan McMahan.

"Who are you?"

"Omar Miran."

"What are you doing here?" He spoke in a mélange of Kurdish and Arabic, but it was understandable if the listener gave it some thought.

"I helped herd some goats to town. We brought them to Number 16 Shahzad."

"Why are you sleeping here?" McMahan actually asked if Harding was sleeping. Harding held up his hands in a gesture of noncomprehension.

McMahan pointed to where Harding was still sitting and was repeating the question when one of the four Kurds with him interjected with the question.

"I have no place to sleep and I am far from home. I thought I would get a start once I got some rest." It was translated.

"Where's your home?"

Harding made a quick decision. North of here or south of here? Where were McMahan and his camels heading for? "I am

far from home. I live south of here, just this side of Hamadan."
He was taking a real risk. Hamadan was about 220 miles from
Mahabad to the southeast, and it wasn't Kurdish territory.

McMahan held a quick palaver with his cohorts. "You lie,
dog. You are not from Hamadan."

"Please, *aga*, please. I speak the truth. I went to Hamadan
with my father when I was a boy to help his brother make
shoes for the farmers there." Harding held up one of his feet.
"My father left me there to work with my uncle. I just finished
visiting my mother back in Naqadeh. She's sick, and I am now
working my way back to my uncle's house . . . Why should I
lie? Who am I that I should lie about where I work or live?"
Translated.

McMahan grinned at Harding and rolled his eyes upward.
This filthy beggar was just like all the rest. They all smelled the
same, and they would talk your ear off if you gave 'em a chance.
McMahan put him to the test. He wasn't about to take the
slightest chance of anything going wrong.

"I need some help with those camels you saw there last
night. We're going in your direction. Food and water if you join
us, and our protection."

Harding knew that McMahan was testing him. If he agreed
quickly to join the caravan, he would be suspect. "You are too
kind, *aga*, but I don't know anything about camels. I am afraid
of them. I pass up your kindness with the greatest of regret."

McMahan relaxed. "Stop your whining. You can come along
to fill the water bags. You don't have to help with the camels.
Satisfactory?"

Harding nodded vigorously in assent as he grinned and
bowed by tipping his head. Why the hell was McMahan so
anxious to have extra men at this point? What if he was all
wrong? What if Pat and the rest of the Americans weren't even
here? He couldn't face the thought of it. He had to find out
damn soon.

He didn't have long to wait. With grunts and shouts within
the caravansary, the camels lurched to their feet and clomped,
one at a time, out through the portal. Ah, they were meharis,
the swift ones, the first two carrying McMahan and his lieutenant, a man wearing one of those high-crowned black

calpacs, and each man carrying a highly visible rapid-fire carbine. The fast, single-humped camels were followed by regular, slower-footed dromedaries, with riders in a hodgepodge of local garb who didn't look a single bit native—and had their wrists tied to the pommels of their camel saddles.

Harding's job, as spelled out for him, was to bring up the two asses carrying water and food supplies, again in the rear. He waited as the parade of camels swayed by, always a mehari and a dromedary carrying a prisoner, one behind the other, with a tether to the bridle of the camel carrying the prisoner.

Harding waited patiently, seemingly not looking, as the parade plodded out and wound its way down the path to the open fields.

The photographs he had studied allowed him to identify immediately the two Secret Service agents, O'Meara and Kenyon. Thank God, he thought. At least they hadn't been discovered and were still alive. They looked especially haggard, though, obviously unshaven for weeks.

And there she was, Patricia Ann Randolph, perched atop a light brown dromedary with her right knee hooked around the saddle pommel, swaying up and back, up and back, heading for a destiny no one knew.

Harding sent the signal.

Chapter 20

"If one word of this gets out, my daughter is dead."

"I absolutely agree, Mr. President. We won't be able to tell the congressional leaders anything."

"I'm glad you see it my way, Tom. On the surface, it's good news, and that's the way it should be looked at, and to hell with the consequences."

"You're right, sir. The fact that Pat's been spotted by our man and that she seems to be unharmed is absolutely great news. But can you imagine what would happen if her abductors learned that we knew exactly where she was?"

The President shook his head. "Tom? How did Harding let us know?"

"He signaled an Israeli undercover commando team that's been following him."

"Oh, my God! Is this safe?"

"Sir, the Israeli unit—there's only four of them—are all graduates of the antiterrorist training school . . . uh . . . you know . . . the Netanyahu Institution. I would say without reservation that they can hold their own with the best of ours, if not better."

"How did they get to Iran so soon after Harding was dropped off? And I can't believe that Harding connected up so quickly. It's almost a miracle, or is Harding a miracle man?"

"I'm glad you're coming around to my way of thinking about Harding, sir. He's a pistol, no doubt about it. About the Israelis: They were dropped in on the other face of the mountain range that Harding was on. Their stealth bomber, sir. You know, the design they were accused of stealing from us through one of our 'great' Americans for five thousand dollars? Well, the plane whipped in unseen, peeled off at a dangerous altitude to drop the chutists, and was back to the coast before anyone knew."

"Why did we get the word from the Israelis?"

"Harding couldn't go in with the dot beeper or any other device that could be carried. But we gave him something to use, albeit of short range, to get the job done."

"You mean, he would be able to signal the Israelis but not be able to reach the carrier or Adana."

"That's it, Mr. President."

"What's it, Mr. CIA Director? What's Harding using to transmit?"

"His jaw, sir." Brockway couldn't help grinning at the President's surprised look. "We had to change Harding's facial appearance, since he had met and even talked to Jones-Armitage, also known as Stefan McMahan, the apparent mastermind in this awful situation. So, we changed his nose, which was easy, and also took an impression of his mouth under his lower teeth. We then cast a mold of plastic that would fit there and at the same time broaden his mandible, effectively changing his facial contours. While we were about it, we fixed it so that if he assumes the highly natural pose of holding his jaw in thought, he can transmit by simply applying slight pressure with his thumb and forefinger."

"And the Israelis? Why . . ."

"They are not only armed to the teeth, but they have with them the communication equipment necessary to assure total and complete contact with any of their overt and covert operations."

"Tom." The President sounded frustrated. "Tom, how come the Israelis are there armed to the teeth as backup to our man and not even our own man has so much as a toothpick for offense or defense? What's going on?"

"It's perfectly simple, sir. Only a man of Harding's abilities and talent could have gotten close enough to see Pat and the rest of the gang, because he looked enough like the people he was shadowing to be accepted among them.

"The last the Israelis saw of Harding as night fell that day was our man leading a couple of jackasses behind the caravan. He had passed the test, obviously, and for some reason, they had taken him on as a helper.

"Now, as for the Israelis, they are a small minority of the vast millions of humans in the Middle East and southern Asia who fall under the broad umbrella of Semites. That's an arbitrary physical label. Has nothing to do with nationality or religion.

"Hell, Mr. President, that dumb expression we gentiles have heard, and some of us have even used, you know, 'he looks Jewish,' is such a load of cow pucks. The Israelis' worst enemies for centuries—even before we called them Israelis—have been fellow Semites, the whole skein of Arabs and their relations.

"What I'm getting at, sir, is that Israelis can make themselves act and be whomever they want in that godforsaken land and environs they call Holy. They know the country. They know the peoples. Right now, the four commandos out there are probably dressed in the military uniform of an untouchable group. They've probably commandeered a vehicle of some kind . . . and I wouldn't be a bit surprised if they have already made a decision as to where to intercept the caravan."

"I hope they're going to let Harding in on their plans, Tom."

"I was only tossing off a thought, sir. I don't think for a minute they would plan anything without the input and concurrence of our man Harding. After all, they're there to support him, not go their own way. They have survived these many years for one reason and one reason only, sir: discipline."

"Fine, you've convinced me again, as usual, Tom. The big question now is, what are the plans to get our people out of there?"

"We must wait, sir. When the Israelis catch up with Harding at a reasonable location, the layout for a rescue plan will be formulated and executed. It will probably have to be a lightning execution because of the alien environment, but, at the moment, I'm just guessing. We'll have to wait for word from Harding."

"What's your estimate as to a time frame for all of this?"

"The whole thing should be over within forty-eight hours, sir, unless something unforeseen occurs. Frankly, none of us, including Harding, has any concept of why that caravan was moving southward. It could mean a difference in our reaction, but we really don't have any way of telling at this time."

The President sighed and changed the subject. "Tom, the leak to the media from our cabinet sessions is driving me close to paranoia. Have any suggestions?"

"That's a tough one, sir. I've thought of suggesting that we screen out different sets of support staff at each session and see what leaks or doesn't leak. But that certainly isn't feasible."

"Wouldn't work. Too obvious. I'd never admit any of this publicly, but that story in the *Times* . . . *New York Times* . . . about the exact number of visits Miss Davis had made to the White House this past month and saying that I had complained about the article at the last cabinet meeting, is something I won't stand for. These cabinet sessions I consider to be sacrosanct as the President's only way to conduct the business of this nation in an orderly and responsible manner. If none of us can say anything that might be considered as negative if made public, we are in deep trouble. How else can we discuss the pros and cons of any issue, any policy, any course of action, if what we say as a devil's advocate, for instance, becomes irreverent public knowledge, and out of context?"

"Aside from the leaks, I hope you are aware, Mr. President, that any more of this talk concerning Miss Davis will place you in the untenable light of carrying on with a woman while your daughter is somewhere out there in mortal danger." Brockway paused and waited. The President did not respond.

"I am truly sorry, sir, if I offended you. I've been worried about you . . ." Brockway fiddled with his horn-rims, one of the handful of persons in public life who had stayed faithful to their eyeglasses rather than have the corneal surgery performed that would correct eyesight without further need for glasses. Randolph remained silent.

"I'll take my leave, sir." Brockway picked up his briefcase and headed for the Oval Office door.

"I haven't excused you." The voice was emotionless.

"I'm sorry, sir. I thought your reticence was my cue for exit."

"I was thinking, Tom. You made me face up to something I've been unable to do till now. Sit down . . . please. Tom, these have been rather difficult times for me, starting with the death of my wife, becoming familiar with this job, having my daughter held hostage for the life of another person . . . Then, along comes a human being who knows and understands all my mental and physical needs at a time when I have no one, privately, to turn to. No one with whom I can be a simple man seeking simple support and comfort. Miss Davis provides that. We have even reached an understanding that once Pat is back safe and sound, we will get married . . ." The President held up his hand to stop Brockway's delighted reaction. "In the meantime, I'm torn between the utter need for her presence and exactly what you said the entire affair looks like. All right, Tom, you tell me what I should do."

"It's not my place to do so, sir."

"Of course, you're right, Tom. I must make the decision, and I have made one, believe it or not. I'm sending Miss Davis away, by mutual consent, of course."

Tom raised his eyebrows. "Where are you sending her?"

"The only place she would consent to go at a time like this. She's flying out today to the Mediterranean Fleet to be aboard the *America* when Pat is rescued and returned there."

Brockway closed his eyes for a moment. "I don't quite see what . . ."

"Come on, Tom. She's out of reach of the poison pens. She's out of my reach. She's out there clucking about on Captain Shield's bridge. And she'd certainly be a wonderful interim reception for my daughter when Pat's brought aboard."

"What's the gimmick, sir?"

"She's going to be called my personal representative in the Middle East, empowered to make on-the-spot decisions about my daughter's deliverance, along with that of Pat's friends and colleagues."

"Is she really going to have the power out there to say yes or no in any given situation?"

"I don't see why not, Tom. She has the mental goods. She has my total confidence, and I know she has my total well-being at heart. What more could I ask of a plenipotentiary?"

"A pleni . . . a plenipotentiary? She'll need Senate confirmation, sir."

"Not as my personal representative, Tom. She isn't representing the United States in a foreign capital. She will be representing me, if necessary, in any situation that requires an immediate, on-the-spot decision concerning the kidnapping."

"Shouldn't we get some advice on this . . . from State, maybe?"

"I kicked the concept around on a hypothetical basis with the people at State. I've got carte blanche, a la Napoleon." Randolph seemed utterly pleased with himself, and why not? With one stroke, he was shutting up the gossipers and eliminating temptation. What harm could she do or get into confined to the deck of a warship thousands of miles away? He wished he could have kept her around. An amazing woman, Allison was . . . is . . . What in blazes is the matter with me?

Chapter 21

Harding tugged lightly at the two jackasses to catch up with the long-striding camels ahead. One of his beasts had an old hackamore for a bridle, and the other had one of braided goat-and-wool hairs. Luckily, the two years Harding had spent as a youth on a horse farm made him totally familiar with the animals he was now entrusted with. An initial show of who was the boss and the asses were entirely tractable thereafter. Much like handling a woman, Harding thought. He had yet to tangle with one who didn't attempt to take over the relationship to dictate terms, activities, and conclusions. The underlying problem was that Harding's tastes and interests were never aroused other than by a woman of obvious intellect, character, and drive, not to mention good looks. Harding had learned long ago that the advice offered in that musical about times past, *Camelot*, that you could "handle a woman" by simply loving her, was not entirely true. You certainly could, if she were a cow and reveled in docility. Forget it, if she had an ounce of brains. That kind had to be stomped on at the outset once the initial miasma of tenderness and breathless anticipation had subsided to the corrosive cadence of casual cohabitation. That's when his partner would begin to seek more, and that's when Harding would lose her because of his unbending reluctance to bow to her efforts to change him. He knew he was never going to marry, not at the rate he was turning them away. And he always harbored the uneasy feeling that each lady had been glad to get rid of him.

He was now nearly two miles behind the caravan, having stopped at a spring to replenish his water bags. The huge bags of goatskin, created by stitching up the belly and closing the

113

openings for the legs in the tanned hide, leaving the neck for filling and pouring, had been employed in the area as a means for carrying water or oil for centuries. If the bags dried up for lack of content, the first time that water or oil was poured back into them, it created quite a dribble of liquid until the hide swelled and effectively stopped the leaks.

Harding estimated that the caravan had traveled about fifteen miles in the hot sun, now sinking behind the mountains to the left. The left? Harding gasped as he realized that the camels were now heading north across open fields. The rolling terrain and his preoccupation with the donkeys had made him lose his sense of direction. But the sun setting to his left was all he had needed.

Harding squinted at the column of camels, barely visible against the sere, light brown background, most of it unseen in the dips of the land, and took a chance. He squeezed off a special signal.

He didn't have to wait long. Four Russian-built vehicles copied from the American Jeep came bouncing across the sandy, sparsely bushed terrain, each sporting the crescent of the Islamic Republic Defense Forces on its bonnet and sides, and each carrying a smartly uniformed officer of the Palace Guard. The lead Jeep came to a stop where Harding remained seated, with all four air-cooled .30-caliber machine guns on each vehicle trained on him.

"What are you doing out here, miserable one?" It was asked in impeccable Farsi by the officer in the lead Jeep. "What name do you go by?"

"I am Ibrahim." Harding played it safe and responded in Arabic.

"Ibrahim? From where do you come?"

"From Al Qubayyat . . . and Shanidar."

The man in the Jeep broke into a broad grin, leaped down, and stuck out his hand. "I'm Margil, sir. Lt. Jared Margil of the Israeli Armored Interceptor Command on special detail. What's going on?"

"Can't tell you much, Lieutenant. They were going south from Shanidar, reached Mahabad, and now they seem to be backtracking, heading north. I hope they didn't spot all that dust you raised getting to me . . ."

Margil shrugged. "Couldn't be helped. Didn't know if you were in trouble. What's the play now, sir?"

"Looks to me like they're going around Mahabad to get back on the road north. We'll do the same, but you've got to get off a message for me right away: To Beanbag. Any word about calpacs?"

Margil signaled, and the convoy stopped after he had sent the message, to await reply. The reply might indicate where they should go . . . other than the direction they were going.

An hour went by without a reply. Harding had shook his head in admiration at Margil's story of how they had strolled boldly into Mahabad, in full military regalia, minus the menorah on their insignia, armed to the teeth, speaking impeccable Farsi and hitching a ride out of town with some Palace Guardsmen. Once alone on the road, the Israelis took over. The head shots had preserved the uniforms, and a discreet exchange of clothes had been made in a grove of trees near the highway. Margil had shook his head at the naiveté of the guardsmen in accepting the Israelis simply because they were walking around among the enemy without attempting to hide.

"Incidentally, I trained with Lieutenant Levin."

"How's she doing? Have you heard?"

"It's secondhand information, but I understand she's going to be fine." Margil grinned. "You know, sir, you think you know all there is to know about someone you've been on duty with for years, but you never really know. Every time she went under anesthesia for the plastic surgery series on her face and body, she kept moaning for a guy called George. None of us had ever heard about a guy called George!" He was shaking his head and chuckling at the mystery of women. The Israeli's sounder began to beep.

The message, weak but clear, snapped back with one word: "Tabriz."

"Make sense to you?" Margil was fishing.

"Remember those dead men back near the grove of oaks near the pass? Every man was wearing a calpac with a blue piping. I had it checked out to see where they made 'em. Tabriz."

"Is that where we go?"

"I'm not sure, Lieutenant, but it is north of here, and I don't think we can go wrong by heading there."

"Let's do it."

"Better find some way to go around Mahabad, though. These are special vehicles you're riding. And sooner or later you've got to dump me somewhere. You're my backup, remember?"

"How could I forget, Ibrahim . . . sir?"

Chapter 22

"Dave, I asked you to be ready this afternoon to give us a report on the general picture of domestic and foreign media treatment of the kidnapping. Are you ready?"

Demery smiled as he shuffled his papers and took a quick scan of the expectant faces around the giant oval table in the Cabinet Room. He'd better be ready, he thought. Then: "Yes, sir. First of all, the domestic press has coined a name for it, 'The Iran Exchange.' It's a takeoff on a best-seller title, but as we know, the press has never manifested the slightest degree of originality. If you remember your history, ladies and gentlemen, after the so-called Watergate hearings, practically every questionable situation that arose in government had a 'gate' stuck to the end of the noun.

"All six cable networks mention the situation daily even if there hasn't been one iota of new information. The print media dishes out at least two full columns of 'news' based almost entirely on rehashed file data.

"Our most urgent worry is that one of those so-called investigative reporters will stumble on something that will tear off the protection we have for our covert activities in search of our lost people.

"The reason for the departure of Ms. Davis to the Middle East was totally misconstrued and blown up beyond all reason. They used such expressions as 'a high official close to the White House,' 'a close friend of the President,' 'an unimpeachable source who has always proved to be right in the past,' and 'a source who demanded anonymity before talking.'

"And the stories claimed that Patricia's release was imminent; Ms. Davis was being rushed out there to accompany her home; that the prince was on his way out there to be exchanged; that the prince was not being exchanged but that the $6 billion in Iran's frozen assets had been accepted; that it was the Iranian government behind it; that it was not the Iranian government behind it; that it actually was the Bulgarians; that it was the Japanese Red Army . . . ad infinitum."

The handsome young director of communications stopped for effect, shook his head, and continued.

"The German and Soviet news agencies have published and broadcast stories about air activity over that entire region from the Mediterranean across the Fertile Crescent, and that none of the countries whose airspace seems to have been violated can actually identify the intruders."

Dave tried to keep a straight face. A chance look at the President, who gave him only the hint of a negative nod, wiped the growing smile from Demery's face. The redheaded staffer loved an inside joke, especially one that most of his audience was not aware of.

"Dave, we're getting a ton of a mail decrying the entire affair, with all kinds of personal condolences about Pat, but what's the editorial stance, in general?"

"It continues to be supportive of you, sir, but some of the major opinion setters, backed up by those ubiquitous polls, are demanding action, whatever that means. They want to know why the CIA, the FBI, the NSA, and the DIA, in concert with the British, French, German, Russian, Japanese, and Chinese cannot get an angle as to what's going on.

"As you know, students around the world have rallied in support of the victims. In Paris, a sedate demonstration before the Iranian Embassy by the Société Préhistorique Française was supplanted for the rest of the week by students from the Sor-

bonne who reverted to their natural state of protest—they ri-
oted.

"In London, a column of students from Cambridge, Oxford,
and the University of London joined in a rare show of cooperation before the Iranian Embassy under the aegis of the Royal
Anthropological Institute for a solid week.

"In Ankara, it was the same thing, hosted by the Ankara
Universitesi Dil ve Tarih-Cografya Facultesi Yayinlari. A calm
two days was all, then rioting.

"In Jerusalem, the demonstrations were led by the British
School of Archaeology, and in Prague, by the Czechoslovak
Academy of Sciences. No riots.

"And, all of us have seen the pronouncements here in this
country by the National Speleological Society, Harvard's Peabody Museum, the Smithsonian, the Wenner-Gren Foundation, and, of course, the National Geographic Society, to
mention a few. Not a single protest rally.

"Incidentally, the students at Heidelberg got carried away
. . . the police say from too much schnapps . . . and torched
both the Iranian and Iraqi consulates in Munich. No one was
hurt.

"In summary, the entire civilized world seems to be in agreement about this, ladies and gentlemen."

"Thank you, Dave. Are there any questions?"

"Yes, I've got one for Dave, Mr. President," the Secretary of
State, Roscoe Barnes, said. "Do you have any idea how the
Washington Post seems to know everything we do here?"

Dave stared at the questioner for a couple of seconds. Barnes
had never liked Demery and had vigorously opposed Demery's
appointment. "I certainly do, Roscoe." Dave took pleasure in
calling Barnes by his first name. "Someone in this room right
now will repeat what goes on here directly to the *Post*. It's as
simple as that."

"Well, that's obvious, Dave . . ."

"If that's obvious, Roscoe, why did you ask the question?
Did you expect me to know who it is? Do you think it's me?"

"Please, gentlemen, that's enough. I'd like to know who it is
also," the President interjected, looking pointedly at every face
in the room. "And, I promise you, whoever it may be, when

you are discovered, and you will be, you will find it extremely difficult to locate a decent job unless, of course, the *Post* hires you." Randolph's visage had assumed a darker shade. "If there are no other questions, we can adjourn . . . Adjourned at twenty minutes past six o'clock, and thank you."

As the CIA director stood up from his chair, the President raised a finger and beckoned for him to follow.

In the Oval Office, Randolph was shaking his head. "I shouldn't have said those things, Tom. I just shouldn't have. Bet you all the dough in the U.S. Treasury that that snitch will have it over in time for the *Post* to use tomorrow morning."

"I wouldn't worry about it, sir. The pipeline won't look good if that comes out in print . . . probably never see the light of day."

"To hell with it, Tom. Now, what about this latest from heartbreak alley? She's disappeared again?"

"Yes, sir, she was last seen going north, to where, we don't know at this point."

"Is Harding coming back to the carrier to make a report?"

"He hasn't indicated as much, sir. For some reason, after Pat and the rest disappeared, Harding asked for something innocuous. He wanted to see if we had found out yet where a hat he had picked up out there had been made. The anthropology department at the University of Texas came up with the answer only hours before Harding requested a reply. The cap was made in Tabriz."

"Isn't that an Oriental rug?"

"Yes, sir. Rugs woven in that city are named for that city . . . like the rugs woven in Hamadan and Isfahan and Kermanshah are named for those cities."

"Well, what's the significance of this cap having been woven in Tabriz?"

"The chances are pretty good that the owner of the cap came from there, and there were more than a dozen men in the ambush group at the pass all wearing caps made in Tabriz. There's nothing special about these sheepskin caps. All towns and villages make their own, and each tribe puts its own private mark on each cap. Harding spotted the same mark, a blue piping, on every calpac at the scene."

"So, what does this mean?"

"It's the only lead he's got at the moment, sir. Dollars to doughnuts he's hightailin' it back north to see what's going on in Tabriz."

"I wonder . . ." Randolph stood with his head bowed.

"Mr. President, you've got to admit he's done tremendously well, so far. You must have hope. Bear in mind that the kidnappers haven't made one single demand or request since they radioed nearly two weeks ago to say they wanted to swap the Americans for the Persian prince."

"Is that good, Tom?"

"It isn't bad, that's for sure, especially since everyone was alive only two days ago. I'm beginning to get the feeling that our abducting friends are in the throes of some kind of a dilemma. Why else have they not contacted us as to when and where they would make their nefarious exchange?"

"You're right, of course. All right, thank you, Tom. I guess there's nothing more to do except wait, and that's a tough nothing. I've come to the conclusion that Milton was blowing smoke when he wrote, 'They also serve who only stand and wait.' "

Chapter 23

The country was rugged and almost impassable, except for the road on which the four Jeeps were traveling. They were able to skirt Mahabad and were only a couple of kilometers beyond, just about where Harding had become a goatherd, when a burst of gunfire from some rocks ahead on the right shoulder sent all four Jeeps into a careening turn to the right, where a stand of dwarf oak looked promising as cover. All the vehicles made it into the trees, but the last one slammed into a boulder and landed on its side, the driver thrown about five yards away.

"Moishe, Moishe, are you hurt?" Lieutenant Margil was running back to the driver who wasn't moving. He went sprawling on his face as another burst from up the road zinged by his head.

"Stay down, Lieutenant! Where in hell do you think you are?" Harding had dragged a rifle from the Jeep's gun rack when he had dived for cover. It was an old M–16 U.S. Army issue rigged with a scope, was well oiled, and looked highly serviceable. Harding crawled to the base of the tree in front of the Jeep and scanned the road. And he saw it almost instantly— the glint of the sun on metal.

There were all kinds of movement and low conversation behind him, but Harding didn't pay attention to anything but screwing the scope until the cross hairs focused sharply on a black sheepskin calpac. He lowered his sight until the forehead and eyebrows became visible. It was about four hundred yards, Harding estimated, and if he missed at that range, he would turn in his Boy Scout sharpshooter badge, he thought, squeezing the trigger. The head disappeared, but the calpac went into a high trajectory. Then, about four yards to the left, closer to the road, another calpac appeared, followed by a full torso and an assault rifle at the ready. Harding's trigger finger wasn't fast enough. The sharp crack behind him and the upward jerk of his target's arms indicated that the Boys from Netanyahu were on the job.

Harding turned his head and looked into the grinning face of Lieutenant Margil, who nodded and then raised his hand as if to ask if Harding thought there were any more gunmen up there.

They waited about two minutes, without any sign of movement among the rocks. Moishe had a broken shoulder, the pain drawing the color from his fierce, mustachioed face. He settled for a rope sling to keep the area as motionless as possible and eschewed any painkiller. It would have sapped his alertness, he said. Shit, Harding thought. The poor bastard was going to lose that to shock in no time . . . but gung ho is gung ho.

"Cover me, men," Harding suddenly announced, wondering if John Wayne would have approved as he stepped out from the trees and walked along the shoulder toward the rocks. Nothing happened. He climbed up the scree and reached the site where the gunmen had waited behind the boulders. He waved an "all's well" back to the Israelis coming up behind him. The man Harding had hit had a hole near the top of his skull with the back blown off. Margil's target had a tiny rip in his tunic in the middle of his chest. Got him in the heart, Harding guessed.

Back among the trees, they held council. The loss of one Jeep didn't matter, but the existence of an ambush, and by people who wore the same caps as the McMahan bunch, gave them a knotty problem. How in hell did McMahan know who they were? Why had he posted a rear guard on the road? Was the ambush meant for Harding? Harding in a Jeep with Palace Guardsmen? How could he know? All five heads took part in the discussion . . . until it dawned on Harding that they had overlooked the most important development.

"Hold it, men. Just thought of something. Do you realize that we're on the right track? We headed north on a guess that McMahan would be heading north. This ambush proves we were right!"

"But who did this McMahan think would be tracking him?" It was the lean, intense Lieutenant Geffen asking. "And why attack a convoy of military vehicles?"

Everyone fell silent. Would it be farfetched for the Ayatollah's top military unit to be in cahoots with the American or Americans? It would, without any doubt about it. Then McMahan, who seemed to know exactly what he was doing, was firing on an enemy that he thought was pursuing him—an enemy of the Americans'. It didn't seem to make any sense.

"Lieutenant Margil, signal the carrier for an armed chopper. I need to catch up with these people, and we won't stand a chance running a gauntlet of ambushes along the way. And I think those Jeeps and the uniforms you expropriated have served their purposes, hey?"

"You said it, sir." Lieutenant Margil sliced off a faint salute with that broad, toothy grin of his. "This is as good a spot as any for your chopper. We'll move up about a kilometer or so and signal for something to get us out of here, too. See you around . . ."

During the nearly ten minutes Harding sat against one of the oaks and waited, he saw smoke curling up to the north. Margil must have destroyed the Jeeps to prevent any quick evidence being available. Harding was starving, having not had anything to eat since the night before. He couldn't even chew on the bark of the oak to ease the pangs. Oak bark was toxic.

He didn't know how it was done, but the Navy gunship, having lurked in wait in Turkey and minus its identifying cocardes, circled once and settled on the road almost opposite Harding. The navigation had been awesomely accurate. Harding nodded in resignation when he saw him. It was Lieutenant Garza, of course, leaping out to greet him. He didn't have anything against Garza. It was just that every time he turned around, Garza was there. They shook hands as they ran to the copter and jumped in.

"Let's point this crate north, following this road," Harding yelled to make himself heard above the racket.

"Sorry, sir. You've been ordered to return to base."

"Sorry, my ass. We're heading north. I think I can pick 'em up along the way—"

"Can't do it, sir. Orders from the CIC."

"The CIC? Since when is the President directing this show? We've got Beanbag in charge . . . or had Beanbag in charge. What happened to him?"

"I don't know who Beanbag is, sir, but you can bet your life that the CIC is running things now."

"Yeah?"

"The President has his own representative now, working directly from the flagship out here."

Harding's eyes widened. "No kiddin'? What's his name? Who is he?"

"Not a he, sir." Garza was grinning. "He's a she. She's somebody called Allison Arnold Davis and comes directly from the White House. And she seems to have the goods, sir."

"Bullshit! You mean I have to work only with her? I don't

have the right to make direct contact with anyone I want back home?"

"Really, sir. I can't answer those questions. You've got to talk to her, and I advise that you go back to the carrier as requested."

Harding threw up his hands, remaining silent but nodding to Garza to get on with it. He didn't know what was going to happen to the trail he was following, but orders were orders, and he had no choice. You can't argue with the commander in chief or anyone directly representing him.

"Got anything to eat?" By the time he had devoured three oranges and picked at a pomegranate, the chopper was out at sea and flashing recognition signals with the fleet visible above the horizon.

No sooner had Harding stepped out of the gunship and saluted the quarterdeck than the loudspeaker on the bridge ordered "the new arrival" to "proceed at once to Wardroom A."

On the two previous occasions he had been aboard, he had had a private little cell where he was subjected to an overseas debriefing via laser scrambler and code. Now, he was ordered to report to the skipper's own wardroom.

Harding was the object of long stares and not a few titters as he shambled to the open hatch at the base of the bridge and took a handhold-and-step elevator up, at the direction of a bos'n's mate. Just aft and below the bridge level, another sailor waved him off the moving vertical belt and toward a passageway forward. It ended at a closed hatch upon which he knocked. A woman's voice told him to enter.

A smile, ever so slight, worked around her eyes as Allison Arnold Davis took in the pathetic-looking creature that stood before her with a somewhat baleful expression. His brutish face with its squat, broad nose and heavy jaws, coupled with the tawdry, bedraggled clothes, including the wide, flat sandals (my God, they looked like tire treads!), and the growing awareness of the stench that began to permeate the room, finally made her gasp in surprise.

"You, you must be Jackson Harding." She was almost hoping he wasn't.

"Yes."

"I'm Allison Davis, President Randolph's representative in the matter you're concerned with."

"Why?"

"Why? What do you mean?"

"Why are you concerned in this so-called matter, lady?"

"Because the President asked me to be, that's why, if you must know."

"You're an expert of some kind?"

She stared at him for an instant in disbelief. "You don't have to know anything beyond the fact that I represent the President."

"Listen, lady, cut out the highfalutin bullshit and explain to me—"

"How dare you address me in those words and tones. Just who do you think you are . . . you . . . you animal!"

"I'm a dumb animal simply trying to do a job, and I need an explanation of—"

"I'll explain nothing to you, you uncouth chest thumper. I'm telling you . . ."

"It's Commander Harding, lady, and I don't take orders from anyone who doesn't know what the hell is going on."

They glowered at each other before she spoke in a low, unemotional monotone. "I'm here at the direct request and orders of President Randolph to take charge, and I will *not* be questioned in this manner."

"Have it your way, lady, but I'm not sure you haven't screwed up the works already."

"Oh? I've done something wrong, according to you?"

"It's not a matter of right or wrong at this point. Only consequences."

"You're talking in riddles. What consequences?"

"You pulled me off the trail of the hostages."

"You can't pick it up again?"

"I was at the point where they could be taken in one of two directions."

"You can't—"

"When I get back there, I'll have to guess which way they went, and it's critical time lost."

The mention of the word "time" brought an immediate

change in her attitude. "This exchange isn't getting us any-where, Commander. If it's all right with you, I would prefer if you were to clean up and find some decent clothes before we sit down and continue this." His odoriferous presence, physical and mental, was becoming intolerable.

"Thank you, I appreciate that suggestion. I would also like something to eat before—"

"A good idea, Commander. Get cleaned up and report back here in a half hour. We'll kill two birds with one stone. We'll talk as we eat, OK?"

Harding found his way to the cell he used, just below the hangar deck, found a change of khakis, along with underwear, socks, and black shoes, took a long shower aft, and had the special SOB unit remove the nose and jaw implants. He felt almost human again. That was a great-looking bitch, he thought. Dirty blond hair, gray-green eyes, more on the handsome side than not, with an ineffable aura, an elegance . . . savoir faire. Tough, too. She hadn't backed down an iota when he took out his frustration on her. Well, she wasn't going to last long in that position. Not with the kind of cold-blooded decisions that could be required before too long. He would probably have to end-run her and link up with Beanbag again when push came to shove . . . In the meantime, he'd take things as they happened.

She was surprised a second time at his appearance. His face was almost handsome now in its natural state, and the rest of him looked trim and athletic in his khakis. Thank God, the smell was gone.

Harding almost forgot his manners at the sight of the roast beef and ham, gravied potatoes, bean salad, coffee, and a ewer of milk. He had to restrain himself and slow down in his intake to make room for sentences.

"Yes, I had to call in my Israeli backup team when Pat and her colleagues were suddenly backtracking and going north. I couldn't understand why our people were being taken south in the first place. Didn't make sense to me."

"Are you sure you're on the right track now?"

"Frankly, lady, I was piss . . . irritated about your preemptive orders to drop everything and report to you." He was sounding peevish again, she thought.

"It had to be done, Commander. I'm sorry that my need to see you immediately forced a delay in your intelligence work."

"What was so important about you seeing me at this moment?" Harding was sure it was going to be a bit of feminine whimsy.

"The abductors, Commander. They are giving the United States twenty-four hours to come up with a decision to hand over the prince or face the consequences. That was about four hours ago." She had to stop and give Harding a fill-in on the ransom demand.

"And if we don't?" Harding knew the answer.

"They will kill one hostage a day, by lot, until their demand is met."

Harding had not expected the little catch: "By lot?"

"Commander, the President's daughter could be murdered in less than twenty-four hours. It comes down to that kind of a time frame."

Harding raised his hand. "It won't happen, ma'am. It won't happen." He called her something other than "lady" for the first time.

"You don't seem to understand." Her voice was cold again. "If they are going to be killed by drawing lots, who's to say that Pat will not draw the death card in the first round? It could happen . . ."

"Never. If anyone dies, you can bet your own life on it, Pat would be absolutely the last one to go."

"I don't understand how you can say that."

"Well, regardless of any feelings we may have about the President's daughter being no better or no more special than any other American, if you look at the whole picture realistically you might be able to recognize one important element: Without Patricia Randolph in their hands, their power to persuade America to give them the Persian prince in a straight swap wouldn't carry half the weight it has now."

"I find it hard to believe, Commander, that we, as Americans in a great democracy, would be less concerned about those unfortunate pawns out there if Pat were not among them."

"I'm not saying that, ma'am." Harding was certain she understood exactly what he was saying but was not about to abandon the flag in which she had draped herself. "The terrorists have a tremendous psychological advantage over us right now because of Pat. They don't need the other twelve in the party. All they need is Pat to pull it off. They might even release the others soon. Excess baggage. Think for a moment. Pat, the only hostage."

"All right, then, if I accept your premise, and I must say I'm beginning to see your point of view, do you think they will kill anyone?"

"If we don't do what they want us to do in the time period they have established, I feel certain they'll kill one of the hostages. They must, you see, to show us that they're not kidding."

"Then, of course, you must go out there and find them, Commander. Find them and bring them back, safe and sound, before anyone is hurt."

He stared at her to make certain she hadn't flipped her wig. No, by gosh, this dame had decided that he would wave a magic wand and get them back, safe and sound, as she had just ordered. He found himself saying, "I shall do my very best not to disappoint you, ma'am. I guess I had better get back there right away, right now."

"Only after we've discussed your strategy. The President keeps asking pointed questions, and I will need to know at least some of the answers."

Harding started grinning. "You're absolutely right, ma'am. OK, let's see. I go back to where I think they were and make a tough choice. The area we were in was at the southern end of the giant salt lake they call Urmia. Go north on the right side and it's about one hundred twenty miles by road to Tabriz, which is where I think those brigands are from."

"Really? If you know that, why hesitate about where they're headed?"

"Because they could go up the left side of the lake and be about eighty miles from where they started, from Shanidar Cave."

"Commander, why would they even think of going back to the cave?"

"Because it's across the border in Iraq."

"I don't understand."

"I may be losing my mind, but I'm coming to the conclusion that since the abduction of our bone diggers, something changed. There are enough new angles to convince me that our Mr. McMahan is playing a dangerous game, and it isn't only with the United States. In making this assumption, a lot of loose ends fall into place."

"You're talking in riddles again, Commander." She was watching him closely. She liked the way he launched into his almost classroomlike expositions.

"I may be in left field, but McMahan may have offered the Persian prince to the highest bidder among those fanatics."

She shook her head. "Why does that make a difference?"

"It makes one helluva difference, ma'am, if he had started out as the agent of just one of those fanatical factions—the government, the Islamic Republic of Iran."

"He wouldn't dare try such a gambit, would he?" Allison Davis expressed herself almost in a stage whisper. "Why, he would be absolutely mad to try something like that with those crazies."

"What's to prevent him? All he has to do is obtain possession of the prince and sell him to the highest bidder, if he hasn't made such arrangements already."

"Then why do you think he would head back to Shanidar?"

"It's across the border from Iran, about twenty-five, thirty miles inland and presumably beyond the reach of angry and pursuing Iranians. Also, it is extremely rugged country and could easily be defended against ordinary attack by a handful of determined, resourceful men."

"Well, then, Commander, what is your best guess?"

"I'm going to head for Shanidar, but I'm not going to go in alone, ma'am. I know what I have to face, and if McMahan and company are heading for Shanidar or are already there, I'll need some direct support and no pussyfooting."

"What do you want?"

"I want Lieutenant Margil and his commando team, for starters."

"Good, Commander. When do you want any of this?"

"Lady, I'm going to get into some green combat fatigues and leave in ten minutes for Shanidar. You will tell Beanbag to let the Israeli command know of my destination and timetable. Do you think you can handle that?"

There was no sarcasm in his voice, at least none that she could detect, so she didn't react that way either. "Leave it to me, Commander, and I want you to know I do not harbor ill will toward you, despite your initial inability to be civil."

Harding let a smile gather around his mouth. "My civility is usually in direct proportion to two factors. The most important is the amount of or lack of food in my belly."

"And the other?"

"The logic and judgment exhibited in the arena wherein I'm forced to be civil, Ms. Davis." He mentioned her name for the first time.

"Good luck, anyway, you insufferable bah-stard."

"Thank you, Ms. Davis."

Chapter 24

Lieutenant Garza didn't recognize Harding at first when he prepared to salute a heavily armed officer approaching the chopper. Harding was clomping along on the flight deck's grating in his heavy boots, combat green from head to foot, an old Kalashnikov rifle strapped to his back, two 9mm Sig Sauers, a half-dozen grenades pinned to his right shoulder (he was a southpaw), and a variety of other lethal odds and ends. The helmet under his arm, with three bars, indicating his rank, would be left behind when he departed the gunship.

The son of a bitch is a commander and he never let on, Garza growled to himself. "Good evening, sir. I see you're going hunting."

Harding muttered something inaudible and then piped up:

"Let's get back to that cave in the mountains, Lieutenant, top speed."

Garza looked at his watch. "We may not make it before sundown, sir . . ."

"If we're not there by sundown, all the better. You'll drop me off during the last possible light as close to Shanidar as we can get."

"Yes, sir," Garza responded, and after the blinking signal lamp from the bridge gave the OK, off the chopper went into the darkening eastern sky.

About an hour later they were still over the eastern end of the Syrian desert, and darkness was descending, as the poet would say, Harding thought.

"Mr. Garza, is there a UN station in Mosul?" He had been scrutinizing the charts with a penlight. Mosul with its own "leaning tower," a leaning minaret.

"Yes, sir. It's the northern frontier security outpost for Iraq."

"What country's got that duty? I'll upchuck if it's the British."

"The Russians, sir."

"Good. Get in touch with the post and see about landing me a vehicle for the night. Use 'Shanidar' as the authorization code."

Garza jumped to it and turned around in his seat within two minutes with an affirmative. "They'll have two blues and a white flare to mark a landing spot for us . . . and we should be coming up to the Mosul mark in about ten minutes."

Harding nodded. He would be about 120 kilometers—less than 80 miles—from Shanidar once he set down in Mosul. Even though it was mountainous country, it would be a fairly easy drive to Aqrah, if he remembered accurately what he had studied, and a rough, dangerous drive on a third-rate mountain road to the backwaters of the dam lake on the Greater Zab, a stone's throw from the Turkish border. Once across the river bridge, he'd have to hide his vehicle and work himself over to the cave. It would be less than a mile away. He was satisfied with the timing. Now, if only the Russkies cooperated.

When the gunship landed on target, Harding stepped out to introduce himself as Ibrahim to three Red Army officers who rolled up in their version of the Jeep. There was no question about anything. They had a similar vehicle gassed up and ready, along with a thermos of chicken soup, two foot-long pork sausages, a chunk of khashar cheese, a long loaf of bread, two fat onions, and a liter of red wine.

Harding gave each officer a hug of appreciation, but that wasn't enough for him to get away. They saw the Russian piece he had strapped on his back, recognized it immediately, and the one officer who could manage some English expressed amazement that an American was carrying around such a weapon—and it wasn't even made in the West. Harding had gone through this drill with practically every military man who saw him with the Kalashnikov. And he had just one word to explain his affinity for the rifle with the long, curved magazine protruding downward from the breech: dependable. That one word was all the explanation needed to anyone who had seen combat.

They slapped his back, gave him what they thought was the Western version of thumbs-up (they used the wrong finger and it was more like "go screw yourself"), and cheered him on his way.

The UN pennant on his right mudguard, with the hammer and sickle on the left, gave him clear passage during the night through two checkpoints and a radio confirmation in Aqrah. After all, this big fellow was armed to the teeth and spoke gibberish about going for a weekend hunt. Once past Aqrah, the combination of pitch-black visibility and a badly repaired road slowed Harding down to 15 and 20MPH. It took him an additional hour beyond his original estimate to reach the Greater Zab and cross the bridge. He was now about a mile, two miles from Shanidar.

Harding pulled over off the road and waited until daylight. The first thing he would do would be to hide the vehicle for possible use later, or get it back to the Russians to save the United States some inflated bill for a lost Jeep. This business of reparations between friendly countries scalded Harding's sense of right and wrong. As he settled down for a snooze until daylight, he recalled the time back a few years when the fleet received a frantic call for help, from the governor of a small island nation, to dislodge an army of rebels solidly entrenched in an olive grove on the southern coast, threatening to pull off an imminent coup d'etat. Since it was the closest, the U.S. Sixth Fleet responded and, with permission from Washington, shelled the grove, dispersed the rebels, and saved the day. Subsequently, a bill was submitted to the United States in the amount of $2.4 million for the destruction of forty-eight olive trees at fifty thousand dollars apiece, and an additional $1.5 million for revenues lost from the future production of olives. What had baffled Harding was the alacrity by the Congress in approving the payment. So much for logic . . . and gratitude.

He snapped awake as light began to grow. He was alone on a beautiful, twisting and turning mountain road barely wide enough for two cars abreast. It was the same road that would run past the mouth of the cave about a mile or so due east from where he was. He found a spot where he could drive the vehicle down a slight slope into some heavy shrubbery. He hid the key and worked back to the road, scuffing up the ground as best he could to hide the tire tracks.

Harding paralleled the old road—some of it evidencing the work of the ancient Assyrian road builders of Sargon II on his punitive expedition against the Kurds about twenty-five hundred years ago—as he approached Shanidar Cave with mixed emotions. He hoped he was right, that the Americans had been brought back—but if they were there, how was he going to extricate them from such a natural fortress without bloodying some of them?

Harding took his time. He had to be careful just in case they were at the cave and McMahan had thrown out some patrols to warn of approaching danger.

It took him twelve minutes to reach the head of the valley called Shanidar, or Sapna on some maps. There was the Greater Zab River again, far below to the right. He could see the remains of an old building that used to be the police post, just above the river, and the sawtooth Baradost Mountains framing the entire, lovely green panorama. The cave would be about a thousand yards to the left, among some towering limestone bluffs. He could see where the gunship had left him with Lenna. The cave was set back and high up from that point.

His orientation came to an abrupt end. A high-crowned black

sheepskin calpac was emerging from among the dwarf oaks on his left. Under it was a casually striding man in one of those ubiquitous shirts of striped purple, carrying a machine pistol hanging from a shoulder strap. He didn't see Harding as he passed him within five yards.

Harding recognized him as one of the Kurds with McMahan in Mahabad. He let him live. No use alerting McMahan at this point in time, since Harding didn't have a plan or a schedule.

He crouched in his tight little bower of shrubs for a quarter hour before the Kurd reappeared and strolled on back toward the cave site. It looked to Harding as if this was the extent of the patrol on this side of the cave. He followed the Kurd, at a good distance, stopping when he knew the cave would be visible at the next step or two—and he might be visible, in turn, to anyone at the mouth of the cave.

Harding took to crawling now. He crawled up the shallow slope leading to one of the bluffs flanking the cave on the left, reached a sort of shelf, and got his bearings. The cave still was not visible, because he wasn't high enough up the slope. He crawled for another ten minutes, certain that he had the height now, and he was right. He could look down with a clear and unobstructed view of the apron of land at the mouth of the cave. He couldn't see anyone inside, but a step outside and the person would be visible to Harding. He made himself comfortable, wedged in between two scrub cypresses, and waited. He wished he had a cover for his close-cropped black hair. The sun was extremely hot even though the air was comfortably cool. He began to doze, snapping awake when his head lolled.

The problem of his sleepiness didn't last long. His first reaction was embarrassment when he felt the point of a knife digging into his back and a heavy voice asking him in Kurdish what he was doing here.

Harding rose from his squatting position slowly and at the same time raised his hands. From his uniform and his weapons, there was no question Harding was a military man. The voice told him to turn around slowly. Harding did and found a six-inch poniard leveled now at his belly by the man he had followed earlier. That was all the time left for recognition. Harding brought his left arm down like a poleax toward the Kurd's head, knowing that the Kurd would be thrusting the knife into his gut. The knife arrived first, but Harding delivered his lethal chop to the Kurd's neck. Harding did not sustain a scratch.

He carefully slipped the Kurd's knife back into the sheath he found on his belt, rolled the body as close to the edge of the bluff as he could without being seen from below, and gave it a kick to send it tumbling and bouncing down the escarpment to land with a thud on the rocky apron in front of the cave. As the body started its plunge, Harding had given a wild yell of surprise in Kurdish. Who knows, they might think he slipped and broke his neck in the fall . . .

Harding crept farther away, upward and among the scrub trees, feeling certain someone would climb up there to see what might have caused their man to slip or be pushed or whatever.

Three of them did climb up there, simply by walking up the side of the cave to the right, where there was a path to the spring.

Harding gazed thoughtfully at Stefan McMahan, the man who had outwitted him time and again, consistently, persistently, and to the total annoyance of the President of the United States, the CIA director, and countless other high muckamucks who never questioned their own unmatched competence in a world of self-ordained and pretentious deities.

Harding watched as the three walked about slowly on the precarious slope, looking for a clue of some kind. Shit. If they wandered far enough over they would easily spot the place where he had spent several hours sitting in the sun.

Apparently they were ready to accept the death as an accidental fall, and McMahan waved to the others to go back down.

Harding could have picked off the three of them then and there. He could not take that chance, however. Gunfire and the bodies of McMahan and the other two appearing in front of the cave, dead, could bring about the sudden death of those Harding presumed were inside. He hadn't seen a soul other than the four today. It was going to be a waiting game, no doubt about it.

The cave had no other openings, not even some kind of a vent in the ceiling anywhere. If Harding was to accomplish anything, he knew that he would first have to get in there, somehow, with

the victims. That was going to be virtually impossible under ordinary circumstances. The cave opening did not have large boulders or trees or shrub or any type of cover in front or at its sides.

For Harding to get into the cave was going to require some
type of diversion . . . or for Harding to manage being captured.
He didn't think too much of the latter concept. McMahan was
no fool. He would most certainly shoot him on the spot if he
got his hands on Harding. Somewhere, McMahan had been
trained to his eyeballs, and his native wit was doing the rest.

He decided to sit it out and wait for Lieutenant Margil and
his merry band of killers to contact him. He found what he
considered to be a safe place high up among three branches of
a tall oak, pulled his trusty rifle around to his front, and waited
for sleep to refresh his sagging spirits.

The dots he squeezed off to the carrier and Annapolis not
only indicated he was alive but also that he had found the lost
diggers again.

He realized as he closed his eyes that the message he sent
was not quite accurate . . . but fuck 'em, he was tired and
wasn't going to spend half the night spelling out what was or
wasn't or could be . . . If only he could speak the tongue of the
Oglala . . . It must have surprised that poor son of a bitch who
tried to stick him with that fancy poniard he had probably
stolen . . . us Yanks are so smart . . . gotta thank Beanbag for
that one when I get back . . .

Chapter 25

"She's raving about Harding, Tom."

"Good or bad, sir?"

"Allison . . . Miss Davis has informed me in no uncertain
terms that if anyone is going to get Pat and the rest of the troop
out, he's the one who'll be able to do it." The President was
grinning.

"She must have met him . . ."

"Yes, Tom, she yanked him from the field to let him know the urgency of the situation, you know, the business about killing our people by drawing lots."

"I hope Harding was able to convince her that it wouldn't be like that . . ."

"It's amazing, Tom. Both you and Harding came up with the same conclusion."

"There was no other way you could cut it, sir."

"Tom. I'm becoming a bit uneasy about your not being in the loop. Since Miss Davis went out there, all the messages have been sent to me . . ."

Brockway hesitated for a moment. "Mr. President, I've got to admit that I was going along with a charade in these conversations with you. Frankly, there was no way that intelligence from the field operatives anywhere in the world, including voice-overs and scramblers, would not be on my desk as soon as it arrived."

The President didn't seem disturbed by Brockway's admission. "I thought that sort of situation existed, Tom, but I wasn't certain. Does anyone else have such access?"

"Two others, sir. My deputy Hotchkiss, in charge of covert operations, and 'Mother Hubbard' at Fort Meade, both for obvious reasons."

Randolph nodded. "Harding . . . or Allison's report seemed slightly vague about the captives. Did you have that reaction, Tom?"

"Yes, I did, sir. I think . . . I'm fairly sure that once Harding was able to determine that McMahan was back at Shanidar, that's all the justification or proof he needed to confirm that he was correct as to where the captives had been spirited. The key is, he didn't flash anything definite about Pat.

"I'll wager, however, that he got there after McMahan had reached the cave, and Harding never saw the captives. It's a big barn of a cave, sir. I was talking to Dr. Maran at Columbia about the cave, and he says it goes back about forty-five yards and is about sixty yards wide, with a four-story-high ceiling."

"What's Harding's next step?"

"Actually, sir, his work is practically done. His job was to find our people . . . let us know where they are, so that we can do what we have to do to free them."

"Of course, that's right! . . . But why did he ask for an Israeli backup team when he went back?"

"Contingencies, sir. The stakes are too high, and he doesn't want to be caught flat-footed. His respect for McMahan has rocketed. In the meantime, I've got our people working up a plan of rescue with advice from that old Israeli rifle, Menachem Goldberg."

"Does Harding have anything more to do out there?"

"Yes, sir. He's not going anywhere until he can send back that one-dot message, bingo."

"Bingo? What in the blue . . ."

"Bingo stands for Pat and pals. Once we get that one dot, we move in with Plan A . . . which we're working on, Mr. President."

"When will this rescue plan be ready?"

"Sir, we have only eleven hours left out of the twenty-four they gave us before someone is killed. Rest assured, Plan A will be operative within three hours, at the most."

"May I ask why such a plan wasn't in readiness days ago, weeks ago?"

"We had no idea what to plan in terms of the rescue locale, sir. Now we know it's going to be a cave on a mountainside in an unpopulated area along a sweeping valley. It could have been in a city neighborhood, a farmhouse, a—"

"You've made your point, Tom. Just one more question: What group are you planning to call in for the rescue?"

"Harding's unit, the Special Operations Branch."

"Are they the best we—"

"They have no rivals short of Superman—with the possible exception of the crack British Special Air Services, Mr. President."

Randolph pondered the reply. "I've heard some rumors about the SOB, Tom. Are you confident they can pull it off? What about the Army's LRRP or our Delta Force?"

"Strictly military operations, sir. Both are excellent. The LRRP works in seven-man teams under Army command employed in military action as its name implies, Long Range Reconnaissance Patrol. The Delta Force needs airports and drop zones. The SOB works under my direction without uniforms, without records, without status, and is known only to a small, highly select group of people at McLean."

"Why didn't we use them before to rescue all those hostages in Lebanon?"

"We've had the three-man units on red alert innumerable times in the past, but let me point out, sir, I am no different from any of my predecessors in running my department. The CIA works strictly in concert with the desires and command of the President and his broader decisions based on international and domestic policies, not to mention military ramifications. Frankly, sir, the SOB feels frustrated, much like most Americans."

"Who are these SOB people?"

"Harding is an excellent prototype of the men in the SOB. They've been culled mostly from the Special Forces, cross-trained so that each man in the trio can do everything his partners can do. They work in complete unison, mostly unarmed, depending on the circumstances, and complete their assigned task . . . or don't come back."

"What does that mean . . . don't come back?"

"If it's do or die, they die in the attempt. There's no quarter, sir."

"What are you saying, man?"

"They are killers, sir. That's the brutal truth."

Chapter 26

The insistent whisper of a buzz slipped into his consciousness, flowing into the widening cracks of broken sleep. Harding groaned as he felt the impressions of the three branches on his body, jerked to alertness as the buzzer went off again, and beeped a recognition signal.

Lieutenant Margil was telling him that he had arrived . . . somewhere nearby. Must be somewhere down the valley, out of sight, Harding hoped. They couldn't carry on conversations by beeper . . . would have to meet.

Harding sent out a burst of beeps. Then he climbed down from his perch and began moving back in the direction from which he had come yesterday. After moving another three hundred feet or so, scrambling along the top of the bluff, he sent out another burst of beeps, and then another every three hundred feet he traveled. Margil's laser beam would be tracking that movement and would know where Harding was going. He was telling Margil to meet him at a locus in the direction of the beeps.

Harding was within ten minutes of where he had hidden his wheels the day before when Margil appeared on the old road with six commandos in two four-wheel-drive wide-bodies emblazoned with the markings of the vaunted Iraqi Camel Corps, a proud unit that had abandoned camels more than forty years ago but which maintained the insignia and heritage. (Much like the 1st Cavalry Division back in the States, Harding thought.) Christ, the Boys from Netanyahu were now parading around as Iraqis. Were they able to speak the Iraqi in the Arabic dialect they used?

The greetings were earnest but somber after the vehicles had moved onto a narrow shoulder. Harding wasted no time. He was assuming that the captives were in the Shanidar Cave, explaining to Margil's raised brows that he had seen McMahan and some of his men but could not see inside the opening. He had had no choice but to make the assumption he had. Margil was aware of the 24-hour deadline for murder. They agreed that plans would definitely be under way in Washington for the rescue, since Harding had signaled the location of the captives. The Israeli officer was certain that plans were afoot, because his former mentor at Netanyahu Institution, Goldberg the Rifle, had been rushed to Washington.

"What's there for us to do?" Lieutenant Margil seemed let down. "Incidentally, you look a lot different without the stuffing in your face."

"I'm not sure . . . I'm worried, Lieutenant. I can't believe McMahan has holed up in a cave with a bunch of valuable captives and guarded by a dozen or so rifles without a plan. What's he waiting for? He couldn't be more cut off, more vulnerable, if he were at sea in some boat without a safe port of call."

"I don't get it, Ibrahim. What are you getting at?"

"OK, so he kills one of the captives within a few hours. And he tells the world he has done so. How would he be able to prove it? How would the White House accept that news without verification?"

"Is McMahan going to invite the press to his supposedly secret cave to exhibit the body? Don't you see?"

"Holy Moses, you're right. You've got to be right, but . . ."

"Lieutenant, I've screwed up! That bastard McMahan has done it to me again!"

Margil was taken aback at the show of snarling emotion by the American. Ibrahim grabbed Margil's arm. "Quickly, now, patch me through on a scrambler to Washington! Quickly!"

In a few seconds, Harding was telling Beanbag to abort plans to attack or attempt a rescue at Shanidar. "The captives are in Tabriz. Over." He slumped against the vehicle's side for a moment.

Margil didn't say a word. It was indeed, as the bullfighters used to say, a moment of truth. In talking it out, Harding had stumbled upon the truth.

Harding finally looked at the Israeli and his men, now in a solemn semicircle around him. "Let's nail those bastards at the cave, Lieutenant. I'd like to have a cozy little chat with McMahan . . . before Washington calls me back and stations me in Nome."

They made their plans. Lieutenant Margil and Harding would go back directly to the cave area in one vehicle, and be dropped off to move on foot to the bluff above the opening. The two vehicles with the six commandos would continue down the valley and fully expose themselves to the occupants of the cave. Then the commandos would move toward the cave, leaving the vehicles when the terrain became impassable. Harding and Margil, in the meantime, would get over to the footpath to the spring up the right side of the cave, and work their way to the level of the cave opening. After that, it would be a matter of action and reaction.

As they began to climb into the wagon, one of the young Israelis—by gadfrey, another woman!—asked if there would be limitations on weapons used, grenades for instance.

"Damned good question," Harding said, holding up a hand to stop everything. "I know that the archaeologists used dynamite to blast some large boulders in the deep trench way back in the 1950s. I know that the blasts didn't harm what they were looking for. I don't know what the effect of a grenade explosion would have . . . It couldn't be much more than a dynamite explosion, though . . . All right—if you are in a position for a grenade and it seems like a good idea, do it. In no case will you allow considerations other than the preservation of your own life. Let's go."

Both details were in position at the Shanidar Cave in twenty minutes, most of the delay caused by Harding's and Margil's scramble high above the brow of the cave. It was 10:35 in the morning, Baghdad time, when a figure, clutching an assault rifle, stepped out of the cave opening to watch the approaching commandos. Four more armed figures joined the first observer.

The commandos kept coming, clearly visible, about fifteen hundred yards away now.

Five more came out of the cave to join their comrades watching the six Iraqi troopers down below.

When the commandos passed the 1200-yard mark—an experienced guess on the part of the marksmen in the drama that was unfolding—the men on the lip of the cave opening dropped to their bellies and aimed their guns.

One man did not drop down. He stood upright, waving at the commandos to stop, to move back. They kept on coming . . . The upright figure also bellied down.

The rifles on the hillock became steady, as the commandos, their rifles at port, moved into the 1100-yard range, the outer limits of accuracy.

But the rifles on the hillock never got off a shot. A double burst of gunfire broke out from their left flank, sweeping a rain of death down the length of the prone figures in front of the cave mouth. It took all of five seconds.

The commandos reached the base of the path to the cave and began what would be a forty-minute jaunt up to the cave.

Harding and Lieutenant Margil carefully surveyed their hand-iwork, and the American eased his head around the cave wall for a peek inside. The sun was almost overhead, but enough light was reflected to show that there was nothing in there resembling a human form, just a herd of frightened horses far in the rear. Three of the bodies in the front of the cave began to emit moans.

Harding couldn't distinguish the tall, heavy body of Stefan McMahan among the prone figures. "I don't see him."

"Could be one of those at the far end . . ."

"I'll bet that sonovabitch left before we got here."

They headed for the far end of death row to determine if McMahan was among the riddled.

Two shots in rapid succession boomed from the reverberating walls of the cave.

Lieutenant Margil grunted, went to his knees, and pitched forward on his face.

Jackson Harding was jerked laterally away from the cave by the impact of the slug into his chest, his body sprawling like a rag doll in the bright sun.

There wasn't a sound, even as Stefan McMahan strolled out of the cave from the trench shelf where he had hidden, leading a horse. He tossed a contemptuous look at the bodies of his adversaries and started down the column of his dead and dying company, drawing his big knife to do what he had to do. He couldn't leave anyone alive to talk . . .

"I say, old boy, up to your old tricks, I see."

McMahan froze in midstride, then turned slowly around to look at Harding, who was sitting on the ground with his Sig Sauer pointed at McMahan's chin.

"I can't believe it! I shot you dead, damn it. I never miss!"

"No such luck, McMahan. Yes, I know who you are . . ."

"Shit, I thought I killed yuh . . ." He just couldn't get over it.

"Forget it, big fella. We're going to have a little chat."

"Forget my ass, you fucking ham bone. Shoot me and get it over with."

"Not a chance, mister. I need to know some things, first."

McMahan laughed easily, as if he were trading bon mots at a cocktail party. "Not from me you're not . . . Ibrahim . . . Covington Clarke . . . Achmed Hamal . . . Hagop or whatever you call yourself, asshole. And tell Beanbag he's full of shit and eats fumunda cheese.''

Harding realized that McMahan knew far more about him than he thought anyone did. And he knew the code name for Brockway. What the hell . . .

"Drop that pig-sticker, McMahan. I'm going to take you in and see what we can squeeze out of you besides all that shit."

"I ain't talkin', and you'll never catch up with her, not that one. So I'll see you in hell, ham bone . . ." His hand holding the knife suddenly went back, and the heavy blade streaked for Harding's chest.

Harding fired one round, blowing away his target's left ear and some of the skull. The American groaned as he saw McMahan collapse to the ground, obviously mortally wounded. He had meant only to hit him in the shoulder.

He brushed aside the heavy knife hanging by its tip from the clothing on his chest and rushed over to the man he had just shot. He turned him over.

McMahan opened his eyes, his face pale and drawn, and smiled up at Harding.

"Had . . . had your number all along," he whispered weakly, still smiling. "Never got your real name . . . gonna wreck all you imperialist assholes . . ." His voice was waning. "Do . . . do me a favor . . . tell my ma in Detroit I was . . . was . . ." He made a small sound and the light faded from his eyes.

Harding never liked to see death close-up, and there he was, Stefan McMahan, the man who had made him jump rope to his tune, lying there, having made one and only one mistake about Harding. He didn't know Harding was wearing a Kevlar padding under his greens, padding that even a .44 magnum couldn't penetrate at point-blank range. He closed the dead man's eyes and moved over to the body of the young Israeli officer whom he had grown to like so much.

His heart quickened when he saw an active seepage of blood from Margil's chest area. Harding turned him over. Margil moaned. He was a bloody mess. When the bullet had knocked him down on his face, the fall had broken his nose, which was bleeding profusely. Harding turned him on his side, so that the blood wouldn't accidentally choke him, and checked the chest wound. The bullet had entered the right pectoral and continued inward. Obviously, it had missed the heart.

The lieutenant opened his eyes. "Who . . . who was that masked man? Did we get him?"

"Yeah, we got 'im. It was McMahan, Lieutenant. Had to kill him."

"Crap!"

"You said it. Probably laughin' at the predicament he's left us in. Is there a medic in that small army of yours?"

"Yeh. Metzenbaum. Thinks he's a doctor cause he's screwing a nurse. God help me."

"You'll be all right, Lieutenant, as soon as I stop this bleeding and we get you back for a patch-up and refill. Mind traveling in a U.S. Navy chopper?"

Harding didn't wait for an answer. He snapped off a series of dots and then ran over to the row of riflemen, looking for anyone who was still alive. He shook his head. Four of them had survived the initial gunfire, but he had waited too long to get to them. Each had bled to death.

Harding went back and sat down beside the Israeli to wait, his eyes staring off into the valley, unable to shake the growing mantle of melancholy about his spirit.

In less than two hours, an American hostage was going to be murdered, and he couldn't shake the blame from himself.

Chapter 27

"He fucked up, sir, and we've paid the price." Secretary of State Roscoe Barnes liked to use vulgarity on occasion to make his point. He felt that the use of profanity or obscenity at carefully chosen times helped to enhance his image as a two-fisted realist.

The body of the young American was found across from the

main portals of the Blue mosque in Tabriz, his throat cut, his hands still tied behind his back.

"Any ID yet?"

"No, Mr. President. The Swiss consulate took the body and is sending it to Zurich for transfer to Washington."

"We are certain the body is one of the captured Americans?" Randolph was asking questions directed to no one in particular among the usual group that met daily about the abduction, augmented this morning by the attendance of House Speaker Davis and Senate Foreign Relations Committee Chairman Ralph Caggiano.

Brockway answered: "The radio announced that the first American had paid the price for our lack of respect and that the body was at the Blue mosque for all the world to witness. A body was found there this morning, and it was attired in a khaki outfit similar to what students wear on such field trips. I don't think we can assume it isn't one of ours, sir."

"Can we assume without any doubt now that our people are being held in Tabriz?"

"At least as of yesterday, sir. No one can be sure . . ."

"Tom, wasn't it your man who thought our people were being taken to Tabriz?" Randolph was asking the question.

"Yes, sir. When he lost them on an initial trek southward, he guessed they were going back north and tracked them with the aid of an Israeli special team."

"And then he lost them again?"

"Not exactly, sir." Brockway paused long enough to carefully weigh what he would say next. "Our operative was at the geographical point where the captives could be taken either to Tabriz, staying in Iran, or taken to the relative isolation of the cave where they first had been captured in Iraq."

"That's when he lost the trail?"

"We pulled him off of it, sir. We ordered him back to the carrier to review the situation and inform him of the death threat."

"Wasn't he able to convince anyone that he should stay on the trail, Mr. Brockway?"

"No, sir."

"Why not?"

"Your name was used as the one issuing the order for his return to base."

"Who used the President's name?" It was Barnes asking.

Brockway stared into the President's face. "I did, sir."

President Randolph returned the stare, startled at Brockway's unexpected assumption of the onus. He looked quickly at the only other person in the room who knew about Allison calling in Harding and saw Dave Demery give a faint yet discernible nod of acceptance. Of course. It was the only thing to do under the circumstances.

"You had good reason for doing it?"

"Yes, sir. It was imperative to inform our operative that he had less than twenty-four hours to find our people, if they were going to be saved. Since he had no communications gear to enable us to contact him, we waited until he called in for a chopper to gain on his quarry. He just happened to call at that critical juncture for him, and that's when we pulled the string. I had to use your name, sir, because I know this operative. He would have ignored all orders if it meant his efforts were being subverted. All except that of the commander in chief."

"You are saying, then, that if he had not required a chopper at that time, we might never have reached him and he might have been able to follow the trail."

"That is right, Mr. President."

"Very well, Mr. Brockway. After we adjourn I want to see you privately, please."

"Yes, sir."

"All right. We have an extremely important set of decisions that must be made almost immediately, gentlemen. The first priority is how we go about getting our people back. We have failed, to date. Any suggestions or observations?"

"I have a suggestion, sir," Barnes said. "We must recall that operative running around ineffectively in the Middle East and replace him with several handpicked squads from our multinational UN forces keeping the peace there."

Randolph was surprised at the moderateness of Barnes's suggestion. The man could be relied on to deliver bombastic, shallow evaluations and wild observations on practically any subject on the table. But in private. In public gatherings and appearances, the man was a veritable Jekyll and Hyde, exhibiting the soul of understanding, patience, and empathy, even to the point of bowing his head rather than respond to a personal public attack. Those who came to know him personally learned quickly the little regard he had for anyone's feelings but his own, and constantly fed an overblown ego with giant servings of sneering insults and heavy harpoons of calumny.

The President had realized long ago that a worse choice than Barnes for secretary of state could not have been found if a contest had been held to select the most tactless boor in the country. The almost fifty-fifty ideological split in Randolph's party during the struggle for the nomination had caused the party leadership deep and valid concern. The bitterness had been so deep that once Randolph had won the nomination, the leadership felt certain he would go down to defeat in the national election with a significant percentage of his party sitting on its hands rather than voting for him. Randolph's faction struck a bargain, and the word went out that if elected, Randolph's secretary of state would be the leader of the losing faction, Roscoe Barnes. That seemed to satisfy the intraparty opposition, and Randolph did win. But at what price, he had thought so many, many times in retrospect. Among Barnes's other negative attributes was an almost childlike, cruel animosity, bred of jealousy, toward anyone who seemed to have closer contacts with the President than he. Barnes seemed to hate Demery but, since the communications director was in a lesser position, tended to save most of his jibes and scorn for Randolph's old friend, Brockway. He seemed to be obsessed with a negativism regarding the CIA man's every word and deed. The President knew that it could not go on much longer.

"Thank you, Roscoe."

"Mr. President, have we heard from your representative out there as yet?" The Speaker of the House was asking about his sister.

"Yes, we have, Mr. Speaker. She filed a lengthy report which we haven't had a chance to review or discuss. Perhaps we should do so now as a basis for whatever new plans we undertake. Is that agreeable?" There was a general murmur of assent. "Fill us in, Mr. Brockway."

"Very well. Miss Davis debriefed our operative after he was picked up and returned to the carrier . . ."

"After he found out he was chasing butterflies, no doubt . . ." Barnes's voice had a touch of acid to it.

"No-o-o, Roscoe, after he and a squad of Israeli commandos assaulted the cave where he thought our people were being held."

Roscoe Barnes didn't know when to stop and listen: "What happened? Did they end up shooting each other? Har . . . har."

"No, Roscoe, there were more than a dozen rifles at the cave. Our operative and an Israeli officer crawled up to the cave while the others launched a frontal attack. They killed everyone."

"Sure. Never thought of grabbing a prisoner or two for interrogation."

"Mr. Secretary. I want you to refrain from further extraneous observations until this report is completed. I do not wish my secretary of state to continually place himself in a position of ridicule."

In the heavy silence following the public reproach by the President, Barnes, red-faced, excused himself and walked out.

"Continue, Mr. Brockway."

"Thank you, sir. Let's see now, oh yes. There were eleven all told. Four of them survived the attack although they were wounded. The Israeli officer and our operative were gunned down at close range by the leader of the abductors, but special protection saved our man. The leader was apprehended, but he tried to kill our man again and died in the process.

"By the time our operative took care of the wounded Israeli, who will live, by the way, and went to the wounded enemy, they had bled to death."

"Tom, where were the other Israelis? Why didn't they help?"

"Ah. The commandos, once they reached the base of the bluff containing the cave, had at least a forty-minute climb to reach the cave opening, where all this was going on.

"The fact remains that our agent found the man who had been leading our people in captivity, and it wasn't the answer. His appearance at the cave was a decoy. Our operative's fear that the hostages might be in Tabriz was confirmed in the most unfortunate way."

"Any ideas as to where they might be? Does our operative still believe they're there?" Everyone at the meeting knew where Tim Rand was coming from. If the captives were anywhere specific, he would love to marshal the entire Defense Department to rescue them.

"Yes, he does, Tim."

"Has he made any suggestions as to our next step?"

"Not exactly. At the moment he wants to hand the baton back to us and come home. He feels he has let us down. He blames no one but himself for the current state of affairs."

"Our operative is obviously an arrogant, egotistical knave . . . Holds himself responsible . . ." DIA's Woodley snorted derisively. "He's done one helluva job, things don't fall into place exactly the way he hoped for, so he wants to quit! I wouldn't let him, Mr. President. I'd hold his ass . . . hands . . . to the fire until the job is done."

The somber faces in the room lit up with smiles for the first time.

"Thank you, Bill. My sentiments exactly." The President looked at the faces about him and obtained emphatic nods. "Now all we have to do is get him to see it our way and get him back to work."

"That won't be difficult, Mr. President." Dave was grinning again. "All you have to do is pick up the transmitter and tell him. From all that we've gathered here this morning, the commander in chief can make him do anything . . ."

"That's an excellent approach, Dave. I'll do it. Does this decision mean, then, that we proceed as before, relying on our lone operative to see us to a successful conclusion?"

Senator Caggiano spoke up for the first time. "Before we agree to the status quo, have any of the countries we've been running across and flying over and shooting up expressed or filed demurrers?"

In the absence of the secretary of state, Brockway answered. "Senator, we've been extremely careful. Our operative has figuratively tiptoed around in discreet areas of Lebanon, Iraq, and Iran. Our aircraft, including stealth, have used the airspace of

Lebanon, Syria, Iraq, Iran, and Turkey. Only the Turks and Soviets have been apprised of our operations, and they are providing us full cooperation and assistance as needed. None has raised a single question, yet.

"Our scowling friends, the Iranians, however, are much like pit bulls on restraint, waiting for a chance to hurt us. Our space satellites have picked up Iranian military chatter about unidentified blips on their scan screens—coinciding with our aerial forays for our agent—but they don't seem to have an inkling about what's going on. They found some dead Palace Guardsmen, but they think it was the work of Kurds."

"That sounds good, Mr. Brockway. One more item, the Israelis. Do we or can we expect any negative reaction from their efforts on our behalf?"

"That's a good question, Senator. No, the Israelis are going to assume all responsibility in any circumstance when and if their people somehow fail and fall into official hands. You can say, without question, they are true friends of the United States. There is no plan to reveal their assistance after this is over."

Caggiano raised his eyebrows at the last remark but thanked Brockway.

The President intervened. "We've got less than twenty hours before the next American is scheduled to die. I am presuming that none of us here is prepared to exchange the young shah for our people?"

Only Brockway shook his head. Everyone was looking at the President.

"I'm sorry, gentlemen. I didn't mean to put you on the spot since my daughter is one of the hostages. Let me say that despite my obvious anguish as a father, I personally could not countenance such an exchange. I will assume that everyone here agrees with me, without a show of hands.

"We meet tomorrow at the same time. Thank you, all."

Everyone left except Brockway. The President buzzed his secretary and asked that Demery report back to the Oval Office.

Randolph didn't exchange one word with the silent CIA director until Demery arrived and sat down.

"I've asked you to be here because of some public-affairs elements that are involved, Dave." The President turned to Tom. "Did you think it was necessary to accept the blame, Tom?"

"I did, without the slightest doubt, sir."

"And you, Dave, you agree with Tom?"

"Absolutely, Chief." Dave looked at Tom. "I've got to hand it to you, Tom. That was a gutsy move."

The President peered over his Teddy Roosevelt spectacles at the pair.

"Mr. President," Dave continued, "if the American people learned that a personal friend of yours, who also happens to be a beautiful woman, used your name to, in effect, confound a covert operation and perhaps cause the death of a young American student, you would be up for grabs . . . your political power would have gone up in smoke, the personal attacks on . . ." Dave stopped at Brockway's loud harumph.

"What Dave is trying to say is that I am in a position to take the heat generated by the Congress, the media, the American people at large, while you are not. Our country can't afford to lose its presidential power. I am honored and proud to serve as the shield in this case, Mr. President."

Randolph was silent again. This decent man, his friend of more than twenty years, with an enormous reputation and record of heroic service to his country, would sacrifice an honorable mention in history for the good of the presidency.

"Barnes asked the right question and you jumped in. I feel totally inadequate, Tom Brockway, inadequate about giving Allison all that leeway out there and inadequate about how I can ever thank you for saving my political hide." Randolph threw up his hands in despair.

Dave took up the slack. "We'll have to decide what public stance you are going to take about Tom, sir. Davis and Caggiano will tell the story privately, swearing everyone they tell to secrecy, and before the day is over, the whole damned town will know. And there'll be a thousand embellishments when it appears in tomorrow morning's papers as a side bar to the killing in Tabriz."

"For starters, Mr. President, I believe that you must censure me publicly, then strip me of my position. You have no other choice."

Dave broke the silence. "Tom's right, sir. I hate to say it."

Randolph got out of his chair and began pacing behind the desk. "It can't be that serious . . ."

"Mr. President, this country has suffered a damned defeat at the hands of some sneaking cowards. The country will be looking for a scapegoat, and it's going to be easy to point the finger at Tom."

"Dave's right and you know it, sir. I suggest that we draw up two statements at once and issue them today in time for the evening news broadcasts. One would state our official position on the killing; the other would be my censure and your request for my resignation."

"I don't think there is need for words to reprimand, Tom. The request for your resignation will suffice. Or, better still, you resign."

"No, Mr. President, you've got to kick me out. It's got to look like that." Brockway's eyes began to mist as he uttered the last few words with a choking sound. He couldn't stand any sign of emotion and snapped erect to mutter an "Excuse me, sir."

Randolph walked up to the stiff figure of his friend and gave him a hug.

"I'm not going to do it, none of it, Tom."

"You must, sir. You can't let us down. It's the only way."

"I'll have a couple of drafts ready within the hour, Chief."

"All right, Dave. Let me see the drafts, but I'm just not going to do it. Absolutely not, and that's final."

Chapter 28

Allison Arnold Davis leaned across the bench desk, extending the radio-laser phone, and said, "The President wants to talk to you."

Jackson Harding took the scrambler handset as he left his seat and squared his shoulders to snap off a "Mr. President, sir

". . . Yes, s . . . Yes, si . . . No, sir . . . Yes . . . Absolutely, sir . . . Thank you, sir . . . I'll do my best, sir . . . No excuses, sir . . . May I speak, sir . . . McMahan knew who Beanbag was . . . Yes, sir . . . Yes, sir, and he also knew several of my cover and code names. Beanbag ought to know that . . . Yes, sir, and thank you again, sir. Goodbye, sir . . . Phew."

Allison was shaking her head in amazement. "I never heard so many 'sirs' in all my life. And you stood at attention as if you were at a parade inspection. I swear all you academy grads act as if the same cookie cutter got you.

"Well, I heard only one 'no' in that whole series. Did you agree to go back?"

Harding nodded, now pacing back and forth in the wardroom.

"What was all that about McMahan knowing who Beanbag is and knowing some of your other names?"

"As McMahan was dying he called me by four of them, and he should have only known about one."

"And Beanbag?"

"I can't say, ma'am. I'm sure the President will tell you if you ask him."

She nodded. "OK, I know it's Brockway. We've got no more than twenty hours until the next scheduled killing. God help us. Do you have any plans?"

"I feel I have one major goal at this moment—Tabriz." Harding didn't want to tell her he was feeling helpless. He didn't want to tell her he didn't know what he could do in Tabriz . . . didn't even know if the Americans were being held there. At this juncture, however, he felt it was as good a starting point as any.

She looked doubtfully at him. "Perhaps we should have some counsel."

"Counsel? Who would you suggest, ma'am?"

"I . . . I don't know, really. Perhaps I could help?"

Harding started smiling. "OK, let's see. If I head for Tabriz, here are some of the elements I must consider: One, how do I get there? Two, who do I go as? Three, do I go alone or do I have a backup? Four, what mode of communication do I use? Five, do I carry arms, and if so, what kind? I could go on, but that gives you a rough idea of some of the considerations without going into such silly little details as where do I go in a city the size of Boston or Milwaukee, where do I stay while I'm there, whom do I contact, how do I get it all done within twenty hours . . . See what I mean?"

Allison's eyes showed that she was impressed, but she didn't vocalize. She stood up, walked around the desk, and gave the still-seated Harding a long bear hug from behind. "Your job seems insurmountable, unattainable," she whispered, stepping around to look at his surprised, upturned face. "How in God's name . . . Is this the sort of thing you're up against all the time?"

Harding's surprise at her sudden expression of tenderness and concern for him evolved into a general reaction of "shucks, it's nothing" and "pshaw, it's all part of the game" to cover his genuine embarrassment. He never felt there was anything "macho" about his work. He thought of it as a combination physical and mental chess game with luck having more to do with the outcome than superior force or superior sense. He kept seeing the surprise etched on McMahan's face when he found Harding alive. He had been lucky to have that Kevlar padding; if he hadn't, life would have been over for him at Shanidar. Luck. Pure luck.

Luck. Like the time he had "drifted" ashore in the Gulf of Sidra just north of Qaminis, clad only in a loose-fitting pantaloon, and walked about five kilometers to the sea side of Bengazi, where he stretched out on the sand after planting a three-inch box of mercury that floated a directional beacon to the heavens. The Libyan patrol had found him sound asleep and this, coupled with his pleas for *baksheesh*, led them to accept him as a harmless beggar and leave him.

Luck. Like the time he realized he was coming down with "something" after squatting for three days at the base of a wall in a squalid, dusty, and heat-baked alley in Beirut, watching a doorway obliquely to his left. On the fourth morning, when he had staggered to his post—nailing the location of the American hostage—three heavily armed gunmen, no more than teenagers, had poked him to his feet, then let him be, disgusted at the sight of the running sores on his body. The Navy doctors had taken care of his "crawling crud," but the White House had done nothing about the located hostage.

Luck. Like the time he knew he was a dead man when the stocky stevedore in Haifa ambling along ahead of him on a quay suddenly turned to face him with a big smile and a big automatic. Harding's last act was to lunge at him, deciding not to die easily. The gun apparently jammed, and the would-be killer, now with a broken back, had plopped into the slime-covered waters of the harbor.

Luck. Like the time he was poking through the rubble of a basement in a bomb-wrecked brownstone in New York with another member of the team, when a double hammer-cock behind him coupled with the words, "Die, you pigs," impelled both to whirl around and dive toward the sound. The gunman fired the first barrel at Harding's colleague, blowing off most of the left shoulder. Harding easily reached the wielder of the 12-gauge in that split-second, smashed him to the floor, and broke his scrawny neck, only to discover he had killed a young woman.

Yes, luck, pure luck that he was still alive.

"Why don't we take five minutes and talk about Tabriz? Maybe it'll give you an idea as we kick it around." She sounded hopeful.

"Sure, why not, ma'am? Let's see now. Tabriz is one of the largest cities in Iran, tucked way up in the northwestern corner, only sixty miles from the Soviet border and one hundred miles from the Turkish line. It's really two cities, the ancient walled city dating back to Roman times, with six or seven gates, and the urban sprawl outside the wall.

"The wall is more or less in ruins but still defines a sharp demarcation between the old and the new. The city sits in an earthquake-prone region; it's been flattened four times in its history and rebuilt each time except for such things as the old wall.

"Tabriz is watered by the Aji river, which isn't exactly sweet. They've had water problems from day one, apparently. It has a couple of magnificent parks and a big train station on the west side, outside the city limits.

"It has two notable features: one of the most beautiful mosques in the world, its dome decorated entirely with a lovely blue faience tile, and another structure which began as a mosque but became a citadel, the Ali Shah, both located in the southwestern center of the city, and both partially damaged by

earthquakes during their seven hundred-plus years of existence. Enough?"

"Is that the Blue mosque, the place where they dumped the
body?"

Harding looked down as he nodded.

"What about the other building, the Ali . . . ?"

"They call it the Ali Shah Citadel or the Arg. It's a fantastic
edifice, ma'am. Its walls are twenty-five feet thick and go up a
hundred and twenty feet, one of the most massive brick structures in the world. It was absolutely impregnable until three
quakes knocked down some of it."

"Is it used for anything?"

"Yep, it has a marginal military use. For at least a hundred
years it was a cannon foundry, cannon for ceremonial purposes, and lately it's been a lovely park."

"Anything else about the city that crosses your mind?"

"Not really . . . Do you know those fancy shopping malls we
have all over our country, covered and air-conditioned and all
that? Well, I don't know what it's like today, but Tabriz at one
time had more than twenty-five miles of its interior streets
covered over so that its bazaars could display their wares regardless of weather. It's called the Ghaza."

She shook her head. "I don't know what you ought to do.
We haven't had anyone we can talk to in Iran since back in the
1970s when they made hostages out of our embassy staff."

"Don't I know it." He sat thinking for a minute or so, got on
his feet, and proclaimed he was going to his room. "I think I'll
have a chat with Beanbag. Got an idea . . ."

Allison obtained clearance, opened the scrambler, and announced that Forty-Three needed to talk to anyone in Beanbag's office, immediately. Beanbag himself responded. Harding
stole a glance at Allison as he took the hand piece and spelled
out his immediate plan and needs. After that, he reiterated
what he had told the President about McMahan knowing
Brockway's cover and four of Harding's deep-cover names.

"I don't like it a bit, Forty-Three. Have any ideas?"

"Looks as if we've got a mole or a transient leak. I can't
believe it. What about moving to . . . let's see . . . Mode Seven?
That ought to throw 'em off for a while."

"All right, Mode Seven it is, beginning at twelve midnight. I'll get things rolling for you. Get your ass to Station Best ASAP. Anything else?"

"Yes, sir. Whatever happened to those shell casings I sent for prints?"

"What're you talking about?"

"Oh, shit . . . excuse me, ma'am . . . I'll check it out here and get back to you when I can . . . Yes, there's another person in on this conversation—Miss Davis. OK? Talk to you soon."

Harding was grinning when he turned back to Allison. "Brockway almost had a heart attack when he heard me make an aside apology to you. He thought I had a girl friend sitting in . . ." His grin grew wider.

"Why did he think that? Have you broken rules before?" They both laughed, then Allison became serious. "Frankly, Jake . . . Commander, I don't know what's going on. At this point, I don't want to know. I'll let someone tell me."

"Miss Davis, ma'am, all I can say is that nobody said it was going to be easy, and it sure ain't.

"Before I do anything else, I've got to find Lieutenant Garza and see what happened to those shell casings I entrusted him with. Then I'm going to shove off in twenty minutes for never-never land. Wish me luck, beautiful!"

Harding tracked down Lieutenant Garza having coffee in the pilot's wardroom. They smiled as they shook hands.

"Lieutenant, I've got a problem which I'm sure you'll be able to fix."

"Yes, sir, Commander."

"What happened to that little cloth bundle I gave you, you know, the bag I said contained casings I wanted sent to Washington for a fingerprint check?"

"I don't know, sir. I did as you asked me. I tagged the bag with the name you gave me, stamped the tag 'urgent,' and put it in the diplomatic pouch for the next flight out."

"When was the next flight out?"

"I caught it five minutes before it left, sir. In other words, it wasn't aboard here for much longer than fifteen minutes."

Harding nodded, deep in thought. Over a week ago and Beanbag hadn't received it yet. The name on the tag was Brockway's. The system hadn't failed in the past. Supersonic bomber from anywhere in the world to Andrews, copter directly to the White House pad or the pad at McLean or the pad at the Pentagon for distribution. What had happened to it?

"Lieutenant Garza, get the exact hour of the day it went out and give all the details to Miss Davis . . . she's in Wardroom A, below the flying bridge . . . and tell her I'd like Beanbag to know about this, rush. Got it? I'll be in the Ready Room in ten minutes for takeoff, Lieutenant."

Harding was ready, wearing a standard flying suit and carrying a small satchel, when Lieutenant Garza stuck his head in the hatch and said everything was ready. As they strode along the flight deck to the now-familiar gunship, Lieutenant Garza informed Harding that he had given Miss Davis the message and that she was probably on the horn as they spoke.

"She sure is a honey, sir."

Harding growled something about bears and ignored the opportunity to exchange verbal leers.

The wind had whipped up to provide white crests for the choppy sea as the gunship lifted off, circled the triple-hulled nuclear carrier, and leaned toward the north, its giant blades propelling Harding to the American airfield in the Turkish poppy fields of Adana.

Chapter 29

"The appeal will be issued within the hour, sir. The United Nations General Assembly has voted affirmatively on the Russian resolution to seek the release of the hostages without further bloodshed or delay."

President Randolph nodded absently. "A lot of good it's going to do. We don't even know who we're talking to."

David Demery shrugged. "It's becoming hard to understand.

American students are grabbed and hustled off into Iran. We know that much. A demand is made for a swap with the Iranian prince. Yet, the Iranian government and the Mujahedeen Khalq, its so-called holy warriors, absolutely deny any responsibility. They were a bit late in denying it, but they now say so in no uncertain terms."

"I wonder what took them so long."

"I have no idea, sir."

"Do you believe them, Dave?"

"Sir, they've never been bashful about owning up to such things in the past. I've got to believe them now."

"I do, too. That leaves us with the burning question, doesn't it, Dave?"

"It's always been there, sir. You know, when we first learned about that IRA chap McMahan, it was a fairly certain conclusion that he was in cahoots with the Mujahedeen and that the government wanted to grab the prince to pay him back for his attempt to overthrow the government. But now, who knows?"

"Hope that Harding fellow comes through for us, but I'm having doubts again. When are we meeting with the Berry family, Dave? That's really going to be tough . . ."

"We've set it up for tomorrow at eleven o'clock in the morning?"

"Why the delay?"

"The family wanted some of his classmates from Yale to be present, sir. We had to make arrangements for that."

"He was only twenty-five?"

"Yes, sir. John T. Berry of Enid, Oklahoma. Majored in physical anthropology and was on his second major dig. Outstanding lacrosse player . . ."

"Poor kid. It's difficult to understand this world. We're only a few hours away from the next execution . . ."

"Yes, sir. We have less than ten hours left. The UN resolution doesn't offer those bastards a thing for desisting from their next murder. It's become a true test of our resolve as a nation with principles." Dave softened his voice. "I can't see how you stand it, Mr. President . . ."

Randolph waved a hand in deprecation. "I just . . . I just don't think about it, that's all."

"Let me change the subject for a moment, sir. I'm baffled by another development. It's rumored all over the government that you demanded Tom's resignation, but we never made a public statement. You killed the statement I drafted. I had the only copies when I brought them to you, and we had Alice shred them."

"Who typed the statements for you in the final?"

"My secretary and personal assistant, who's been with me for six years, Mrs. Delmar, and I'd trust my life with Sherry, sir. Talk about a clam!"

"All right, what about ribbon cartridges or the discs in computers?"

"No ribbons, and the disc was erased when I got back to the office minutes after you made the decision not to issue a statement. Sherry was still at her desk, had never left it while I was with you, and it was erased in my presence."

There was a long chasm of silence between the two. Then the President spoke. "I'm going to have the FBI and the Secret Service look into this matter. Did you know that some stuff sent from the Middle East by Harding for a fingerprint check can't be found? Yes, Tom informed me last night. He got an inquiry from Alli— Miss Davis, who had asked on behalf of Harding."

Dave looked at Randolph steadily. "Hamlet said it a long time ago. There's something rotten . . ."

"All right, Dave. Let's get into our daily sweat session with the troops."

Chapter 30

Abou sur Biroglu sat motionless in the dusty, hot confines of the outdated Wagon-Lits passenger train, awaiting his turn to have his papers examined by the Iranian border guard at Qotur. He had already gone through a similar procedure a few minutes earlier by the Turkish guard on leaving that country. It was interesting to Abou to see how little love was lost between the soldiers of these two Moslem countries, obviously because the Turks were mostly Sunnis and the Iranians were almost all Shiites. Another reason was, of course, the centuries-long enmity between the countries, with the Turks frequently attempting to annex the entire northwestern section of Iran. And both had to be constantly on their guard against the rebellious antics of the Kurds, who had claimed that area long before the Turks and Persians established their dubious boundaries.

Biroglu answered the perfunctory questions asked by the two guardsmen with perfunctory answers. He was returning from Van, yes, on a business trip. Yes, rugs, his family business in Tabriz. Yes, his address and place of business was right there, on that card. Oh, yes, thank you, the trip was successful. Just a minute. Here, these are new and should replace those for better protection. Don't mention it, my pleasure. Peace go with you.

The Irani rug dealer had noticed that the handkerchiefs with which the soldiers were covering their holstered handguns were frayed, and he had given them two new ones. It was common practice to use pieces of cloth or handkerchiefs to protect firearms from the fine, wind-blown dust that never abated.

The train jerked to a start once again and began rolling. He estimated he would be in Tabriz in about two hours. He closed his eyes, slipped downward in the old velveteen bench seat, and went to sleep. No use staying awake and being conscious of the heat and what he was about to do.

The slowing down of the train was enough to disturb his light slumber. It was preparing to switch onto the main line between Jalfa and Tabriz, which would then continue on to Teheran. Ten minutes to go. He checked his briefcase, straightened his tie, made sure his mustache was firmly in place (it would have to be steamed off when he had no further use for it), tapped the heel of his left shoe to feel the lump (it would give him a slight limp when he walked), and waggled his jaw to feel the plastic implant for the umpteenth time. Yes, Jackson Harding was ready.

The train trundled across the bridge spanning the Aji, and he could see the brick-red range of hills that provided the northern backdrop to the handsome city. The old diesel engines, in double yoke to traverse the mountains, finally groaned to a stop in the palatial, high-topped Vagzal terminal, with signs in Farsi, Turkish, English, and Arabic proclaiming that this was Tabriz, although one sign would have sufficed.

Harding stepped down and followed the few other passengers toward the main rotunda and the taxis to Tabriz, twenty minutes away. He had been working on an idea, but he knew better than to board a taxi and order the driver to take him to the place he had in mind. After all, he was a rug merchant, and rug merchants went back to the bazaar after a trip out of the country . . . not on a sight-seeing trip.

So he waved to the line of Mercedes taxis waiting in front and asked to be taken to the Ghaza, the main bazaar, where he hoped he would be able to find the address of the rug place he was supposed to represent and be an owner of. When he was told politely that he couldn't be taken all the way, Harding nodded indifferently and said, of course, take me as close as you can. He was left on a side street, apparently leading to the maze of streets that served as the city's huge bazaar or marketplace.

The well-dressed man nodding to him the first time they walked past each other could certainly be chance; seeing the same person leaning against the rail in front of the teahouse as he walked by was a coincidence that Harding did not accept. Coincidences were highly suspect in his business, and now he kept his eye out. When he saw him the third time, walking away from him in another part of the crowded bazaar, he walked rapidly to catch up and touched the man's shoulder. He turned around and smiled.

"Ah, Biroglu Aga. I was hoping you would recognize me."

"What? Recognize you? Why do you follow me? How do you know my name?"

"If that is your name . . ." He was still smiling. "Let us repair to a private place where we may talk."

Harding felt a combination of elation and trepidation. He was elated that someone knew him in these strange surroundings. He wasn't sure he would survive such recognition. He had to wait and see.

Harding followed the man, who looked to be about forty, through an ever-changing mass of moving humanity in the bazaar. The spoken words that Harding heard were mostly fragments of Azeri, a bastardized Turkish, and Farsi, but there were dollops and smidgens of Arabic, Armenian, Kurdish, and Russian. The man finally stopped at a narrow doorway just off the milling bazaar and beckoned Harding to follow him in.

It was a two-story building of red brick with apparently thick walls, for it was relatively cool once Harding stepped inside. The stairway up was fairly broad, and the man led his visitor through one of three doors on the landing to a large, airy room with thick Oriental rugs on the floor and hassocks and large pillows along the walls. Harding was motioned to sit, and a clap of hands brought tea and small sugar cookies carried by an unveiled woman in her twenties.

It was weeks and weeks since he had heard it on the beach, but the man opened the conversation with the quiet words, "Nighttime would be safer."

"It's a nice day for a walk," Harding responded . . . and waited.

"Ibrahim?"

If the late Stefan McMahan hadn't dropped all those code names of his, Harding would have relaxed when he heard this one, but it wasn't going to be good enough now.

"The stag at eve had drunk his fill . . ." He waited.

"Where danced the moon on . . . how do you say it . . . Moonan's rill?"

The American burst into contained laughter. It was the damndest thing listening to a Near Easterner reciting English poetry with an accent. They both grinned.

"Who are you? I wasn't told anyone was going to hook up here."

"My name is Abdul Ali Baad. I am a Turkish silversmith, and I have been asked by my superiors to lend you any assistance I can."

"Your superiors? The Iranians, the Turks? Who?"

"I am an agent for the Soviet Committee for State Security, or, as you Americans call us, the KGB."

Harding sat where he was, stunned. "What the hell are you saying? What's going on?"

"Nothing is going on. I am merely attempting to assure you that you are no longer alone and can rely on me for assistance, if you require it. That is all."

"All right, Abdul, tell me first how you knew who I was. You must guess that it bothers me that you picked me out of more than a half-million people here."

"I am afraid to say it, but it was very easy, my American friend. Out of total boredom I wait around the train station and sometimes the airport and see who comes and goes. They are usually the same people, day after day, week after week, month—"

"So you saw me get off the train . . . Why follow me?"

"I don't have anything else to do. You will excuse me for saying this, but in your attempt to look local, you were as a clown. Nobody wears suits of that Russian cut. Haven't worn that style in years. Then you get off the train wearing one of them. If you had ever looked back as you walked you would have seen so many passersby look back at you and giggle."

"How did you find out who I was? You have my ID code, Ibrahim, as well."

"It is so rare for me to report anything to my regional office that I decided I would tell them about you. They knew who you were right away. You are the man with the Kalashnikov rifle who made contact with our truce team in Mosul. They are impressed that you are alive and in Tabriz.

"Frankly, dear man, my chief wants me to help you get the President's girl back and also to keep an eye on you just in case you are thinking of other mischief.

"What is bothering my chief and therefore bothering me is why you are in Tabriz. Is it conceivable that the President's girl is in Tabriz?"

"Abdul *aga*, it's my best and only guess. If the Americans haven't been brought here, I'm lost. Remember, they were here long enough to have one killed."

"Who would have brought them here?"

"That I don't know either. I had followed the people who had captured the Americans at the big cave in Iraq, and I took my eyes off of them for a short period of time. When I found them again, I followed them back to the cave. The abductors were there but not the Americans. The only other place I assumed they could or would go to is Tabriz."

Abdul Baad and Harding sat sipping their tea for a while, not exchanging a word. The American noticed two pairs of large, solemn brown eyes peeking at him through a part in the door curtain whence the tea had come. He winked at Abdul and announced in a loud voice in Turkish: "I have two silver rials here made especially for little girls. I wish there were some little girls here so that I could get rid of all this weight, Abdul *aga.*"

"What a wonderful surprise," Abdul said. "I think there are two of them right here . . ." And he waved the two blushing, squirmingly shy girls, six and seven years old, from behind the curtain to accept the coins and run back out of the room.

"Do you realize that this city was in Russian hands five separate times during the last century?" Abdul Baad looked pensive.

"Do you realize that the majority of the population in Tabriz speaks Azeri, a hodgepodge of Farsi and Turkish with a touch of Russian? And do you know that every time there is a rebellion against the natural government, it seems to have its roots right here in this crazy, wonderful city?"

"Tabriz is the usual center of rebellion, you say?"

"Absolutely. Going back through the previous century, there were six revolts and all of them started here. The revolts first were aimed at the shah, then the usurping shahs, and now the Islamic republics."

"Then, Abdul *aga,* I am in the right place. I feel confident that the hostages have something to do with a plan to shake the central government."

"Whose plan?"

"Don't know yet."

"It is getting late, Ibrahim. Their plan is to kill another of your friends by morning."

"I don't think that will happen, Abdul Baad. I have a hunch—a feeling—that they will adopt an air of civility and see what can happen to impel us to make the swap for the young guy."

"I hope you are right. Do you have any specific plan at the moment?"

"Yep. I am going to visit a couple of spots. Advise me, please. What is the most inconspicuous way I can travel about in this town, without drawing unnatural attention?"

"I would say a bicycle, but you're not dressed for it."

"A bicycle?"

"My friend, you are in the land of the Bible, the Koran, and Zoroaster, where even hatreds take centuries to change . . . and only for the worse. Bicycles and donkeys are still a common mode of transportation . . . well . . . mostly in the outskirts. I think I will secure a bicycle for you as well as the proper clothes to go with a person who cannot afford a car or a motorcycle.

"You will be a guest in my home until I can accomplish this."

Harding thanked Abdul Baad. This was a start, anyway, he thought.

Chapter 31

It was shortly after President Randolph had called the Federal Bureau of Investigation to meet with him and the Secret Service, to discuss what could be a real problem, that he called for a meeting of the National Security Council in session with the Joint Chiefs of Staff, the Defense Intelligence Agency, the Central Intelligence Agency, and several individuals whose identities were unknown but vouched for by the President and the CIA.

There was no question about it. It was one of the most serious breaches of national security since the 1980s, when the

Walker family had sold out the Navy to the Soviets for a few paltry dollars. Every word that had been spoken above a whisper in the Oval Office, apparently, had been audible for the past two years.

The bugging had been ingenious. The areas that had been bugged were those that had been repainted in time for the arrival of the new occupant, President Randolph. The room in question had moldings and wainscots in keeping with the general decor. To make certain that the paint on the flat surfaces did not encroach on the moldings—painted a slightly different shade—a strip of masking tape had been applied along the edges of the moldings, a common enough procedure.

It turned out that the masking tape was uncommon—or at least that was the conclusion the FBI arrived at after looking into the whole matter and discovering along the molding edges a hair-thin filament that had been painted over. They concluded that the masking tape had contained the filament along one edge of its total length when applied. When it had been taken up, the filament had remained. No other conclusion could be drawn as to how that wire had been applied to the President's office space.

Most interesting was the power source for the bug. Caulking, ostensibly to smooth over rough spots, was loaded with minuscule filings of the identical filament and spread across the deep windowsills in the Oval Office to collect solar energy.

A check with the painting contractor, a pleasant and outspoken man who had been doing this work at the White House for a dollar a year, had reduced him to a state of shock. He told the investigators about the difficulty he had had in hiring good workers—painting was considered too menial in the state of affluence the American population had attained—and had practically hugged this one job applicant who had demonstrated her abilities by brushing perfect circles or an absolutely straight line in quick, deft strokes. She was fairly new to the country, and her English had a definite accent, but one didn't have to speak well to paint well. Of course, there was no record or trace of Lisa Bangala or whatever her name was.

A baffling element to the sorry situation was that a sweep by a variety of detectors, conducted every other week as a simple, routine precaution, had not unearthed the system. Once the existence of a bugging device was seriously entertained, it was found. The wires and the power source were discovered within hours after several of the scanners decided not to accept the FM signal that they had picked up over the years as coming from the radio station located in northwest Washington. Sure enough, the signal from the bugging system had a sideband, which had misled the checkers constantly and consistently.

Once it was established that there was a signal being transmitted from the Oval Office, the hair-thin filaments around the moldings were discovered by an agent playing Sherlock Holmes who scrutinized the woodwork with a large magnifying glass. It had been easy to see that the system had an extremely low power output. Its signal could not have possibly gone much beyond the walls of the White House.

The first step was to find how the signal got out of the Oval Office. This portion of the search created the damage to the floors, walls, and ceilings. As it turned out, the damage had not been necessary. In a previous administration, an electric-coil space heater, about a yard square, had been set into the wall near the executive desk to keep the chief executive's lower extremities warm. He had had a case of diabetes and a problem with cold feet. Two innocuous wires were strung across the heater, one along the top of the opening, the other along the bottom, parallel to each other. The ends, joined seemingly for some purpose known only to a heating man, were touching a field of caulking that reached the filament. As the Secret Service expert who finally spotted it said: *"Voila!* I give you the transmitter!"

There was a studied rush out the basement doors into the gardens and lawns behind the White House, with everyone now looking for two specific items: a receiver (to catch the transmission from the Oval Office) and an amplifier combined with a directional transmitter to boost the weak signal to a megahertz frequency to reach a destination miles away if necessary.

They found them. Two ordinary-looking spotlights, one pointing toward the White House (the receiver) and the other pointing aimlessly off to the east (the direction gave it away), completed the system.

It was immediately obvious that if the White House had issued the statement announcing Brockway's resignation, no one would have been the wiser. But someone had spoken too soon and had given away the whole cabal.

What bothered the Secret Service chief, Atwater, was that the Brockway statement had become a matter of government-wide rumor in Washington.

He pointed out that a foreign power or powers might have had the wire installed, but apparently government employees—or at least one—were privy to whatever was being snatched from the airwaves.

"We cannot assume that this bugging was necessarily the work of a foreign country. We must keep open the thought that it could have been perpetrated by an American national for reasons unknown but including espionage," Atwater stated in his precise manner. The slight breeze made his empty left coat sleeve flap as the group stood in a rough circle in the Rose Garden. He had lost the arm when he had thrown himself in front of the vice president six years ago to take the brunt of a burst of gunfire from a would-be assassin who mistook the VP for the President.

"Will they be through with the electronic scrutiny today?" The President sounded dubious. He didn't like having to meet in the Rose Garden on matters of national security because the offices of the leader of the greatest power on the globe was the last place to hold a confidential conversation.

"It's been completed, sir. Worked through the night. What is delaying us is the patchwork and painting to repair the necessary damage we caused to various portions of the walls, floors, and ceilings. Business as usual tomorrow morning, sir."

"I suppose the Iranians who are doing the repair work have been properly cleared?" The President's acidulous joke brought a careful titter from his audience.

"And one more thing. Presumably the leaks to the *Washington Post* will be a thing of the past? May we assume that the wires were the source of the leaks?"

"Can't assume that, sir. If we do, it could imply that the *Washington Post* was in some way, somehow involved in the placement of the tap. I, for one, do not believe that an institution as ingrained in our history and service as the *Post* could ever countenance or be a witting recipient of information from such a source." Aside from the Joint Chiefs, everyone in the group nodded in acceptance of Brockway's statement.

The President turned to Brockway. "Have all operatives and posts in the field with direct access to this place been warned not to transmit until they get an all clear?"

Brockway nodded. "Not only that, sir, we changed all codes and modes."

"Any word from Harding?" Randolph had pulled Brockway a few steps away from the gathering, out of earshot.

Brockway's mouth tightened before he spoke. "I've come to the conclusion that I should have resigned from this job, sir. I must inform you that we have word about Harding, but it's not from any of our sources."

"Speak up, Tom. What do you mean?"

"The Russians, Mr. President. The Russians were the ones to tell us that Harding had arrived safely in Tabriz."

Randolph grimaced.

"Thank God, they were sharp enough to inform us by hand delivery rather than any form of oral communication. It seems that Harding was spotted by one of their agents in Tabriz and that the Russian and the American are now working together."

"Tom, is it that easy to spot one of our covert operatives?"

"I really don't know what to say. He's one of our best, yet he must have been recognized practically upon arrival . . . If the Russians spotted him, I wonder if . . ."

"Let's hope not, Tom, let's hope not. Now tell me, what could Harding and the Russians do together that Harding wasn't able to do alone?"

"If you think it over, sir, I believe the addition of the Russian is a plus. If the Russian is good enough to spot a covert agent of ours, he should be good enough to become an extension of Harding's potential."

"That's good, Tom, that's good . . . How much time left in the twenty-four-hour death watch?"

"I was hoping you wouldn't ask. Less than an hour. I have a feeling they won't kill any more, not for a few days, at least."

"Let's fervently hope so, Tom."

Their prayers were not answered.

The body of Edwin Genereau of Amesbury, Massachusetts, graduate student of physical anthropology at Stanford University, was found on the steps of the Blue mosque, with death due to severe lacerations across his throat.

*   *   *

Electronics genius Samuel Hankin was reeling from the unexpected blow to his prestige as the Man-in-the Know at the Department of Commerce and Labor. When he had picked up totally unexpected conversations on his personally rigged omnirange radio receiver in the department's audio-visual division and had come to the conclusion that he was listening to people talking in the Oval Office at the White House, he had kept the startling development to himself. But he had made constant and unerring public predictions about the President's programs and prospective actions. His so-called rumors had spread quickly throughout the federal government, and he had gained a special standing among his fellow workers, not to mention several assistant secretaries who bought him lunch on occasion. When his predictions had suddenly ceased, and he could not explain his abrupt lack of information, awe had given way to disbelief and finally to cold shoulders. And none of it had been premeditated on his part. Hankin wanted to cry.

Chapter 32

The ruins of the Blue mosque were in the Sirkhop section of the city, so Harding focused his search there. Shortly after he had declared with some certitude to Abdul Baad that there wouldn't be more killings for a while, it was Harding himself who discovered the body of young Genereau well after midnight.

Abdul had provided him with the clothing of a shit collector, called a *hamall* in that part of the world. He had escorted him to a barn, just beyond the sprawling Ghaza, where some heavy bargaining by Abdul rented Harding a bicycle for the day. Astride the rickety machine, Harding nearly touched the ground with his feet as he rode off, with the relatively sharp saddle telegraphing future pain.

He must have missed the placement of the body in public view by minutes, he estimated. The body was still warm and the blood still glistened about the neck. The boy had been killed elsewhere. There was no blood on the steps.

Harding had to peer intently into the dead face to recognize the student in the darkness. He had memorized all the faces before he left the States, and each hostage had a code number preset so that a simple transmission of any of the coded numbers would mean that the person had expired. As he was making the identification, Harding rifled through the dead man's clothes as if he were robbing the victim. When he couldn't find anything, he enacted a small dance of frustration and kicked the body before he mounted his bike and rode off. He cursed Brockway and the President and Allison Davis for the kind of situation he found himself in—having to kick the body of a young American who had just been murdered—to protect his own identity.

Well, he had better let them know . . . He brought his right hand up to his jaw and squeezed out the dead man's code, repeating it twice more to make certain it wasn't missed.

Jackson Harding was feeling a bit grim. He was riding a bike that really wasn't big enough for him in a strange city alien to his customs and mores, seeking brutal and heartless killers. He could have ridden by one or more of them that day before night fell, and he had absolutely no way of identifying them.

Would he have to expose himself to draw the killers to him? It had not worked too well back what seemed a thousand days ago in the Kaleshin Pass. What other choice did he have? Ride around in circles as he was doing now and . . .

Too many of them had whizzed by his head for him not to recognize the sound of a bullet. There was no report of any kind, not even a blip.

He slid off the bike on the side away from the direction whence the bullet came, grabbed his jaw and held on, cuddling as close as he could to the flimsy buffer provided by the bicycle.

Another bullet zipped by and Harding snarled in hate. The bastards were using either full metal jackets or dumdums, either one providing that telltale bumblebee warble as the slug tumbled by. A hit would have churned up his body tissue and torn up everything.

Harding desperately wanted to look and see where the shots were coming from. There should be a muzzle flash even if the slug went through a silencer. But he knew that whoever was shooting at him had an excellent vantage point, and his curious head would invite an instant slug. He wondered how the gunman or gunmen had missed with the first shot . . . probably his erratic movements on the bike.

He still held on to his chin but permitted a slight bit of exposure to the shooter as he bent downward with his free hand to dig out a weapon of his own.

The bullet creased across the hide of the saddle and tore across the side of his ribs. Harding let go of his jaw, threw his arm into the air with a heavy grunt, and lay still on his back, one arm propped across the bike and his other hand under the folds of his bloody blouse. He hoped it would work. It seemed to be his only chance.

It was around three o'clock in the morning under a starlit sky without a soul to be seen in the narrow streets surrounding the mosque. There was no sound or movement of any kind for at least five minutes, Harding estimated, trying hard not to move or show breathing—thank God for the dim light. He knew if he blinked it would be over in a flash.

The careful sound of crunching gravel tiptoed toward the American. Harding kept his eyes staring into the night sky, but his peripheral vision saw two heads coming into view. Not heads so much as darker masses in the darkness. Peripheral vision can pick up images in the dark with greater clarity than can direct sight.

"Is he dead?" The whispered question was in Azeri.

"Shoot him again to make sure . . ."

Harding's hand came up like a cobra strike. The four explo-

sions from his 9mm Sig Sauer shattered the stillness and all
four kneecaps of his would-be assassins. He savored the high-
pitched screams and then the protracted moans and groans of
the two he had shot. The wounds were among the most painful
that can be inflicted by bullets, and they probably would never
walk again without artificial assistance—not that Harding
cared.

He stood up, holding his bleeding side, and sauntered over
to the howling, whimpering pair. He looked down at them
without expression and finally said just two words: "Javid
Shah."

The squirming pair didn't seem to care too much, but they
understood perfectly well when Harding squatted down beside
them and casually asked where the Americans were being kept.
He held on to his jaw again, letting go his side.

No response. They continued their wails of pain.

Harding asked them again, quietly, almost politely.

They were not talking.

Harding shot off the left elbows of each of them.

Their pain was certainly not feigned, but both shook their
heads when Harding asked again.

These bastards were prepared to die, Harding thought. He
realized he could spend the rest of the night chopping them up,
and he still wouldn't get an answer. He didn't make another
sound or another move, just waited.

The filthy melon truck, redolent with the stink of decayed
casabas, chugged up and squealed to a stop.

Three men leaped from the truck. Even if he hadn't recognized them, Harding knew who they were from the soundless
impact of their feet on the pavement; the coordinated scanning
of the immediate area with the middle man eyeing the central
zone and the flankers covering the right and left sides; the
casually lithe, alert look they had; and the fact that all three
were forty-five years or more. They didn't act the part: poor
farmers in loose-fitting garb, shod with sandals cut from old
tire carcasses.

"It took you long enough," Harding said, raising his right
hand no higher than his chest in greeting.

"Lost you when your signal went dead." The big man in the

center spoke in a laconic drawl. "Are we too late?" He had gestured toward the moaning duo on the ground.

Harding let a smile cross his face. So, Brockway had pulled the string. Instead of Israeli commandos, he had sent in an SOB unit as his backup. The big man was Bill Smithson, and the others were Leo Trovato and Jim Westcott. This was only the second time he would be working with this trio, but he nodded his approval.

"Not late at all. Need those two for questioning . . ."

Two quick pops from Trovato's automatic brought everyone to their knees as they turned to focus on the archway behind them in the mosque. Two figures slumped outward into plain sight.

"Had their guns on us." Trovato shrugged by way of explanation.

"Collect those bodies and let's get out of here."

They bound the shattered joints of the wailing wounded, handed them onto the truck bed, collected the bodies in the arch and tossed them aboard, and Smithson drove the jouncing truck north toward the river. The truck climbed into the hills north of the city and pulled into a grove of cedars containing three goatskin tents. The SOB trio was efficient. One cleaned and bandaged Harding's superficial wound; another cleaned and covered the smashed joints of the wounded pair, now quiescent from the deep trauma overcoming their bodies; and Smithson dragged the bodies off the truck to be buried.

When Harding saw the two bodies being dragged away, he called out, "I'd like to examine them carefully in daylight. Let's get some sleep."

Three hours of sleep was all they needed. After a quick breakfast of goat cheese and pita, they stripped the two bodies and examined everything. The male and female couldn't have been much older than twenty. The clothing was nondescript, mostly of a coarse woolen weave. Harding would have been shocked if any of the items had a label. Nothing.

The female had large, almost flaccid breasts despite her youth, and her well-defined and deep hips were portents of what would have been a Rubenesque maturity. Nothing.

"Notice anything about the guy?" Harding waved at the thin but sinewy body.

They stared for a moment, then Westcott turned to look at Harding with widened eyes. "He's not a Moslem!"

"Or a Jew, for that matter," Trovato chimed in with a chuckle. "The prick isn't circumcised, if you'll excuse the pun."

"So what the hell have we got here?"

"Can't be a member of the Mujahedeen or anybody with the Islamic Republic government. Say, check those two before they come to. I wonder . . ."

The pantaloons of the wounded captives were untied at the waist and pulled down briefly for a look. Not circumcised.

Harding shook his head. "Never thought of checking the men we killed back there at Shanidar."

"What's it mean? Do you think it's significant?"

"I really don't know. They don't have the light coloration of Circassians. They could be Armenians . . . hell, they could be anything! And it could mean a lot and it could mean nothing. We'll have to wait and see."

Smithson pointed to the wounded pair. "I don't think those guys are going to last. We haven't anything to treat 'em for shock. I don't think they'll ever come out of their comas."

"They weren't about to talk. Maybe I can get something out of them in their present condition." The wound on the side of his chest was giving him pain and throbbing badly as Harding knelt beside the shooter of the night and shook him. You can't rouse a body in a coma by shaking it. He got a vial of ammonia from a first aid bag and tried that without effect. He pulled the body to a sitting position and that did it. The man's eyes fluttered open, and he groaned. He was about twenty-five with deep pockmarks on his thin face.

"Where are the Americans? Where? Where?" he asked in Azeri.

The eyes closed for a moment, then opened wide.

"The Americans. Where did you leave them?"

"You . . . you know . . ."

"Where?"

"You said . . . you told me . . ." He sighed and closed his eyes.

"The Americans. Where are they?"

He could not be revived.

Westcott expressed his puzzlement. "What the hell is he talking about? Did you understand?"

Harding was thinking out loud. "I think he was saying that I knew. That I had told him . . . All I did was ask them the same question when I brought them down. And they wouldn't tell me."

"That's all? Nothing else?"

"I did thumb my nose at them at first. I rubbed a little salt with a smart-ass opener. I simply said *Javid* Shah."

"*Javid* Shah?"

"Yep. *Javid* Shah. That's exactly what I tossed off at them. Nothing more, other than asking them where the Americans were."

The bedraggled group of "farmers" and the "shit hauler" stood silent, pondering their next move.

"Take me back to the city. I think I'd better get back to the *America*, get this side of mine patched up, and regroup. Anything you want me to bring back?"

Smithson shook his head. "You realize there may be another dead American by the time you return." It wasn't a question.

Chapter 33

The nuclear carrier USS *America* was steaming back from Malta, escorted by the guided-missile cruiser USS *Mobile Bay*, the guided-missile destroyer USS *Lawrence*, the fast combat-support ship USS *Seattle*, and the frigate USS *Joseph Hewes*, when the gunship settled on the carrier's rear elevator with Comdr. Jackson Harding, USNR, aboard. He looked like anything but a naval officer as he limped across the flight deck to the starboard hatchway on the island. The badly cut suit with the wide lapels and baggy pants, the broad, drooping mustache, and the slight limp all added up to someone who didn't belong on a modern fighting ship.

Harding made his way directly to Wardroom A, greeted Allison Arnold Davis with a handshake, and launched into his report. She was looking at him intently, and he couldn't help but think how damned attractive she was with the sun from the porthole striking the back of her head.

"Got much to talk over with you, ma'am. You and Beanbag switched my backup, but I'm not complaining. Only wish Beanbag . . . Brockway . . . could be here. I need his insight in some of these things."

"Why don't we try to raise him on the speaker here? Wouldn't that help?"

"That's a great idea, but it would be about one-thirty in the morning back in Washington."

"If you think it's important enough to have Brockway listen to what you have to say, he won't mind losing a little sleep. I'm going to get him on the scrambler. What's the new mode?"

While she was setting it up and waiting to reach Brockway, she pleased Harding with a request. "I'll call you Jake if you'll cut out that ma'am stuff and call me Allie . . ." He grinned and nodded acceptance.

Brockway's voice broke in. "Thanks for getting ahold of me. I'm going bananas. What's the good word, Commander?"

"I thought you ought to hear my report to Miss Davis, Tom. There are some elements that we need to get our heads together on."

"Excellent. Shoot, but tell me about the Russian first."

"You've heard? OK. Looks as if our people aren't up to date about what the Russkies are wearin' these days. A KGB agent picked me out of a crowd at the Tabriz station the second I got off the train. He said I looked like the caricature of a Russian going back to the 1950s.

"He has all the outward appearances of a Turk, Tom. Looks like a deep mole to me, probably planted back at the end of

World War II when the Russians gave up a four-year occupation of Tabriz."

"How old would you say he is?"

"About forty."

"The Reds must have left behind his dad, who probably spoke some Turkish. Must have melted into the population. What's your estimation?"

"Looks as if Abdul Baad is on the level with me. Took me to his home. Got me a change of clothes and a bike, and I took up riding the streets.

"Found the boy on the steps of the Blue mosque. They had just killed him, Tom. But I wasn't able to pull it off in my disguise as a . . . excuse me, Miss Davis . . . shit collector."

"Stop your kidding, Commander, and . . ."

"I'm not kidding, Tom. How do you think people in that part of the world get rid of their human waste? There isn't anything like indoor plumbing and no water closets to flush. Their solid waste goes into buckets, and men go around from house to house collecting and disposing of it. I was disguised as one of them."

"I'm sorry I asked. So what happened?"

"After I identified the body, I was ambushed. I knocked down the two guys that came out to see if they had killed me. Hurt them badly, sir," Harding said, stealing a glance at Allison, "but they wouldn't reveal where they're holding our people. My backup arrived, and we carted them off with the bodies of two more we killed as they were watching us from the mosque." Harding began to see two Allisons.

"Now, Tom, here's what's bothering me. The people we dragged away may not be Moslems at all."

"Not Moslems? What else could they be? Wait a minute. Did they say they weren't Moslems?"

"Yes, Tom. When we strip-searched the dead man—the other was a woman—and checked the two wounded, none of 'em was circumcised."

There was a long pause at the other end as the intelligence sank in. "Well, I'll be that proverbial uncle! What are we dealing with, Commander?"

"Just a minute, please," Allison's voice had an edge to it.

"What're you two carrying on about? What's the big deal about being or not being circumcised?"

Brockway chipped in. "The good book of Islam, the Koran, calls for all males to be circumcised for the sake of cleanliness. And you ain't no believer if you ain't. It's part of the religion, the same as the Hebrews."

"Then what you must be thinking is that the people who dragged off our archaeologists can't be Moslems and therefore have no connection with the Iranian government or the Mujahedeen Khalq." Allison beamed back at Harding, who had nodded with a grin at her summation.

"Precisely and not quite precisely. Any ideas, Commander?"

"Tom, if they're not from either of those two groups, then what other group would want the pretender to the Persian throne delivered to them? Why don't you pose that question to the young prince right away? He just may have a notion about all of this."

"Good idea, Commander. Now, what else?"

"Another bit of a puzzle, Tom, Miss Davis. One of the prisoners the next morning was able to talk briefly. I pushed him again about where the Americans were. The gist of what he said in response was that I knew. That I had told him." Harding was feeling faint.

"What did you say to him?"

"After I had shot the pair of them, I was rather sore, Tom. They had been firing dumdums or full metal jackets at me. So I greeted them with 'Javid Shah' before I got down to asking about our people." Harding was entranced by Allison's eyes. Probably what was making him feel far away.

"OK, Commander, what does it mean?"

"Translated freely, it simply means long live the Shah or the Shah forever. Nothing more. Come to think of it, it was a wasted jab. Hell, they were in too much pain to care about anything at that point."

"That's it?"

"That's it. That's all I said other than repeating 'Where are the Americans?' and 'Where?' over and over."

"We'll have to think about that. Oh, yes, Commander, my investigation concerning the prints—"

"He can't hear you, Mr. Brockway!" Allison's voice had risen a notch or two. "He's passed out and on the floor. I'll call you back as soon as I can, over!"

Allison rang the board for the sick bay and gasped at the sight of blood pooling near Harding's body when she knelt beside him. He was unconscious.

She got back on the horn to Brockway at four in the morning Washington time to inform the anxiously waiting CIA director that Jackson Harding was going to be all right. He hadn't told anyone about the bullet wound he had along the side of his chest when he came aboard. Yes, he had been hit by a tumbling bullet. It had ripped into his side and slipped out again leaving what looked like a superficial four-inch gash. He had been leaking blood internally and had passed out from the loss of blood and its concomitant shock.

"He says he needs to get back to Tabriz, Mr. Brockway, but I'm going to keep him here until tomorrow."

"By all means, Miss Davis. Tell me, is what I heard all that he had to say before I was called?"

" Absolutely. He had expressed regret that you couldn't hear some of what he was about to report to me, and I suggested that you should be called, despite the hour."

"Thank you, Miss Davis. May I say you are a gem. Good night— Good morning, ma'am."

Harding was up and about by late afternoon, ignoring the orders of the flight surgeon and the pleas of Allison. Didn't anyone give a damn that another American hostage was going to be murdered within a few hours? He probably wouldn't make much difference if he were back in Tabriz, but at least he would be where he was supposed to be.

He was back in Sick Officers' Quarters within five minutes. Captain Shields, or "God," as one is known as when one commands a capital ship of the Navy, simply ordered Commander Harding to report to Flight Surgeon McConnaughy and remain under his command until further orders. It was that simple.

Harding stopped fretting when he realized that his brief ambulatory excursion had sapped his strength and he felt better on his back. Allison joined him. Harding apologized for having ranted about his confinement, and the two kept smiling at each other without saying a word.

"You certainly make life interesting for me."

"I'm not trying, ma— Allie."

"That's what makes it so special, Jakey. You mind your business and I get a kick out of it."

"Well, that's something I haven't tried before on the opposite sex. How does it go again—I mind my own business and that turns you on?"

"Come now, Jakey, You're being flip. I was merely trying to be supportive of someone who gets shot in the line of duty and fails to tell anyone."

"Actually, I didn't think it was anything more than a scratch. I had no idea it had punched a hole in me."

"Well, you really scared everyone when you keeled over. Frankly, it was great theater, fine drama."

"I planned it that way, Allie. A man's got to catch the eye of beautiful females any way he can. I found out a long time ago that next to being a good-looking hunk, a little bleeding and a well-timed slump to the deck will get 'em every time."

"Humph."

"It worked with you."

"Bilge water, as you might say, mister! I'm doing my job for the President, and part of it is to see that you do yours. Nothing more." Allison was delighted at the look of dismay that flitted briefly across his face.

"And another thing, Mr. Navy Commander Hero Who Bleeds On Order! I don't fall for any of those pat labels such as beautiful female."

"Enough, ma'am, enough. I'm sorry I transgressed. I shall hence—"

"Oh, we're back to ma'am, are we?" She grinned broadly at the forlorn look his face had assumed, a face that had become almost that of a little boy. "Come on, perk up, all is not lost, Jakey. I do love ya, you know."

It was his turn to grin. "You do, huh? Well, I love ya, too. When shall we get married?"

"Is that a proposal, Commander Harding?"

"Don't ask questions, m'dear. I don't ever recall asking that question before . . . in my whole life . . . to anyone, drunk or sober."

"Thanks for the warning, m'dear yourself. You're neither drunk nor sober. You've been sedated, drugged. You seem to achieve a special attraction in that state of mental incompetence. That's a warning, sir. Once it wears off, I won't care a tinker's dam about you, understand?"

"Not quite, me darlin' . . ."

"Not quite what don't you understand?"

"What the hell's a tinker's dam?" Harding realized he was crazy about the iron-assed bitch.

"Stop being so flip, you idiot. I guess this is as good a time as any to have a serious talk with you." Her eyes had suddenly become solemn and searching.

She stared at Harding, and he returned the stare, appraising her physical self carefully for the very first time: an almost childlike face, innocent in cast with a sensuous mouth, especially the full lower lip; round gray-green eyes; head topped with a clutch of light brown hair that refused to stay put, strands slipping over her eyes on occasion. No question about it, she was a veritable delight to behold and a brain to boot.

She stood up, walked around the desk, and they stood face-to-face, almost nose-to-nose, with unflinching eyes. Then they embraced, chins on shoulders, hugging and holding and holding and hugging for what seemed like an eternity, her pair of hands and his lone hand each softly caressing the other's back. Time was sweet and poignant, and the only sounds were soft, whispery sighs venting what apparently was weeks of ineffectual, unstated, unknowing longing.

And then they kissed, still standing, still silent as their mouths searched and felt and tasted, their heads rolling slightly to capture the total essence of the other's desire. She emitted small sounds as if she were crying, and he responded with short moans, his hand dipping under her blouse to rub her back. Then, as quickly as it had happened, they stopped, looked into each other's smiling face, and sat down together on the only place they could, the edge of her table desk.

Even as they smiled, both seemed to have a touch of discovery in their expressions, prompted by the warmth of their embraces and kisses, sparking the discovery of feelings they did not know they had shared for one another. Harding's fingers were lightly caressing her knee as they sat looking at each other, then moved to a stroking, and she didn't resist when his hand slipped under her blouse and caressed her smooth, flat belly. She didn't resist when his hand moved up to her breasts and massaged her nipples through her bra. She gave no resistance as he kissed her long and fervently and his hand searched for the silken folds encasing her sex. Both seemed slightly short of breath, breath taken by the rising tide of passion.

"It's almost eight bells, and perhaps we should stop this and . . ." Harding was fishing. He didn't know what he should do. He knew what he wanted to do . . .

"You're absolutely right. Why don't we get into some fancy dress and join Captain Shields for dinner before we call it a day?" She was looking at him with those big round eyes of hers, telegraphing her vulnerability.

"Great idea. I'll pick you up in . . . twenty minutes OK?"

At a white-linened dinner table with candles and an array of silver, Captain Dara Shields had Miss Davis on his right, Commander Harding on his left, and his executive officer, Commander Joseph Budget, across from him. The lady was attired in a high-necked, floor-length sleeved ensemble of silk or chiffon; the men were dressed in formal whites, their chests bedecked with Navy Wings of Gold over rows of medals of various hues and shapes, their meanings mostly a mystery to the civilian world. It was required adornment as part of the dress uniform, and Allison had murmured a barely audible "wow" with a big grin for Harding's benefit when they had encountered each other on the gangway to the captain's quarters.

Dinner was a carefully orchestrated affair under the joint ministrations of Captain Shields and the warrant officer in charge of the mess, both of whom anticipated every need. The quiet, calm demeanor of Captain Shields on the bridge, seated in his swivel chair, was transformed at the dinner table into an affable, good-humored Captain Shields with a ready smile and a constant twinkle in his blue eyes.

Once the small talk accompanying the quality, taste and texture of the first four courses had been deftly handled by all, and the chocolate mousse was disappearing, the skipper turned to Harding, saying he had always wanted to ask someone in Harding's business a question.

"Tell me, Commander, without breaking any confidences, how do you manage to escape detection in hostile territory?"

"Class distinction, sir."

The answer broadened the smile on the captain's face. "Yes?"

"Whether it's New York City or Beirut, Paris, or Prague, people do not pay attention to beggars or other obviously lowly persons, especially if there's no plea for alms. It's usually the best disguise."

"I gather you're a brave man, Commander, but tell me, honestly, does fear ever enter your mind?"

"It's constant, Captain. I'm always afraid at the prospect, the anticipation of getting caught."

"I take it, it must be a hindrance . . . ?"

"If you can control it to any extent, it is an important ally, sir."

"Yes?"

"Fear pumps you up with big dollops of adrenaline, giving you faster reaction time both in thought and body. It's almost a saving grace, you might say."

"Ah . . . Commander, you mentioned something about control."

"Yes, sir. I control my fear by acting."

"Acting? Like being on stage?"

"Exactly, sir. I become Sean Connery or Errol Flynn or Tom Cruise, depending on the circumstances. I become detached and collected, allowing the initial introduction of adrenaline to take its course. I hope I'm not laying it on a bit too thick, sir."

"Not at all, Commander. Not at all. I suppose you have special feelings about the abductors of our people?"

"I'm not sure exactly how I feel about them. I fear them more than I would if I were facing a professional soldier, for they are fanatics and cowards, two dangerous traits in any enemy one has to face."

Captain Shields shook his head, smiling. "Your answers are most interesting, Commander . . . Ah, the coffee is here . . . I shan't bother you with any more questions, Commander. Miss

Davis, tell us a bit about life in Washington these days. . . ."

That's the way the day ended for Harding and Allison. He had a bad time trying to sleep. Her face continued to float across his consciousness. He wasn't sure why such things happened, only that it had happened only once before in his lifetime, and he wasn't at all sure whether such happenings were commonplace or equally rare among all humans inhabiting the earth. He had accepted long ago that all creatures had been endowed by a higher being with an innate attraction and need for the opposite sex. The only question seemed to be the degree of attraction and the mutual level of reaction between the specific individuals feeling that need.

Was she for real? Did she feel about him the way he was feeling about her? She seemed to, but one never knows about the mutuality of feelings.

It was settled for him the very next day when the intercom ordered him to report to Wardroom A. Allison greeted him with a brief hug. (That was a good sign, he thought. She didn't have to do that.) and said that Brockway was coming on in two or three minutes.

Brockway was down to business immediately. "Miss Davis, is Commander Harding there? . . . Good. Now listen to this: The little bag of shell casings you sent, Jake, was found in an unused diplomatic pouch at State. The only answer we could get was that the item had been overlooked by Secretary Barnes's staff when the pouch was opened and its contents distributed to the various agencies to which they were addressed.

"The casings are being checked as we speak, and I am trying to run down how anyone could have overlooked that little bag. That's it, and President Randolph sends his regards to both of you. Hopes you recover from your wounds quickly, Jake, over."

"I thought we should have a little talk, Jakey." Her eyes were solemn, searching.

"By all means, Allie, I've been . . ."

She held up her hand. "I must set some matters straight, Jakey. I am spoken for. The President and I have agreed to marry once Pat is returned. I love him dearly and have for several years without his knowledge.

"But ever since I met you I have marveled at the experience of discovery when I'm with you. I have led a celibate life for several years now, and I thought I had achieved a level of existence that suited me. Then I met you and rediscovered animation, quickness, joy, curiosity, appreciation, interest, attraction . . . in short a reawakening to life.

"I'm thrilled with you and by you, Jakey, and I don't ever want to lose you. I love you, my dear man." She had rushed through her little speech and was somewhat breathless, awaiting his response.

Jackson had recoiled inwardly when she opened with her declaration of undying love for Randolph. He recovered some of his hope for her when she spelled out his impact on her life and then tossed him for an emotional loop with her protestation of love. She was a puzzlement, and he toyed desperately with the idea of kissing her and walking away. Did she love Randolph or Jackson more? Was it possible for her to love both men with equal intensity? If he walked away now, it was all over. He would have lost her. If he approached her as he had done yesterday—touched her again—she could throw him out. The result would be the same in any case.

He took three steps to stand in front of her, kissed her gently on the mouth, and began unbuttoning her blouse. She stood erect and still, not saying anything, not helping him, not stopping him. His heart was pounding now as he removed all but her pantyhose. He noted thankfully that she had a wholesome sense of herself and wasn't a bit bashful about her nakedness, at least none that he could sense.

She was truly superb in the nude. Her breasts had an elegant sweep upward with perfect nipples and a symmetry that reminded him of the later works of the ancient Greek sculptors. Her hips were classic and lean, tapering to the sculpted columns that were her thighs, framing the delicate tuft of brown at her vee.

But it wasn't her naked beauty that set her apart from all the women he had known. It was her face, even more glorious with the softness in her eyes that seemed to ask for acceptance and tenderness.

He turned her around and led her to her bed, where, seated,

he whispered into her ear to ask if she would kindly help with her pantyhose. That did it. She kissed him deeply, smiled, and removed the last of her garments before she crept under the covers, watching him as he began removing his clothes. He had difficulty removing his shorts in front of her. He did, however, averting his eyes only to catch a grin on her face at his obvious discomfort.

He was under the covers in a flash, pulling over the sheets on his side, and they found themselves holding on to each other with an almost desperate strength. They were both motionless for minutes and speechless as well, appreciating the other's physical closeness in an almost osmotic ecstasy. Then both relaxed, each seeking the other's lips, and they inhaled in long drafts—tasting, biting, lips sucking lips in gentle leisure. His hand began to move, his fingers sliding delicately down her back to feel the growing roundness of her soft bottom, feeling the smoothness of her thighs, then back, his fingers rubbing and then tweaking a nipple. She was making tiny sounds continually, and he was moaning softly. He let his hand drift to her sex, his fingers gently exploring and probing her wet opening. He had a sudden desire to taste her sex, a desire he had never experienced for an act he had never performed with the women he had come to know carnally. He reluctantly left her lovely face, went to her breasts, where he circled and circled her nipples with his tongue before nibbling and sucking at them and moving downward to her soft, flat belly, where he placed his cheek and held her before allowing his tongue to roam and rove to her vee, where he traveled over and around and across, spreading her thighs wide to finally bury his face there, dampening it, foraging with his tongue between her swollen labia, and instituting a rhythmic motion with his tongue and lips on the pink protrusion that swelled there.

Her tiny sounds were almost guttural in unison with the movement of her hips, and Jackson felt an ocean of contentment roll over him at the realization that he was pleasing this alabaster goddess, that she had accepted him, that she was giving of herself with unstinting generosity. She was now making sounds like a muted kitten, her thighs pulled up and spread wide, her eyes half-shut, her breath coming in short takes, her hips moving in a small counter rhythm.

She suddenly took his head in her hands and returned him to her side, whispering that she missed him away from her lips, and poured words of affection and I-love-you in a constant repetition between kisses. Each kept asking what else would please the other. Suddenly she turned over onto her knees and offered up her lovely bottom. It was a pose he was never to forget, a view that remained etched in his memory, perhaps because it seemed to symbolize the gift-giving of her total self to him. He positioned himself between her drawn-up knees and entered her in ever-deepening strokes until he felt her wetness and warmth completely, in her inner depths. He varied his probes with bursts of quickness, then carefully measured rhythms, directional changes, shallow thrusts, deep thrusts, symphonies and combinations until the sweat gleamed on both, their bodies sopping from head to foot after more than an hour of it. Then, heeding her worries about impregnation (he had never gotten around to telling her that he had complete control of his functions), he turned her over, drew up her thighs once again, and caressed her sex with his tongue as he applied a simultaneous dual-digital penetration of both her orifices for total arousal.

It worked within a few minutes. She reached an arching climax, revisiting the peak again and again and again until she finally came back to earth for a last, long groan, collapsing happily as he came back up to her face.

He was enjoying himself immensely, reveling in the pleasure he had afforded her. It had not occurred to him that he had not reached a physical climax until she whispered something about it being "his turn." She tried to move to a position where she could reach his member with her lips, but he gently restrained her and continued to hold her close. She finally slipped off into sleep, murmuring driblets of words that contained "I love you" and "not fair."

He could not believe the metamorphosis, the psychological transformation of this woman in bed. One moment she was the unapproachable, dignified, witty, and sometimes acerbic person whom some might even call bitch. Then, in bed, in the arms of her lover, she was totally docile and submissive, generous and giving—completely entrancing. A total woman, he thought, one to be treasured as a mate forever.

Harding vowed he would never let her go, as he gazed at her face, her hair matted by perspiration, her beautiful visage flushed and hot. She opened her eyes and smiled weakly at him: "I love you."

"I love you, too. Now, go to sleep. I'm going to leave you alone." He leaned over, kissed her on her wet forehead, slipped into his clothes, and left, foregoing a shower, to retain her spoor as long as possible.

Late that afternoon, they were together again, to return Brockway's signal. The shell casings had been wiped clean! "No help for you, Jake . . . Yes, we have the culprit, but I am not at liberty to reveal it at this time . . . No, it has no bearing on your assignment. Good luck to both of you."

When Allie and Harding met again that night, they were totally content merely to hold on to each other, kissing now and then, but talking about life and death and the fantastic and overwhelming elation that inundates the senses of two people in love. They agreed that having such feelings for each other was just about the finest experience a human could have. They had reached the point where they cared not if others on board noticed their attachment. They parted near midnight.

Chapter 34

"It's going to mean trouble for you, Mr. President. He was the one man you named for appointment to buy off the—"

"I know, Tom. I know. I have no choice, however. What he did was indefensible, utterly childish, and criminal, as far as I'm concerned."

"It certainly is difficult to believe that a member of the cabinet would stoop to—"

"Tom, there is absolutely no doubt of his guilt?"

"It's totally circumstantial, but there is very little else that can be drawn from the evidence."

"Then I'm going ahead with it. I'm going to call him in, confront him with the evidence, and ask for his resignation on the spot. And I'm going to do this alone, Tom. I don't want anyone present."

Brockway nodded. It was going to hit the fan when it got out about Barnes. One doesn't resign suddenly from being secretary of state without the truth coming out eventually. Brockway almost smiled at that thought. The truth might undergo some reshaping by the media, since the actual truth was too ludicrous to accept at face value.

The discovery of the small cloth bag containing the shell casings in an apparently empty diplomatic pouch weeks after it had been sent from the Middle East could have been chalked up to simple human error or oversight.

But when the casings were checked for the prints that Harding had expected, Brockway's technicians had found that they had been wiped clean. Not even a smudge. Not even a trace of whorls at the rim of the casings, where Harding had held them.

So, in the interval between the placement of the evidence into a diplomatic pouch in the Mediterranean and its removal from that pouch in Washington, someone had opened the little package, wiped clean the shell casings, put the casings back in the little bag, and tossed the bag back into the now-empty diplomatic pouch.

Left at that, it would have been moot who had done such a thing.

But the tag with Brockway's name as the addressee had been handled by at least four persons. The distinct print of a thumb, twice, on the tag could not be explained away. The secretary of state had most certainly handled the little bag of shell casings.

No matter what kind of a face, what circumstance, what reason was applied to relieve the secretary from culpability in the matter, it didn't wash.

What had angered the President was the realization that this act had occurred while a desperate search was being conducted for his daughter and her colleagues. And the only explanation that anyone could sanely provide was that Barnes was highly jealous of Brockway's position with the President and perpetrated that almost treasonous act to prevent Brockway's plans from succeeding.

Barnes was in Philadelphia making a speech but would be back in the early evening. He had been informed already that he was to report to the White House at 5:30 P.M. upon his arrival.

"Dave, I'm of the opinion that this situation will not become a matter of public notice or information until I'm ready to announce it."

"Right, Mr. President. From the day we discovered the bug in here, the intragovernmental rumors have ceased."

President Randolph nodded quickly. "But not leaks to the *Post* when we hold cabinet meetings or other affairs here . . ."

"That's right, Chief. I've got an idea about how to nail the bastard, sir, but you've got to give me some leeway until I work it out."

"You nail this person, Dave, and you'll have my undying gratitude. It's become a real joke around here."

Chapter 35

The death of the second hostage was too much for the American public. It was convinced that all thirteen Americans would die now, unless the prince was handed over. Nearly 47 percent of the people in representative groups polled by press and broadcast media organizations felt that the prince should be sacrificed instead of the Americans. About 40 percent felt the

President wasn't doing enough to save the hostages. Five percent felt that the honorable way out was to nuke Iran, and the remainder had no opinion.

Dave Demery knew that another killing or two, at the most, would make the presidency unbearable. Not one newspaper or broadcast station had broken ranks about the United States standing firm in its resolve not to bargain with terrorists. But a few editorials had closing sentences to the effect that perhaps the country should take another hard look at vanishing alternatives. Of course, there weren't any, other than handing over the prince. That's what it was going to come to.

Dave flushed up in anger at the *Post* story that had shown up this morning. The pipeline was at it. Brockway had left for Greene County in New York to have a chat with the prince about the puzzling development that the terrorists didn't seem to be Moslems. He was going to go over the entire scenario with the young man in hopes that something important that had slipped detection would be spotted by the prince.

The trip was to be in absolute secrecy. Brockway, in fact, left for Greene County by way of stops in Knoxville, Cincinnati, Detroit, Ottawa, Montreal, and finally to the safehouse in the vicinity of Catskill, New York. At four of the changes, the aircraft took off with someone doubling for Brockway. And complete changes of pilots, aircraft, clothes, and baggage were made along the route to prevent the possibility of a planted transmitter. Brockway would eventually have five tubes of toothpaste, five toothbrushes . . . five of everything by the time he returned home. And it wasn't going to be a simple return flight, either. From Catskill, he would be flown by chopper to Fort Devens in Massachusetts wearing Air Force mechanic's coveralls, transfer to another chopper, which would take him out to sea and to the deck of one of those brand new submersible Hovercraft DEs, which would disappear from sight and surface off Norfolk, where another chopper would pick him up and bring him back to Washington.

The visit with the prince would take approximately two hours. The trip, to and from the safehouse, to maintain its integrity would take almost two days. There wasn't a person in the organization who felt the steps taken were too much. Some even felt that they were not enough.

But the devastating fact was that the *Post* had learned that Brockway was going to "a secret destination" to meet with the Iranian prince (it's a wonder the story didn't mention Greene County, Demery thought) and that the reason for the "urgent flight was obvious." The only possible reason that one of the top confidants of the President would be traveling to visit the prince would be to seek his acquiescence to being swapped for the hostages.

The horror of the story staggered Dave. He knew Brockway was going to see the prince. It had nothing to do with a swap. Dave knew that the prince would once again beg to be swapped. But the upshot of it all would look as if the President had sent his man to seek agreement for a swap, and when it did not happen, the country would come to the conclusion that the prince had said no and, in effect, said "Let the Americans die; I'm too important to die." God, what a rotten setup!

Dave had thought of calling in the editors to give them the inside dope on all that was developing and asking them not to print or air certain elements, for the sake of national security. But in such cases, it had to be left to the final judgment of the media chiefs as to whether certain facts should or should not be withheld. And if one of them printed or aired a fact that was being held back, then all of them would come out with that and additional information. It would be a terrible trial for both the Administration and for the media chiefs involved, especially those who wanted to honor the concerns of the government.

He knew one action he would take immediately. He sat down and personally tapped out a news release that he would get the President to approve. It might help pull the fangs from the inaccurate dope story the *Post* had run on the basis of the inadequate leak:

PRINCE BEGS TO BE SWAPPED

President Randolph, in a statement today, said he "could not in good conscience accede to the plea of Prince Pahlavi to exchange him for the Americans being held hostage by terrorists."

The President said the Prince had pleaded with him from the very first for the exchange, weeks before any American lives had been lost.

"I am touched by the sincerity and bravery of this young man. My not acceding to his wishes in this matter is something I believe all Americans can and will support," the President said.

Dave then tapped out a statement by the President to be covered by the terse press release and trotted up to the Oval Office to see the President, other commitments notwithstanding.

For the first time since his appointment, Dave was beginning to dislike his job. Circumstances can sometimes alter intentions, and he was beginning to think that the Israelis were not as right about dealing with those PLO bastards as he had believed all along. Matters of state had a hollow meaning when it came to bargaining with a handful of stateless killers for the lives of a handful of your own citizens.

Chapter 36

Brockway's expectation that he would be with the prince no more than a couple of hours was not realized. Five hours later, they were still going at it, with pauses for a dozen or so calls he put through to Washington and to the Sixth Fleet. If anyone had been the slightest bit interested in measuring the sudden increase in radio and telephone traffic from a twenty-eight-acre estate deep in the bluffs along the Hudson, it would have been easily assumed that something was up.

An unanswerable question raised by the prince, when Brockway had recounted what was going on, had prompted Brockway to ask for the laser transmission of all of Harding's debriefing tapes to the high-speed copier at the safehouse.

While they were waiting for the material, Brockway walked the compound, which was heavily wooded with pine, oak, and elm from the river to the state highway. The property had been purchased from the DEA years ago, after it had been confiscated in a raid to crush a huge drug manufacturing operation on the premises. What had made the property most attractive was that the house was approachable only by a mile-long driveway. It seemed to be a perfect hideaway for the prince. The fourteen-room colonial had a separate guest house and a twelve-stall horse barn, which had been converted into a six-bay garage. The security team had rooms in the basement of the house, with headquarters and communications in the guest house.

Brockway was taken aback when he asked the question for which he thought he knew the answer. "I suppose things are fairly quiet around here, Jim?"

"Well, yes and no, chief," the man in charge of security, Jim Taylor, replied. "We're getting a lot of foot traffic around here."

Brockway did not say anything. He stared at Taylor, waiting for an explanation.

"Treasure hunters, sir. People looking for Rip Van Winkle's lost treasure."* Taylor knew that wasn't enough of an explanation, but before he could get off the next word, Brockway was on him, his words tinged with contained fury.

"Cut the shit, mister. We're not playing games here. What the hell are you talking about?"

"It's the truth, Mr. Brockway. I didn't believe the interlopers at first. Thought our entire operation here had been blown. I battened down the hatches, ready to call for an evac, but I had to check first. I bought a bag of groceries in town and sauntered into the county's legislative office building.

* The Lost Treasure of Rip Van Winkle was an actuality in Greene County, New York, from 1984 until its discovery early in 1990.

"That's where the info about the treasure was supposed to be, according to the people we questioned. And sure enough, the head of the county government, Bill Hagan, verified the story. He's an old Washington media hotshot who found his job here a bit on the sleepy side. So, to drum up more vacationers to this neck of the woods, Hagan dreams up this scheme of Rip's adventure to include a lost treasure. Well, a rock with *RVW* carved on its face is secreted somewhere in the county, and a gold tenpin worth about a hundred thousand dollars is the prize for anyone who can find the rock.

"Well, sir, the value of the tenpin is now about a quarter-million dollars, and the rock still hasn't been found. They've got an out-of-print booklet that provides clues. The five-ninety-five booklet is now worth a lot more, if you can find one."

"Well, I'll be . . ." was all that Brockway could say. Then: "Why's the treasure hunt in this area?"

"It's the location of the fictional character Washington Irving created. Hagan had Irving's story doctored up with clues, and the revised version has Rip Van Winkle steal one of Henry Hudson's golden tenpins. Rip falls asleep and can't find the pin when he wakes up. The tenpin, created by Hagan and his county cohorts, was "found" at a spot now marked by the *RVW* rock, and the tenpin is on display at the local bank, to be awarded to the finder of the rock."

"How many treasure hunters have you counted, Jim?"

"The average is 4.33 at this time, sir . . . per day. Before the summer is over, I expect the average to perhaps double."

"Unacceptable! Absolutely unacceptable! We'll have to get the prince out of here!"

"Excuse me, sir, but why? We have a fairly accurate profile now of the average treasure hunter—we've been running everything through your new RWAC, and I'm certain we'd be able to spot a ringer."

"Tell me, Jim. Do you have any reason to believe the treasure is somewhere on this property?"

"I checked that out, sir. It cost the agency five hundred dollars, but I was able to buy a copy of the booklet from one of the treasure-hunt officials, named Martin Smith, who handles our oil-heat needs here . . . Yes sir, we checked him out, of course.

Totally reliable, hard-nosed Yankee who's not averse to making a buck through us city fellers.

"The treasure is nowhere near here, Chief. It's on the side of a mountain with such an obvious name, the rock should have been found years ago. It wasn't easy locating it, though. It took us all of three days to figure it out, because of the misdirections among the clues. It's several miles from here and nowhere near the river."

Brockway thought it over. "Are they planning to make a media event if the treasure is found?"

"Yes, sir. That's part of the whole deal."

"All right, Jim, we have a choice. We either get the hell out of here, kit and caboodle, or bring this attractive nuisance of a treasure hunt to a screeching halt."

Taylor began to nod. Brockway continued: "We tell someone exactly where the treasure is, let it be found, and we have no more treasure hunters. Then, if we find anyone around here continuing to 'look for treasure,' you can put the screws to him . . . or her."

"I wonder who we can give this treasure location to without it being traced to us?"

"I'm going to leave that up to you . . . and the minute I get back to headquarters, I'm going to find out the name of the dumb sonovabitch who selected this area as a good place for a safehouse . . . smack in the middle of a treasure hunt! God help us!"

Brockway returned to the main house, mumbling and muttering about the state of the world and his fortunes in particular.

He spent hours with the prince, listening to the tapes and some transcriptions, mostly from Harding. When they got to the part where Harding was repeating, verbatim, the last words of Stefan McMahan, the prince had the tapes repeated three times.

The prince's was an intense personality. There was a softness in his brown eyes that didn't match the hardness and drive he exhibited in his thoughts and actions. His big hawk nose, characteristic of his family, was such a prominent feature that it would be difficult to disguise him. In fact, his resemblance to his father, the late shah, who had died in limbo—truly a man with-

out a country—was uncanny. The young man had become an
excellent pilot, flying supersonic aircraft; played polo well
enough to be a member of a U.S. touring side out of Oak Brook;
climbed the northface of the Eiger solo; and was graduated
summa cum laude, from Stanford, in political science with a minor in astrophysics. Brockway was totally aware of the young
man's stern dedication to the idea of some day reclaiming the
Peacock Throne and returning the land of his fathers to the
greatness it had once enjoyed centuries ago. It was this over-
riding thought that was impelling the young man to offer himself to the kidnappers with the certitude that no Persian would
or could kill him. His ill-fated attempt to invade Iran, overthrow
the Islamic Republic, and restore the throne was something he
attributed to ill fortune rather than hostility or refusal by the people to accept him. When Brockway had sent in a small rescue
team to snatch him from certain death as the armored land force
closed in, the prince had to be literally overpowered and
dragged to the gunship, he was that certain that once the attacking force realized who he was, they would cease hostilities and
carry him in triumph to the palace in Teheran. His father had
gracefully passed on the baton of the monarchy to his son, who
had turned out to be all that any man could wish of a son.

The prince looked at Brockway after the third rerun.

"I believe the people who have abducted the President's
daughter are communists or socialist extremists of some kind.
The dying man uses the phrase 'imperialist assholes.' I find the
use of the word 'imperialist' of extreme significance. I am certain it has a bearing on what's going on.

"As for something else he said . . . 'You will never catch up
with her, not that one . . .' Have you given any thought to the
idea that the dying man was not referring to the President's
daughter? That he was, perhaps, referring to a female in charge
of the terrorists. Think about the phrase 'never catch up with
her, not *that* one.' 'That one.' If the phrase had ended, 'never
catch up with her,' well and good. But he adds 'not that one.'
Which one, you may ask? The President's daughter? She isn't
going anywhere by herself. The dying man was referring to
someone else; I am positive about it." The prince brought his

head up and down as if his nose were stroking an aerial excla-
mation mark.

Brockway was impressed. "Your Highness, do you have any
thoughts as to who might be the leader? We were certain it was
the dead man, McMahan, but the operation had used him as a
decoy, so it couldn't have been him."

"Mr. Brockway, you have deprived me of a telephone and
any other form of communication since I was placed here for
my own protection. This is no better than a gaol . . . and I
realize why you are doing this. If I had not expressed a strong
desire to be handed over to those who would harm innocent
Americans, I suspect I would have been in a less confining
environment.

"What I mean to say, Mr. Brockway, is that I believe I could
obtain some information relative to this matter that could be of
immense importance to you if I could contact some of my people in London and Paris."

"That's out of the question, Your Highness. Such calls can be
traced easily. To comply with your suggestion, we would have
to bring you to Washington, and the exposure there is not
acceptable. Personally, I feel great regret and embarrassment at
the treatment of your person, albeit we both know it is meant
totally for your own protection.

"The President of the United States is taking personal responsibility for this nation's concern for your safety, especially in circumstances that involve any ultimate perception that he eased
the way to save the life of his daughter in exchange for yours."

It was a demonstrably sad young man who brought up his
hands in a small sign of surrender and suggested that they
proceed with the tapes.

The very last tapes, of the conversation among Harding,
Brockway, and Miss Davis, brought the prince to his feet, excitement in his movements.

"Just as I thought! I was not certain before, but I am certain
now! Yes, they are not Moslems! Of course! I know who is
behind this terrible tragedy, Mr. Brockway!"

Brockway was standing up, also, the excitement generated
by the prince now permeating his being as well. He waited.

"The leader is a woman, all right. She is called Sulmass Ochi

Pishavari, leader of the dead or moribund Tudeh party. It was a Marxist-Leninist cell that went underground when my papa ruled as the shah.

"She has to be the one, Mr. Brockway, and she has to be seeking the rebirth of the Tudeh party."

"What makes you so sure, Your Highness?"

"Members of this party renounced their allegiance to Islam and Mohammed. With that renunciation, they abjured any ceremonies or rituals dictated by the Koran. Therefore, the men in the party are not circumcised."

"Couldn't there be others, like the Mujahedeen Khalq, for instance?"

"I thought of them immediately. That's why I wanted to call London. But the fact that the terrorists are not Moslems eliminates the Mujahedeen. They are the so-called People's Holy Warriors, but their leadership was ousted by the late Ayatollah Khomeini because of their own fanciful interpretation of the Koran into a mishmash of Marxist socialism. During that terrible war between my country and Iraq, they sided with the enemy. Excuse me, the point I want to make is that they continue to observe the rite of circumcision."

"You've convinced me, my boy . . . Your Highness. But tell me, why is Tabriz the locus for this horror story?"

"Mr. Brockway, read any history of Persia and modern Iran, and you will find Tabriz has been the center of rebellion against any and all governments. It doesn't seem to matter who is ruling from Teheran or Shiraz or Basra—Tabriz is where antigovernment fomentation begins. My family's dynasty was started in that very city.

"The Tudeh Communist Party was founded in Tabriz, and it was more Marxist than Marx, more Leninist than Lenin. The party went underground after its leader, this woman's father, was killed following World War II."

"Very good, Your Highness. I'm convinced that we must concentrate our efforts on rescuing our people in Tabriz. Do you agree?"

"Most certainly, Mr. Brockway. I am extremely well informed about the entire city, and request permission to lead the rescue activities there."

"Do you mean to tell me that you know where the Americans are being held."

"I do."

"How do you know? Tell me?"

"I know from having heard Commander Harding's tapes."

"Well . . . tell me . . . tell me where they are."

"I will, sir, if I am allowed to join forces with my friend Jackson Harding in Tabriz."

Brockway's eyes opened wide for a moment, with the simultaneous dropping of his jaw. He recovered in a flash. "Why, that's impossible, Your Highness. It's ridiculous to contemplate. How would you expect to enter? What could you do other than tell us where you think our people are being held? Please, Your Highness, be sensible . . ."

"Ask President Randolph if I may return to my own country to save the Americans. Call him now." The prince was standing as straight as a flagpole.

"Please, Your Highness, it—"

"Call him now!"

Brockway and the prince stood about a yard apart, staring into each other's eyes. "Very well, I'll call him," Brockway said softly.

Calling the White House direct required a different procedure from his other calls. He called St. Louis, was relayed to St. Paul, interrupted and transferred to Ft. Meade and then to the Oval Office.

President Randolph sounded desperate and disbelieving. "You mean that he knows where my daughter is being held and he won't tell us?"

"Please, take it easy, sir. He wants to go there and help Harding rescue our people."

"I believe there's something wrong with that suggestion of his . . . isn't there, Tom?"

"There certainly is, sir. The prince isn't trained for that kind of work. It's not as if he's leading a squadron of jets into attack or charging across a plain in a rumble of tanks."

"Have you told him that?"

"I have."

"And . . ."

"He insists on being allowed to join Harding."

"Let me speak to him."

" . . . I'm sorry, sir. He will not come to the phone. He says there is no longer time for words. There must be action."

"Goddammit, Tom . . . I won't have it, do you understand? I won't have it!"

"Yes, sir . . . ?"

"Tell him it's no dice . . . Tell him to go to hell! If he won't tell us, we'll settle with him after this is over. Get your ass back here and to hell with covering your tracks."

"Excuse me, sir. What shall I tell him?"

"I told you . . . Tell him to go to hell!"

President Randolph was a bit angry.

*   *   *

Jim Taylor lost his job a week later. He was recalled to Washington to supervise an innocuous file room in a minor division of the CIA.

His downfall began with the arrangements he made to have the Rip Van Winkle treasure "discovered" by a couple of plants carted in from Erie, Pennsylvania, and converted into a public photo event by Greene County's Kaaterskill Foundation, sponsor of the treasure hunt. The gold, jewel-encrusted tenpin would be presented to the lucky couple in a ceremony at the local bank. Saturday being a "slow" news day, coupled with the feature aspects of the story for Sunday exposition, brought the media from as far away as New York City, Buffalo, Boston, and points in between.

Taylor and two of his assistants drove to Catskill to witness the result of his handiwork in removing the treasure-hunt nuisance from the area of the safehouse. They parked the Caprice behind the bank and went around front to stand on the fringe of about two hundred people, including twenty-five reporters, cameramen, and soundmen, to watch the unsealing of the box verifying the authenticity of the rock before the treasure was awarded.

Meanwhile, the trunk lid of the Caprice popped open and the prince emerged after a careful look around and headed for a phone in the closed-off office area of the bank.

Two hours after the reporters and Taylor had left, a two-door gray Acura drove into a Mobil station near the bridge on Route 23 and the prince slipped out of the men's room, hopped into the driver's seat, and drove off in search of the New York Thruway and Kennedy International Airport.

His twin-engine private jet was being put through its check-list in preparation for a short hop to Montreal.

Chapter 37

"It has to be Dr. Baines, Ursula Baines, professor of anthropology at Georgetown University. She's the only older woman in the group."

"Same place?" Harding could see the body in his mind's eye on the steps.

"Yes, and murdered in the same way." Allison was learning to be emotionless. "I never met her when I was at the university."

"Don't you think I ought to be getting back? Sixteen hours on my back is long enough."

"If Dr. McConnaughy says it's okay, Jakey. What would be the sense of your going out there and collapsing? If you're going to be of any use, I think it's imperative that you're able to walk around without fainting in the arms of the first pretty woman you see . . ."

"Gadzooks," he said in a display of feigned gentility. "How you carry on, Scarlett!"

"What did you think of the idea the prince had of joining up with you?"

"Allie, I hate to work in tandem, but I would have welcomed him with open arms if he had some of the skills needed in this work. Willingness alone will only get you killed or destroy the chances of success. If he were a Lieutenant Margil or a Lieutenant Levin, we'd be able to operate back-to-back and get things done."

"Brockway said he had never, ever seen the President so angry as when the prince tried blackmail to get his way."

"Did he believe the prince? Does Brockway feel that the prince knows where they are?"

"Yes. And he, the prince, claims he spotted it from your verbal reports."

"OK. It must have to do with the two gunmen I shot up. The one I talked to said I knew where they were. Unbelievable!"

"Has to be, must be. Let's listen to that part of your report. Brockway said the prince had parts of your tapes repeated up to three times."

Harding was allowed to leave SOQ to go to Allie's quarters, where she had the machine set up for the tape review. They sat silently listening six times to the place on the tape where he mentioned his attempts to get the gunmen to talk.

"I don't get anything from this, Allie. But I understand why, now. Both of the gunmen I shot and the prince picked up something. And they're both Iranians, and both are familiar with Tabriz. That's got to be it. I must get back there immediately and try it out on my Russian friend, Abdul Baad. I'll bet he'll pick up the same thing!"

"We'll see what the flight surgeon has to say." Allison's eyes softened as she looked at the blue-black stubble of his unshaven face. The haggardness around his eyes was lessening and his color was returning.

Harding saw the softness creeping into her gaze, her eyes becoming rounder, and embraced her gently before they kissed. Their union of body and soul had been complete in the hours they had spent together. Neither had mentioned a word about their future or the consequences of their actions. They simply reveled in each other's company.

"What did you say?"

"Nothing, Allie . . . I was thinking about how I was going to crack this damned puzzle. Come on, sweetheart, we've got to make a case for me getting back there."

Harding was back in Tabriz by noon of the day after Dr.

Baines's body was found. His friend Abdul was not to be found at the train station so he hailed a two-horse droshky for the ride to the Ghaza, wondering who had ever thought of red and green as the right coloring for the buggy's leather seating.

Abdul was not at home when Harding made his limping way to his house, and Harding would not accept his wife's invitation to enter and wait. It would have been a breach of etiquette to be alone with another man's wife. He walked back to the first open street beyond the huge bazaar area and hailed a taxi this time instead of an open droshky. The cab was one of those tiny, Soviet-built Moskvich cars, well over twenty years old and still in service. He told the driver in Turkish to take him for a ride in and around the Blue mosque and to point out areas of interest if there were any.

Traffic on the cobblestone streets was heavy, and the going slow, what with automobiles, droshkies, bikes, and pedestrians all assuming equal rights and ignoring the strident honks and yells of fellow travelers.

The first thing the driver did was take him to the very steps where Harding had been shot and tell the tale of the murdered Americans being found, one a night, there. He said a gang of cutthroats, led by the son of the dead shah, had captured nearly a hundred Americans and was killing them one by one until America gave the gang ten thousand American dollars for the release of the captives. Harding cluck-clucked at the audacity of the gang in seeking such a huge sum.

"Ten thousand dollars, you say? And in American money? Unbelievable how greedy those monarchists can be. Does anybody know where the Americans are being held?"

"Oh, certainly, everybody does, but nobody is going to give it away until the money is collected. Then the gang will be attacked and robbed of its ill-gotten gains, and the money distributed among the needy."

"Ah, how just and worthy of our Lord Mohammed for his people to have reached such a proper and good conclusion in such a sorry incident. Tell me, are you among the chosen who knows where the rich Americans are being held?"

The driver turned his head quickly to give his passenger a knowing look and noted that some questions should never be asked, especially by strangers. Harding nodded, grinning into the rearview mirror for the driver's benefit.

The small, dark red vehicle entered the Khala section of the city and creaked down a shallow decline where the crumbling walls of what must once have been a gigantic edifice loomed to the right. The driver, pointing to it, noted that the Arg was built centuries ago as a mosque but that it had become a citadel, so powerful was its construction. "Oh, yes, it has walls more than eight yards thick where they still stand . . . on the other side . . . and they rise forty yards. In fact, mister, it came to be called a citadel after the great one who had it built, Ali Shah . . ."

Harding stopped listening, his mind in a sudden whirl of excitement. The moment the driver uttered the name of the citadel's builder, he knew where the Americans were being held. The young pretender to the throne of Persia had been of help, despite everything. It was uncanny and a great bit of fortune. He gave his jaw some special squeezes, smiling at the furor the message would cause.

His excitement was transmitted to the driver, whom he told to rush him back to the western opening to the Ghaza. He hoped Abdul would be back by the time he got there. Harding paid the driver triple the fare, for unwittingly having solved the problem for him, and dashed down the narrow, crowded streets to Abdul's house.

Abdul was there, nervous and impatient, awaiting Harding's return.

Harding grabbed Abdul's arm. "I know where they are, old boy!"

"How did you find them?"

"I didn't find them. Yet, I know the place where they are being held."

"Good, good. What's your plan of rescue?"

Harding stopped. "I'm sorry, Abdul. I'm so elated at having found where they must be captive, I've given no thought to anything else. Frankly, I'm way ahead of myself. It's a big place, and I have no idea where they are in that big place."

"What do you mean, my friend?"

"They're somewhere in the Arg."

"Ah!"

"But I have no idea where in the Arg."

"Ah."

"The question is, how will I be able to poke around in those ruins and not be noticed immediately?"

"Ah."

"And those bastards know me despite any disguise I assume."

"Ah."

"I know that if I run down Sulmass Ochi Pishavari, I've got the ringleader."

"What? Did you say Sulmass Ochi?"

"Yep." It was Harding's turn.

"She's engineering this kidnapping?"

"Yep."

"I think you are wrong, my friend."

"Nope."

"You must be."

"Nope."

"Please, Ibrahim . . . or is it George, now . . . stop that and tell me what you know."

Harding scowled. "You know already my code-name change? What the hell are we doing wrong in Washington? Abdul, she is the daughter of the late leader of the Tudehs. The Tudehs have been underground the past forty-odd years. You can see what's been going on now relative to this hostage-taking."

"How were you able to identify her?"

"The prince, the pretender did." When Harding saw the puzzled look on Abdul's face, he continued. "It is a long story which I'll tell you as soon as I get my bearings. I've got to find out exactly where our people are being held without them knowing that I'm looking. See you later."

Harding half ran and half walked back to the west portal of the Ghaza, holding his jaw off and on as he went. The melon truck was there in less than a quarter hour, and they sped back to the camp in the foothills. Smithson could see that matters had taken a new turn when his passenger suddenly asked how many hours before the next American was to be killed.

"Six and a half if they stick to their schedule."

"I had to make sure of that. I've got to get word to the fleet, and then we've got to get back to the city. To the southwest section near the Blue mosque."

"Is that where they are?"

"No, but close by. They're somewhere in the Arg."

"You mean the war memorial and park in that old pile of rubble?"

"We're almost there. I'll fill you in when we head back." They leaped out of the truck cab and raced to the tent where the communications gear was set up. Harding sat at a makeshift table for a minute, sketching. Then he sent out the call letters for the USS *America* with the scramblers set, spoke tersely for forty-eight seconds, agreed on 110.5 megahertz, and signed off.

"Let's do it. Let's see if we can save a life tonight. Full gear and black faces." The truck headed back into town.

Among other items, they brought along a laser-powered directional signal and a supply of concussion grenades.

The truck rolled into the Sirkhop section, went past the Blue mosque another quarter mile to approach the Arg, in the Khala, and ground to a stop to allow two of the riders to get off and fix the rim of the right rear tire near the ditch that served as the street curb. When they leaped back on the truck, a four-inch gray box half-full of mercury was sitting among some large stones, sending an absolutely vertical signal into the heavens. It was situated at the northeast quadrant of the rectangle occupied by the Arg.

The truck turned down the first side street on its left and disappeared from the view of anyone who might have been watching from the citadel.

High above, at fifty thousand feet, an SR-71 recon plane opened its bay, and machines and instruments whirred and clicked for no more than a split-second.

Harding got the word from the plane on his headset, sitting in the back of the truck with some radio gear. "Repeat, northwest corner. Correct. Thanks."

He turned to the waiting men. "Our people are in the northwest corner of the Arg. I should have guessed, but you can't take chances. That's the only large section of the ancient walls still standing."

"We looked over that place." Smithson sounded puzzled. "I didn't see anything resembling a habitat of any kind . . ."

"The walls, the walls. They're twenty-five feet thick. Some time ago, a cavity must have been dug to accommodate people or animals or whatever. The hostages are there. The question is where is the entrance or entrances, what is the layout? We have about three hours before they kill the next one. What do you think, men? Any thought as to how the killing is done? I mean, do they kill with the hostages looking on, or do they take the victim out of sight and earshot and do it?"

"Would it make a difference?" Trovato asked.

"It could be the difference between life and death. If everyone is jammed into a small area, the killing could take place outside—outside, where we might be able to stop it."

"If the killings were done outside the detention area, they would have to take place in the courtyard. You couldn't cut someone's throat in plain view on a street corner, which would be the location of the outer wall." Smithson carried the conjecture a step further.

"Yes, let's work on the premise that the entrance into the wall cavity where the prisoners are being held is located somewhere inside the courtyard. And let's also assume that the killing will be done outside the detention area. That gives me an idea. But let me continue for a moment. I cannot believe that they have been in that hole all this time without some kind of external warning system, sentries."

"You're right," Smithson said. "They've got to have some sort of lookout. But we had at least four pairs of eyes scanning the location as we went by, and none of us saw anything resembling a human being on top or anywhere near the place."

"OK, check this line of thinking. They don't seem to have any lookouts, yet they are able to leave their victim on the steps of the Blue mosque a quarter-mile away. There's only one answer. There's got to be a tunnel between the Arg and the mosque. That's it. They take their intended victims into the tunnel, kill 'em, and emerge at the Blue mosque, where it doesn't take more than twenty seconds in the open to drag a body to the steps. Let's get there, on the double!"

The truck had pulled over on a side street and was back at the

Blue mosque in five minutes. The vehicle was parked, again on a side street, a block away, behind some houses, and the deadly force in tattered attire, their weapons well concealed, sauntered back to the mosque.

When they reached the ruined edifice with its arches and columns and walls with no roofs, and large chunks of masonry everywhere, they made final plans. Once it got dark, each man would be stationed among the ruins in a location that prevented him from seeing any other member of his unit. The concept was that it would be practically pitch-black when they could expect action, and any movement anyone saw would have to be the kidnapping gang's. The first man to see anything would do two things. He would utter a number, the number assigned to his location, loud enough for his throat mike, wait five seconds, and fire off a quick-burst flare to illuminate the whole scene. The rest of it would depend on what happened when the lights went on.

A careful examination of the ruins did not provide any indication that Harding's surmise was correct. There was no dried blood anywhere, no scuff or drag marks, nothing. The American almost called for a return to the Arg, but he squelched the thought. They were at the Arg, for sure, but they *had* to be using this location for entry and exit. It made sense. The worst part of the operation lay ahead, an hour before darkness and then probably another five or six hours before the bastards showed up with the result of their grisly game.

They sat together for the remaining parcel of daylight. Harding looked at the faces around him. Their quietness and what he knew they could do to an enemy gave him some assurance. But he felt this particular setup was a real screw-up. He was not supposed to initiate any kind of military or paramilitary action or plan. His job was to find out or indicate or determine whatever information his country required, and the United States would take over from there.

But there wasn't time for that if there was any possibility of saving the life of the next victim and simultaneously rescuing the rest.

"Whaddaya think, men? Am I going to foul this up?"

"One never knows." Westcott was the cynic.

Everyone heard it. The sound of stone scraping on stone. The unit had huddled together toward the front of the ruins, near the broad steps, waiting for darkness before taking up their posts. They were sitting amidst some rubble with unbroken walls on two sides. The sound seemed to be coming from somewhere behind the walls to the rear of the unit. It sounded close, but it could be anywhere in there, because of the echo effect on bare stone.

There was no need to indicate silence. The troop crouched as much as it could among the stones and broken brick. Except for Harding. He began a crablike crawl to the corner of the wall to find out if anything could be seen. It was twilight now, but there was enough to make out movement, at least. He slowly poked his head out at the end of the wall, quickly pulled back, and crawled to the troops.

Even as he whispered "Section 2, one guy, pulling back the lid," they could hear the scrape of stone on stone again.

The scuff-scuff of sandaled feet grew nearer. The person was going to pass within yards of Harding. Harding held up his right hand and signaled like a metronome. That meant no guns. He changed it instantly to a one-finger-up poking movement.

As the figure suddenly loomed in front of them, passing by, a thrown rock thudded off his skull. Without a sound, the figure collapsed in a heap of black cloth. And Harding had not said a word. The value of close camaraderie and tight training had shown its results.

Trovato, the pitcher, moved instantly to haul the unconscious body out of sight, back to where they were.

Harding and the rest moved to where he had seen the stone lid being replaced. It was difficult to find until it was noticed that the bits and pieces of rubble scattered over the surface area were loose except where the rubble covered the lid section. On that part, the rubble had been cemented to the lid, so that movement of any kind would never disturb the seemingly loose scree on the lidtop.

"We were right, for once," Harding whispered. "I don't believe they would have any reason to be guarding this end . . . Let's see if we can move this thing."

After much groping around, they found the key. Some of the

rubble at opposite sides of the roughly four-foot-square slab of slate had been arranged to form subtle handles. Once they were discovered, it was easy work to lift the slab about three inches and slide it away. There were stone steps, steep but serviceable, disappearing below.

There was no light now to help them. Westcott carried a penlight. They decided to take a chance and use it.

"Remember, men. Try not to off anyone we find in the tunnel. Leo, stay with that guy." Harding was hoping there wouldn't be anyone along the length of the tunnel. A feral confrontation would certainly result in noise traveling back to those presumably guarding the hostages—and that could be the end for them.

There was no need to worry about a light being seen in the tunnel. It had been cut aeons ago in twelve-foot lengths at 45-degree angles to zigzag straight toward the Arg, its design also serving as a bearing wall to carry any conceivable load above. The tunnel was exactly four feet wide and five and a half feet high, causing them to stoop as they moved toward their goal.

Ten minutes later, they knew they were getting close. The deathly stench of human waste began to dominate the air in the tunnel. The penlight was doused, and Harding, in the lead, felt his way from predictable corner to predictable corner.

About two minutes later, still in total darkness, they heard it. A heavy shout of pain and voices ahead.

Harding gave up worrying about making noise at this point. He made one more corner, saw a lighter area at the next bend, ran like hell for it, and came upon a scene that jerked him into action.

Two figures in skullcaps and pantaloons were holding a man, bare from his waist down, with a knife handle protruding from his chest, trying to make him loosen his grip and release a third pantalooned man, whose face was being held deep in a pit full of human waste.

The tunnel had opened up into an area three times as wide and about eight feet high.

Harding's first two shots dispatched the two holding the

man with the knife in his chest. It was the Secret Service agent, O'Meara.

Harding didn't waste a second in stopping or looking. He dashed for the opening at the other end. Empty.

There was no Sulmass Ochi Pishavari to be found.

There were no other Americans.

And there was certainly no Patricia Ann Randolph.

Chapter 38

"Report, Mr. Harding. The President is with me."

"Found the main hideout where the hostages were being held, Mr. Brockway. Prevented the latest execution and rescued O'Meara.

"They had split up our people into six units and spread them about the city. Captured one of the terrorists. Made him talk in twelve minutes after a bit of persuasion . . . No, sir. A plastic bag and piece-of-paper method . . .

"Know only the general neighborhoods of four hideouts but know exactly where Patricia is being held . . .

"No, sir. We can't affect a rescue of Patricia until we can pinpoint the locations and rescue of the others. Once we find out, we would hit all locations simultaneously . . . Yes, sir, split-second timing . . .

"Looks as if Patricia is with the leader, Sulmass Ochi, and we are assuming that the other female hostage, Ferrick, is also with her . . .

"Yes, sir. If we hit Patricia's location first, it could tip off the others, and I'm certain the rest of our people would be killed . . .

"No, sir, we covered that possibility. We brought the body of one of the killers we had to shoot, changed his clothes with O'Meara's, slit the throat for effect, and left him on the steps, like the others . . . The Swiss will be sending you a body, which you can dump . . .

"Yes, sir, I'm afraid we'll have to go along with O'Meara being the fourth victim for now. O'Meara was knifed, but he'll be fine, sir. Have him aboard now in the hands of our surgeons . . .

"Yes, sir. It was O'Meara who filled us in. The hostages were taken initially to one of the Armenian neighborhoods, Khala, where the Arg is situated, the center of the old section of the city. They were passed off as a sight-seeing group, each hostage walking arm in arm with a captor . . .

"O'Meara says that after they killed Berry, a beautiful woman showed up in the Arg and he figured she was the leader from the way everyone acted . . . Sulmass Ochi, of course.

"Patricia and Miss Ferrick were picked out and left with Sulmass Ochi and her entourage. Then, at intervals of an hour, Dr. Caldwell and Nasvik were paired up and taken away, followed by Gilmore and Labelle, Spooner and Isenstein, and Kenyon by himself, leaving Dr. Baines and Genereau with O'Meara.

"That tends to jibe with our reluctant informant's information that the hostages are being held in four or five other locations . . .

"We'll need five SOB squads and an additional three for contingencies . . . Operating out of the foothills north of the city . . . Yes, sir, I believe I can handle the search and rescue operation . . . Thank you for your confidence in me, sir. Need the squads ASAP, preferably within five or six hours . . . and a stash of rials. We'll be on the streets and will need spending money.

"And, Mr. President, we will bring your daughter out if it's the last thing we do here . . . Rest assured, we will take care of ourselves, thank you, sir."

Harding signed off and switched off the scrambler in the communications shack of the *America*. He turned to look at Allison. "I feel we're going to win this one, Allie."

Her face was etched with solemn concern. "Brockway told

me the SOB squads consist of only three men each. You asked for only five units. What are you going to do with only one squad for every hostage location?"

He grinned. "Don't worry, kid. We really don't need all those men for a localized rescue. But we need enough to cover more than the hundred square miles that make up Tabriz. Our first job is to find exactly where the four remaining hideouts are located."

"What about the Arg?"

"The squad that worked with me on the rescue there is keeping a close eye on the tunnel entrance in the mosque. I'm hoping that we will be able to keep a lid on things until we mount rescue operations. Once those slime realize that none of their comrades have been heard from since the last American was killed, anything can happen."

"You have some idea as to where our people are being held, I take it. You told Brockway that—"

"Allie, we know for certain where Sulmass Ochi's headquarters is. It's on an estate in the fancy section of the city, on Shapour Avenue. It's a safe bet that Patricia and Bernice Ferrick are being held there.

"Two other hideouts are in the city's slum section, Gajil-gabsi. Another is supposed to be in a neighborhood called Lilava, another Armenian enclave, and a fifth location is somewhere on Gulistan Avenue. That's about all the information we could drag out of our prisoner. He didn't seem to be kidding us."

"Do you think you might get additional information from him?"

"Not a chance, Allie." Harding turned away and changed the subject. "As soon as the men arrive, we'll hold council and make our move."

"How long do you think it's going to take to find our people?"

"Could be hours, days, or even a week, but we'll find 'em. The sooner we clean this up, the sooner I'll be back with you." Harding reached out to touch her arm.

"See you then," she said, jerking her arm away to avoid his touch.

Chapter 39

They arrived in straggling ones and twos—most on foot, a few on bicycles, one astride an ass—as motley a group as Harding had ever seen gathered in one place. Undistinguished and certainly undistinguishable in a crowd was the best way to politely describe them. They were all older than Harding, bunched in the fiftyish age group. And they were attired, if that was the word for it, in the most tattered, filthy, drab, and badly fitting raiments conceivable. Most were shod in the *kaloshes*—the tire-tread sandals—indigenous to the area and of the poor.

It was the sixth hour since Harding had asked for them, and it took most of the day for them to arrive. For some of the arrivals, it had been a fairly easy task getting to the camp—they had been in Teheran and Meshed in Iran, so there were no borders to slip across. Six of the groups had been flown into Adana and had crossed over into Iran by the train from Van, all carrying the necessary papers. Gunships had carted the rest from a pickup rendezvous in Israel, where they had arrived from Beirut, Amman, Damascus, and Port Said. They had been dropped off in four locations north of Tabriz near the Soviet border.

Harding couldn't help a smile as he watched them. As they trickled into the camp nestling in a copse of stunted oaks in the hills overlooking the city, the newcomers had quietly joined up in groups of three, barely exchanging salutations and hardly looking around.

He knew many of them but not entire groups. There was Orsolak with two he didn't know; there was Svenson and De-Lucia with a stranger; MacLeod, the Medal of Honor holder, with Giannatsis and Gibbs; Maloof and Stewart and Pace and Smythe and Zablonski and Rubinstein and Wyrocki and Telford and Williams . . . When he finished scanning the arrivals, Harding shook his head. Brockway had sent him ten SOB squads, not counting the unit at the Blue mosque. Hell, he thought, he had a small army, and he wasn't sure how to handle such a large group. He waved to have them gather around, and they sat in a semicircle facing him.

Harding introduced himself as Forty-Three and got down to business, laying out the problem in general. Then he spelled out some details:

"One, the headquarters of the terrorists, on Shapour Avenue, should be the easiest to locate, since it's in a prestigious neighborhood and should have more activity than an ordinary household.

"Two, another hideout is on a long, busy thoroughfare called Gulistan Avenue, so that should help concentrate the search, somewhat.

"Three, another is in the Armenian neighborhood of Lilava, about five square miles, and the language difference between the terrorists and the inhabitants should help.

"Four, the central hideout in the center of town, called the Arg, is already in our hands, and we are keeping tabs on it with one of our groups.

"Five, the toughest nuts to crack, as far as we can tell, are the two or more hideouts in the slum section of Gajilgabsi, covering about fifteen square miles. That's going to require some intense surveillance.

"The terrorists all seem to wear black calpacs with dark blue piping. But many others do the same, so that will be of small help. Another thing, our targets speak Azeri, not much help, either, but it may help eliminate some prospective suspects. And, oh yes, the men we seek are not Moslems, so they won't be kneeling in the direction of Mecca when the muezzin calls the faithful to prayer five times a day with his chant praising Allah and his prophet . . .

"When? An hour before sunrise, at noon, at about five o'clock, an hour before sunset, and an hour after sunset. OK?

"Now, our first task is to find the hideouts. You've been at this kind of operation much longer than I have, so let me make the following suggestions, and we'll kick it around.

"Five groups will spread out in the Gajilgabsi slum, one group to Shapour Avenue with a second group for backup purposes, two groups to the Lilava section, and one group to Gulistan Avenue. Any questions?"

"What's the drill, once we find a hideout?"

"Two remain on watch, one returns with the information. Signal and radio silent."

"How much time do we have?"

"As long as it takes, but it should be soon. We will not launch rescue operations until all hideouts have been located and cased. We will not act until we know where all of them are, *all* of them."

There was a perceptive change in his audience: shoulders squared up a bit more, the men sat straighter.

"Once we know what we're up against, we'll lay plans accordingly to get our people out. I know what you're thinking. What if we find all but one hideout? Will we move on those we've found? Let's not think of that contingency until it arises. I feel we can do it, men, come hell or high water.

"Our best information is that our people are being held in pairs. We believe Miss Randolph and Miss Ferrick are together on Shapour Avenue. Dr. Caldwell and Nasvik may be paired, and so, too, Gilmore and Labelle, and Spooner and Isenstein. Kenyon may be alone. Yep, he's the Secret Service guy. I've photos of all of them for you to memorize. Remember, they may not be paired where they're being held—which will make our job that much more interesting.

"For the moment, let's get a rundown of language skills before we assign sectors."

It was a toss-up. They all had a command of literary Arabic; four also spoke Turkish and Farsi; one spoke Armenian; and the other languages—Spanish, Italian, French, German, Japanese, Mandarin, Russian, and a dialect of Vietnamese—didn't seem to count in these circumstances.

Harding made some quick calculations and divvied up the squads.

Assigned to Shapour Avenue: Alpha Group - MacLeod (Farsi), Giannatsis, and Gibbs (Turkish); Bravo Group - Orsolak (Farsi), O'Brien, and Ciampa.

Assigned to Lilava district: Charlie Group - Maloof (Armenian), Junker, and Kachel; Delta Group - Stewart, Berube, and Stone (Turkish).

Assigned to Gulistan Avenue: Echo Group - Smythe (Farsi), Williams, and Zablonski.

Assigned to the Gajilgabsi slum: Foxtrot Group - Svenson, DeLucia, and Bradford (Turkish); Golf Group - Pace, Ogden, and Raffa; Hotel Group - Kuhns, Rubinstein, and Sheehan (Farsi); India Group - Young, Billings, and Wyrocki; Juneau Group - Telford, Vivian, and McDonald.

"All groups except Alpha, Bravo, Charlie, and Echo will check the locations of their assigned areas, check their gear, and leave immediately. Those remaining will give me clothing and shoe sizes so that you can meld with the scenery. And, in the meantime, you can go down to the river and clean up . . . no more than a pair at a time. I'm going into town to pick up the new duds."

"One more question: What about the gendarmerie and the military?"

"The police don't patrol. Available on call. The citizens of this town rarely call the police, a carry-over from the days of Savak. Those who call are taken to headquarters and treated with almost the same suspicion as an apprehended criminal."

"And the military?"

"They're the same as in most cities in this part of the world. They're visible during daylight hours, walking in pairs with rifles strapped to their backs but not on any specific assignment. You'll see them on Gulistan Avenue and in the crowds of the bazaar. You won't see them in the Gajilgabsi or on such swanky avenues as Shapour, Pahlavi, or Karashenk."

"Where will you be?"

"There's little need for a command post the first or even the second day, I don't think . . . won't be that lucky. I'll be circulating on my own in all the sectors. We will not recognize one another, unless you need to talk to me. If you kneel down and retie or restrap a shoe, I'll follow you to a spot you select, where we can talk unseen."

"Is the group mode in effect?" It was MacLeod who raised the key question.

"Definitely negative. Each man is on his own. Most of the time, you presumably won't be in contact with each other. You'll be living on the street. DeLucia has distributed enough rials to keep you going for at least a week. If any man gets into trouble, we will not go to his aid other than in absolutely natural circumstances . . . and the circumstances will dictate your action. I hope that's clear.

"We are initially conducting a search mission only. If all hideouts haven't been located in a week's time, starting from 2400 hours tonight, we will meet here at 2400 hours for another confab."

Harding realized what a kick in the ass it was for the men not to be able to operate in the group mode, their vaunted MO. Working in lonely groups of three, their record of clandestine achievement was one of the incredible hallmarks of American covert action. What was truly incredible was the casualty rate: Only two operatives in the past twenty-odd years. Their record was even better than that of the Army's Special Forces, which lost only 208 men in the stinking jungles of Vietnam . . . where Harding and the SOB had also operated to a smaller extent.

"Anything else?"

"What if you don't show up a week from now?" It was Smythe, the hard-nosed Cherokee from Oklahoma, who was the only Native American Harding knew with a truly red face.

"Thanks, it hadn't crossed my mind," Harding said with a grin. "I've got Smithson over at the Arg who speaks Farsi, Arabic, and Turkish, and we've got Gibbs, Stone, and Bradford here who speak Turkish, and there's you, Smythe, and MacLeod, Orsolak, and Sheehan who can handle Farsi.

"If I can't make it, I have no preference as to which one of you should take over. Just bear in mind that a *concerted* rescue effort must be the topmost priority."

"Just in case, have you thought of how such a city-wide rescue action could be orchestrated if we maintain radio silence?"

Harding grinned, shaking his head in appreciation: "We've got a built-in timer, gentlemen: The clock tower in Shahrdari Square near the Arg. It bongs away the time every hour on the hour. It's amplified and can be heard in every part of Tabriz. How's that for a start? Think about it.

"OK. I'm off to pick up some clothes. Good luck to you who won't be here when I get back."

Chapter 40

Harding jounced and jiggled on the rickety motorcycle up the badly rutted road that led to the hidden camp among the oaks. He was riding the three-wheeler with a box trunk used by messenger services around the world. Three-wheelers tend to be a bit tipsy on turns, and Harding agreed to buy it because his friend Abdul, his bargainer, had convinced him it was just about the only way he was going to be able to cart the dozen or so suits, slacks, shirts, socks, and shoes that the men required. It was that or an automobile or truck, and a vehicle required official ID. The melon truck was enough of an attractive nuisance, and they ought to get rid of that, anyway. It was stolen, and it would be simply a matter of time before it was spotted.

He stared all the way back down the hill he was climbing, saw nothing following him on the three-mile open grade of reddish earth, and turned off for the stand of oaks.

Harding did a double-take and whistled softly when he clattered to a stop near the communications tent.

The melon truck was there . . . and so was Smithson . . . and so was . . . by God, the prince!

The tall young man in a bedraggled gray business suit, his large, soft brown eyes etched with near exhaustion, strode rapidly over to Harding as he swung off the bike. "Commander Harding! My friend, Commander Harding!"

"Your Highness . . . Riza . . ." The two embraced as if they were long-lost brothers. Harding finally held the prince off at arm's length, mindful of the silent audience, and asked weakly: "What the hell are you doing here?"

"I've come to help you rescue the hostages. I know I can help and—"

"Did Brockway give his OK? The last I heard, your request to come here had been denied."

"No one helped me," the man with the chiseled hawk nose of the Pahlavis said with a tinge of sadness in his voice. "My supporters in America and Europe paved the way."

"How did you get here?" Harding looked at Smithson as he asked.

"He showed up at the Arg," Smithson volunteered. "We didn't know who he was, but Westcott, who was watching the citadel, saw him walking around there for a whole day, and, you won't believe this, he finally appeared at the Blue mosque to grab some sleep."

Harding nodded at the prince. "So you figured it out from the tapes when I was shouting 'Javid Shah.' Tell me this, Your Highness: What did you think you could accomplish all by yourself?"

"Not much, I admit, Commander. Frankly, I was hoping and expecting to find you, and I have found you, at last."

Smithson piped up: "It was touch and go, for a while. We were beginning to think he was one of the terrorists trying to make contact with his tunnel pals. We were going to muss him up a bit to be on the safe side, and drag him here for questioning . . ."

"I heard an American accent in his Farsi," the prince said, laughing. "Then I said I was looking for you, so Mr. Smithson brings me here. I was hog-tied, as you Americans would say, on the way over. I am glad you are not taking any chances."

"Now that you're here, I don't know how you can help us, Your Highness. I'm working with professionals in trying to find where the hostages are."

"It would be safer and easier for all of us if you called me Riza, please. I believe I can be of help. I know exactly where Sulmass Ochi resides."

"We know she's somewhere on Shapour Avenue."

"Ah, but I know the exact house—it is a mansion—and I know the interior layout as well. It's a big compound with a high, pink wall around it, No. 18."

"Now how do you know that?"

"It is the home of the former minister of culture and education, a man named Birya, who was the co-leader of the Tudeh party with Pishavari, Sulmass Ochi's father. Birya escaped to the Soviet Union when the Tudehs were outlawed, but my father eventually allowed him to return. Sulmass Ochi was orphaned in 1949 when she was two years old and was later taken in by Birya. I'm certain she's still occupying the mansion. She's an actress in motion pictures and hasn't been identified with any political movements. The Islamic Republic hasn't touched her."

Harding clapped his hands. "One down, four to go. All right, men. Find the clothes that fit you and let's get moving to our sectors. Smithson, Riza will stay with you at all times. Cart the men to convenient drop areas in town, swing by the Arg and let Trovato and Wescott know that you will be holding the fort here with the prince. Need only one group on Shapour Avenue. Bravo Group remains here.

"I'm going to Shapour Avenue to see about the lay of the land. I should be away from there by the time Alpha Group shows up. Good luck." Harding shook hands with the prince, straddled the motorcycle, and was off for the city's northeastern area, where Shapour Avenue began.

Fifteen minutes later, he was turning onto Shapour and beginning a slow, careful crawl down the middle of the avenue. In no time, he found the place: pink walls rising about eight feet, embracing an area of several acres, dominated by a white stucco three-story mansion with red barrel tiles.

As Harding passed the high, center-opening iron gate, he noted some activity far up the driveway. He rode on another quarter mile, made a U-turn, and went back to take another peek as he rode by the gate. The second he went by and spotted three men watching the "window" presented by the gate, he knew he had goofed. The putt-putting two-cylinder cycle was too distinctive a sound for that quiet street. Passing by once had not been attention-getting. But twice?

Harding had not traversed another quarter mile when a white sedan emerged from the gate and speeded up behind him. Harding couldn't give them further suspicions by trying to outrun the car. He slowed down, seemingly looking for an address, pulled over to the sidewalk, stepped off, rummaged through the box trunk, and pulled out a box of shoes he had saved for himself. Then he casually strode up the long walkway to the house he had selected to stop in front of, outwardly oblivious of the white car, which now had almost come to a stop, watching him.

Damnation! The house was unoccupied. He acted as if he were at a loss, scratched his head in perplexity and turned back to the motorcycle. A thin man in a business suit and wearing a calpac was sitting on the box trunk, smiling at him. Two others were still in the car.

"You are lost?" He spoke in Azeri. Harding recognized him as one of the men in the camel caravan.

"I think so," Harding replied in Farsi. "I am to deliver these shoes to a Number 11, but there are no numerals on these fine buildings."

"Do you have a name?"

"Marashi." Harding picked one of the most common names in Iran.

"Cannot be of help," the thin man said and walked back to the sedan. He got in, and the car made a U-turn and started back to the walled compound. As Harding redeposited the shoebox and straddled his bike, the sedan down the avenue suddenly screeched into another U-turn and roared back to the motorcycle, automatic rifles trained on him from both side windows.

Chapter 41

The hour for the next hostage execution came to pass, and a body was found on the steps of the mosque. The staff at the Swiss consulate was highly agitated at the putrification that had already set in when the body was brought to them by the police for shipment to the United States. The body was undoubtedly that of Dr. Caldwell, the expedition leader, from the papers that were found on his clothing. Everyone had agreed that Dr. Caldwell had been murdered days before.

The relative peace that prevailed among the nations on earth for the past few years had created such a pervasive feeling of good will that the radio broadcast beamed to the President of the United States brought a tremendous outpouring of anger and rage from all corners.

It was heard that Sunday noon, casting a genuine pall on most Americans. It announced that with the killing of the fifth American hostage, Dr. Caldwell, the killing would stop. The terrorists had a new offer.

They still wanted the Persian prince. And they would exchange Patricia for him, unharmed, in a neutral country's consulate or embassy. But they assured the President that if their demand was not met, they would still free his daughter and the remaining hostages. There was another *but*. Her face and body would be horribly disfigured with knife and flame, she would be made barren, and her Achilles tendons would be severed so that she would never be able to walk without mechanical assistance. And the President was given two weeks to think it over. They would not be that insensitive.

The President issued a plea to the terrorists, suggesting that holding or harming Patricia could serve no real political or other purpose. An agreement, other than an exchange of persons, could possibly be worked out, the President announced, breaking the pledge of no deals with terrorists for the first time in U.S. history.

But the country was with the President, as were the majority of the world's powers.

There was no response from any of the kidnappers.

The Secretary of Defense was all for dropping the entire 82nd Airborne Division of 16,000 men on the ancient capital city for a house-to-house search.

Another one of those polls had 22 percent of the public now

approving a nuclear attack on Iran to wipe out that country if any harm should come to Patricia—and approving the President's announcing this to the world.

The nation was wracked by mental horror pictures of Patricia Ann Randolph in a variety of hideous poses. Hate for the terrorists mounted with a concomitant buildup of frustration that began to take the form of attacks on anything or anybody that seemed to be of Iranian blood or manufacture.

It was becoming a jolly good time for rednecks, north and south, east and west. Iranian-American groups removed their identifying signs if they had any and stopped mailing Iranian newspapers because some postal people were fingering recipients. Arab associations had to keep repeating that Arabs were not Iranians and Iranians were not Arabs, that Arabs and Iranians spoke vastly different languages and so on. To the great numbers of poorly educated Americans, these were fine points that really didn't matter, and the frequency of bombings, fires, smashed store windows, and hate marches began to remind many of the savage outbursts during Hitler's rise and the ascendancy of the Nazi party.

Patricia Randolph had to be rescued. That was the only answer to the violence that was visiting the United States.

At the emergency meeting called immediately in the Oval Office, the President first sought advice and opinions as to the sincerity of the announcement. Would they really do such a thing?

It was Brockway's unenviable task to assure the President that they certainly would. It would be a living death for Patricia and her family, the heartless act of someone with a coldly sadistic mind.

The feeling of helplessness was exacerbated by the knowledge that the whereabouts of the Persian prince was unknown. Since his disappearance from Catskill, New York, no one, neither family nor friends, had seen him.

Brockway admitted that he had launched a search for the man about twelve hours after he dropped from sight, but there was nothing to report.

Even if anyone wanted to trade him for Patricia, it was, at the moment, out of the question.

Chapter 42

"How's he doing?"

"OK, I guess." Pace, from Golf Group, had reported back to base with the news that one of the hideouts had been located with the attempt by the terrorists to murder Dr. Caldwell. An orientation sweep by the fifteen men assigned to the Gajilgabsi slum area had taken a full day. Two marginally likely places had been spotted: A second-floor window, in the rear of a slouching masonry building full of families, had new three-inch-wide wooden slats nailed as makeshift bars to it. About a half mile away, another family tenement had a third-floor window continually draped, day and night. Not much to go on, but surveillance was immediately instituted.

"We've got him under wraps at the tunnel. Caldwell almost shit when I hit his two escorts at the stone manhole and sent 'em to hell." Trovato spoke in a monotone. "They showed up, in that broken-down old Ford I came in, around eleven o'clock and brought the old man up the steps, arm in arm. Switched clothes with one of 'em and dumped him on the steps. Westcott's with Caldwell in the cavern under the Arg."

"We were right about the barred window being one of the hideouts," Pace said. "But developments present us with a problem. If they're going to cart their victims to the Blue mosque to kill them, we'd better beef up our welcoming committee there. It was damned lousy seeing them stuff Caldwell into the car and not being able to follow them. We lucked out at the mosque."

"If that's the MO, we wouldn't have to find the hideouts, but I don't think so. It might be the MO for those being held in family settings, but we can't count on anything until we know for sure." Smithson was holding council with Trovato, Pace, and the reserve group of Orsolak, O'Brien, and Ciampa. The prince was taking it all in.

"Looks as if Nasvik is still OK there, as long as the terrorists continue to feel safe. We're running out of time, though. We can't go on forever wiping out those killers without someone asking why they haven't come back."

Pace spoke up: "Got Ogden and Raffa on Nasvik's hideout, front and back."

"Good. Get back there right away. Trovato, find Juneau Group and ask them to cover the Blue mosque with you and Westcott. That'll leave twelve to find that other hideout in the slum." Smithson didn't sound too sure. "Where in hell is Harding? Not a word from him or of him in two days."

"We must do something," the prince volunteered.

"Negative, Your Highness. Harding made it very clear at the briefing that it was every man for himself. We could tip our hand if we start looking for him, especially if he's in the Shapour Avenue area. He'll have to take his chances, if he has any left.

"I'm going to signal the fleet to let them know that Harding is missing, and that Caldwell is safe." Smithson turned to the prince. "You want me to tell 'em you're here, Your Highness?"

The prince smiled. "That is fine with me, but please do not make plans to send me back. I am in my own country. If you believe I am in the way, let me know and I shall leave."

Smithson raised both his hands. "Certainly, Prince. No deals. I'm pleased to have you with us. Your sketches of the interior of the mansion are extremely valuable. Could save a life or two." He was grinning.

The sun was setting when Smythe pedaled up in a stolen bike. The hideout on Gulistan Avenue had been located. It had to be in one of those elite wrestling clubs, called *zourkounes*. The city had many of them, somewhat like health spas but confined to the fine art of Greco-Roman wrestling and body building with weights. They were meccas for the young and the sturdy, mostly classic endo-mesomorphs. That was what brought the *zourkoune* to the attention of Zablonski, one of the Echo Group.

With little to go on, the SOB men had kept an eye out for men wearing black calpacs with blue piping, even though many were seen on the avenue. When two relatively taller and much thinner gentlemen in business suits and telltale calpacs appeared for a short visit in the morning, and the same duo appeared around noon and again at supper time, and at each visit were carrying a paper bag, it was curious. When the visits were repeated the next day, coupled with absolutely no obeisance to the muezzin's chant at noon, Zablonski felt his team leader should know.

"It's got to be it, Smythe. You can handle Farsi. Get back there in the AM and see what it looks like inside when you ask for membership in the club. We might get lucky. You might be shown around the facilities."

About an hour later, Svenson of Foxtrot Group walked into camp. The third-floor draped windows had to be a hideout. Bradford, the Boston Brahmin scholar who spoke Turkish, Greek, Latin, and Japanese, squatting in fly-covered, fetid squalor for a whole day without food or drink, had heard snatches of Azeri conversations among playing children from the building. "American Jew" and "the Americans" piqued his interest. The next morning, when he staggered back and fell in a heap, feigning illness, near the same spot, one of the little boys with latent entrepreneurial instincts was offering a peek at the Americans for a price—candy, gum, a toy, whatever. That had been enough for Bradford.

Including Shapour Avenue, that accounted for four hideouts, leaving only the one in the Lilava neighborhood.

It wasn't until the middle of the next morning, the sixth day of the search, that Maloof, the American with Syrian Christian parents, appeared, his sport clothes immaculate, his face wreathed in a wide grin. The holding place had to be a second-floor room overlooking an alley behind the ovens where they baked Armenian *pideh* all day long. While he was buying bread on his third visit, a man had come through the rear door leading to some back rooms, picked up four loaves of the flat staple, and retired, not paying but saying thank you in Azeri. The Armenian baker had not paid the slightest attention to the man but had grimaced at the "thank you." Nothing much to speak of. Maloof found Junker six blocks away and instructed him to buy bread early in the morning and around noon, hanging about as much as possible. Junker had seen the same little play enacted at noon. Stone, in Delta Group, who spoke Turkish, was located and sent to the bakery at supper time. Nothing. But Maloof, now loitering in a shirt borrowed from Stewart, saw the man he had first spotted walk out of the bakery, wearing a black calpac. He followed him easily to the tenement off Karashenk Avenue, the one with the makeshift bars on the second-floor windows, where Nasvik was being held. That was enough.

Smithson felt that all hideout locations had been found. With one man left to stake out each hideout, everyone else was called back to formulate rescue operations.

After a half hour of deliberation, the plans were set, but some materials vital to the rescue operations were needed. Dr. Caldwell's report that he and Nasvik had been chained constantly from ankle irons to a pipe made chain cutters imperative . . . just in case.

Thus, when MacLeod, Orsolak, and Sheehan, all of whom could speak Farsi, took the melon truck back into the city, they had an odd shopping list to fill: five heavy-duty chain cutters, one box of thumb tacks, two double-bed-sized dark blankets, one heavy-duty glass cutter, one four-inch manual suction cup, one metal scroll saw, 30 feet of six-strand nylon rope, and four pairs of running shoes, two size 9s and two size 10s.

Chapter 43

Harding was feeling uncomfortable in a variety of ways. His hands were tied behind his back, there was a gag stuffed into his mouth, he was parchment dry, not having had a drop of water or a morsel of food for what seemed an eternity, and worst of all, there was a chain around his ankles from which he was suspended upside down three feet from the floor. Yet the most devastating aspect of his peculiar incarceration was unspeakable. Harding was intensely embarrassed. He knew that if he ever got out alive—and he had a strong feeling he would not—he would never find it possible to tell anyone that while he was hanging upside down, his bodily functions had reflexed and he groaned in despair as the solids slid downward to lodge at his belt line while the liquids seeped through, with some trickling by his ears and dripping to the floor. There was something about that happening that made Harding want to die immediately. He had been reduced to the lowest human condition, literally soaking in his own waste.

At one point in time, he knew that someone had entered his place of confinement—it was pitch-black—and had retreated without a word. Harding's body had smartened up in the interim, and it had not expelled another bit of solid waste, although a tiny trickle of urine expressed itself once or twice. Harding couldn't smell anything anymore, having become inured to his environment. He realized that this could be one way of killing him, even though it didn't make sense. He had been knocked out quickly and had regained consciousness in the position he was in now.

He had no idea about time. He could not tell how long he had been in this position, only that he heard exaggerated sounds, such as a faster and louder heartbeat in his ears, coupled with a weeping noise that he had never heard before. Pain seemed to have left him, unless he moved. Then the lancets of pain made him groan. If his mouth hadn't been stuffed, he could have obtained some clue of the passage of time by checking his beard growth with his tongue.

His mind began to go. He would become conscious in fits and starts and utter words and phrases in a variety of languages and dialects, mixing them up in muffled noises until, suddenly, the rag in his mouth, dry and shrunken and without the thong, which had loosened also, slipped out and fell to the floor. The lack of a gag didn't make much difference. The words he formed were emitted as croaking sounds and were getting weaker by the hour.

He seemed to be dead when a torchbearer approached the

suspended body, spat in disgust at what he saw and smelled, and released the overhead hook to allow Harding's body to clump to the earthen floor in an awkward, disjointed sprawl. He was kicked to flatten out his body, and the torchbearer left.

About an hour later, four men carrying torches gathered around Harding's body. They were lackadaisical at first, talking about what was the best way to carry him to avoid the smell and dirt. Then one of them made the observation that he must be dead, for sure. That galvanized them into an immediate investigation that included touching to see if the body was warm and taking his pulse.

He was alive, and that seemed to be what mattered at the moment. One of the men left and returned moments later with a large blanket. Harding was placed on it, and the four grasped the corners and carried him up a flight of stairs to what turned out to be the English basement level.

A man with a stethoscope was waiting in a small windowless room that had a table and two chairs in it and was lit by a single bulb hanging from the center of the ceiling. Harding was laid out on the table.

The stethoscope was applied to his chest and back; his blood pressure was checked, his pulse read, and an anal thermometer was used to take his temperature.

None of his clothing was removed. Where necessary, it was pulled away to complete the examination. The physician left, closing the door. Harding had not moved or made a sound during the entire time he was gathered up from his cell, carted to the room, and examined.

Hours later, the door opened. A tall young woman stood just inside the door and stared at the filthy specimen of a human being, clad in a shirt that had once been white, dark blue pants that had been part of a business suit, black socks, and black shoes. His head was puffed up with a sickly blue-gray cast, red capillaries lacing the skin. His hands had been untied, but they were still puffed up and blue, like sausages. A closer look showed that his shoes had a peculiar appearance, distended by the puffed-up feet. He was covered with brown streaks of excreta, now dry and crusty.

She said not a word, made not a motion of any kind, just turned around sharply and left.

The doctor returned almost immediately. He revived Harding, wet his lips with water, then dribbled some into his mouth, and finally fed him some consommé, which Harding immediately vomited up.

It took three days to bring Harding around to the point where he could sit up and conduct a conversation without reeling and almost falling from the chair he sat in. He was never bathed; his clothes were never changed.

On the fourth day, the woman returned to the room and sat down opposite the now somewhat coherent, rational Jackson Harding. He knew her instantly to be Sulmass Ochi Pishavari, the lady with the blond streak on the left side of her head, the lady with the lovely features: dark eyes, exquisite cheekbones, sensuous, budding lips accented by a finely chiseled nose, and a complexion that rivaled Poe's Annabel Lee.

Neither spoke for a good two or three minutes. Then she spoke, in Farsi.

"You are a difficult man to kill." Her voice was low and gentle, and her tone had the intimation of a remonstrance.

"Everyone does his best to stay alive."

"Some lives are not worth the effort."

"Truthfully said, but each person deems his own as most worthy."

"You are a Hye?"

"No, I am an American."

"Where did you learn to speak our tongue so well?"

"I learned it in American colleges because I love to speak and understand foreign languages."

"Why do you love foreign languages?"

"Languages give one an insight about the people who speak them."

"Is that why you hate us?"

"On the contrary, linguistic familiarity draws peoples together."

"You say these things, but you are extremely efficient in murdering my people."

"Your syllogism has gone astray. I did not kill anyone on the basis of their nationality or religion or race. I killed people who were engaged in criminal acts, and I killed people in self-defense. But never on the basis of their nationality or religion."

"But you do admit that you killed some of my people."

"Certainly I admit that, just as you were killing defenseless students and teachers, people with their hands tied behind their backs and whose only crime was that they happened to be Americans in the wrong place."

"I am certain that you feel you are correct in what you have done. What I want to know is why you Americans are being so foolish about the prince. Why would you allow Americans to die for that worthless excrescence?"

"Americans don't bargain with knives at their throats."

"Those in power may feel that way when the knife is not at their own throat." Sulmass Ochi looked smug.

"You know damn well the President doesn't feel that way."

Sulmass Ochi didn't respond for a moment; she looked at the tabletop and said, "I am not planning on keeping you alive much longer, or I would have had you cleaned up and given you a fresh set of clothes. I shall not be seeing you again. Is there any last request that I might consider?"

"Thank you, yes. I am about to lose my life in a situation that I have been unable to understand in several respects. Would it be too much to clarify a few points for me?"

She smiled, and Harding couldn't get over the softness and beauty of her face. "Knowing what happened, I'm certain you and your colleagues must have been puzzled. I will give you no more than two minutes."

"Thank you. First, how was Stefan McMahan involved?"

"Mr. McMahan was an agent of the IRA who was closely associated with the Palestinian fight for independence. He was responsible for the wiring in your President's offices. He conceived of kidnapping the students when the President's daughter arrived at Shanidar.

"His offer to hand over the pretender to the government in Teheran for 50 million dollars in gold was accepted with alacrity, as long as the government would not be implicated in the kidnapping.

"McMahan kidnapped the party and was taking your Americans to a special holding area when my agents approached him with a better offer."

"Ah. That's why he suddenly changed direction and turned north."

"He had little choice. We were holding his mother hostage in Detroit, and he was to get five million in gold from us when he delivered."

"Why did he go to Shanidar after making the delivery?"

"For two very good reasons. He was being hunted by the Iranian government for disappearing with the hostages, and if he had come to Tabriz, the government would certainly have tracked him down. Thus, we decided that Shanidar was as safe a place as any to remain until everything was over. Since the cave was in Iraq, he felt the Iranians would not dare start another war by sending troops across the border after him."

Harding nodded, then asked casually, "Is Patricia Randolph safe?" He wasn't about to mention Miss Ferrick.

"She is in good hands. This conversation is over."

"Just one more question, please. What good would it do you to have the young shah in your hands?"

"It goes back to 1945. I am the daughter of the founder of the Tudeh Communist Party, the only cell that's left preserving the original concepts of Marx and Lenin. We planned to gain tremendous popularity among the people by capturing the young shah to show that the Tudeh party can accomplish what no one else has been able to. The Albanian and Bulgarian governments are behind my efforts.

"The revolution we would have started here would have spread across this land, and my father's dream of a Marxist-Leninist government with total equality for all would have become a reality."

Then her eyes glittered. "I have special plans for the prince. It was his father's soldiers who seized my father, tortured him for days, then hanged him. I will return the favor to the shah's son. You Americans will have to give him up. The prince is not worth your President's daughter, and you all know that. You will ultimately bend to my will as I kill your precious people, one by one." She sneered, "You understand now why you will have to die." Her eyes were glittering again.

"You seem to have a penchant for killing, madam. I know you were the one in the darkness at Kaleshin Pass. Was it a rifle or pistol butt you used to smash up the female lieutenant? And only a cold-blooded stone-age savage would have resorted to that nicety of peeling the skin off her breasts." Then Harding heard himself saying, "You're a bitch, Sulmass Ochi!"

Her unflinching stare dissolved into a fit of laughter at Harding's remonstrance.

"What language! George Pulver . . . Oh, yes, I know who you are . . . I cannot resist telling you this: The man called Jones-Armitage was never Stefan McMahan. Jones-Armitage was his exact twin brother, John . . . I will not be seeing you again. You will die in the malodorous state you are in, wearing those filthy clothes as a reminder of the kind of life you have led.

Sulmass Ochi had made a serious error.

Chapter 44

"We hit all five targets simultaneously at 0300 hours.

"The three chimes of the Shahrdari clock tower will be the only signal.

"Two groups, operating as one, on each target.

"Each dual unit plans its own rescue operation.

"Alpha and Bravo, with the prince, Shapour; Charlie and Delta, Lilava; Foxtrot and Golf, second floor, Gajilgabsi; Hotel and India, third floor, Gajilgabsi; and Juneau and Echo, Gulistan.

"Three post-rescue vans will be ready for you. I'll pick up first at Shapour, then swing down Gulistan and pick up Smythe and company.

"Trovato, with Dr. Caldwell aboard, will pick up Maloof and company at the Lilava bakery.

"Westcott will be on Karashenk Avenue in the Gajilgabsi, picking up Svenson's crowd and swinging over six blocks for Kuhns's company.

"We rendezvous at the Blue mosque, no later than 0400, clock-tower time.

"Two transport Hueys will touch down just east of this camp-site at 0500. No time leeway.

"Channel F for radio contact but strict silence until rescue operations completed.

"Keep wet-work to minimum, silent mode unless it can't be helped.

"We will all wear black calpacs, business suits, and white arm bands supplied by Harding's KGB ally, and that includes the vans."

Smithson stopped. "Any questions?"

"Why do we rendezvous at the Blue mosque? Why not proceed to base?"

"In case of loose ends. We have no certain idea of what we'll find at these hideouts, as you well know. Some of you may not pull it off in the ten minutes I know all of you are expecting to do it in—that would be my time frame. If the van that comes for you has rescued personnel aboard, and you are not ready, the van cannot sit on the street. It will go directly to the Blue mosque, transfer its cargo to another van, and roll back to the pickup point with some backup people, just in case."

"What's the color of the vans?"

"You'll see pretty soon. You'll be riding into town in them. They're white two-ton panels with the Red Crescent on their sides."

"Do we know who we're rescuing?"

"Really doesn't matter, does it? We think the two women are in the mansion; that Nasvik is alone in the second-floor slum tenement. Spooner and Isenstein could be in the third-floor wrack-up . . . base that on a kid mentioning an American Jew. Could be Isenstein, but he happens to be a German Catholic. Then we have Gilmore, Labelle, and Kenyon, the Secret Service man. It's an unimportant toss-up, men.

"OK, we have about seven hours for you to make plans for your specific targets. Select whatever gear and arms you think you'll need, and don't forget that each unit should take along one of those chain-cutters."

Smithson paused again as the men began to break up into their groups. "MacLeod," he called out to the leader of the Alpha Group, "you might want to bring back Harding's body if it can be found."

None remembered the prince. He was not around.

Chapter 45

It seemed as if hours had passed since Sulmass Ochi had left, but there was no further contact with him. He prowled around the little green room with the single light bulb suspended from the center of the ceiling. No window, no light from the outside, which left him unsure of the time of day. Of course, his wristwatch had been taken. He went to the door and, with great care, attempted to turn the knob with finger and thumb. It was locked, of course. He examined the keyhole. It was a cheap, standard lock with a skeleton key tumbler, and the key was in the lock on the outside.

Harding had no idea what was on the other side of the door. Probably a hallway. Was there anyone in the hallway? If he pushed out the key in the lock, would someone see it happen or hear it fall? Who knew, but he was going to try it. He had nothing to lose beyond his life, and that was already forfeit.

He got on his knees and peered under the door. He could make out a dim light. That was heartening. He thought for a while, then took off his shirt. That would have to do. He then picked up one of the two wooden chairs at the table and smashed one against the floor. After waiting to see if the noise attracted anyone—it didn't—he examined the splinters and found a sliver that would allow him to penetrate the keyhole.

He spread out his shirt collar, that part being the stiffest, and did what any Grade B movie hero would do: he slid it under the door as far as he thought it could go without wrinkling up, and played with the keyhole until the splinter pushed the key out. Harding heard it hit the floor. He gently pulled back the portion of shirt he had pushed out. No key was on it. He went quickly to the pile of splinters and pieces of chair and selected the longest splinter he could find that might slip under the door crack. It was about a foot long and it did the trick. He stuck the splinter straight out under the door and swept the outside as if with a windshield wiper. He lost the key halfway back, but another try and he had it.

The slight exertion he had undergone left him panting, gasping. He sat in the other chair for a moment to regroup, holding the key in one hand, the sliver of wood in the other. He couldn't believe that he was on the verge of tottering as he took the few steps to the door, turned the key, and opened the door a crack. Hardly any light. He opened it wider and peeked. It was a dark hallway, with light, daylight, cascading down some steps at the far end. There was a door across from his. He tiptoed over and tried it. It opened into a room exactly like his except that this one had a window, a heavily screened window.

Harding checked the window. It was at chest height, and he was looking out on a street beyond a wall almost at the height of the windowsill. He bent down and unlaced one of his shoes, grasped the flat lace at one end, and split it down the middle as if it were a lamp cord. He then pried at the inner sole of his shoe until it came out, kneaded the flat shape into a kind of rope, opened the window, and ran the rope down one edge of the screen, across the bottom, and up the other edge. He bit off a piece of what had been his shoelace and stuck it into one end of the thick rope. Then he peeled off the heel of one of his shoes, selected a wooden match with a yellow head from its center, and stuck it under the lace in the rope. He closed the window, tiptoed to the door, listened, fixed his loose shoe with a piece of the lace, opened the door, put the key in his pocket, and retrieved a chair leg, for defense purposes, from his room before he crept carefully down the hall toward the steps.

A doorway to the stairwell opened onto the hall Harding was in, and he was lucky. He was able to hear footsteps on the stairs, and quickly pressed against one side of the doorway, holding the chair leg over his head. The footsteps never came down to his level. There must have been several floors that the stairwell served. Harding crept into the well, painted yellow, with opaque glass-brick sections for light, and decided he had no other course but to move up. He heard some more footsteps, changed his mind, and made a dash for his room, leaving the key on the outside but the door unlocked. It would be better if he waited for nightfall. Nightfall. He wondered what time, what day it was. Had the men found all the hideouts? When would they be coming? Would he be alive when they came?

It seemed to take an eternity for it to get dark, an experience somewhat akin to the watched pot never boiling. During the wait, he came to the realization that perhaps the estimable Sulmass Ochi was simply going to allow him to starve. No fuss, no bother. Send someone around to his room in a few days and pry his body off the door. He'd see about that. When it was dark enough that he couldn't make out the stairs from his door, he made his move.

Up the stairs on tiptoe to the next floor, and he was lost. It was too dark to see anything, since there were no lights in the hall. He used his sharpened sense of smell to guide him toward what seemed to be food of some kind. He kicked a tray on the floor. It was next to a door, and the remains of a repast was sitting there awaiting a pickup. He groped on the tray, found something soft, smelled it, didn't care, and stuffed it into his mouth. He coughed it out. It was a paper napkin that had absorbed some kind of gravy. He couldn't find a morsel, and he wiped his hand clean on his filthy pants.

There was no light under the door where the tray was, so he tried it. It opened. He was overcome by the heavy scent of a cologne or an after-shave, he wasn't certain which. He closed the door behind him.

"Is that you, Mansour?" It was a man's voice.

"No, wrong room, stay well." And Harding slipped out.

Once again he didn't have any idea what time it was. If he could only hear the Shahrdari chimes indoors. . . . It seemed to be too early for anyone to have gone to bed. He tried the door across from the one he had just closed. Snoring.

He went back to the stairs, climbed to the top floor and struck pay dirt. He could see a light shining from under the door on the right side of the hall. Harding had misgivings, but he gripped the knob tightly and turned it ever so carefully to prevent a click or any other sound. Then he pushed the door open slowly until there was enough of a crack for him to see something in the room.

What he saw was the reflection in a large dresser mirror of a scene that might have been staged in a blue movie, except that the sexes were all mixed up.

Sitting on a chair against the opposite wall was a young man, not much more than boy, watching, with bright black eyes and glistening lips, the two women Harding had come to find.

Patricia Ann Randolph, completely naked, was spread-eagled on a large bed. Her wrists and ankles were strapped to the top and bottom bed posts. She was crying.

Standing over her was Sulmass Ochi Pishavari, wearing a headband to keep her hair clear, and nothing else. The dim light cast shadows on her tawny skin. She was making feral sounds as she approached the helpless girl, and in her hand she held a leather quirt.

A slight movement drew his attention to a second bed. It was Bernice Ferrick, also unclothed, bound to the bed by two sheets, her turn apparently finished. Harding could see welts across most of her torso. He eased the door shut, trying to think. He had no quick way of reaching the man before he gave an alarm. By the time he got rid of him, the woman would have given him away. No. Neither hostage seemed to be in mortal danger. Only the agony of sadistic revenge painfully experienced. He would get them out of there once they were alone. He tiptoed back to the stairwell and waited, as the minutes passed. He was feeling tired and weak and wondered if his ebbing strength was going to be his downfall.

He didn't have any idea when the door had opened, but he was suddenly aware of sound in the hallway. He could not see anything, but he was sure he heard two voices that vanished with the sound of a door closing. Were the girls left alone in the room? Was the door unlocked?

Harding crept to where he remembered the door to be. He groped along the door frame and found the knob. It was locked. He fished in his pockets and found the key he had taken from one of the other doors. They were usually interchangeable and this one was, with a little jiggling.

He slipped into the darkness of the room quickly and dropped to the floor, waiting. He made out the sound of soft whimpering. He crawled toward where he remembered the beds to be. He slowly stood erect, facing the side of Pat's bed, with the chair leg raised, and softly called her name. If anyone was with her, he'd have to handle it.

At the sound of her name, she began to whimper a bit louder, a lining of fear now evident.

"Shhh. I'm Commander Harding, United States Navy. No noise, please, Patricia, Bernice." Harding had given his name and rank. In the dark, it could be reassuring.

Patricia gasped. Bernice sighed. There was now no sound.

Harding leaned over to where he thought Pat's face was. He didn't want to touch her—she'd had enough of that. "Are you tied up?"

Her answer was a tremulous "Yes."

He went to the top corner of the bed, remembering the cords he had seen, found the nylon rope, and untied that corner. He worked his way to the other three and loosened those cords, too. "Can you take them off of you now?" She whispered that yes, she could, and Harding asked her if she knew where her clothes were.

She began a soft whimpering again and finally articulated that neither she nor Bernice had had a stitch of anything to wear after they were brought there.

"All right, all right, you're going to be fine, now. Give me those ropes you've got somewhere on the bed. Good. Now stand up . . . Can you? . . . Good. Get that bed sheet off and put one end on top of your head—like they did when you were on those camels, remember?" He was boiling mad. She was almost a blob of jelly, poor baby.

She understood immediately, and Harding tied a piece of rope around her forehead to hold the top of the sheet, much like a *chador*, then brought up the long folds, wrapped them around her, and held the whole thing in place with another rope around her waist. They had reduced her to a whimpering child.

Then he turned to Bernice, who began to cry softly. He found and untied the bed-sheet knots and had her dress in the same manner as Patricia. As he was tying a piece of rope to hold her headgear, Bernice put her arms around Harding and sobbed convulsively. He put his hand on her mouth and begged her to be quiet.

"Now listen, you two. Your life and my life will depend on utter silence. You follow me by holding on to my shoulders with your right hands in the dark. You can't go wrong in that manner. Let's go."

Harding opened the door, spent a moment listening for sounds, eased out with the women in tow, then closed the door. They crept toward the stairwell, reached it without a sound, and went all the way to the basement without incident. Patricia was shaking like a leaf in a windstorm.

Harding went to the room across from where he had been imprisoned, and once inside, he turned and gave each woman a big hug. "You'll be OK now, if I can help it. You rely on me, and we'll all get out of this alive."

"Are you really from the Navy?" Patricia sounded a little better. He certainly didn't smell like Navy—more like an out-house.

"Yeah, your father sent me, but later . . ." He opened the window as far as it would go and peered into the darkness. There was no moon, and the street beyond the wall didn't have lamps. Harding wasn't sure the street was safe, but it had a greater safety potential than the house they were in. He fumbled around to locate the matchstick in his pocket, found it, and then searched for and found the piece of shoelace he had stuck into the plastic rope he had fashioned.

Then he remembered something. He whispered to the women to wait a minute, and slipped out of the room and across the hallway, and returned with the other chair. "We'll need this."

The PETN detonating cord that had been his shoelace worked perfectly when he lit it, setting off the plastique "rope" he had rigged up around the iron-mesh grill. It went up in a whoosh (instead of a bang, thank God), and Harding lifted each woman up and through the opening, over some inhospitable jags of hot iron. He handed Bernice the chair and clambered out himself, taking a few jabs of hot metal in the process.

Now for the most perilous part of their escape. There was about fifty feet of open lawn to the wall, without a tree or a shrub in the area—and an eight-foot wall to climb—all in the open.

It was a starlit night, which didn't provide much light at all, but it was enough to see, since their eyes had not been exposed to artificial light for a while.

Patricia couldn't make it, even as Bernice went directly to the wall. She was unable to get up from the ground. Harding leaned over, whispered words of encouragement such as "You can do it, old girl," lifted her to her feet, and had her lean over his right shoulder. He stood erect and carried Patricia like a sack. He was surprised at how little she weighed. He carried the chair in his other hand and staggered to the wall without incident, his back prickling at the prospect of a bullet from one of the windows. No sound, no lights, no bullets.

At the base of the wall, he planted the chair and stood up on it, still carrying Patricia. The ground was hard and dry, and the chair hardly made any impression in it. It wasn't going to work, because of Patricia's weakened condition. He stepped down, leaving Patricia to remain standing on the chair, had her turn her back to him and sit on his shoulder. Her sheet kept blocking his vision.

"All right, Pat. Use the wall to keep your balance. I'm going to get up on the chair, and you should be able to reach the top of the wall. Let's try it."

When Harding was fully erect, standing on the chair, the wall was at Patricia's waist. She couldn't swing a leg up. He asked her to lean over the top and stay there until he got Bernice up there, too. He had Bernice sit on his shoulder the same way Pat had and boosted her atop the wall. She was heavier. Both women were now head and shoulders over the

top, their bottoms facing the lawn behind them, waiting for
Harding to get up there and get them over.

Harding never got up there.

Two bullets smacked into the wall near his head. "Do not
move or you are dead." Lights appeared in the windows of the
mansion, and the grounds were suddenly floodlit.

There was Harding, his arms extended to chin himself to the
top of the wall, and there were Patricia and Bernice on top like
two sacks of potatoes. The flaring whoosh from the window
screen he had burned off must have awakened a light sleeper in
the mansion.

"Go for it!" Harding yelled, hoping the women would wrig-
gle over the wall as he whirled around, diving for the ground.
He knew it was all over for him as well as the women.

There was a crescendo of gunfire, and bullets tugged at his
body. Even as Harding lay conscious but motionless on his face
in the grass, the firing continued, interspersed with howls of
"*Javid* Shah!" "*Javid* Shah!"

What the hell . . . It was the prince! He had stepped out from
behind a cypress tree, firing an automatic weapon at the two
gunmen who had shot at Harding.

The two went down. The prince began backing to the wall,
angling toward Harding and the two women still atop the wall,
his weapon pointed toward the mansion windows. He was a
sitting duck in the open under the glare of the floodlights.

A head appeared at the near corner of the mansion. The
prince snapped off one shot, and a body with a hole in the head
slumped into view.

All the lights went out within the mansion. The prince
reached the wall near Harding, sat down against it, and continued to scan the building.

The crashing of glass and rapid fire from one of the second-
floor windows ended almost as abruptly as it had started, the
prince having sent three slugs into the aperture the split second
he heard the glass shatter.

Glass began to shatter in at least four or five more windows.
As the prince started rapid firing, the burping of his weapon
was augmented by three more weapons firing at the house
from the wall above him. Then suddenly the Uzi slipped from

his hands, and his chin came to rest on his chest, as if he had decided to take a nap.

The gunfire stopped immediately. Three men in natty business suits and calpacs swarmed over the wall, telling the women to stay put and ignoring the two men at the base of the wall, heading for the mansion. Three others, similarly attired, all with white arm bands, appeared from the rear and entered the mansion, tossing concussion grenades as admission fees.

The Shahrdari Square clock tower struck three.

Harding had been on time, almost.

Chapter 46

The Shahrdari Square clock tower struck three.

Charlie and Delta groups swung into action.

The Euphrates Bread Bakers in the Armenian neighborhood of Lilava was a typical family enterprise, handed down for generations, with everyone in the family working at it. The ovens, the dough-mixing and kneading room, the sales counter, and the storage room for the flour and condiments, were in the front of the two-story brick building. The family lived in the back and upstairs. There were the father and mother, the father's maiden sister, three adult sons, a teenage daughter, two daughters-in-law, and three grandchildren.

The building had a back door that served occasionally as the entrance to the living quarters. All indications from similar situations in the past pointed to the holding room for the two hostages being upstairs. There had to be a spare room in addition to at least seven bedrooms for the family.

Stone, who spoke Turkish, sat across the street from the storefront.

Berube stationed himself alongside the bakery, in the alley.

Kachel stayed opposite the entrance to the living quarters, leaning against the rear of the outhouse so that he wouldn't be visible from the front door.

Maloof, Junker, and Stewart approached the door, and Maloof knocked. He had to knock repeatedly before a voice asked who was there, in Armenian.

Maloof responded in the language. "Tell your son we have come to take away the Americans. It is time."

The door was opened a crack. The three pushed into an unlit foyer without ceremony, and Maloof asked where the Americans were. Light flooded the area when a door was opened on the left side, silhouetting a women, and the elderly man who had opened the front door pointed to the stairs on the right.

Junker stayed put. Maloof and Stewart, the latter carrying a chain-cutter, bounded up the stairs after finding the light switches.

They tried all the doors. All were unlocked. No help there.

Stewart remained in the hallway as Maloof entered each room and snapped on lights, looking for a secondary room. Sleepy occupants were too dazed to react, at first.

Maloof found the room with the man whom he had seen in the shop the first time. He was sitting up in bed, transfixed by the nozzle of a .44 magnum pointed at his head.

"Are they in there?" Maloof asked quietly, pointing to a door with a chain on it. The man did not answer.

"Stewart. Bring the cutters." He didn't take his eyes off the man in bed.

Stewart bounced in, ran to the chained door, snapped the chain, and slammed it open.

Gilmore and Labelle were standing up expectantly, chained to a cast-iron stove in the center of the room. They were round-eyed, expecting the worse.

"It's OK. We're Americans," Stewart said as he went about snapping the fetters. "OK, let's go!"

Maloof waved the magnum at the man in bed. "You're going with us."

The hallway was now crowded with the family, looking apprehensive. As Maloof pushed his half-naked captive through the crowd, the elderly man began to shout, "I told you . . . I told you . . . You have brought shame on our heads . . . You and your communist murderers . . ."

Once they were outside, Kachel pushed the man into the outhouse and cut his throat.

The rescue had taken exactly seven minutes and forty seconds.

The van with Trovato at the wheel appeared two minutes later, and the bakery site was left just as screams indicated that the body had been found.

*   *   *

The Shahrdari Square clock tower struck three.

Echo and Juneau groups swung into action.

The Loyal (changed from Royal after the revolution) Wrestling Club or *zourkhoune* on Gulistan Avenue was open daily except Saturdays until midnight, catering to those who enjoyed the fine art of classical wrestling as once performed naked at the ancient Olympics. The plush foyer, with its leather sofas and deep carpets, belied the large, austere gymnasium, which could handle thirty matches at a time. The wrestling pads were ringed at the walls by weight-lifting paraphernalia. A central door in the rear wall of the gym led to some handsomely tiled Turkish baths, featuring both hot and cold water immersions, massage tables, and dressing rooms. The gymnasium had a skylight and a heavy metal door in the rear, the entrance for the custodial employees, masseurs, and referees, opening up into the dressing room and locker section. The gym was devoid of rear windows. The building was hugged on either side by two- and three-story structures housing a sporting-goods emporium and a men's clothing store featuring the latest cuts from London's Bond Street. There was a long alley backing the buildings.

Smythe had observed most of the layout after he had handed over a 500-rial initiation fee and was taken on a tour, promising to fill out an application later, when he had more time. The place had indoor toilets. What had sated his curiosity had been the sight of a suit-clad man in an undoffed calpac seated with legs crossed in front of a dressing room.

Zablonski was stationed on the avenue, casually sauntering

up and down, alternating with the sidewalk across the street.

Down the block and up the next street to the alley entrance was where Vivian patrolled as lookout.

The rest of them walked up the alley to the back of the club building, and Williams climbed up the clay drainpipe with a heavy rope coiled on his shoulder.

He tied the rope to an iron vent pipe on the flat roof, and Smythe, Telford, and McDonald hauled themselves up. You can't trust a drainpipe to take too much lateral pressure.

A four-inch suction cup was slapped on an end pane of one of the skylights, a glass cutter did its job, the glass was snapped to allow a tungsten steel blade to slice through the wire mesh embedded in the glass, and the pane was yanked out.

Smythe stuck his head into the opening to see what he could. "There's nothing worth stealing here, you Ay-rab monkeys."

Smythe pulled back out of sight. The three on the roof looked at each other. "Sounded American to me . . . What do ya think? Can't take a chance."

Smythe went back to the opening and jabbered away in Farsi, asking if he was the night watchman.

"Oh, shit, more Greek . . ."

That did it. Smythe pulled the rope around to the opening, ready to drop it through. "Are you alone?"

"Who the hell are you? You're talkin' American."

"Are you *alone?*"

"Naw. I'm dancin' with a two-hundred-pound weight. They give me the run of the gym at night."

"OK, grab the rope and get up here. We're some assholes sent to rescue you from the bad guys." The vernacular had to be street talk to convince the voice below.

In less than a minute the head and then the muscular body of Donald Kenyon, the "Baltimore Bullet," as he was called as an All-American guard at Penn, clambered onto the roof. He had been held at the club solo.

The rope was used for the exit down the back. When all seven emerged on Gulistan Avenue from the side street, they were just in time to see Smithson's white "taxi" recede from view. The exercise had taken all of fourteen minutes.

*   *   *

The Shahrdari Square clock tower struck three.

Foxtrot and Golf groups swung into action.

Dr. Caldwell had not been able to tell them much about the exact environment of the cell where he and Nasvik had been held. They had been blindfolded when brought there. He knew it was on the second floor and he had seen children and adults beyond the door when it was opened by one of his jailers to bring food and water and remove the bucket of waste once a day. He didn't know there were wooden bars outside the window, a window that was completely boarded up and covered with cloth on the inside. The only favorable aspect of the setup was that the window was at the rear of the brick tenement building, and that was not saying much. Nasvik and Caldwell had sat and slept on the opposite wall to the window because of the pipe to which they were chained. Caldwell guessed that someone was always asleep at night across the door of the cell, and there could have been two of them, judging from the symphony of snores and gurgles that he heard.

The decision had been made to hit the cell through the window—too many women and children to wade through in the interior. Some of the menfolk might get brave . . .

The last clock chime had barely faded across the city when Svenson and four men moved to the back of the building, leaving Bradford out front with his knowledge of Turkish.

They were quick and precise in their actions. Ogden stooped, facing up close to the building wall; DeLucia leaped up on his shoulders, and Ogden straightened up, allowing DeLucia to pin a poncho, with thumbtacks, across the window below the barred one.

Raffa, like a cat, clambered up the backs of Ogden and De-Lucia, reached the barred window, and stuck six quarter-pound RDX cubes, each imbedded with cigarette-sized detonators, charged by lithium wafer batteries, and all strung to a digital Timex watch set for twenty seconds. Each of the wood slats now had a plastic explosive halfway up. Pulling out nails, breaking glass, and pounding on paneling would have been fatally nonproductive.

Raffa leaped down from the window. Ogden and DeLucia hugged the wall.

The blast had barely subsided when Svenson scrambled up the human ladder, now extended outward at the base again, with two 9mm Sig Sauers strapped to his chest.

He reached the window. The blast had cleared away the slats, the glass frames and panes, and the flimsy wood cover on the inside. He slipped in like an eel, with one hand out the window, signaling.

Five seconds had elapsed since the blast.

Svenson trained his guns on the door as Ogden crawled in with chain-cutters.

It was pitch-dark in the room, with a smoky tang of burnt vegetable oil in the air. But the darkness wasn't enough to mask the door's opening ever so slowly.

Svenson pumped four rounds into the door's midsection. The sound was deafening.

Ogden crawled quickly to the opposite wall, calling Nasvik's name in a stage whisper.

The door was now wide open, the sill jammed with two moaning bodies.

Nasvik wasn't moving. Ogden found the chains and snapped twice to free his ankles and sever the restraint attached to the pipe.

As Ogden dragged Nasvik to the window, Svenson held a gun as far away from his body as he could and fired to see what the flash would reveal. There was a fleeting outline of someone half-crouching behind the two bodies.

Svenson's other gun, poised for just that image, fired once again, and there were now three bodies in the doorway.

"I'm dropping him out of the window . . . catch!" Ogden said as he followed through, then swung out himself, hanging from the sill and then dropping to the street.

Svenson backed to the window, watching the door, swung out a leg, still watching, swung out the other, and hit the street like a trapeze artist.

There were some popping sounds out front.

Svenson let out a sharp whistle, Bradford came running, and

the group marched quietly up the next alley, Raffa and DeLucia carrying Nasvik.

They had to wait nearly four minutes for Wescott's van to show up. In the meantime, they pulled out a large wooden splinter that had penetrated Nasvik's back, and patched him up.

The entire rescue had taken five minutes and ten seconds.

The only aspect of the action the group mentioned to each other was the fact that only one window within their view lighted up after the explosion.

*   *   *

The Shahrdari Square clock tower struck three.

Hotel and India groups swung into action.

There was little to go by except that it could be the room with the heavy drapes in the center of the third-floor rear. The kids playing on the street had been the tip-off. Judging from the number of children—they had counted at least sixty coming out of the tenement—the place would be jammed with families living in extremely close quarters.

The rescue procedure would be simple. Walk into the building, go up to the third floor, find the rearmost apartment, and take it from there.

Wyrocki sat down on the front stoop, keeping an eye on the front hallway.

Billings stopped at the second landing in the structure, which was quiet except for the insistent cry of a baby. One weak bulb lit each hallway.

Young stayed at the top of the third-floor stairs.

Sheehan, who spoke Farsi, walked to the rear of the hallway, with Kuhns and Rubinstein tagging along with the chaincutters.

So far, so good.

Sheehan tried the door. Locked. He pulled out a set of police keys, opened the door with the second try, and stepped into an apartment hallway jammed with children sleeping on the floor. There were four doors, two on each side of the hallway, and a door at the far end. Ordinarily, that could have been a bathroom door, but not in this slum neighborhood. Outhouses were in the backyard.

A burly young man was sleeping on the floor in front of the door. The three intruders, keeping their feet flat on the floor as if they were using skis, pushed through the sleeping children to make sure they weren't stepped upon. One of the children was awakened and began to whimper after seeing the large forms barely visible from the outer hall light.

Sheehan moved forward quickly, reached the burly sleeping form, and sapped him with his gun butt. He reached over and tried the door, fished out his keys, and unlocked it after six attempts.

The room was occupied by a middle-aged man and woman and three little children.

Sheehan raised his finger to his lips to signal quiet to the man, who had suddenly bolted upright. The man couldn't see Sheehan's face. He yelled out in Azeri something Sheehan couldn't understand.

Sheehan leaned over and snarled one word: "Americans."

The man looked frightened all of a sudden, but his eyes flickered twice in the direction to Sheehan's left.

Kuhns and Rubinstein had to draw their weapons to stop three men from advancing on them from the hallway.

Sheehan stepped back out of the bedroom to the first door on his left, crowding Kuhns and Rubinstein in the process. All the children on the floor were now sitting upright watching the big men and their guns.

The door did not budge, and Sheehan did not see the need for silence any longer. He stepped back and slammed his right foot into the door with a karate snap.

The door swept open halfway, banged into something on the floor, and began closing. It saved Sheehan. A gun began banging from inside the room, but the bullets chipped away at the thicker lip of the door.

Amid a chorus of screams from the growing audience, Rubinstein, just next to the lethal doorway, opened up with his Uzi, aiming at shoulder height. A grunt and a thud seemed to indicate that the unseen gunman had had it.

Sheehan dropped down and crept into the room.

"Watch out behind the door!" The warning was shouted from within.

Sheehan rolled over to his right and planted four rounds into the door. A naked man fell over.

Kuhns's hands reached into the room and found a light switch.

There they were, Spooner and Isenstein, smelling like skunks and badly in need of shaves, on the floor and chained to the wall on the left. Their live-in guards were dead.

Rubinstein performed the chain trick. The two hostages could walk. Waving automatics and machine pistols, the invaders paved their way down to the second floor.

Billings was making a continuous, slow surveillance of the hallway as the parade walked down the stairs, his M16 at the ready.

As Billings turned to follow the rear man, Rubinstein, down to the first floor, a door burst open across the landing and a machine gun chattered angrily.

Billings collapsed on top of Rubinstein.

Rubinstein held on to him with one arm and moved two steps up so that his eyes were on the level of the second floor. He saw some legs moving toward the stairs, waited until two pairs of legs were almost at the banister, and shot all four legs to pieces with cool precision. Then he cradled Billings as best he could and moved down the stairs again to catch up. The others had not waited, because there wouldn't have been room for more than one Rubinstein and Billings on the stairs at the same time.

Wyrocki took up the guard position as the group filed out. He dropped to one knee suddenly and slammed some rounds up the stairs. Two bodies and two East German Buhag guns tumbled down to the front hall. Wyrocki joined up, and everyone gathered to regroup in the next alley. Kuhns and Rubinstein worked furiously to stop the bleeding from three holes in Billings's upper chest.

The action had taken twenty minutes and fourteen seconds, but Wescott's van was waiting. It had sounded like a war, but Westcott and Smythe had not budged to see what was up.

The men of the Special Operations Branch did not expect the cavalry when in trouble.

Chapter 47

President Randolph went on national television to make the official announcement of the rescue.

"I am delighted to announce that at approximately three o'clock in the morning, Teheran time, eight American students and two college instructors were rescued in the Iranian city of Tabriz.

"Yes, you are hearing correctly. There are ten rescued hostages.

"It can now be revealed that the announcements by the terrorists of the deaths of Dr. Jonathan Caldwell and Robert O'Meara were false. The two hostages had been rescued, but, for obvious reasons, the deaths were allowed to stand so as not to jeopardize our undercover operations.

"Our joy today must be tempered by the fact that the loss of even one American under such evil and criminal circumstances cannot be tolerated.

"Our hearts and deep-felt sorrow are extended by all Americans to the families of Dr. Ursula Baines of Poughkeepsie, New York; John T. Berry of Enid, Oklahoma; and Edwin Genereau of Amesbury, Massachusetts, who are not returning.

"One of the students, James Nasvik of Pittsburgh, was hurt slightly during his rescue, but the doctors assure me that he will be fine.

"All of our rescued people will arrive at Andrews Air Force Base at seven-thirty this evening and will be taken to the Naval Hospital in Bethesda for complete physical and mental checkups. They all are suffering from malnutrition, dehydration, and a variety of skin problems.

"None will be available to the media until their health has

been fully restored. Immediate family members will be able to visit with them the moment they arrive at Andrews.

"Two of the so-called students were undercover members of the Secret Service and engineered the escape.

"The kidnappers are members of a defunct Bolshevik organization called the Tudeh, with headquarters in Tabriz.

"I will now take some questions."

"Did the Iranian government have a hand in the kidnappings?"

"We are not certain at this time."

"How were they taken out of Iran?"

"We sent in a couple of large helicopters and lifted them from a spot just outside Tabriz."

"Did we have the cooperation and permission of Iran?"

"No, we did not have its cooperation, and we certainly did not ask its permission or anyone else's."

"Were we in violation of Iranian territory?"

"We were."

"Wasn't the United States taking a chance of an armed confrontation with the Iranian armed forces?"

"We were."

"Did the Congress say it was OK to do that?"

"The Speaker of the House and the chairman of the Senate Foreign Relations Committee were aware of it. But I want to make one thing absolutely clear: We had some American college kids—yes, and one of them was mine—and some teachers being murdered one by one in a country that lately hasn't demonstrated the slightest bit of decency and justice, and I wasn't about to wait on formalities or by-your-leaves to get our people out. Yes, I had F–16s and gunships from the USS *America* flying cover for the two transports we sent in. Would anyone in the United States feel that I overstepped the bounds?" President Randolph stood at the podium, his jaw stuck out, his eyes blazing. There was a moment of awed silence at the unexpected emotion exhibited by the usually calm, monotonic man.

"Did the Secret Service agents have help in the rescue?"

"As far as I know, the rescue was executed by the agents."

"How were they able to do it since they were hostages, too?"

"I don't know. That's all the details we have at the moment.

All we know is that one of them, Robert O'Meara, was wounded during the escape."

"Who did the escapees contact to get word out that they needed transport from Iran?"

"That's another element of the escape we know nothing about. I think you have all the information available at this time. Thank you, ladies and gentlemen."

The President shook his head when he was alone with Demery. "There are too many unanswered questions concerning the rescue, Dave. You heard them. We'll have to work up a good story, and we'll have to get the cooperation of the hostages. Otherwise, our clandestine operations everywhere will come into question."

"I suggest, sir, that we do nothing. Let the hostages tell their stories. The media will have a confusing set of facts, based on the word of, at the most, nine people—your daughter won't talk, I'm sure—and it will be the worst mishmash one could imagine. I think the only things they will agree on is that the Middle East's version of the Red Cross—the Red Crescent— had a hand in their rescue, because of the vans, and that two giant American helicopters carried them away to safety. Brockway's men aren't talkers, sir, and everything was pulled off around three o'clock in the morning in pitch darkness."

"What's the latest word on Harding and the prince?"

"The prince is fine, sir. He suffered a bullet graze on his skull from a ricochet. He's recovering nicely. Harding's another matter. He sustained seven bullet wounds, one of them in his right lung, and it's touch and go at the moment. The prince is insisting on staying with him. Feels responsible because he didn't kill the two men in time before they got Harding."

"When can we expect Brockway to return, I wonder? Thinks a lot of Harding, doesn't he?"

"Yes, sir, he certainly does. The word is that Harding had been hanged by his ankles until he was near death. That was before he was shot up so badly."

"If Commander Harding lives, I want to meet him."

"Yes, sir, Boss. I'd like to meet him, too. Almost lost another SOB man, Billings, in the rescue operations, and he may pull through. Tough bunch . . ."

"What's Brockway accomplishing going out to the Mediterranean . . . other than to cluck-cluck over Harding and Billings?"

"I guess it's that other matter. There wasn't a trace of Sulmass Ochi when the mansion was stormed."

"I would leave her to heaven, at this point."

"You could be right, Mr. President. Let's see what Brockway has to say when he gets back."

"I assume Patricia and Miss Ferrick will be well enough to return with Brockway and Miss Davis."

"I'm sure they will, sir. The boys at the Adana base were just being extra careful about the two girls."

"Good."

Chapter 48

The administrator at the United States Air Force base hospital in Adana wasn't about to permit Patricia Ann Randolph and Bernice Carter Ferrick to leave the premises, even for the short haul to the USS *America*, where the rest of the freed Americans had been taken. Even Nasvik was let go to the carrier, though he had suffered a nineteenth century–type wound once routinely acquired in naval engagements between wooden ships.

The hospital staff had come to the unanimous conclusion, no doubt inspired by the international attention the base would get, that the young women had taken severe mental and physical beatings and required complete rest and close observation. They were most concerned, of course, with the weight loss suffered by Miss Randolph. She weighed in at just over ninety pounds on a five-foot seven-inch frame. And that was not good.

Jackson Harding was sent directly to the carrier, he being Navy property. It was just as well, the Air Force thought. He was terminal as sure as shooting. Let the Navy take care of its own. There was no glory in a body bag.

It was a cold-eyed Prince Pahlavi, looking heroic in a heavy bandage around his head, who accompanied the rapidly sinking man he considered a friend, aboard the gunship to the carrier and its first-class sick bay. Lieutenant Garza was on the flight also and was reluctant to leave Harding's side after the litter was off-loaded and carried below.

Comdr. B. W. McConnaughy, known as "Bilge Water" because of his initials (typical Navy, Harding had snorted when he heard it the first time), was a crusty medical officer from Down East Maine who had chosen to stay in the service after a double hitch in Vietnam, realizing that too many good physicians opted for civilian life, leaving the services devoid of enough good talent.

McConnaughy shook his head at the sight of his former patient. He read the tag made out by the triage officer at the Adana base. What caught his attention was the observation that the still slightly swollen head, the bluish-gray tinge of the complexion, and the facial tissue laced with hairline red capillaries indicated that Harding had been hanged from his ankles—attested to also by the deep welts there.

The bullet that had passed through the upper right corner of his right lung had only added to his peril, since he had been close to suffocation already from the near-collapse of his intercostal muscles during his hanging ordeal.

McConnaughy marshaled his top crew of corpsmen and nurses and prepared Harding for emergency surgery—muttering about the excreta still clinging to the dying man's body in spots—with blood transfusions to stabilize his pressure and drains to prevent him from drowning in his own blood. After four hours, the pressure and pulse indicated a small degree of hope that the surgery would not kill Harding in the process.

Harding survived the six-hour marathon of patching up his lung and chest, his stomach, his small intestine, his lacerated left bicep, his anterior left thigh muscle where the bullet had nicked the bone, a cracked right thigh bone just above the kneecap where the slug had torn away the cartilage, and a clean hole through the right calf.

After the patient had spent six hours in post-op, McConnaughy was not satisfied with his condition. That enforced inversion seemed to be having negative effects on the recovery cycle. He came up with an idea. He had his corpsmen strap Harding on the seesaw with a greater tilt toward the feet and rock him to see what the result would be. He watched the battered body for a few minutes and then went about his business. Five hours passed, and the whirring of the seesaw apparatus had become part of the environment when a feeble voice reached the surgeon's ears: "Whose fucking idea of fun is this . . . ?" And when McConnaughy walked in, ". . . I should have known, Doc . . ."

"How do you feel?"

"I won't know until you let me offa this yo-yo . . . I'm seasick!"

"That's great. We'll get you down in a minute, mister. Hold on now." He called a corpsman, and they slipped him onto a gurney, his hairy legs protruding from the gown he was in. His dark eyes were sunken, as were his cheeks.

Harding stared about him and McConnaughy stared at his patient until Harding suddenly seemed to come alive and piped up with concern: "How's the poor baby girl? How's the little girl doing, Doc?"

"She's doing just fine, mister, just fine. She's OK. Now, I'm going to let you have a few sips of chicken broth for starters, and we can go from there. How does that sound?"

"Fine, Doc, fine. Any chance of seeing her?"

"I don't think so, mister. For one thing, she's not aboard, you know. They kept her at Adana . . ."

"Is she that bad off, Doc?"

"Not really, mister. It looked to the medical staff there that she had been sapped of her physical strength, and her psyche seemed to have been badly trampled. . . . Talk about a wreck! You two made a pair, mister."

"I got her out, Doc. I thought I was going to kill her trying.

But it was better that than what she was going through." Harding's voice faded.

"Were they beating her or something?"

"Forget it, Doc. I want to . . ."

"You said it, mister. At least you're back. Mind answering a few questions?" Harding nodded. "You were hung up by your feet, right? How many days? I guess you wouldn't know, in total darkness and nobody serving you breakfast in bed. You were covered with crap . . . OK, OK, I won't ask. You know, I can never believe how the human body reacts when it has to . . . lugging her around when you should have been in a wheelchair yourself. Adrenaline certainly does wonders . . ."

Harding smiled weakly. "You're right, Doc. I began to fall apart two or three minutes after we crossed the border into Turkey. Then, suddenly, I felt like a bag of shit with a hole in it . . ."

"Well, perk up, mister. Your sidekick left you a note."

"Sidekick?"

"Miss Davis, the President's rep. She flew to Adana to be with Patricia. Gad, they had everything except a twenty-one-gun salute when she arrived. You've got to hand it to those Air Force guys."

Harding tried to keep his voice calm. "Is she planning to come aboard, do you know?"

"Haven't heard, but I don't see why not. She and Captain Shields struck it off well. And there's you, too. I'll let you know when she's coming."

"Thanks." Harding was eaten up with the prospect of seeing her again. He began to fidget and fuss and couldn't stay still for long, something that didn't escape McConnaughy's notice. The flight surgeon couldn't guess the reason for Harding's agitation, however, and he decided his patient needed something to quiet him down.

The small sedative that Harding was given, along with an intravenous feeding, was enough to knock him out for nearly eighteen hours. When he came around, he learned that Miss Davis had packed up Patricia and Miss Ferrick and returned to Washington on the two-hour substratosphere flight. No, she had not visited the carrier.

He wasn't able to hold and read the note from Allie for three more days.

"Dear Jakey," it read. "I feel we should not see each other ever again. I love him and am returning to him. I am deeply sorry and regretful for the pain I must be causing you now, but there is no other course for me to take. I would be hurting him as much as I am hurting you if I were to be yours. I am devastated for having had my cake and having eaten it, too. Please try to forgive me. I love you with all my heart." It wasn't signed.

Harding stood on the flight deck forward, the wind tugging at his clothes, chilling the tears wetting his cheeks, holding on to the prince.

Maybe McConnaughy would let him get back to Tabriz early if he promised to get himself shot for good.

I wouldn't care, not anymore, he said to himself.

Slowly, a smile began to form. Hell, it wouldn't have lasted. He could never care for too long for any woman who called him Jakey.

She had certainly fooled him. He was so sure she loved him, cared for him. It was a facade. She wanted sexual attention and obtained it. It would have looked cheap if she hadn't said she loved him. That was all, for sure. She didn't really care for me. Well, I don't really care for her, either. Unfortunately, Harding knew he didn't believe any of this.

McConnaughy permitted Harding to be visited by Brockway, to make his report, in SOQ, where the flight surgeon had created a special setup for Harding.

After a round of warm greetings, Harding and Brockway sat down for an eagerly awaited report, which Brockway would transcribe. A transmitter was also set up, and Harding became impatient with the outpouring of questions about his health. When he suggested that "we get on with it," Brockway said he was stalling until . . . "Here he is now, Jake; the President wants to talk to you."

"Hello, Commander Harding, how are you doing?"

"I'm doing fine, Mr. President, sir."

"'That's good, my boy. I'm calling you to express my deep and eternal gratitude for having saved my daughter and the entire company. Words cannot express my feelings, Commander, and I want you to know that if there is anything that I can do for you that's within my power, it is yours to command, understand, my boy?"

"Thank you, very much, Mr. President. I was extremely fortunate in being able to resolve the matter, and you don't owe me anything, Mr. President. I was doing my duty as ordered, sir."

"Well, I wish everyone conducted themselves and performed their duty as you did, and, Commander, you will permit a grateful parent to express his tremendous feelings of gratitude and joy to the person responsible for it. God bless you and keep you, and carry on. Good-bye, my boy."

"Jake, I want to add my own congratulations for a job well done. Everyone in Washington had a stake in the action, and we were going to rise and fall with your success and failure, how 'bout that?"

"You were all on shaky ground, sir. I was sure I had bought it a couple of times."

"Jake, Patricia has been questioned . . . They really did a job on her, Jake . . . and she's vague about so many things, we need some facts to clear up this whole matter."

"I don't know where to start, sir. But I've got a question for you. What the hell was the prince doing in Iran?"

"We lost him at the Catskill safehouse. We let down our guard . . . it's a long story . . . and he disappeared, absolutely disappeared until we got the report from Smithson in Tabriz."

"Well, he saved my life, that's for certain, and also Patricia's and Miss Ferrick's. It's astounding that the rescue drill had been set for 3 AM, and I was unwittingly ahead of the schedule by only a few minutes."

Brockway nodded. "I wish there was something tangible we could do for the prince . . . but I'm afraid those days are just about over."

"Have you talked to him, Tom?"

"Oh, yes. He's been outside your quarters day and night. He's got a tremendous sense of loyalty and obviously a lot of guts. How did you find Patricia?"

"I didn't. The Sulmass Ochi gang grabbed me on the street off of my motorcycle. When I regained consciousness . . . they

had me hanging by my ankles for a while . . . I found myself in
a basement room where this Sulmass Ochi dame, a beauty, sir,
interviews me and allows me to ask a few questions.

"Remember when I was with the McMahan bunch carrying Patricia southward and McMahan suddenly started going
north? Simple explanation. McMahan had cut a deal with the
Iranian government. He would receive $50 million if he deliv-
ered the prince to them. So that's what he was doing, trying to
get us to give up the prince, when Sulmass Ochi made him
change his plans. She grabs his mother in Detroit as a hostage
and persuades McMahan to deliver the prince to Sulmass Ochi
for a five-million-dollar discount price.

"But I learned something that cleared up what had been
bothering me from the moment I learned about McMahan. How
could he have been sitting and waiting for me to show up in
what I can describe only as a stinking armpit of a location called
Al Qubayyat in Northern Lebanon? It never made sense until
Sulmass Ochi did a little bragging to a man she was certain
would be dead in no time.

"Listen to this: Stefan McMahan has a twin brother, John
McMahan, who has the sobriquet of Jones-Armitage. He was
the one who engineered the bugging of the Oval Office. So
correct your files, if you can. Apparently, Jones-Armitage was
never in the picture after the first round."

"How did you break out with Pat and Bernice? Were you left
alone or something?"

"Tom, I've got to thank the gods for them not taking my
shoes. Yeah, that's right. I used the inner sole for the explosive
wire around the iron mesh in a basement window, the yellow
match for the detonator, and the shoelaces . . . yeah, the PETN
. . . for the detonator cord. Worked fine. It was actually our
only chance short of carrying the two out the front door."

"Where'd you find her?"

"Up on the top floor, the third floor of this big mansion."

"Yes . . ."

"They were in a bedroom with two guards. I waited until
everybody was asleep and crawled in and got them out of there
through the basement, where I had already rigged the window."

"Jake, this can go no further, but Patricia and Bernice were sexually molested."

"I know, sir."

"You . . . You know?"

"Yes, sir. Can I get by with a simple statement of fact? Sulmass Ochi is a lesbian."

"You are certain?"

"No question, sir."

There was a long silence. "When are you going back to Washington, Jake?"

"I'll be around this neck of the woods for a while longer, sir, if I have your permission."

"To hell with nailing her, Jake. You did your job, and it's about time you came home and got some real rest. You've earned it, lad."

"I've got to nail her, Tom. I must."

"What's the big deal? She'll surface somewhere, and we'll nail her in our own good time."

"Please, sir."

"Again, what's the big deal?"

"She was hurting the girls, sir. She was getting a kick out of it."

"Go to it."

Chapter 49

"I've called you here for one last time in regard to the terrible hostage situation we underwent personally and as a nation.

"I want to thank each and every one of you for the tremendous support, moral and otherwise, that you provided me during those harrowing weeks.

"I was hoping to have the man who managed to save the hostages here today, but Tom is keeping him out there to finish the job. Yes, to bring the ringleader to justice.

"Perhaps we can salute the man at a later date; we shall see."
The President began to beam. "I wish to report that my daughter Patricia is now an outpatient and feels she will be able to return to her studies at the University of Texas in another week. She's feeling fine, thank you."

"I have some more good news," Randolph continued, looking around at the faces of Brockway, Atwater, Rand, Woodley, Demery, and Allison Davis. "Dave, will you do the honors, please?"

Dave Demery stood up, smiling. "Tim," he said, nodding to the Defense Secretary, Tim Rand, "you were one of the twelve cabinet members to be given an FYI package upon the successful conclusion of the hostage situation. Remember? Nearly two weeks ago? If you remember also, each of the packets contained exactly the same information, information that was going to be used by the President as background for his summary press conference that was to follow in two days.

"As we all know, the important points covered in the packet appeared the very next morning in the *Washington Post.*

"We did not consider the leak vital or important, but it gave us the culprit." Dave was grinning. So was the President.

"No, no Tim, it wasn't you. It's just that you are the only one here today who received a packet. Here's how we nailed the leak . . . or plugged it, if you will.

"Each packet contained the name of the leader of the terrorist gang, Sulmass Ochi Pishavari. It's not a common name, as you can see. What I did was run off special pages with a different spelling of her name for each packet. In other words, State's packet had the name spelled with two els. Defense had the correct spelling. Justice had two els and one ess. And so on. We made a record of who got what, of course.

"The *Washington Post* story spelled her name Salmass Ochi a total of fourteen times in the story. It was the misspelling in the packet given the Secretary of the Treasury . . . Mr. President?"

"Thanks, Dave. I'll take it from here. I called Secretary Elton, and she was too mortified to say anything. Her deputy secretary has a live-in boyfriend who turns out to be a *Post* reporter, and she was providing him with what she considered tidbits. On top of that, her father has been a member of the White

House household for years, and the chitchat he passed on in-
nocently to his daughter ended up in the ear of the reporter.

"I want to thank David Demery for a job well done. We will
figure out some sort of reward . . . Sectretary Elton is looking
for a new deputy. No, I'm not doing anything about the household staff. His was a human error.

"One more item and I'll let you all get back to work. Dave is
working up a Special Day of Mourning for the three Americans
who lost their lives. Its theme is going to be that freedom has
always had a price, and we, as Americans, must be willing to
pay that price.

"Thanks, everyone."

Chapter 50

Jackson Harding had had enough of his enforced recovery
period. He was pacing off ten miles a day on the flight deck
with the prince, beginning at 4 A.M., before launch operations,
and was feeling fit. McConnaughy always shook his head when
Harding brought up the subject of active duty, but the surgeon
shocked him today with an OK.

Harding rushed to the special communications shack and
put in a priority call to Brockway. "They're letting me off this
damned scow, sir, and I need a few things. I need one backup
man, either a Turk or an Israeli, it doesn't matter which, and I
want to make certain that Level One communications are in
effect during the entire period I'm out there. No, sir, I just want
to make sure that if I cash in, you will know exactly where and
when. That may give you a small chance to follow up and nail
her. I just don't want to kick myself all the way to hell without
some hope that you're closing in on her, OK?"

"Jake, do you know what you're asking? The whole damned world will know exactly where you are, and that includes the bad guys."

"Affirmative. That's why I asked for a backup."

"You asked for one person, Jake. Hell, you'll need an army to cover your back."

"No, Tom, I'm not going to be stopping somewhere for an ice cream soda. Look, even my backup will have trouble keeping up with me."

"Negative. I can't give you Level One. You'd be wide open for no good reason. If you have enough doubts about nailing her, let's call off this Lone Ranger bit and . . ."

"OK, OK, you're right. I'll go in as per Stage One. A chopper should be over the border in case I signal. I'd like a com relay for my jaw set, if that's OK. Too many know my face."

"You got it, Jake. I'm not happy with any of this, but if you want to go out there and get killed, I'm not going to stop you."

"That's very kind of you, sir. Do you think we can coordinate by eighteen hundred hours?"

"Certainly, I can. Now tell me, what are you going to do about the prince?"

"What do you mean by that? The prince isn't my responsibility."

"Oh yes, he is, Jake. He's been sticking by you ever since the rescue. And he's there now. I don't think he plans to leave you as long as you are out there."

Harding thought for a second. "Never mind the backup, Tom. I know the prince will be tickled pink to take over that slot."

"I don't like it, Jake. He doesn't have the training, the special skills to give you what you need."

"Tom, when I saw him in action covering my ass, I was impressed. He may be short on some skills, but he has courage. I'll settle for that."

"OK, Jake. It's your ass."

"Thank you, sir."

Harding repaired to the special unit section, where he had his nose flared again and the jaw broadened with the radio transmitting insert. No mustache but soft-lens eye caps that changed his eye color to gray-green. He also donned a Kevlar vest next to his undershirt. It was going to be hellishly hot, but he was going to take as many precautions as he could. Besides, the nights would be cold, anyway.

He had special buttons replace the ones on the dark business suit he was going to wear, had a flat strip of C–4 explosive sewn between the two faces of his pants belt, and scuffed up a new pair of black shoes fitted with the special goodies. A knife and a Sig Sauer 9mm with two extra clips, and he was ready to move. Five minutes after he had obtained a new set of IDs, conforming to his new face, he was boarding the gunship, accepting the smart salute of Lieutenant Garza. He wasn't aware of it, but Commander McConnaughy was standing in an aft bay watching him take off with the prince and continued to watch until the chopper disappeared.

At Adana, a Turkish gunship joined Harding's, and he was in the outskirts of Tabriz in no time.

Smithson, Trovato, and Westcott were waiting for the two. There was genuine delight on the faces of the trio. None had expected to see Harding alive, and the action of the prince at the mansion had impressed the entire SOB.

What Harding and the prince needed was an all-wheel-drive vehicle. Yep, they were going to the cave at Shanidar. Where else could Sulmass Ochi and the remnants of her gang escape to under the circumstances? Tabriz was her only home, and the location seemed untenable at the moment. Her mention of Stefan McMahan being alive gave Harding the only clue he had as to her whereabouts. McMahan and his brother John must have exchanged information about the cave, and it could certainly be the only place McMahan might suggest as a temporary haven for her. No more than a month, he might have suggested, until things cooled down. Then she could go back to her home, for that matter. It could be fixed up in the meantime.

Harding clung to the idea of Shanidar. None had a better idea, especially the prince, who knew the area and the people better than any of them. So it was decided. Trovato found a Rover (with the spare on its bonnet), salutes of farewell were made, and both groups went their ways, the trio to a jump-off point for copter pickup, and the Rover south by the great salt lake, Urmia, for the Iraqi border and Shanidar.

Chapter 51

It wasn't until the occupants of the Rover were well past the town of Naqadeh, and had left the road for the open fields about five or six miles from the border, that they saw the first signs that other vehicles had been there recently. There were six or seven sets of tire tracks in single file. As they neared the Kaleshin Pass, Harding pointed to a pile of huge boulders as the spot where Lieutenant Levin had been battered. A mile or so more and they passed the ghastly remains of the men who had died attacking the wrong grove of trees in the night. The lack of scavenging animals and birds in the region was evident. As they approached the head of the Shanidar escarpment after skirting the ghost town of Birkim, the Rover was driven into a thick cluster of bushes and dwarf oaks and hidden. Both Harding and the prince were in combat fatigues of the Iranian Defense Forces.

The two gathered their equipment and set off on foot, approaching the cave area from the rear.

Harding had misgivings about the prince being with him. This was going to be a simple search and destroy mission. Why risk the life of the young man? But the prince had insisted on tagging along. They agreed that once it was determined that the cave was occupied, Riza would drop back a good hundred yards or more, depending on the terrain, and do nothing but cover Harding's rear.

The Baradost range of the Zagros was formidably rugged to begin with, but the two had to keep their eyes on constant sweeps ahead, which made it a trial since the simple act of walking and climbing over the rocky terrain required concentration.

They melted into the low shrubbery together as both saw him at the same instant, a man wearing one of those high-crowned black calpacs, standing as big as life with a rifle cradled in his arms, having a smoke. He obviously wasn't taking his sentry duties seriously. The two nodded to each other. The trip to the cave had not been a waste of time.

Riza stayed where he was, and Harding crawled forward in his odd style, like a crab, without his torso touching the ground. He was able to get within forty yards of the sentry when he had to stop. From where he was, the sentry would be able to see him easily if he went forward another yard. He waited, and the sentry accommodated him eighteen minutes later, by Harding's timepiece, when he laid his rifle down, sat on a rock, and began rolling another smoke. Harding sprinted for the seated figure, who scrambled to his feet, trying to get his rifle into service, just before Harding's Bowie found his throat. He had been at least four yards away when he had to throw it. He removed the dead man's calpac and put it on.

Harding and Riza remained apart, and they both adopted more of a creep than a walk. It was going to be a difficult approach. They were still a good half mile from the brow of the cave's bluff, and the sentry they had encountered meant the gang had others strung about. Harding unlimbered the Kalashnikov, just in case, and stood erect. He might be able to pass as a sentry from a distance. Creeping was sapping his strength. Another hundred feet and a tall man with his rifle at the ready approached him. Apparently he wasn't sure about Harding because of the brown uniform. Two single shots banged away what cover Harding had. One was his, knocking down the approaching man, the other was from Riza's Uzi, knocking down another rifleman, who had materialized to the left and behind Harding. Still remaining in tandem, they bent over and headed swiftly for the bluff.

Harding reached the bluff over the cave opening without further contact. He was on his belly now scrutinizing the area from the cover of a bushy clump. Far below, in the valley before the cave, were eight vehicles of various types, parked in a row, with two guards visible from Harding's view. He could not see the lip in front of the cave opening—the lip where the riflemen had been slaughtered on another day, as they awaited the oncoming frontal attack. The cars indicated that the cave was occupied. Was Sulmass Ochi there? It really didn't matter to Harding at this point. No friendly lives were at stake. If she were there, fine. If not, the people certainly were part of her gang.

He crawled back as far as he could to escape notice from the valley and crept to his left to find the path to the spring that would also take him to the cave-floor level. He could not see Riza. He held his assault rifle in his right hand and his Sig Sauer in the other, ready for anything, and moved slowly down the path, a path with plenty of brush and scrubs to cover him.

A burst of gunfire behind him, no more than twenty feet away, sent him sprawling on his face from the impact and shoved him into the brush off the path. Two men, talking excitedly, approached what they considered a dead body. The body came alive with two brief bangs, and the surprised men dropped dead. Harding's back was riddled, but the Kevlar had saved him. He knew something wasn't right with his back after the walloping it had taken from the rain of bullets, but he was able to stand and move down the path.

He came face-to-face with a heavy-set man running up the path, perhaps to investigate the shots. The big man died without ceremony, and as he fell toward Harding, his killer lowered him gently to the ground.

Harding was nearly at the end of the path. Three more steps and he would be in the open. Were they waiting for him? They certainly were. A grenade bounced into the path, almost at his feet. Harding leaned over and swung it back in one motion, the missile exploding before it reached the ground beyond. With that exercise, Harding leaped into the open, assuming a crouch with the muzzle of his Kalashnikov swaying back and forth, looking for a target. There was a body, probably that of the grenade thrower, and nothing else. The opening of the cave was five feet away on his right. At that moment, he heard gunfire farther back up the path. He retreated quickly, took a few steps up the path, and waited. Riza was involved back there, and he wasn't going to give anyone in the cave the free information that there were two of them. That kind of info is earned with blood. After two minutes, he stuck his head out and found the cave front still empty. He assumed his crouch and worked his way to the cave opening . . . and peeked in. Couldn't see a thing in there, even though the sun was still high to the west.

Harding knew the inside of the cave like the palm of his hand. There were a lot of passenger seats in the cars parked below, and he hadn't accounted for any sizable number of passengers up here. If any of them were in the cave, they could very well be hiding in the trench shelf, but that could hold no more than six or seven.

Where the hell were they? The skin at the back of his neck began to prickle. He had that sixth sense that some people have, which if they're in his line of business, helps them stay alive. He was falling to the ground and twisting over as three or four bullets winged by where his head had been. He landed on his right side with his 9mm barking at a crowd of riflemen who were pouring out of the cave, firing at him. Harding's marksmanship had always been uncanny, from the days when he learned how to shoot at the academy—uncanny from any position he happened to be in—and the riflemen died one after another as they tried hitting a difficult target, never realizing that Harding always fired his next hollow-nosed round at the man whose rifle's aim seemed to be locked on him. Harding didn't wait a split second after he knocked down the last man in his view. He rolled to the wall even as he fished for another clip of fifteen rounds to slip into his gun. He wasn't going to wait to find out if he had any bullets left.

A quarter hour later, he was still waiting. No sound, no movement. Not a sound or any indication that the prince was around, either. He wondered if Riza had bought it in that last firefight he had heard behind him. Could have. So be it. He stood up . . . and went into a crouch.

As he raised his Kalashnikov he felt the muzzle of a gun pressing into his neck. "Drop it and stand up, carefully." The words were in Azeri with a girlish pitch. Harding did as he was told. There was no room for reaction with a muzzle sticking into you. "Move down there into the open." Harding did as he was told.

Sulmass Ochi, dressed in a black jumper and white blouse, stepped around in front of Harding and snapped her fingers at him. "McMahan was correct. He said if we came out here, you were sure to follow."

"You went to a lot of trouble."

"Not at all, Mr. Pulver, not at all. You had become truly a problem to me. Now you shall die."

"I'd like to talk to him, first, if you don't mind." The voice belonged to either John or Stefan McMahan who stepped into the circle wearing a Detroit Lions cap, a small blond mustache across the top of his thin lips, his towering, massive body clad in light khaki and safari boots. The sonovabitch lacked only a riding crop and a monocle to carry off the presence he was attempting to manifest with such savoir faire, Harding thought. He had been in the cave all along.

"And which misbegotten son of poor Mrs. McMahan might you be, fatty?"

"Thank you, I decry the lack of discernment in this man who is about to die. Why do you hate me, George? Because I led you on a merry chase to hell and back? Frankly, it should be the reverse for what you visited on my brother."

"Save it, McMahan. It really doesn't matter which brother you are. You're both horseshit. I just want to know one thing, something that's been bothering me since the very beginning. How did any of you know in advance that I would be using A1 Qubayyat in Lebanon as my jump-off point? You had infiltrated the British station there even before I left the States. I realize you had the Oval Office bugged, but I know such details weren't discussed there until after the fact."

The smile on McMahan's oval face kept broadening into a beaming moon. "Since you're not long for this world, I'm going to tell you. Did it ever occur to you bozos that the White House wasn't the only place we tapped? We were able to wire up the Israeli Embassy on International Drive. You jerks are so hidebound that even though you plan a top secret caper—tipping off only the Israelis because you need them—one of your ge-

niuses at the State Department goes by the book and informs
the military attache at the Israeli Embassy on an FYI basis. You
know, what really baffled us was that someone felt that your
State Department had to be kept informed, ostensibly because
foreign governments were involved. You guys still don't know
how to play this game. You ought to take some lessons from
the SAS in London."

McMahan turned to Sulmass Ochi. " Do with him what you
will. I'm not going to have any part of it."

"Even though he killed your brother?"

"John died as he lived, taking his chances. I understand he
plugged this guy and another one before he got his." He looked
at Harding. "Yep, I'm Stefan. I thought I had a handle on the
prince trade until you came along. But revenge is for children."
He waved his hand as if to wash his hands of the entire matter
and turned away.

"I suggest strongly that you stay, Mr. McMahan." Sulmass
Ochi had raised a hand, and some of the rifles were now pointing at him.

"I'm sorry, Madame Pishavari, but I have given you enough
of my time. Goodbye, for now."

"Stand where you are. You shall die with him, Mr. McMahan. You are a dangerous man who knows too much about me.
You see, I do not believe one word about you not seeking
revenge."

"But you had nothing to do with the death of my brother . . ."

"Not revenge for your brother, Mr. McMahan. Revenge for
your mother. For having held your mother hostage and having
fed her only cheese sandwiches for two weeks. We know you
were raving insanely about her condition when she had to be
rushed to the hospital later.

" Shoot them at the edge there so they will drop out of my
sight. Go!"

The two were hustled to the edge of the apron to the cave—it
was about nine hundred feet from the plain below—and the
gunmen stood back to give themselves some shooting room.

Harding bumped into McMahan. "Drop to the ground on the
count of three, shithead . . . one . . . two . . . three!"

Harding's hopeful guess paid off. The second they were

down, Riza's Uzi began its blurred snapping from the base of the spring path. There were seven in the firing squad and eleven others. They fell on top of and about the two condemned prisoners, some dripping blood over their intended victims. Simultaneously, there was a mad dash for the cave by Sulmass Ochi.

"You OK, fat one?"

"I'm OK, motherfucker. How come you saved me?"

"Later, shithead, later."

"I wouldn't have done that for you."

"Later, I said. That bitch is back in the cave. See anyone in there, McMahan?"

"I'm not looking too hard. You can get killed doing that."

"You damned Irish are so aware of your mortality . . . ever since you tangled with the English."

"That wasn't my Irish talking, smart ass. That was my Polish half exercising good judgment where my Irish half might have charged waving an effing flag." Then he took a good look at Harding's companion.

"My God, it's Prince Pahlavi!" McMahan couldn't believe what he was seeing. "What the hell is he doing here? Is he crazy?"

"I've got connections, fat one. Watch him, Riza. We can't trust him. Let's see about Sulmass Ochi . . . Step out from there and give up yourself."

"I am coming out. I have one young friend left, who will not make trouble." Her voice was soft and as mellifluous as ever. She stepped out into the opening with a young man following closely. Harding recognized him. He was the one who had been sitting in the bedroom with wet lips, watching Patricia being . . .

Sulmass Ochi suddenly screamed in hate as she spotted the prince. "I'll kill you! I'm going to kill you!" She lunged past Harding, her hands reaching for Riza's throat, but sprawled on her face instead as Harding tripped her. She scrambled up from the dust and tried again, groaning and grunting in gasping, sobbing frustration. Harding stopped her by placing a boot on her rump and keeping her down. She calmed down, finally, and Harding yanked her to her feet. She was still sobbing.

"McMahan. There are at least two of her gang down there by the cars. Guard the path over there so we won't be surprised."

McMahan didn't say a word but tossed Harding a salute of acknowledgment and trotted over to the head of the path.

"We keep changing roles, madam. Why is that, I wonder?"

"Perhaps because the gods are fickle. I really don't care, at this point. I only know that Americans cannot kill a woman in cold blood."

"Said with some degree of perception, but it begs the question, madam. Are you a whole woman or only partially a woman? If the latter, it would be much easier to dispatch you to your own special hell."

"That is a laugh and not worth comment."

"Not worth discussing, for certain, but not at all mirthful. No, madam, it would not be difficult to kill you, but I would like the families of the three Americans you murdered, their friends, and all the citizens of the United States to see you hanged by the neck. And I, personally, would like to see you in that final predicament, because of the President's daughter." He paused, staring into her eyes until she looked aside. "Yes, we understand each other."

He unbuckled his belt, pulled it off, slipped the tongue end through the buckle, slipped the loop over her head and drew it firmly but not tightly around her neck, like a neck brace.

He held on to the end with the buckle holes. "Now listen to me. This is a special belt. If you try to run away or yank at it, you will die instantly. Do you understand? I am not making an idle promise, madam."

He turned to Riza: "What should we do with this monkey?"

"I say shoot him, but I couldn't. He's a sissy."

"You couldn't shoot a sissy?"

"It's almost like shooting a girl."

"Would it help if we dropped his pants so you could see his balls when you shot him?"

The prince was laughing. The youth knew he was the subject of the conversation and brightened up a smidgen when Riza started laughing. The one they had hanged upside down a while back had gestured toward his goodies. That could be a favorable sign, but you never know about these wild foreign-

ers. In the meantime, he stood a bit behind Sulmass, instinctively seeking her protection.

Harding didn't have the heart to keep looking at the forlorn
duo. There is something about a defeated foe, perhaps their
manner, perhaps a certain look in their eyes, or perhaps the
body language—a slight stoop in the shoulders—that saps the
will of the conqueror to kill. It was only a matter of weeks since
this handsome female had slaughtered three of his country-
men, viciously molested the sanctity and person of two young
women, and literally hung him out to dry. Harding watched
them, his gorge rising at the thought of killing the two. They
had become, suddenly, God's creatures, with their abject mien
and downturned heads, covered with dust and grime. She was
right, the bitch. He killed without a flicker of hesitation, without doubts, when his life was pitched on the line. But what
Sulmass Ochi didn't know was that he couldn't kill the young
man with her, much less her.

He took a deep breath, sighed, and held up his hand to call
McMahan back. His hand stopped at midelevation. There was
no McMahan at the top of the path. Just as he gestured to Riza
to go and look, the sound of four gunshots wafted up from the
valley below. Riza changed his direction to look down the prec-
ipice. Harding couldn't do anything, since he was holding Sulmass tethered to the belt.

"Our slippery friend is gone. He hoofed it down there, shot
three men apparently guarding the vehicles, and he's taken off
in that direction, Aqrah and Mosul," Riza said, pointing.

"He can't get away now. We'll radio his description."

"What are we going to do with these two, take 'em with us?"

"You said it, Your Highness. Get on the radio there and call
in the cavalry. Make certain you specify how many we have all
together here."

Riza stepped away, out of earshot, to signal. Harding motioned Sulmass Ochi to the ground . . . carefully . . . don't
yank the belt . . . and he sat close enough to hold the far end
of the belt, with the youth sitting behind her, supporting her
back.

It was not according to the best of plans. The worst of unin-
tentions occurred.

Sulmass Ochi Pishavari lost her head, literally, blown completely off by a charge of C–4 plastic in the belt at the buckle end. Crap! Way too much plastic!

The young Iranian sitting up against her was horribly smashed by the explosion, only a foot away from his face when he had managed to surreptitiously loosen the belt noose. You can't do that. There is no metal tongue sticking through a belt hole to act as an anchor, and pulling it loose only makes the metal prongs holding the belt buckle lose contact inside, completing the circuit and detonating the charge.

Jackson Harding was still sitting where he had been, covered totally, on the side facing the explosion, with flesh, bone particles, and a heavy coating of blood. The prince had raced back, looking in revulsion at the scene. He knelt down beside the American, afraid to touch him lest he find out his friend was dead.

"Com . . . Commander?" The prince's voice was shaking, barely audible.

"Persians suck lemons, screw goats, and . . . " Harding's faint words trailed off.

The prince launched into a rain of Persian invectives, all in Farsi, with tears streaming down his cheeks. "Stay alive, stay alive, you crazy Turk, you son of a dog whelped on a dung heap . . . please."

He stopped venting his concern long enough to signal for a copter and medical assistance, thanking his stars that Harding had instructed him.

Harding fell over. There were so many holes in him along his side, where the Kevlar doesn't cover, it was going to be nip and tuck until he could be patched up.

Riza sat by him, cradling the bloodied head, until the Navy gunship took a dangerous chance and settled on the precarious apron of the cave, its rotors inches away from the bluff.

All the ubiquitous Lieutenant Garza could say when he saw Harding was, "Oh, my God!"

The prince sat beside the American's stretcher, muttering to himself under the incessant roar of the chopper blades.

Lieutenant Garza finally broke the soliloquy with, "What was that, sir?"

"I just want to know if he really is going to live."

"Don't worry, sir. You can't kill this guy. I think he talks to God."

Epilogue

The President of the United States was feeling better than usual these days. His daughter was safely back home and in school; he seemed to have mastered the situation concerning Allison; his new secretary of state, whom he had personally selected, had been approved unanimously by the Senate; the GNP, the CPI, and the prime rate were in favorable long-term upward or downward trends; the War of the Drugs was finally winding down in Colombia, Peru, Bolivia, and Mexico, and, best of all, the startling side bars in the *Washington Post* had ceased.

*   *   *

The White House director of communications was kicking himself incessantly after his brief moment of triumph in unmasking the leak from the White House. Dave realized later that he should have slipped the information to the President without revealing how he did it. From Cabinet members on down, if the paper they were perusing or discussing had been channeled in any way through Dave's office, there were immediate and unsubtle comparisons to make sure Dave wasn't up to something. You can't win for winning, he thought.

*   *   *

Central Intelligence Agency Director Thomas Pierpont Brockway decided he had had enough, and his resignation was accepted only on condition he did something about changing the rules regarding the appointment of big fat guys as case workers (never call 'em agents) and making the Special Operations Branch less elitist and broader-based. Tom didn't understand

what that meant (some pen-pushing asshole in the White
House basement must have come up with it), but he knew how
to do it. Simply change the name to White House Special Service, and everyone would love it and congratulate him on a job
well done.

*   *   *

To say that Allison Arnold Davis was a bit miffed these days
was putting it mildly. She was as puzzled as she was angry and
frustrated at the distance Randy had put between them since
her return with Patricia. It was becoming apparent that his
need for her had been in direct proportion to his need for
emotional solace during a period of deep concern for his daughter. The President didn't seem to have time for quiet White
House dinners with her anymore. He found it easy to have
unbreakable schedules when it was a matter of finding time to
see her, and their phone conversations were brief and, on many
occasions, abrupt. Wedding dates were never topics of conversation, and this was perhaps the underlying reason for bitterness on Allison's part, since they had agreed to her having a
baby before her biological clock ran out. Time had become a
thief in more ways than one.

*   *   *

Patricia Ann Randolph continued to excel in her studies at
the Austin campus, but everyone who had known her before
her additional fame as a rescued hostage said she was different.
She had withdrawn completely from ordinary social contacts
and associations, including her fellow students, faculty, and
former friends. She had so much trouble sleeping that her
roommate had moved out, wondering who was the Harding
she frequently cried about during periods of fitful sleep.

*   *   *

Prince Riza Pahlavi II was back in the United States, the toast
of Washington's power brokers, the military, and most of all,
President Randolph. To the consternation of the Iranian government, the United States had announced that the prince had
been the leader of a private group of Americans who had res-

cued the hostages. Best of all, the ordinary people of Iran began making comparisons between life under the Ayatollahs and life under the late shah, and the shah fared much better in the surveys of memory. The golden feathers of the Peacock Throne were losing their tarnish.

*   *   *

The Soviet Committee for State Security discovered a major flaw in its policy covering deep moles in other countries, re-called Abdul Ali Baad and his family from Tabriz (much to Abdul's despair) and assigned him to the Soviet Embassy in Washington (much to his delight) to spy on the Turkish Em-bassy (why?).

*   *   *

Dr. Geoffrey Maran issued a tongue-in-cheek ukase to his department at Columbia banning any future digs of any kind anywhere unless the region had been free of political and/or military disturbances for at least one hundred years. He only shrugged and produced an enigmatic smile when it was pointed out to him by Columbia's harried PR man, Avery, that the definition eliminated practically the whole world, except possibly Sweden, Finland, Monaco, Liechtenstein, and Swit-zerland . . . and who would want to dig in those locations?

*   *   *

Lt. Jared Margil was placed in charge of the field assignment bureau at the Netanyahu Institution (named for the com-mander of the daring hostage rescue at Entebbe airport, where he was the only one killed). The staff wondered why he had a large sign behind his desk that read, *"Who is Ibrahim?"* Was he crazy? All he had to do was check the Old Testament to get a full rundown on the great Hebrew prophet.

*   *   *

Lt. Lenna Levin had lost that fetchingly mysterious loveli-ness that had been her hallmark before the bashing she re-ceived. Her nose, once of delicate aquiline shape, had been recast as an ordinary, almost straight, ski-jump variety that left her beautiful in the eyes of many more men but also left her indistinguishable from the rest of the world's beauties. She wondered if she was going to meet Ibrahim, or was it George, when she went to Washington next week at the invitation of the White House. She flushed at the idea, then tossed her head with the reassurance that there were plenty of other fish in the sea.

*   *   *

The Kaaterskill Foundation was reinstituted in Catskill when the town fathers decided that the sudden fame bestowed upon them by the prince and the discovery of the treasure was a good reason to launch another treasure hunt. It was good fortune the CIA had chosen that estate as a safehouse. Now that it was up for sale and was being called the Palace of the Prince of Persia, everyone was having fun calling it Greene County's rest room.

*   *   *

Capt. Dara Shields, USN, skipper of the super nuclear carrier USS *America*, was feeling more like the commander of a capital warship these days. It was nearly a month now, and creepy-looking characters were no longer debarking from one of his gunships or transports and walking, limping, crawling, or being carried b'low decks for whatever the special intelligence people were up to. They hadn't covered over the last one they had carried below, and he could see the bloody mess. Even the good captain had no way of telling that all those weird characters he spotted on his deck were the same man, someone he knew as Comdr. Jackson Harding.

*   *   *

Monte Billings of the Special Operations Branch died aboard the USS *America*. Billings had smiled when he opened his eyes briefly and saw his uncle, Brockway, standing by his bed. The CIA chief sat with his man to the end, holding Billings's hand. The smile never left the dying man's face as both men held on, neither saying a word for several hours until the hand relaxed in death. The SOB man's death had been special: He had not died alone.

*   *   *

Jackson Harding was alive and well and getting ready to go home. After three weeks of treatment and recuperation, he was ready for anything except the confines of a warship at sea, no matter how big it was, no matter how many things of a civilian nature it had to offer an off-duty officer. They had brought a neurosurgeon aboard, from a Turkish hospital in Ankara, to handle some complications arising from injury to his spine, but that was taken care of, and the rest required healing time. Some of the bone fragments and a part of the belt buckle had penetrated in so many places that the surgeon had a difficult time finding all the punctures. The one of McConnaughy's observations Harding had remembered was, "You certainly find new ways of getting hurt! Is this part of a belt buckle?"

Harding wasn't too happy about going back to his job at NASA, but it was better than anything else anyone had to offer. He thought of Allie and thought of her and thought of her and kept saying to hell with it, her happiness comes first. Occasionally he remembered the bag of bones he had bundled out of that mansion in Tabriz in the middle of the night, and a smile would cross his face. The poor kid. I hope she's all right, he would think. Might look her up when I get back to Houston. After all, Austin was only a few miles away, if you reckoned the way Texans do. Yep, might take her out for some lunch or a spot of dinner, if it's OK with the President.

His spirits were picking up already.